THE SAME PLACE

THE LAMB AND THE LION
BOOK TWO

GREGORY ASHE

H&B

Published by Hodgkin & Blount
https://www.hodgkinandblount.com/
contact@hodgkinandblount.com

Published 2020
Printed in the United States of America

Trade Paperback ISBN: 978-1-63621-005-6
eBook ISBN: 978-1-63621-004-9

For that which befalleth the sons of men befalleth beasts.
All go unto one place; all are of the dust, and all turn to dust again.

Ecclesiastes 3:19-20

1

Teancum Leon was sitting on his balcony in the morning dark, staring across the Salt Lake Valley, when the knock came. The May air was cool. Dawn had just outlined the spine of the Wasatch Mountains. The peppermint tea trembled in his hand as he jolted upright and stumbled inside. Scipio, his black Lab was barking furiously — probably with the expectation that whoever was standing in the hallway had treats and was desperate to give them to him, if only that damn door weren't in the way.

When Tean answered the door, Mrs. Wish was standing there. His neighbor from down the hall, she was normally a specimen of starch and hairspray. Right then, though, she looked like a ball of yarn after her army of cats — nicknamed the Irreconcilables — had really gotten going: her long white hair stood out in a million directions, and her housecoat was misbuttoned, exposing white calves and blue veins.

"It's one of the babies," Mrs. Wish said and began to sob.

Tean stared at her for a moment. Then, pressing the mug of peppermint tea into her hands, he said, "Let's go take a look."

As a wildlife veterinarian for Utah's Division of Wildlife Resources, Tean had to be an expert on a wide variety of animals. More than that, he had to be capable of learning what he needed to know quickly so that he could understand and address problems in the state's diverse ecosystem. On any given day, he might have to deal with elk poaching, complaints about the steelhead population, or a California condor struggling to hatch her eggs. Maybe all three, in fact. To date, nothing had come anywhere close to the challenge that Mrs. Wish presented.

When they got to the end of the hall, Mrs. Wish fumbled with the mug of tea, still sobbing, and tried to open the door. Tean gently nudged her aside, took her keys, and let them both inside. The apartment was sixty-percent cat dander, thirty-percent potpourri, and ten-percent livable space. From one wall, a larger-than-life President Woodrow Wilson stared down at them from his portrait. He looked just as worried about the Irreconcilables as Mrs. Wish.

After settling Mrs. Wish at her small dining table and making sure she took a long drink of the peppermint tea, Tean headed for the closet where they had set up Senator George H. Moses's birthing box. Tean had been here for several hours in the middle of the night, doing what Mrs. Wish insisted on calling 'supervisorial vigilance,' although Tean hadn't really done anything except eat store-brand chocolate chip cookies straight out of the package, listen to Mrs. Wish's rambling invectives against Teddy Roosevelt's mustache, and let the Senator handle her own business. Barring an emergency, the cat knew better than Tean how to deliver her litter; she was biologically programmed to do it. And she'd done it just fine. Once the Senator and the kits were settled in the birthing box in the closet, Tean had given some basic instructions and caught a few hours of sleep.

"Not in there," Mrs. Wish said through her tears, waving him away from the closet. "I moved them."

Tean frowned. "I told you to leave them alone and keep an eye on the other Irreconcilables."

Coloring faintly, Mrs. Wish said, "I had to make sure the babies were all right. And it's a good thing, too. I woke up to the most horrible noises. By the time I'd gathered the courage to get out of bed and turn on the light, one of the kits was gone. You have to help me find her."

"Why don't you wait here?" Tean said. "I'll take a look. The birthing box is in your bedroom?"

Mrs. Wish took a sip of tea and nodded. Through more tears, she said, "This is very weak, you know. You're not brewing it correctly."

At the end of the hall, Tean paused at the door to Mrs. Wish's bedroom. Senator Poindexter, a nasty, brutish Siamese who started pretty much every scrap in the apartment, was lurking in the doorway across the hall. He hissed when Tean looked over.

"Watch out," Tean said. "If she says the word, I've got a pair of nail scissors that'll go through your balls like they're butter."

"What's that?" Mrs. Wish shouted.

"Nothing," Tean called back.

He let himself into the bedroom, barely closing it in time to prevent Senator Poindexter from squeezing past him. Lace, especially lace doilies, were a prominent part of Mrs. Wish's overall decorating scheme, but she had taken it to a new level in the bedroom. Waterfalls of lace. Huge, ruffled explosions of lace. Tean wondered if psychologists already had a name for a phobia of lace. They'd have one for sure after they institutionalized him.

At the side of the bed he found the birthing box. He searched the room. Then he approached the box carefully and looked in from a distance. Then he sighed. Moving the box hadn't been enough for Mrs. Wish. She'd washed the kittens, in spite of Tean's instructions to leave them alone, and she'd cluttered the nest with tiny toys. She'd even added treats, although she must have known that the kittens weren't weaned. Senator George H. Moses was crouched between Tean and the kits, and when she saw him, she hissed. Blood stained her whiskers.

Tean checked the food and water in the box and then let himself out of the room. He made his way down the hall. When Mrs. Wish saw his face, she started to cry again.

"Mrs. Wish—"

"Oh, she's dead, isn't she?"

"I think so."

"What happened? I didn't step on her, did I? Or do something in my sleep?"

"No."

"Well, what happened? I made absolutely sure that the door was closed. I told Senator Poindexter quite clearly that he couldn't sleep with me. He was very upset. I suppose I'll have to get everyone together and hold a funeral." Tean wasn't sure if everyone meant Mrs. Wish and the Irreconcilables or Mrs. Wish and her enormous extended family—with her, either one was possible, or both. "Where did you put her poor little body?"

"I don't think you understand. Sometimes, when a kit is sick or already dead, the mother disposes of it."

"She couldn't have buried the poor thing. She hasn't been outside."

Tean drew a deep breath. "Many animals will eat their young in extreme conditions."

It took a moment, and then Mrs. Wish's cheeks pinkened. "I should think not."

"It does happen."

"I don't believe it. Senator George H. Moses is their mother. She has a mother's instinct. She never, never would have hurt her own kittens." With a kind of exalted certainty, Mrs. Wish raised her chin. "I know it in my heart."

"Well," Tean said, "right now, my recommendation is to leave the kittens with their mother, but if you see any sort of behavior —"

"Certainly," Mrs. Wish said, standing, shoving the mug along the table so hard that it skittered. "Certainly. She's their mother, Dr. Leon. To think I would allow anything else . . . I just honestly can't believe what I'm hearing from you. I can't believe this constitutes your professional, medical opinion. Is this what they teach you in schools these days?"

"I think I should go."

"You said if the kitten was sick, but earlier, you told me they all looked healthy. Did you make some kind of mistake? Is that what this is? You're trying to cover up your own shoddy work."

"Good night, Mrs. Wish."

He reached for the mug, and she slapped his hand. A horrified look flitted across her face, as though she couldn't quite believe what she'd done, and then it was gone, and her expression hardened.

Tean thought about telling her why it had happened: stress, stress, stress. The stress of the birthing box being moved. The stress of having the kittens taken away one by one, bathed, and handled. The stress — Tean imagined — of Mrs. Wish rising in the middle of the night to check on the kittens again and again.

Instead, though, he kept his mouth shut and headed for the door.

"I can't believe I thought you'd be an acceptable match for Violet," Mrs. Wish said to his back. "She might be a bit gimpy, and she's got a droopy mouth, and she's older than dirt, but at least she has the milk of human kindness. She's not a heartless beast like you, imagining the absolute worst, most impossible things. As though one of God's own creations could do what you've just suggested. As though a mother could do such a thing, Dr. Leon. Their own mother."

From the hallway, with his hand on the doorknob, Tean said, "Mrs. Wish, the best thing you can do right now is keep your bedroom door shut, sleep in the guest bedroom, and only check on

Senator George H. Moses to fill her food and water and clean out the litter box."

"I certainly don't need any more instructions from you, you . . . you Communist pig."

"It was a flyer from the socialist party," Tean muttered as he dragged the door shut. "And someone just put it under my windshield wiper."

2

Tean had to hurry to dress and walk Scipio before work. Their walk was pretty standard; today, it included Scipio chasing a squirrel when Tean let him off the leash at Liberty Park, and then, a few minutes later, Tean rescuing Scipio when a goose cornered him. The black Lab had been pressed up against an old oak, barking wildly at the goose until Tean reattached the leash and led him away. As soon as they'd put a few yards between themselves and the bird, Scipio started bounding and frolicking, his tail going like mad. He obviously considered himself the winner of that particular skirmish and was unbearably proud of himself.

When Tean got to work, he found himself immediately caught up in a fresh conflict. Norbert Smith, eighty years old, who frequently forgot to shave and—even more noticeably—to bathe, had worked for DWR for over forty years. He'd handled a lot of the state's poaching complaints, especially from the northwest quadrant, and he'd done a good job of it until a bad fall and a broken leg in December. Everyone, Tean included, had expected that to loosen Norbert's death grip on his job, but instead of retiring, Norbert had clung on. Now he was back, using a walker to navigate the DWR building, unable to drive long distances let alone hike into the back country to catch poachers. And from the hints he had dropped, he was obviously hoping someone would try to fire him so he could sue.

Instead, Tean had put him in a clerical job, digitizing old records. It was work that needed to be done—although from what Tean could tell on his initial review, all Norbert had managed to do was scan the blank backs of hundreds of pages and include them all in the same file. More importantly, it kept Norbert clear of DWR's daily operations.

Except for this morning. And ten other mornings just like it over the last two months.

"I know you think I'm a bitch," Hannah was saying. She was Tean's colleague and friend, a biologist specializing in native aquatics. Her chestnut hair had a million flyaways today, and her face was splotchy. "Just say it, Norbert. You think I'm a bitch. But I don't care. I don't know how that phone call got routed to you, but you have absolutely no right fielding calls from the public and authorizing them to do whatever they want to do."

Norbert sank down in his chair, an eighty-year-old sullen child. "Can I go now? Got work to do."

"She's right," Tean said. "Your job isn't to handle calls from the public."

"I've done this job longer than either of you's been alive," Norbert said, his sunken eyes cutting back and forth as though he couldn't quite fix on Tean. "It was a simple question. I know my years of experience don't mean bullpucky to either of you, but they ought to count for something."

"Well, that's fair," Tean said, darting a look at Hannah. "I do value your experience, and I know that many times, people call in with the same questions, so I'm sure you felt comfortable answering—"

"The man wanted to go fishing with dynamite," Hannah shouted. "And Norbert said yes."

"It's those damn burbot," he said, referring to an invasive species of fish. "Let him blow them all to hell if he wants."

"That's illegal and unethical—"

"Ok," Tean said. "Norbert, it's not your job to answer the phone. If you do, and if you're fielding questions from the public, you need to give answers in line with DWR policy. Is that clear?"

"Wasn't like this back in the day," Norbert said, slouching even lower in the chair.

"Is that clear?"

"Yes."

"And talk to him about the paperwork," Hannah said.

"The paperwork?" Tean said.

"He's not doing any of the clerical work he's supposed to be doing. He's supposed to be processing surrendered turkey tags, and—"

"Young lady," Norbert said, "if they got a tag, and if they didn't get a darn turkey, why should I care what happens to the tag after?"

"Because it's your job."

"All right," Tean said. "Hannah, thank you for raising your concerns. Norbert, even if you don't think the task is important, it still needs to get done."

"I don't have time for this," Norbert said, easing himself up from the seat and grabbing his walker.

"That's right," Hannah said, "you need to hurry back to your desk and look at those Japanese *Playboys* you keep in the top drawer."

Tean covered his eyes.

Norbert huffed, and it sounded like he might say something, but then the door opened, and the walker creaked away. He slammed the door behind him.

"Well, you were a lot of help," Hannah said.

Dropping his hand, Tean said, "Don't start with me."

"He ought to be fired. I wasn't joking about those pornos, either. He really does have them in his desk."

"He wants to be fired, Hannah. And then he's going to sue for ageism or who knows what."

"He was only ever good for one thing, and that was rousting poachers, and he was only good at it because he did half the poaching himself. He's a nightmare with public calls. He's a disaster with clerical work. The Division has perfectly legitimate grounds to fire him."

"You know it's not that simple."

"He's creating a hostile work environment," Hannah said. "He objectifies women, especially with those magazines. I feel sexually harassed. I'm going to sue."

"Look, I will make him get rid of the magazines. I didn't even know about the magazines. And I had no idea you felt like this was a hostile work environment. We're going to—"

Hannah screamed as she got up from the chair. "I get so sick of being the only one around here with a pair of balls."

She slammed the door even harder than Norbert had.

When the ringing in his ears died down, Tean got back to work on his most recent project: controlling an outbreak of canine distemper that was affecting populations of coyotes and feral dogs around Heber City. It was starting to get into the domestic populations, and there would be hell to pay if the virus worked its way north into Park City and someone's designer Chihuahua caught it. Worse, it threatened a population of kit foxes along the Wasatch Back, and they were a species of concern in the state. He was just digging into the research around controlling outbreaks when his door flew open again.

Hannah gripped the handle, her face even splotchier than before, her hair like she was building up a static charge. She just stood there, breathing hard, arms folded across her chest. Tean braced himself. He and Hannah had worked together for years, and until recently, they'd gotten along well. She was smart, capable, dependable, and funny. Something had changed, though, and over the last weeks and months, she'd displayed a temper—not always unjustified, as the case with Norbert had shown—that was nevertheless out of character. A couple of weeks ago, she'd taken two sick days without any explanation, when she hadn't taken sick days in years. She had dark rings under her eyes all the time, and although Tean felt like a bad person for thinking this, she'd put on a little weight.

Then Hannah stepped into the office, shutting the door behind her, and started to cry.

Lurching out of his seat, Tean made his way around the desk and hugged her. She cried for a long time, sobbing against his shoulder while he patted her back. His whole body was locking up at the sheer amount of contact with another person; he summoned up memories of the Darwin Awards to keep himself from climbing out of his skin. The guy who had tried to build his own rocket car. The guy who had performed experimental surgery on himself. The guy who had tried to chew through an overhead power line to prove that squirrels weren't any better than humans.

Finally, Hannah squeezed his arm and pulled back. "I'm fine," she said thickly, wiping her face. "I'm really fine. I just hate that I fell apart like that."

"It's ok."

"It's not ok. It's this horrible female stereotype, and I hate playing into it."

"I cried the other night when Jem made me watch the same episode of *The Simpsons* for the fourth time in a row."

Hannah laughed, and then she coughed, and then she laughed some more.

"Want to sit down?" Tean asked. "Have some tea?"

Hannah nodded and said, "Not that horrible homemade nettle tea."

"I'll just go borrow some from your office then."

So he sprinted to her office, stole two foil-wrapped bags of Morning Jazz, and sprinted back. He filled the electric kettle. While the water heated, he got the mugs and unwrapped the tea bags.

"How is Jem?" Hannah asked, obviously trying to keep the disapproving note from her voice and not quite succeeding.

"He's the same as always. He breaks into my apartment whenever he wants, and I come home to find him and Scipio napping on the couch together. He makes me spend money I don't have on clothes I don't want, and then he proceeds to tell me I have no butt and gives me ridiculous orders about how many squats I should be doing. Oh, and he eats like he's fourteen. I think if I took a blood sample, I'd see Big Mac special sauce running in his veins."

Her eyes narrowed. "Why is he talking about your butt? Is that a gay thing? Is he making a move?"

Tean rolled his eyes. "We're just friends."

"As my grandmother used to say, 'You can fool yourself, and you can fool your mother, but you can't fool me.'"

"We're just friends."

The kettle whistled, and it was a nice excuse for Tean to turn away from the look in Hannah's eyes. After pouring the hot water so the tea could steep, Tean sat and said, "Is this about Norbert?"

"No. I mean, not really. I hate that old bag of bones, and I think he's doing a terrible job at something I care about. He's this awful reminder of how things used to be—a good-old-boys club where all you had to do was ride around in your truck and bust people who weren't your friends. But it's not enough to get worked up over."

Tean chose not to mention the screaming that had taken place fifteen minutes earlier.

Fiddling with the tag at the end of the tea bag's string, Hannah stared off into space for a moment. When she spoke again, she said, "I honestly feel like I'm going crazy, Tean."

"You have seemed upset for a while now."

Hannah laughed. "You're too nice. I've been a bitch for months. I know I have. I've had a lot going on. That's not really an excuse, no reason to treat people badly. But it's the truth. No, this is something else. It's just been the last little while."

"What?"

"I think someone's following me."

3

Jem was stocking men's shirts in Snow's Department Store, in the men's section, under the watchful eye of Mr. Kroll.

"No, no, no," Mr. Kroll snapped. He stood with perfect posture, hands clasped schoolboy style at his waist, his graying hair shiny with pomade. "Mr. Berger, have you been paying attention at all?"

"Yes, Mr. Kroll," Jem said. "I've definitely been paying attention." He'd been paying attention, for example, to the way Mr. Kroll watched his ass when he bent over to arrange the shirts on the display table's lower shelves.

"Well, it's very hard to tell from the sloppiness of this work. Can you please try a little harder?"

"Of course, Mr. Kroll."

Jem was hoping that would settle the matter—sometimes Mr. Kroll just liked to poke his nose in long enough to remind everyone that he was the manager of menswear at Snow's Department Store, which was apparently the retail equivalent of being the king of England. Instead, though, Mr. Kroll just stood there, smelling like baby powder and gardenia, until Jem started to sweat. His back was itching like crazy, and he couldn't breathe in a shirt and tie and jacket.

"For heaven's sake," Mr. Kroll said, pushing past Jem to grab a shirt that was still wrapped in its plastic. He shook it in front of Jem. "What does this say?"

"Giroux," Jem said. He'd memorized that one quickly. "And the rest of these are Giroux too."

"Not the brand, ignoramus," Mr. Kroll said, moving closer until his body pinned Jem against the display table. Jem had front-row seats to the broken capillaries in Mr. Kroll's nose, to the faint wrinkles around his mouth, to the way he ran his tongue inside his upper lip when he raked his eyes up and down Jem. Mr. Kroll tapped a finger against the packaging. "This. What does this say?"

Jem's face heated. He was learning—with Tean's help—but it was still hard, and he was slow. He still had to work out the sounds in his head most of the time. Decoding, Tean called it. And it was extra hard because Tean also insisted that Jem was dyslexic, although Jem didn't think that was the case. Nobody had ever told him before that he was dyslexic, anyway.

Mr. Kroll was still staring.

Sweat prickled under Jem's arms. He resorted to his usual tactic in these situations—his number one, charm-the-shit-out-of-a-bear smile.

"LinenTouch," Mr. Kroll said. "And what about this one?"

That one was easy because Tean made Jem read everything at the grocery store. "Cream."

"And is LinenTouch the same as Cream?"

Jem had something smart to say about that, something about Tean, who probably would have worn LinenTouch pants with a cream-colored shirt and ivory loafers, but he just smiled and shook his head. Now that Mr. Kroll had pointed out the difference, Jem could see the slight variation in the colors of the—what he'd thought of, until now, as white—dress shirts he'd been stocking.

"And I don't suppose reading each shirt's color and then putting it in the right pile, I don't suppose that's too much."

"No, Mr. Kroll."

"And it's not too much to assume you can read, is it?"

Jem's face was on fire, but he still smiled. "No, Mr. Kroll."

"And it's not too much to hope you can finish this job in an efficient, timely manner, without my standing over you to make sure you do it properly, is it?"

The old perv would have loved that, Jem knew: standing there, mooning over Jem's ass, snapping out orders that Jem had to obey. Once, he had made Jem pick up pins after another clerk had knocked them on the floor. Mr. Kroll had stayed to observe the whole thing. He hadn't picked up a damn pin himself; he'd just stood there, swallowing obscenely whenever Jem looked up from where he knelt on the floor.

All Jem said, though, was, "No, Mr. Kroll."

"Then see that you do it."

With a snappy little spin—about a half-inch shy of clicking his heels together like a good Nazi—Mr. Kroll headed over to ties, where he was already ripping into Sydney. "If our patrons choose to buy a poorly manufactured tie from a margarita-swilling, beach-bum crooner, that's their own business—and their own poor taste in judgment," Mr. Kroll was saying. "But the Snow's Department Store menswear will go up in flames before we display those ties next to the Stefano Riccis."

"What got in his garter?" a voice asked behind Jem. Mckenna was barely twenty, Tongan, with glossy black hair that came to her waist. She was also stunningly gorgeous, which seemed to be Snow's Department Store's primary requirement for female employees. Distantly related to Jem's neighbors, the Latus, Mckenna had helped Jem get the job at Snow's in spite of his lackluster track record—this was his sixth job in three months.

"It's a phase," Jem said. "He's just going through that forty-year-long, involuntary celibacy phase. You know, when creeps like him are awful assholes because they can't get anybody to look at their junk."

"I think he wants you to do more than look at it."

Jem gagged.

"Oh shit, he's looking over here," Mckenna said. And, true, Mr. Kroll was glaring at them and already abandoning Sydney, who was sobbing into a rack of Margaritaville neckwear.

"Pretend you're whispering something," Jem said.

"Why?"

"Because I told you to."

"No, I mean, why pretend? I can just whisper something for real."

Mr. Kroll was getting closer.

"Then whisper something for real," Jem growled.

Mckenna leaned in and spoke softly into his ear: "I swear to God he's getting a boner just thinking about yelling at you."

"You're the devil," Jem said, fighting a smile as Mckenna slipped away.

"I'm sorry," Mr. Kroll said as he approached. "Did I miss something? Did I overlook a staff notification that this time is meant to be used for idle conversation and fraternization? This is Snow's Department Store," invoking it like the name of God, "and that might not mean anything to you, Mr. Berger, but it certainly does to me. Your behavior reflects on the menswear department as a whole and on me personally, and I'm starting to believe I made a grave error—"

Jem let the rest of the words float past on a cloud of baby powder and gardenia. He might not be able to read LinenTouch—not yet, anyway—but he could read people, and Mr. Kroll couldn't have bluffed his way past a middle-schooler.

"I'm sorry," Jem said, lowering his voice and laying a hand on Mr. Kroll's arm. It was painful, really, the sudden flush in Mr. Kroll's wrinkled cheeks. "I'm really sorry. I just heard, though, and I thought you should know. Everybody else wanted to let them catch you with your pants down—oops, I mean, you know, unawares; sorry for the vulgarity—but I just don't think that's right. You take care of us; we ought to be taking care of you too."

The cocktail of flattery, physical touch, and conspiracy hit most people hard; Jem had used it plenty of times before. It hit Mr. Kroll harder than most, practically flattening him.

"Yes, well, I don't—you'll have to—it's not entirely clear—"

"Surprise inspection."

Mr. Kroll's eyes shot open.

"Mckenna thinks it's only a sixty-percent chance. She didn't want to freak you out. But I think the only responsible thing to do is to get ready."

"Good heavens," Mr. Kroll breathed, fanning himself. "Merciful heavens."

"It's too bad we don't have much time," Jem said, "because I was talking to the CEO's secretary—we bumped into each other when I was filing my HR paperwork—and she told me how much he loves See's caramels. I'd run over and get some, but—"

Jem threw a dispirited look at the display table with the dress shirts.

"Go," Mr. Kroll whispered fiercely. "Hurry. And get two boxes. No, three."

"My credit card—"

"Go." Mr. Kroll was strangling on the word as he shoved cash into Jem's hands and pushed him toward the door. "Mr. Snow himself," he breathed, the Messiah coming again. "Hurry!"

Jem jogged toward the door. He waved the cash at Mckenna as he passed men's active wear and winked.

She rolled her eyes.

4

Jem spent the afternoon dicking around. Normally, he would have used a beautiful spring afternoon to hit up some of the sheep around Temple Square; if he were lucky, he could pull in a few hundred bucks before he needed to clear out. But ever since realizing that Teancum Leon thought he was a scumbag, he had tried to reform. A little.

Instead, he walked through City Creek Mall, the billion-dollar development in the heart of Salt Lake, watching shoppers: a young woman with four kids and a stack of shoeboxes, obviously trying to outfit the whole herd in one go; a middle-aged man examining expensive watches and, in between rounds, bitching out the poor salesman who was trying to help him; a teenage couple on what might, possibly, could have been their first date, the boy's chest puffed up, his face practically glowing as he clutched the girl's hand. She was going to need a hacksaw when she wanted it back.

At five-fifteen, he walked back to Snow's, carrying two boxes of See's chocolates in a plastic bag, and waited in the parking lot. Spring in Utah was beautiful and ephemeral—it came late, and summer was already hammering on the door. But today, the weather was mild, the sky was clear, and the cherries were just reaching the end of their blossoms. Jem thought they still had a little of their fragrance.

When Tean picked him up, the doc was in a foul mood. His dark, brushed-back hair showed signs of stress—he'd obviously been running his hands through it like crazy—and his big, ugly black glasses were even more crooked than usual. The doc was wiry but stronger than he looked; right then, he was gripping the steering wheel so tightly that his knuckles were white.

"For the fourth time," he snapped as they waited at the traffic light to get out of the Snow's parking lot, "I do not want a chocolate wingding or whatever they're called."

Jem nodded, popped the offending chocolate in his mouth, and said, "Thanks again for doing this."

"And don't talk with food in your mouth."

"Oh. Right." Jem had to slurp up some chocolatey drool before continuing, "Thanks. See, this is why we're best friends."

"We're not best friends." Tean hit the gas a little too hard, and the white Ford lurched forward. He had to brake to keep from hitting the Volvo in front of them. "We're friends."

"Really good friends."

"A normal level of friends."

"But with a special past."

"With a past where you lied to me and took advantage of my good nature just so you could drag me into a murder and conspiracy that almost got me killed."

"I know you keep saying that we're just friends, but when you say stuff like that, it sounds awfully romantic." Jem grinned at him. "I think we might secretly be really good friends and you just aren't willing to admit it. This is an epic bromance. You're going to see."

Without looking over, Tean said, "You have nougat in your teeth."

Jem was still laughing—and checking his teeth in the visor's mirror—when his phone buzzed. He answered.

"Mr. Berger?" Mr. Kroll's voice sounded snappier on the phone's speaker.

"Hi, Mr. Kroll. Sorry I didn't make it back before the end of my shift; a bunch of conventioneers were at See's, and the line took forever. The convention sounded really interesting, though. CHL. Clean Herbal Living. Have you already been? I thought of you."

Tean's eyes were huge as he eavesdropped, and he had to shove his glasses back up to keep them from falling off his face.

"That's very interesting," Mr. Kroll said. "I was wondering who your source was."

"Oh, I can't tell you that."

"Because there was no surprise inspection."

"Huh." Jem gave it just enough of a pause. "Well, like I said, it was only a sixty-percent chance."

"I talked to my own source," Mr. Kroll said. "Apparently there was zero chance of a surprise inspection happening today."

"Weird." Jem was fishing another chocolate—this one with caramel inside—out of the box. "Well, because I was running so late, I dropped off those boxes of chocolates with that secretary, you know, the one I met at HR. And I signed your name on the card, so at least you'll get some brownie points."

"Mr. Berger, it has come to my attention that you've been appropriating clearance merchandise."

Wincing, Jem closed his eyes. "What? What does that mean?"

"Several departments have reported missing clearance merchandise, and I have eyewitnesses who saw you taking it. You're fired, Mr. Berger. And you should expect a visit from the police."

"Mr. Kroll, this is a huge misunderstanding. I would never—"

The call disconnected.

Jem slid the phone back into his pocket and began searching for one of the chocolates he knew Tean liked.

"What was that?" Tean said.

"Oh nothing. Here, have this raspberry crème. You like those, right?"

"I'm trying not to eat sugar."

"Why?" Jem asked.

"Because death by diabetes is a horrible way to go."

"But you don't have diabetes."

"Yes, but I'm—"

"And you're not at risk for diabetes."

"Technically, we're all at risk if we eat enough—"

"I think you're just grumpy and not eating the chocolate out of spite."

The struggle on Tean's face was real; Jem kept his own expression clear. After a moment, Tean snatched the chocolate and shoved it in his mouth.

"You're welcome," Jem said softly.

Tean glared at him around a mouthful of raspberry crème.

They drove another block, heading further away from the mixture of retail and office buildings that made up much of downtown Salt Lake City. They were heading west, and the city showed the socioeconomic shift: strip malls with payday loan stores, tattoo parlors, Dollar Generals, and—increasingly—boarded up store fronts. The infrastructure showed the same shift, as the asphalt became cracked, the potholes poorly patched — or not patched at all — and the sidewalks choked with weeds. On the yellow brick of a vape shop, someone had painted a mural of a can of pinto beans as the Virgin Mary, with Our Lady of Goya in gothic letters arching overhead.

"Oh my gosh," Tean finally exploded. "You really aren't going to tell me?"

"Tell you what?" Jem poked through the box. "There aren't any more raspberry crèmes?"

"That you just got fired."

"Oh. That."

"Yes, that."

"Well, I thought, you know, I'd spare you the unpleasantness. Because you're my best friend."

"I am not your best friend. I am a normal friend —"

"You're shouting."

"I am a normal friend," Tean continued, obviously trying to control his volume, "and I'm a normal level of upset that you have gotten fired from your sixth job in three months."

"The McDonald's doesn't count," Jem said. "I was my own best customer. They shouldn't hold that against me."

"You ate four Big Macs on one shift and didn't pay for any of them. After the manager told you not to."

"I want you to be completely honest here. You know how delicious Big Macs are. And you know I'm weak willed. Is it really my fault?"

"Yes! And it's also your fault that you stole a five-gallon bucket of their special sauce."

"We can agree to disagree."

"And before the McDonald's there was the construction job —"

"That guy never proved I took his wallet."

" —and before the construction job, there was the office job at the tech start-up —"

"Ok, those people should have had enough common sense to know I wasn't really an investor whiz kid. And they definitely should have known better than to pay me cash."

" —and before that there was the job selling cotton candy at Jazz games —"

"I love cotton candy. Sue me. And you know what? Those corporate boxes weren't being used anyway, so I don't know why I can't score something extra on the side by renting them out."

"—and now Snow's. Stealing merchandise. And what else? What else happened?"

"Hold on. I'm not a thief."

Tean's bushy eyebrows looked wilder than usual as he shoved his glasses back into place. The effect gave him a slightly deranged look.

"Ok," Jem corrected. "I am a thief. But they were just going to donate that stuff to DI; why does it matter if I take it?"

"Because it's not yours!"

The shout echoed through the truck's cab. Jem reached over, squeezing the nape of Tean's neck, letting his hand rest there.

"You're having a bad day."

"Get off."

"You're really tense."

Tean knocked his hand away, and Jem just rested it on Tean's neck again, his thumb massaging lightly.

This time, the doc did a lot of squirming and shifting like he wanted to slip out from underneath Jem's touch, but he didn't knock his hand away. Progress. Maybe one day the doc wouldn't want to crawl out of his skin when someone showed basic physical affection.

"What happened?" Jem said.

"You got fired, and—"

"That's not what you're upset about."

"It is, actually." They turned into the parking lot for the Royal Mounties Lodge, an apartment complex, and Tean parked the truck and killed the engine. He sat still for a moment, and then he shoved his hair back with both hands. "You're making really good progress, Jem, but you need a job—"

"I've never needed one before."

"—and you need an apartment—"

"I have an apartment."

"—an apartment where you're not squatting—"

"Ouch."

"—and a retirement account and health insurance and—"

"Ok, ok, ok." Jem shushed him, running his thumb up and down Tean's neck. "So what's going on with you?"

"It's Hannah." Then, before he could stop himself: "And Ammon."

A horn blatted down the street. When Jem spoke, his voice was even. "I thought you weren't talking to Ammon. I thought you cut things off."

"It's complicated."

Jem released a controlled breath.

"It is. We've just been talking on the phone. He called me late one night, and I was worried it was an emergency. Then he started calling more often—"

"Which explains why you've been exhausted lately."

"—and he can't say it, but he's going through a really bad time right now."

"Oh, you mean the big fucking shitstorm he made of his own life? The one that he completely deserves?"

"This is why I didn't tell you."

"I want you to tell me! If you're upset and you're worried, I want you to tell me. But I also want to shout about it because I hate that fucker, and he deserves to have his balls run through a gristmill."

"This, right now, this is why I didn't tell you."

Jem shook his head a few times and finally managed to say, "What about Hannah?"

Tean told him in a few short sentences about his conversation from earlier that day.

"But she hasn't actually seen anyone following her?" Jem asked. "I mean, not the same person, no one she could identify."

"No. But she's freaked out, and she's not the kind of person to freak out."

Jem had met Hannah Prince, and he agreed with that assessment. "Well, it's pretty easy to figure out if someone's following her."

"Oh yeah?"

"Yeah. Have somebody follow her, and see if they spot anybody else doing the same thing."

Tean grunted. "Yeah. Maybe."

"We could do it this weekend if you're really worried about her." Jem grinned. "My shifts just got canceled."

"It's too early for jokes about that. Come on or we'll be late for our appointment."

As Jem opened the door, he paused and said, "Hey, Tean, thanks for doing this."

In the apartment complex manager's office, Tean helped Jem fill out the rental application. Reading the application itself was a challenge, but the content of the questions was almost as difficult. Jem didn't really have references, although he did put down Tean and Chaquille, a weed-dealing grad student at the U. Even basic stuff like his Social Security number was tricky—Jem hadn't even known what his was until a few months before, when Tean had helped him get the information from the Division of Child and Family Services foster records. For that matter, Jem still didn't know what the number was—he had to check the card—but Tean, of course, had it memorized.

The real issue, though, was that Jem didn't even understand why this mattered so much. The apartment, yes, but really, any of it—the health insurance, the bank account, something that Tean called a Roth IRA, and he talked about it like he was referring to the Holy Grail. As Jem filled out the forms—well, as he wrote down what Tean told him to write—he glanced around. If the apartments looked anything like the office, with inches of paint over its old paneling and a mustard-colored ceiling, Jem wasn't sure that living in an apartment that he legally rented was going to be any better than squatting in the empty unit where he currently lived. If anything, it looked a fair bit worse. But this was another of Tean's manias, and Jem, for reasons he couldn't fully explain, found himself willing to do a lot of crazy things to make Tean happy.

"I know it's not much to look at," Tean said quietly; he must have noticed Jem looking around the room. "But it's in your price range."

When they got to employment, Jem started working on the S in Snow's—it still took a lot of concentration to keep his handwriting from looking like a grade-schooler's—when Tean whispered, "Put down self-employed."

The apartment complex manager was a sallow-faced man in middle age, and his accent made Jem think he was from Pakistan or maybe India. He accepted the form when they completed it and asked for the credit check fee.

"The website didn't say anything about a credit check," Tean said.

"I'm sorry, but this is our policy."

"When I called, I was told—"

"It's fine," Jem said, and he forked over thirty bucks.

Two minutes later, the manager shook his head. "I'm very sorry, sir, but we cannot offer you a contract today."

"What do you mean?" Tean said. "Why not?"

"Unfortunately, the gentleman's credit score falls outside a desirable range."

"Let me see," Tean said.

Nodding, the manager pushed his chair back and let Tean approach the monitor. Tean's dark eyes roved over the screen and then he glanced up at Jem. "Did you default on a Wells Fargo credit card?"

Jem shook his head.

"What about a Chase Visa?"

Another shake of his head.

"What about—"

"I've never had a credit card," Jem said. "I've never had any kind of loan, actually."

"Crap," Tean said. "This is a mistake. This isn't—"

"I'm very sorry," the manager said, "but this is his Social Security number, correct?"

"Yes, but—"

"And this is his name, correct?"

"Yes, but you don't understand—"

"Then I'm very sorry. We cannot offer him a contract today."

"I'll co-sign," Tean said.

Sighing, Jem stood and caught Tean's arm. "Let's go."

"If I co-sign," Tean said, "you can offer him a contract, right?"

"We will have to run a credit check," the manager said.

"Ok. I'll write down my—"

"No," Jem said.

"It'll just take a minute."

"No," Jem said. "I don't want you to do that."

He said it a little too loudly. Tean's dark eyes were wide, and he pushed his mane of hair back with both hands.

"Let's just go," Jem said more quietly.

Back in the truck, they drove in silence for a few minutes.

"I'm sorry I yelled," Jem said.

"No, I'm sorry. I shouldn't have gotten so pushy."

The truck whumped over something—a foam cup, Jem saw in the side mirror. Sunset lit up the valley in shades of orange and gold. The mountains were a wall of fire.

"Did it have an address?" Jem asked. "For those credit cards."

Tean hesitated. Then he said, "Tooele."

"That's what I thought. LouElla." Jem's last foster mother had expensive tastes and a habit of taking in extra kids just so she could get the state's money. He hadn't known, though, about the credit cards. He hadn't known something like that was even possible.

"It's identity theft," Tean said, "and fraud. She could go to prison."

"Ok."

"We'll figure it out."

Jem wanted to ask why they should even bother; he was suddenly tired of the whole thing. But all he said was, "Ok."

With a suddenness that surprised Jem, Tean turned into an AutoZone lot and parked the truck. He took out his phone and placed a call, and then he said, "Hannah? Yes. I've got an idea. How would you feel about hiring someone to look into, you know, what's going on? Just for the weekend. Maybe it'll make you feel better." He listened for a moment and said, "No, his rates are very reasonable. And he happens to have just finished a job, so he's completely available. Ok. Ok. Perfect. Yes, I'll tell him. We'll be there tonight."

When Tean put away the phone, he had a small smile. "I think I just got you your next job."

Jem arched an eyebrow.

"What? Why not? You're good at this kind of stuff—you proved it with everything that happened with Benny. And Hannah's desperate for help. And it'll be easy money. She's probably imagining the whole thing, and by Monday, you'll have some cash in your pocket, and she'll feel better, and maybe my life at work will go back to normal."

Jem smiled. "You don't have to worry about me. I promise I can take care of myself."

Tean studied his hands on the steering wheel, a shy smile playing across his mouth, and said, "Well, that's what friends do, right?"

"Best friends."

"Don't push it."

Laughing, Jem patted Tean's leg. "Thank you. But why do I get this sick feeling in my stomach that you're determined to make an upstanding citizen out of me?"

5

Hannah lived in a brick Craftsman bungalow on the east side of Salt Lake, in a neighborhood called Wasatch Hollow. Jem had been there once before, when Hannah had invited him and Tean over for dinner with her and her husband, Caleb. The house was on a street of similar Craftsman bungalows, all versions of the same design: dormer windows, exposed rafter tails, wide porches. Kids were playing a game of rollerblade hockey in the middle of the street, and a girl with pigtails gave Jem and Tean a nasty look when she had to lug her goal out of the way. It reminded Jem of one of his foster homes—the one where the man had tried to force his way into the bathroom with Jem.

"Those kids could get hurt," Tean said, "playing in the street like that."

"This isn't exactly a high-traffic area."

"It just takes one. Where are their parents?"

"Probably devoutly canning apples. Or warming up their prayer pads for a really good jaw session with the Lord."

"I don't even know what a prayer pad is," Tean said.

"It's my idea," Jem said. "For people who spend a lot of time on their knees. Don't try to steal it; I already patented it."

"I think you're safe."

"It can also be used for other things."

"Ok."

"Sex things."

"Yep. I said ok."

Jem let the moment drag out before saying, "Mouth stuff."

"Oh thank heavens," Tean whispered as he pulled to the curb. "We're here."

Caleb, Hannah's husband, answered the door. He was another classic Utah boy: skinny from running too many miles, clean shaven, his mousy hair in a conservative cut and part. He owned a half-million-dollar home in a nice part of the city, wore an Omega watch, worked for the Huntsman Cancer Institute in pediatric oncology, and probably thought of himself as pleasantly middle class. In the background, Divorcee, Hannah's teacup Yorkie, was barking. Caleb nodded when he saw them and said, "Listen, guys, I think we've had a misunderstanding."

"No," Hannah said, appearing behind him. She was flushed, her eyes red, her whole face puffy. Jem wasn't sure when he'd seen her last, but she'd definitely put on some weight. "No mistake. Come on in."

Caleb didn't make a face, but his lack of expression communicated enough. He stepped aside, and Jem and Tean followed Hannah into the house. Divorcee pranced around them until Hannah picked her up. She led them to a living room that fit the perfect, middle-class home in the perfect, middle-class neighborhood, with the perfect, middle-class family: a leather sectional, an enormous TV, glossy paintings of Jesus done by Liz Lemon Swindle and Minerva Teichert. Two sets of Mormon scriptures were conspicuously set out on the coffee table, complete with highlighters and pens and pencils — all the trappings necessary to ensure the neighbors that, yes, scripture study was a daily part of their lives.

An older man and woman were sitting in the living room, waiting. The woman was obviously Hannah's mother: the same chestnut hair, the same shape of her face, although thirty years older and nicely kept up with surgery and the right dermatologist. The man looked like just about every Mormon man over fifty that Jem had ever met: balding, pink cheeked, not a whisper of facial hair, and substantially overweight in an expensive suit. Jem immediately pegged him as having some sort of church position of authority.

"My mom, Virgie," Hannah said, "and my dad, Howard."

Everyone shook hands and sat, and it wasn't until Jem was pressed up against Tean, sitting closer than Tean probably would have liked, that Jem noticed how tense the doc was. Jem threw him a look, but Tean stared straight ahead, ignoring him.

"Caleb called my parents," Hannah said, "when I told him that Jem was going to be looking into things."

"Absolutely right," Howard huffed. "We appreciate the offer, boys. We really do. But if something's genuinely wrong—"

"I told you that something was wrong," Hannah said. "I don't know why you act like there's still a question about it."

"—but if something is genuinely wrong, we'll handle it in the Lord's way: first, you rely on your family, then you rely on the ward, and only then do you look outside for help. Caleb and Hannah's ministering brothers will make sure that they get all the help they need." He had his hands folded over his belly, and he was smiling. "So while we appreciate you coming all the way out here, there's really no need."

"What the fuck is a ministering brother?" Jem whispered to Tean.

"Excuse me," Virgie said, her fingers crimping the hem of her skirt, "but I would appreciate it if you didn't use that kind of language in my daughter's home."

"This is a disaster," Hannah said. "I'm sorry, Tean. I didn't know this was going to happen."

"I don't know why you're apologizing," Caleb said. "Tean, I like you, I'm grateful you're willing to help Hannah. Jem, I know we've only met once, but you seem like a good guy."

"I'm not," Jem said.

"He's really not," Tean said.

"But we've got a good support system," Caleb said. "And right now, any problems we have, we're going to solve them as a family." He smiled, glanced at Hannah, looked away. "I really think we're getting all worked up over nothing."

"Unbelievable," Hannah said. "All three of you: you're unbelievable."

"Stalking isn't nothing," Tean said. His gaze finally came up from the floor, moving from Hannah's parents to Caleb to Hannah. "Hannah and I have worked together for a long time. She's gone out into some pretty remote areas all by herself. She's always handled herself without a word of complaint. She's never been spooked, not in the entire time I've known her. I don't understand why you aren't taking this seriously."

Virgie and Howard looked at each other. Caleb and Howard looked at each other. Virgie and Caleb looked at each other. Nobody looked at Hannah, who was staring at her hands locked around Divorcee.

"Thank you boys for coming over," Howard said, maneuvering his bulk toward the edge of the cushion and then standing. "I've always been outspoken about the need for our different communities to cooperate—"

"Wait," Jem said, "is he telling us to take a hike because we're fags?"

Tean groaned and covered his eyes.

"I really won't stand for that kind of language," Virgie piped up.

"Now listen," Howard was saying. "We've been very polite up until now, all of us, but I think it's time for you to go. The fact that you'd try to prey on my daughter during a difficult time, to take money from my daughter during the dark night of her soul—"

"That's it," Hannah said, shooting to her feet. "We're done. Jem, Tean, I have my own money. I'll pay you. Mom, Dad, go home."

"Hannah," Howard said. "We need to talk about this."

"Yeah," Caleb said. "We need to talk about this."

"What's your rate?" Hannah said to Jem, setting Divorcee on the floor.

"I—" Jem began.

"Seventy dollars an hour plus mileage," Tean said.

Jem blinked.

"Fine," Hannah said.

"Seventy dollars an hour?" Howard said. "That's highway robbery. Hannah, let's call some of the brethren and ask them if they can recommend someone—"

"Fine," Hannah said more loudly. "I'll write you a check for a retainer. Just a second."

As she moved out of the room, Caleb, Howard, and Virgie turned identical glares on Jem and Tean. In the stillness, the only sound was the ticking of a clock somewhere in the house, and then the creak of floorboards as Hannah made her way back to the living room.

"Will fifteen hundred dollars be enough?" she asked, already filling out a check.

"Um," Jem said.

"Yes," Tean said. "And Jem will provide you with reports showing how it was spent."

"I will?" Jem said.

"I'll type them," Tean said.

"Oh. Then, yes. I will."

"That better not be coming out of our Deer Valley deposit money," Caleb was saying.

Howard was digging out his wallet. "If anyone's going to pay for this kind of ridiculousness, it ought to be her father."

Scribbling her signature, Hannah leaned back from the check and examined it once more. Then she handed it to Jem. "There. Done. Do you need me to sign a contract?"

"Howard," Virgie was saying, "Howard, I really think Brother Shepherdson could help. He was in the Army, after all."

"Yes, yes, yes," Howard said. "Hannah, let's ask Brother Shepherdson. He's been ministering to our family for thirty years, and—"

"And he was in the Korean War, Dad," Hannah said. "He just had his second knee replacement."

Something seemed to snap inside Caleb, and he said, "I don't understand why you're making such a big deal out of this."

"Of course you don't," Hannah said without looking at him.

"How can I?" Caleb shouted. "You won't talk to me. You'll barely spend five minutes in the same room with me."

"I need some air," Hannah said to Jem and Tean. "Come on."

They followed her to the door. Howard was huffing, and Virgie was crying. Jem had to give her points; he recognized a fake cry when he saw one, and Virgie was in the Elizabeth-Taylor league. Caleb came after them.

"Hannah, just wait. I shouldn't have yelled."

But Hannah just grabbed a jacket and stepped out into the night.

"What are you doing?" Caleb shouted, grabbing Tean and spinning him around. "What is this weird game you're playing?"

Tean's glasses had slipped to the edge of his nose, and he blinked at Caleb.

"You've made some pretty dumb mistakes tonight," Jem said, checking his pocket for the paracord with the hex nut, the telescoping antenna, the barrette with the sharpened tip. "You don't want to make another."

"Caleb," Tean said, "she's upset. Let us talk to her and make sure she gets back safely."

"And in the meantime," Jem said, "get your fucking hands off of my best friend."

"My ears," Virgie wailed.

"Just a regular friend," Tean muttered.

His face twisted with anger and helplessness, Caleb released Tean. Jem caught Tean by the elbow, whispered, "Glasses," and steered Tean toward the door. Tean caught his glasses just before they fell off his nose.

The night was cool, smelling like irrigation water from the sprinklers, spring grass, and the jubilee roses starting to bloom under Hannah's front windows. Hannah stood at the end of the driveway, hugging herself against the chill, just a silhouette as the last daylight died in the west.

"Come on," she said when they reached her. "I want to show you something."

6

Tean and Jem followed Hannah up the block. The streetlights were coming on, shedding pale cones of light. The Craftsman bungalows glowed, the windows warm and yellow against the night. The mountain breeze picked up, carrying the smell of frying onions. In the short time that Tean and Jem had been inside Hannah's house, the roller-hockey kids had packed up and gone home, and Tean found the silence oppressive. He'd known Caleb and Hannah for a long time, and he'd never seen them fight. Ever. Her parents, from what he had gathered, had always been a difficult factor in Hannah's life, and with the toxic combination of President Howard Lackey and Sister Virgie Lackey taking sides in Hannah and Caleb's fight, Tean couldn't imagine how that encounter could have gone any worse.

Hannah turned north at the end of the block, and at the next intersection, she turned east. The street ended at a split-rail fence with a narrow opening for people to enter on foot. A sign said Wasatch Hollow Preserve, and a trail followed the sloping ground across a manicured lawn, past a playground, to the cottonwoods and oaks along a creek. The water looked high with the spring melt.

"Emigration Creek," Hannah said as she started down the trail. "I'm not really in any condition to go jogging right now, but I used to run along here. Now I take walks."

"This is a nice spot," Jem said. "Did you grow up around here?"

Hannah nodded. "Two streets up from where I live now, in the fine tradition of all Utahns."

"You said—" Tean began, but he stopped when Jem threw him a look that he didn't completely understand. He recognized the nonverbal *stop* in the expression, though. "Um, you said you liked this area."

"Yeah," Hannah said, looking around her as though she'd never seen the place before. "I guess I do."

"One of the foster homes where I lived," Jem said, "there was an irrigation canal on some undeveloped land. Some of the older kids would swim in it, but I was way too scared."

"Gosh," Hannah said, "that's so dangerous. And nobody said anything?"

"I don't even think the foster parents knew. They were pretty good people, but they had kids of their own, and four fosters, and they were just pulled in a million directions all the time."

"I can't even imagine." They walked another yard, the only sounds the ripple of the creek and their shoes on the worn asphalt trail. "If it were up to my parents, they'd crawl inside my skin and run me like a puppet."

"That's an image," Jem said, laughing.

"Kind of like the *Loa loa*," Tean said. "The African eye worm. It lays eggs in the skin, and the worm can migrate through the human body for ten to fifteen years. Sometimes you can actually see it in the eye as it crosses the sclera, and the dead worm bodies can build up around the brain and — why are both of you laughing?"

Neither of them had the decency to answer him.

After that — since his contributions to the conversation were clearly not required — Tean decided to be an observer. In the weak light that filtered through the new leaves on the oaks and cottonwoods, Hannah's cheeks were hollow, her eyes dark, her shoulders slumped. Jem, on the other hand, still looked like Jem: his dirty-blond hair in a hard side part; his beard neatly trimmed; not muscular like somebody who hit the gym every day, but with shoulders and arms that said he knew how to do hard work — although, in Tean's field studies, he'd never seen Jem doing anything even approaching manual labor. Jem was more inclined to sack out on the couch with two Big Macs, an extra-super-double-whatever-they-called-it order of fries, and a Coke roughly the size of Utah Lake.

Jem glanced at Tean, his eyes sharply curious, as though he had sensed Tean's scrutiny. He very well might have; he had an uncanny degree of instinct. A smirk pulled at the corner of his mouth, and even though his lips didn't move, his eyes said, *Busted*.

Tean flushed and stared straight ahead.

For a while, they just walked, and Jem did what he was good at: he seemed to be talking, but mostly he was listening, asking questions, using Hannah's name. Making her trust him. Tean wasn't even sure that Jem knew he was doing it—at least, not anymore. It was second nature to him now. And there was no malice in it; it was just Jem being Jem. Put Jem in a roomful of people, and they'd all be writing him checks and trying to set him up with their daughters—or sons—by the end of the night. Put Tean in a roomful of people, and by the end of the night they'd all be scrabbling at the doors and windows, trying to claw their way out.

Something in the conversation caught Tean's attention, and he tuned back in as Hannah said, "This is what I wanted to show you."

The trees grew close together here, casting thick shadows; Tean was surprised to realize he could hear nothing of the city, although suburban homes were probably only a few hundred yards in every direction. The air was chilly and, for Utah, humid; Jem was chafing his arms through the ridiculous turquoise-and-pink windbreaker he insisted on wearing.

"I can't really see anything," Tean said. "Let me turn on my light."

"No," Hannah said. "Don't. I want you to see it the way I saw it. I was standing right here, around this time of night, about two weeks ago."

"Do you remember what day?" Tean asked.

"Friday or Saturday. A weekend night because I wasn't worried about getting up for work the next day."

"Ok," Jem said. "What happened?"

"I looked behind me. Go ahead and do it."

Tean glanced back. The sodium-vapor lamps from the playground threw off a hazy cloud of light where the trees thinned and the path climbed back up away from the creek. The effect was like looking along a dark tunnel and spotting the relative brightness at the mouth. A bird moved nearby in the trees—a nightjar, Tean guessed—twigs crackling to announce its passage. Jem swore, and then he laughed, scratching his beard, when Tean and Hannah looked at him.

"Well, I'm not a Super Scout like you two," he said. "And this place is creepy as hell."

"It is, isn't it?" Hannah said. "I'd never thought of it that way. When I looked back, I saw someone standing there. Just an outline, silhouette, you know."

"Man or woman?" Tean said. "Tall or short? Bulky or thin? Distinctive clothing, hair, physical traits—"

"Oh, yeah, like was it the Hunchback of Notre Dame?" Jem asked.

Tean tried to punch him, but as always, Jem was too fast.

"I really don't know," Hannah said. "I couldn't make out any details."

Jem and Tean shared a glance, and Jem jogged back the way they had come.

"What's he doing?" Hannah asked.

"Just wait," Tean said. When Jem had positioned himself at the end of the trail, he was nothing but a silhouette. "Was the person facing the trail, the way Jem is right now?"

"I think so."

"Profile," Tean shouted.

Jem turned to the side.

"No," Hannah said. "They were definitely facing the trail."

"As tall as Jem?"

She shook her head.

"Shorter," Tean shouted.

Slowly, Jem squatted.

"Like that," Hannah said.

"Stop," Tean called.

Jem froze.

"About the same width?"

"Definitely not," Hannah said.

"Bigger?"

"No, definitely thinner."

"Ok," Tean called. "We're good."

Jem contorted himself into a Quasimodo-style pose and shuffled toward them.

"You're embarrassing yourself," Tean called.

Jem, however, was committed, and he shuffled the rest of the way back.

"I'm not going to be embarrassed for asking if this person had a distinguishing physical trait."

"Of course you aren't," Jem said, laughing as he straightened up.

"Both congenital and acquired traits are important ways of identifying—"

"Yep, it makes perfect sense that the Hunchback of Notre Dame would be hot on Hannah's trail."

"I didn't say—"

"It's really good detective work, Doc. A-plus."

Tean decided to wait this time. He needed the advantage of surprise.

"Five-four," Jem said to Hannah, "or five-five. That's my guess based on how far I had to hunch—get it?—before you said it looked like the right height."

"I'm five-six," Hannah said.

"So maybe a little bit shorter than you," Tean said. "Either a woman of average height or a man who's below average."

Hannah nodded slowly.

"Do you have an idea of who it might be?" Jem asked.

"No."

Even with the darkness hiding most of Jem's reaction, Tean knew what the other man was thinking: Hannah had just lied to them.

"What happened after you saw this person at the end of the trail?" Tean asked.

"It looked like she—this person had something in their hand. I thought it was metal because of the way it caught the light."

"A knife?" Jem said.

"Maybe. Or maybe some sort of tool. I guess somebody could be coming down here to work on the trail, dig up a plant."

"In the dark?" Tean said. "Without a flashlight?"

"I know," Hannah said with a sigh. "I've been trying to explain it away. This person started down the trail, and I freaked out. Normally, I go about halfway along the trail and turn back; the full distance is a little too long for me when I just want a nice walk. But I was scared. Terrified, actually. And the other end of the trail lets out on a subdivision street, so I just went as fast as I could. Then I cut back around, staying in the subdivision, and made my way home."

Jem spoke next. "Why do you think this person was following you?"

Hannah let out a breath she didn't seem to know she'd been holding. Some of the tension went out of her shadowy figure, and when she answered, she sounded like she was on the edge of tears. "Thank you for asking me like that. Caleb immediately tried to convince me I was being hysterical. My dad too. You saw, well, you saw how they acted. They don't believe me. They don't want to believe me. For my dad, it's because — well, it's complicated. Because I'm a woman. That's a lot of it. But I've been . . . unreliable in the past. In his view, anyway. My mom goes along with whatever my dad says. And Caleb — I don't even know if he hears me sometimes."

"Why don't you tell us what happened after you saw this person on the trail?" Tean asked.

"I stopped. Twice. I was scared out of my mind, but I was also trying to be rational. This is a safe neighborhood. I grew up here. I'm nobody important or special, and there's no reason somebody would want to follow me, let alone hurt me. But both times I stopped, I heard the footsteps stop too."

"That's interesting," Jem said.

"Right? I think they had to be following me. They didn't want to get too close, so they stopped and waited until I started moving again."

"I think that's a good sign," Jem said. "I'm not sure this person is trying to hurt you. It seems to me more likely that they were following you for another reason."

"Or, like many psychopathic killers and serial killers," Tean said, "this person was simply rehearsing the kill, enjoying the pleasure of partially acting out the fantasy. It's a frequent early step before the actual killing, a kind of transitional period where the pleasure of the fantasy is starting to fade, but the potential killer still isn't quite ready to — ow." Tean rubbed the back of his head. "Jeez, Jem, what the heck?"

"I saw a bug," Jem said flatly. He was trying to communicate something with a look. A very irritated look.

It took a moment. "Um, oh, you know, actually, I think Jem is probably right. This person was probably just interested in you for some other reason."

Hannah burst into tears.

"Hey," Jem said, putting an arm around her, "we're going to figure this out."

"I am not helpless," Hannah said.

"I know."

"And I'm not defenseless."

"I know."

"I broke a cinderblock with my bare hands," Hannah said. "Tae kwon do."

"Construction sites of the world," Jem said, "watch out."

"And I have pepper spray."

"If you need a test subject," Jem said, "Tean will volunteer."

"With my luck," Tean said, "I'll probably get blinded and stumble into traffic and get run over by a gang of teenage hooligans."

"This isn't about you," Jem muttered. "And hooligans? How old are you?"

Hannah laughed a little at that, wiping her face, and they headed back down the trail. "I've seen a car following me," Hannah said as they walked. "After that night, I mean. A green car. Dark green."

"Make and model?" Tean asked.

Hannah shook her head.

"Anything else?" Jem said. "Strangers who look like you might have seen them before? Unusual traffic on your street? Phone calls? What about your trash?"

"My trash?" Hannah said.

"Have you noticed that anything is different?"

"I don't know. It's trash. We just wheel it down to the street once a week."

"Well, you might want to keep an eye on it."

"Jem loves digging through trash," Tean said. "He's really cute when he does it. Like when Scipio is trying to dig down to get a mole."

"I don't love it," Jem snapped. "And I'm not cute—I mean, that's—you're missing the whole point. I'm just saying people throw away a lot of stuff that can be personally revealing, so just bear that in mind."

Hannah nodded. "Gosh, this is the first time in two weeks that I've felt even vaguely optimistic."

"We're going to figure this out," Jem said.

"That's not a legally binding guarantee," Tean said. He shrank when both of them looked at him, but he added, "Just to be clear."

"We'll stick close to you all weekend," Jem said. "But if we're doing our job right, you probably won't see us. That doesn't mean we aren't there, though."

"We?" Tean asked.

"Yes, obviously," Jem said absently. To Hannah, he said, "Do you want us to start tonight?"

"No," she said. "The Turners across the street are having a family party; there are a million cars I don't recognize, and I wouldn't know where to tell you to start. Tomorrow will be fine."

"Get online," Jem said, "and order some security cameras. They're cheap, they're easy to set up, and it'll help us figure out if the same person keeps coming around the house."

"I'll do it as soon as I go inside," Hannah said as they stopped in her driveway. Her parents' car was gone. She glanced at the dark windows, sighed, and added, "Right after Caleb and I fight this out to the death."

Jem and Hannah hugged; Tean and Hannah hugged. She squeezed Tean extra tight and whispered, "He's amazing. Don't screw this up."

And before Tean could even start figuring out what that meant, she was hurrying up the walk.

"What's this we business?" Tean asked as they went back to the truck. "You're the one who's getting paid."

"Yes, but I'm like Sam Spade, and you're like my girl Effie Perine." Jem adjusted his seat belt. "You're willing to do this out of your pure love and devotion to me."

"A normal-friend level of love and devotion. Actually, no devotion at all. And just friendly friendship feelings. No love. And Effie got a paycheck."

"And besides, what else were you going to do this weekend?"

"I was going to stare up at the empty skies and think about how the universe is endlessly spinning us farther and farther into a cold, merciless void and about how we're all going to die and how meaningless everything is. Just a normal weekend."

Grinning, Jem rested a hand on the nape of Tean's neck, squeezing lightly. "Let's get some ice cream."

That was when Tean pounced. The punch got Jem in the ribs, and the blond man rocked back in his seat, groaning.

"That's for the hunchback stuff," Tean said.

"I've got a punctured lung."
"Good. You deserve it."

7

Jem woke early in the West Valley apartment where he squatted. Someone was hammering on the front door. He had slept in a pair of shorts—the ambient heat of the building kept his unit plenty warm, especially in the spring—and he padded to the door and glanced out the peephole. In the hallway, a small woman was examining a clipboard. She had bottle-blond hair, and her mouth was a slash of bright pink lipstick. She knocked again, called, "Hello," and then tried the key. It worked, and Jem slid to the side as the door opened. Then the chain caught, keeping the door from opening more than a few inches.

"What in the world?" the woman said. "Hello? Is someone in there?"

Jem had played this game before; he stayed out of sight and waited.

Grumbling to herself, the woman finally let the door fall shut, and the sound of footsteps moved along the hallway. She'd go get a maintenance worker, and they'd eventually be back with a pair of bolt cutters. It wouldn't be fast, though; Jem always chose apartment buildings that showed signs of neglect, where it was obvious that nothing happened in a timely manner.

The bummer was that Jem had liked this apartment. A lot. He made his way through the unit, dressing, shoving clothes in a duffel, grabbing the few toiletries that were worth taking, mostly hair products, because they were expensive. He left the mattress and bedding and the fan. That stuff was all easy to come by. Then he opened the window onto the fire escape, slid the duffel out onto the landing, and climbed out of the apartment.

As he went down the fire escape, he wondered if maybe Tean was right: maybe it was time to get a real apartment. In a few days, Jem would be twenty-eight. That meant he'd been doing this shit for ten years. Ten years of wondering if he'd have running water, ten years of stealing electricity, ten years of shoving everything he owned in a duffel bag and climbing out the window. Right then, with the duffel's strap digging into his shoulder, ten years felt like a long time.

On his way down, he stopped and rapped on the Latus' window. Kaelo, who was about Jem's height but otherwise twice his size, opened the window. He was in a Dodgers t-shirt, and he was eating a rice cake with peanut butter.

"Hey," he said, a grin crossing his big face. "You going on a trip?"

"Kind of. Somebody—new manager I guess—tried to get into the apartment today."

"Oh," Kaelo said, crunching the rice cake down in two bites. "Bummer."

"Yeah. Just wanted to get this back to you," Jem tugged on the extension cord that had run from the Latus' window up to his own. "And say thanks."

"Come on in," Kaelo said. "Amelika and Sammy are going to want to say goodbye."

"No, I should—"

But Kaelo just picked him up under the arms and pulled him inside the apartment like Jem was a toddler. As Jem steadied himself, the big man moved across the apartment's front room, calling out for his wife and daughter. When Jem repeated his story, Amelika started to cry, and then she immediately launched herself into the kitchen.

"You're such a dork," Sammi said, who was sixteen but looked much younger, lurking by the hallway that led to her bedroom. Her arms were folded, and her chin was down. "Why can't you just pay rent like a normal person?"

"Sammi," Kaelo said.

"Well, why can't he? I mean, then he could just stay here."

"I'm going to heat up some of that pork," Amelika said.

"I'm sorry," Jem said. "I really don't have time."

"Nonsense."

"He says he doesn't have time," Kaelo said.

"You stay out of this."

"I should go," Jem said. "Thanks again for everything."

"If you need a place for a day or two," Kaelo said, "we've got the sofa."

"I really couldn't—"

"Oh yes you could," Amelika said. "Kaelo's baby brother stays here all the time when he's sleeping one off."

Kaelo shrugged and nodded.

"All right," Jem said. "Thanks. Let me see what happens."

"Just leave your bag right here," Amelika said.

Laughing, Jem climbed out the window again. "I'll see what happens. Thanks again."

Amelika caught him and gave him kisses on his cheeks, and then Kaelo reached through the window and hugged him so hard that Jem's spine cracked. Sammi shot him the finger from where she was still lurking.

Jem finally disentangled himself, dropped down from the end of the fire escape, and headed toward his bike. He kick-started the Kawasaki and made sure he didn't look back, not once. He pushed himself hard all the way to Tean's place, splitting lanes, taking turns too fast. And when he got to the dumpy Central City apartment building, he felt hot, flushed all over, and he sat on the bike taking huge breaths. Then he went upstairs.

Scipio lunged toward him as soon as Tean opened the door. The Lab went wild, licking Jem's hands, giving half-hearted, abortive jumps and then circling around and nuzzling into Jem's legs like a bulldozer. Even though Jem had been through this routine a hundred times now, every time Jem saw the dog, he still felt himself tense, his hands clenching into fists, his heart rate accelerating. His last foster mother, LouElla, had kept a dog named Antony on a chain in the basement, and Jem had been locked down there more than once. He still had the scars to prove it.

"Ok, ok, ok, you big dummy," Tean said, ruffling Scipio's ears. The doc's hair was wild and brushed back—standard—and he was wearing jeans and a polo that were the exact same shade of blue—also standard. "He knows you're here. Give him five seconds." Then Tean did a double take, and Jem recognized his own mistake; he should have left the duffel with the Latus. "What happened?"

"Nothing."

"Are you going on a trip?"

Laughing, Jem dropped the duffel in the living room and knelt, bracing himself against the initial burst of panic as Scipio licked his face and crashed into him.

Tean's hand settled on Jem's shoulder. "What's wrong?"

"Just, you know, making some changes. Hi, hi, hi. Yes, hello. Do you need to go on a walk?"

"No, he doesn't need to go on a walk. He had a very stimulating walk this morning. A teenager made a bad throw with a frisbee, and Scipio thought he was being attacked. You should have seen the big coward. Did you have to leave that apartment?"

Jem heard how Tean stepped around the issue, picking the words carefully. He felt hot again, and he buried his face in Scipio's fur. Ten fucking years of this. And Amelika giving him those kisses on his cheeks.

"Just, you know, time for a change. I've already got a great spot picked out."

The doc's hand slid down, feather-light on Jem's back, always so uncertain when it came to simple things like this, always willing to try even though it made him uncomfortable. "Ok. Where?"

"I'll show you some time." With a mock growl, Jem gave Scipio a tiny shove, and the dog went wild, pouncing for his basket of toys and coming back with a rope for tug of war. Jem caught the other end and let Scipio yank him around while he got to his feet. "Ready to go?"

"Jem, where are you going to stay?"

"I told you: I found a new place. I really like it. We're practically neighbors."

Judging by how those insanely bushy eyebrows went up, Jem didn't think Tean believed him, but all the doc did was shove the glasses higher up his nose and nod. "I was going to make us some breakfast."

"Please God, no."

"What?"

"I mean, you don't have to do that."

"I have some oatmeal from yesterday I can heat up, but I might have put too much powdered cloves in it. It was a little strong. And I have some unsweetened almond milk. I bet I could do something with that."

"I have absolutely no doubt you could 'do something with that.'"

"What does that mean?"

"Let's go. I'm buying breakfast. Sausage biscuits, hash browns, coffees."

"I don't really —"

"With eight sugars and a bunch of cream for you."

Tean's eyes brightened, but then he said, "I really shouldn't —"

"You weigh like a hundred pounds," Jem said, encircling Tean's wrist with a thumb and forefinger. With a shove to get the doc started, Jem herded him toward the door. "And you're eating the whole damn biscuit."

Twenty minutes later, they were in Tean's truck, parked down the block from Hannah's house. Tean ate the biscuit and drank his coffee. His only comment was, "It just seems wrong to make it taste so good." Jem rolled his eyes at that and didn't bother trying to understand what he meant. He ate his own sausage biscuit, polished off both hash browns, and sipped his coffee.

It was a Saturday morning in the Salt Lake Valley, and it was a beautiful spring day. Hannah's street, with its Craftsman-style homes and tidy yards, was mostly inhabited by respectable Mormon families. And, Jem was starting to remember from various foster homes, Mormon families loved to do chores on Saturday. Men and women and children were outside up and down the street: mowing the grass so that it looked as clean-cut as any Mormon missionary's hair; weeding flower beds; picking snails off a rosebush; digging up a damaged irrigation pipe. Two men had stopped along a property line and were looking at Tean's truck, talking.

"I think we might have made a mistake," Jem said.

"Hmm?" Tean said.

"Well, Mormons are a pretty tight-knit community, right?"

"For the most part. The congregations are geographic, and in a part of the world with a dense Mormon population, that might consist of only a few blocks. These people are all likely part of the same ward."

"And don't they have assignments to make sure other families are ok?"

"Yes. That's what Hannah's dad was talking about last night; they call it ministering."

"And what do you think the odds are that a tightly knit community would like a couple of strangers showing up on their street and just sitting there, watching them?"

Tean must have noticed the two men walking toward them now because he said, "Oh. Dang."

"Mind if I handle this?" Jem said.

"Not at all."

The men could have been brothers — in a place like Utah, in fact, they might have actually been brothers. Or cousins. Or whatever. They were stocky, both dressed in shorts and shirts that were obviously meant for yard work, already stained with grass and dirt. They carried themselves in a way that Jem recognized. He'd first spotted that way of moving in Decker, the juvie facility where he'd spent several years as a teen. Kids came into juvie walking like that, like they were tough shit. The first time the lights went out, though, they learned things were different, and they didn't carry themselves like that anymore.

"Hi, guys," Jem said. "Beautiful day, right?"

"Can we help you guys with something?"

"We're just here to do some necking," Jem said. "And maybe some heavy petting if we have time."

The guys made identical, straight-guy revulsion faces at each other.

"This is a nice street," one of the guys said.

"This is a nice place for families," the other guy said.

"Hold on, hold on," Jem said, flashing a smile. "Before you run me out of town, we're here to help Hannah and Caleb with something. We're not creepers, ok? If you don't believe me, just ask them."

The men exchanged a long look. The first one said, "Wait here." The second one nodded, leaning against the Ford's door, obviously still trying to look tough.

"You ever have to do any edging?" Jem asked the guy who had stayed with the truck. "Like, along the sidewalk?"

The guy snorted. "Every week."

Across the street, his buddy was at Hannah and Caleb's front door, talking to Caleb. Caleb looked stiff as a scarecrow, and he was speaking in what looked like short, sharp sentences. After a minute of that, the guy turned around and came back. He didn't even make it all the way to the truck; he just nodded and waved, and his buddy pushed off from the Ford's door.

"I hated edging," Jem told him. "Worst fucking chore of the week."

"Watch your mouth," the guy said as he walked away. "There are kids out here."

Jem grinned and gave him double thumbs up.

"Will you stop antagonizing him?" Tean asked, pushing his hands down.

"What? Edging sucks ass."

Tean groaned.

"So, that's really interesting, right?" Jem said.

"What?"

"The fact that the Utah Gun-Loving Bros Association made a personal visit when we'd been here for less than fifteen minutes."

"It's interesting that for some reason you think you're charming but still manage to make people want to shoot us."

"There's no way that somebody has been sitting out here watching Hannah's house."

Tean was quiet for a moment. "Unless it was someone who had a reason to be here."

"Like someone on the street? You think one of her neighbors is following her?"

"Maybe." He hesitated and frowned. "Crypsis."

"Blade."

"What?"

"I thought we were naming sexy vampires."

"Why would we—never mind."

"Lestat."

"Crypsis is—"

"Edward Cullen."

"Will you cut it out?" When Jem held up his hands in surrender, Tean said, "Crypsis is the term for—"

"Angel. Sorry, that's the last one, but I couldn't leave him out."

Tean took a deep breath. "Crypsis is the term for an animal's ability to avoid detection or observation."

"Like a chameleon."

"Yes, camouflage like that is one example. But it can also be behavioral—nocturnal activity is a form of crypsis, and so is subterranean activity, or mimicry. Some species of squirrels will actually rub themselves with snakeskins to disguise their scent. And the red knot, a sandpiper, alters the chemical composition of its preen waxes to hide from predators. I thought you'd appreciate that because of all the wax you put in your hair."

"I'm going to ignore that because having a bird preen your hair would actually be an improvement." Jem thought for a moment. "Is it like when one animal looks like its surroundings so it's hard to see?"

"Yes, exactly. So maybe we're dealing with a case of crypsis. Someone who looks like they had business on this street, or someone who people have a special reason to trust: a gas company employee reading meters, someone in a bright orange vest marking property lines for the county assessor, a cable technician —"

"A Mormon missionary," Jem said. "It can't be that hard to get one of those little tags they wear on their shirts."

Tean frowned. "Why a missionary?"

"I don't know. It just popped into my head."

"There would have to be two of them."

"Why?"

"Have you ever seen one by himself? Or herself?"

"I guess not."

"And I think Hannah would have noticed if they were dressed in white shirts and ties."

"Maybe. Maybe not. They're kind of like background noise out here."

Tean frowned some more. He had little frown lines that looked like parentheses on both sides of his mouth.

So Jem told him.

"What?" Tean said.

"They're adorable. Like parentheses. You know?" Jem traced the shape in the air.

"I know what a parenthesis is."

"You acted like you didn't. Hey, maybe you should do some frowning on all of these hot dates you're going on. I bet those guys would like your frown lines."

Tean looked like he wanted to frown but was now struggling not to.

"And then maybe you'd get a second date," Jem said.

"I'll get a second date when I want a second date," Tean said.

"Of course you will. Especially with those cute frown lines."

"Can we please not talk about lines on my face? Or anything on my face? Or my face at all? Or second dates or dates or anything? Let's just not talk about anything for a while."

"I was trying to give you a compliment."

"To get back on topic," Tean said, his voice betraying an effort to sound normal, "I thought we had decided that it was likely a woman who had followed Hannah on the trail."

"Or a short man."

"Ok. Well, she only saw one person."

"Short people can have friends too."

"I don't know."

"No, they totally can."

"I meant I don't know why someone would dress up as a missionary. I mean, it wouldn't be hard at all. Almost all missionaries keep their name tags after they come home, so it'd be a simple matter of getting them out of storage or stealing them from someone. But why? Mormons are nosy about missionaries; they don't like seeing them waste the Lord's time, so if they were loafing around, someone would probably approach them and try to figure out what they were doing."

Jem thought about this for a moment. "So you still have your name tag?"

Tean's knuckles were white on the steering wheel.

"Oh my God," Jem said. "Oh my God!"

"No. Whatever you're thinking, no."

"Tean, this is perfect. For Halloween, we can dress up as missionary companions."

"You didn't go on a mission. You don't have a name tag."

"I'll steal one. Oh my God, this will be perfect. The absolute perfect costume for best friends. And it'll be ironic."

"It's not ironic at all. And best friends don't dress up for Halloween together. And you'd have to shave your beard."

"Well—"

"And the only acceptable friend costumes for us would be if I were a katydid and you were one of those caterpillars from Ecuador that look like bird poop and together we looked like bird poop on a leaf."

"Did you just make a crypsis-slash-poop joke?" Jem said.

"No, it was a fashion recommendation."

"Cryptic poop. That's better. Did you just make a cryptic poop joke?"

Tean lowered his head to rest it on the steering wheel. "Get out of the truck. Go away."

"That's not a very nice way to talk to your best friend-slash-missionary companion. Also, Hannah is pulling out of the garage."

Tean sat up, started the truck, and put his hand on the gear shift.

"Hold on," Jem said. "We're waiting to see if anybody else follows first."

"I know. I just want to be ready."

Hannah glanced both ways as she backed out onto the street, and her gaze slid over Jem and Tean without seeming to register them. She was driving a blue Ford Focus, the paint on the hood flaking and, in many places, already gone. Hannah's car made Jem think of Caleb's Omega watch, made him wonder what the hell kept the two of them together. He adjusted the truck's rearview mirror, checking to see if anyone was pulling out to follow Hannah, but the street remained empty. When Hannah had reached the next intersection and was signaling to turn, she still didn't have anyone following her.

"All right," Jem said, and Tean eased the truck away from the curb.

They spent the day tailing Hannah as she ran errands: Nordstrom, Wasatch Dry Cleaners, a clothing consignment store called Grandma's Dusty Muffin—Jem tried to talk about the name, but Tean turned on classical music and played it so loudly that Jem finally gave up—REI, and ending with groceries at Albertsons. She stopped halfway through the day for lunch at Kneaders, and they used the time to run back to Tean's apartment and let Scipio out. On their way back to the Kneaders, Jem, luckily, spotted a Sonic and made Tean pull in. Jem liked their tater tots, and Tean was practically glowing as he talked about trans fats and the increased chances of his heart exploding from a blocked artery, or something like that.

All in all, it was a great day, with only one exception: there was no sign whatsoever that someone was following Hannah. In their initial conversation, she had mentioned a green car, and although Jem had seen many green cars, none of them had come close to tailing Hannah.

It was early evening, the May day mild, the smell of cut grass and gasoline floating in through the Ford's open windows, when they parked on Hannah's street again. The sky behind the Wasatch Mountains was dark blue, smoky with clouds. When the breeze died down, the smell of grass and gasoline faded, and Jem could smell what had been driving him crazy all day: the slight fragrance of sagebrush and range grass and pine that clung to Teancum Leon. The doc was frowning again, and Jem traced the lines around his mouth with a mental fingertip. What would it be like, Jem wondered again, to wear everything on the surface like that?

"This was a mistake."

For a shattering moment, Jem thought Tean meant this, the two of them. Then Jem cleared his throat and said, "What?"

"We shouldn't have brought my truck—it's got the DWR logo on it, and it's way too obvious. And we shouldn't have parked on her block and drawn attention from the neighbors. If Hannah does have a stalker, they probably saw the whole thing and decided to try again another day. We never had a chance."

"Ok," Jem said. "In hindsight, I'm realizing I don't make a very good stalker. That's normally a good thing, right?"

Tean's phone buzzed, and he accepted the call. He spoke quietly for a few moments and then disconnected. "That was Hannah. She says she's not leaving the house again tonight, not even for a walk."

"Maybe she and Caleb are going to have sexy times."

"It didn't sound like it. It sounded like they were in the middle of another awful fight. He was still shouting in the background."

The doc's eyes were shadowed, and he looked so upset that Jem squeezed his shoulder. After about ten seconds, Tean squirmed out from under the touch. Progress.

"If you're right," Jem said, "and we spooked Hannah's stalker, do you think he'll come back tonight?"

Tean hesitated and then shook his head.

"Then let's do this," Jem said. "Let's try again tomorrow, but we'll do a better job. Can you borrow a car from someone?"

"Yes. I guess."

"Ok. That's the plan."

They drove back to Tean's apartment, when they got out of the truck, Jem headed for his bike.

"Hey," Tean called after him, "what about your duffel bag?"

Jem pretended not to hear as he kick-started the bike, and then he drove into the city, heading to the Apollonia. He was friends with one of the bartenders, and the hotel was about halfway between Temple Square and the Salt Palace Convention Center. Jem always had good luck picking up closeted businessmen there, and he could leverage sex into a bed for the night. He thought, briefly, about the Latus' offer of the sofa. He thought even more briefly about asking Tean if he could crash. But ten years of taking care of himself won out. It wouldn't be the first time he traded sex for a place to sleep. It wouldn't be the last.

8

The businessman, who sold HR training packages for a company based in Boise, complained about vertigo and cried a lot after sex. Jem slept poorly, and he woke before dawn, showered, and went through Roy Allen Kitchell's wallet, examining the Idaho driver's license, the Red Cross donor card, the deck of Visas and MasterCards, and then the cash. Jem counted it—eighty-six bucks—and folded it twice. When he shoved it in his pocket, he suddenly had a vision of Tean's face, the disappointment. It was confusing as fuck, and it only made Jem grumpier.

He knocked on Tean's door just before seven.

"Hi," Tean said, wrestling Scipio as the Lab desperately tried to reach Jem, "come on in."

Five minutes later, when Scipio finally seemed to think he had successfully communicated his boundless love to Jem, Jem wiped an arm across his face and said, "Oh no. Not again."

"What?" Tean said.

"This," Jem said, pinching the sleeve of Tean's blue polo. "And this." He swatted the blue jeans. "You wore this yesterday."

"These are clean," Tean said, blushing.

"I'm sure they are. How many of these polos did you buy?"

Tean bit his lip. "They were two dollars each, so—"

"How many?"

"Seven because you said blue is a good color—"

"Come on," Jem said, pushing Tean into the bedroom. He threw open the closet door and started sorting. He pushed all the khaki-colored stuff to one side—that was most of it, and it constituted Tean's work outfits. A very small section at the back contained clothes that Jem had either given to Tean or forced the doc to buy—

under duress, as Tean was quick to point out. Jem raked through the clothes quickly and said. "You want a polo today?"

"Actually, I'm totally good. I can dress myself, and—"

"Ok, fine, a polo. And you're determined to wear that pair of jeans?"

"I like these jeans. They were three dollars and fifty-seven cents, and I've had them for ten years, and they don't even look like they're wearing out."

Jem buried his face in the hanging clothes and screamed.

"And they've got these nifty copper rivets."

Dragging a polo off a hanger, Jem said, "Don't say nifty."

When Tean caught the polo, he held it up and made a face.

"Put it on," Jem said. "No arguing."

"It's pink."

"I said no arguing."

"It's too bright. I look flashy."

"Well, if you weren't so fucking cheap, we could buy you some clothes that you like and get you a pair of glasses that aren't always falling off your face. And you could live in a way nicer apartment. With two bedrooms. And we could go out to eat more. And you could have furniture that you haven't had since college."

Tean stood there, still holding up the shirt, locked in place.

"Wow," Jem said. "That was really shitty. I'm sorry."

Scipio stumbled into Tean, and Tean petted the dog mechanically.

"Look, I didn't sleep well last night."

"In your new place."

Jem just wiped his mouth.

"Will you get out of my room so I can change?" Tean said.

"Yeah. Right."

In the front room, Jem dug through the duffel he had left there the night before. He found his Super Mario tee, black jeans, and a denim jacket, and he took it all into the bathroom and changed. When he came out of the bathroom, Tean was still in the bedroom, so Jem put his dirty clothes in the duffel and sat on the couch. Within about five seconds, Scipio had climbed up and stretched out across Jem's lap: eighty pounds of Lab, rolling onto his back and kicking his legs like a puppy, giving Jem a what-are-you-waiting-for look. Jem scratched the dog's belly.

When Tean came out of the bedroom, he was wearing the pink polo. Scipio thrashed around, threw himself off Jem's lap, and charged toward his bowl. Once Tean had scooped out some kibble, he said, "Let's go," and stepped into the hall. He hadn't looked at Jem once. Scipio on the other hand, stopped devouring his breakfast long enough to stare at Jem.

"Don't you start," Jem muttered as he headed out of the apartment.

Instead of heading for Tean's DWR truck, Tean led Jem to a brown Mercedes parked in one of the visitor stalls. The car had to be thirty years old, minimum: it was boxy and small, and the upholstery looked shiny from wear. But the tags were current, and when Tean turned the key, it started right up.

"It's my grandpa's," Tean said as he started toward Hannah's house. "But he doesn't drive anymore, so it mostly sits in my parents' driveway."

Jem ran a hand over the dash, which was slightly warped and cracking in places. "It's kind of bitchin' actually."

"Great. I'll tell him."

"Come on, I said I was sorry. Don't be mean to me all day."

Tean just shook his head.

"Ok, you can be mean to me for one hour," Jem said.

"I don't want to be mean to you. Just stop talking for a while, please."

As they drove past McDonald's, Jem opened his mouth. Tean shot him a glare so quickly that Jem shut his mouth, but at the smell of frying hash browns, his stomach rumbled. Tean shot him another look. Jem put a hand over his stomach and tried to look contrite; he still wasn't very good at that one.

"You can't be quiet for five minutes?"

"It was my stomach! And it was McDonald's. I can't be held responsible. Listen, I'm going to up my deal: I will personally buy you breakfast, and you can be mean to me for one hour, and you can cut up my purple t-shirt with the old lady hats on it."

The tires thrummed. "What?"

"It's my favorite shirt. Well, one of my favorites."

"I don't want to be mean to you. And I don't want to cut up your shirt. I just want to be angry at you and feel all my feelings and then be done with it, ok?"

Jem's stomach grumbled again. "I'm not trying to rush you, but is there any chance you'll finish feeling all your feelings before they stop serving—"

At the next intersection, Tean turned right so hard that Jem forgot what he was saying. They went around the block, and on the next pass, Tean turned into McDonald's. At the drive-through, they ordered—well, Jem ordered, and he got doubles of everything, plus lots of sugar and cream for Tean's coffee—and then they drove toward Wasatch Hollow and Hannah's house.

It still wasn't eight by the time they parked the Mercedes on a cross street, right at the corner where they had a good view of Hannah's house. The neighborhood was quiet. Jem had lived in a place like this once or twice as he bounced through the foster system, and he knew what Sunday mornings were like. In some imaginary ideal home, the parents were already up, devoutly reading their scriptures, praying over cantaloupe wedges, dressing in white shirts and ties or conservative dresses. The children were probably well into their second hour of pure, unadulterated childlike prayer and reflection. In reality, the parents were probably trying to find clean socks, and the kids were still asleep, and by the time everyone was ready for church, they would have already had a few really good fights, and the day would be ruined.

As Jem unwrapped an Egg McMuffin, he said, "Call Hannah and tell her to let people know we're parked out here. You know, so we don't get the Doobie Brothers breathing down our necks again."

Tean made the call.

When he finished, Jem held out the second Egg McMuffin, the waxed paper cuffed back.

"I'm not hungry," Tean said.

"I know; you're never hungry. You still need to eat."

"I already ate."

"What did you eat?"

"Breakfast."

Jem tried really, really hard not to roll his eyes. He lost. "What specifically did you eat for breakfast?"

"Food."

"God, you are really on one today."

Tean folded his arms. Unfolded them. He seemed to consider the pink polo, and he gave it a solid yank.

"Let me guess," Jem said. "You and Scipio split a bowl of kibble."

Tean hesitated; then he decided on folding his arms again.

"No, no, no. I've got it. You had one lentil. One mushy, overcooked lentil that you saved in the pot from dinner last night."

Faster than Jem had expected, Tean turned on him. The glasses slid straight down to the end of his nose and balanced precariously on the tip. "I don't ever want to talk about money with you. Do you understand that?"

"Um. No. Not really."

"What don't you understand?"

"Why?"

"That's not your business."

"You're my best friend; everything in your life is my business."

"Not this. I don't want to talk about money. I don't want to joke about it. I don't want you teasing me about it."

"Are you still feeling your feelings?"

"Yes," Tean shouted. "Obviously."

For half a second, neither of them moved. Then a tiny smile escaped; Jem couldn't stop it. After another second, Tean flushed, the rigid lines of anger in his face replaced by embarrassment. Jem used his knuckle to bump the glasses back into place.

"God, you are adorable," Jem said.

"I'm a thirty-six-year-old man. I'm not adorable. And I'm not hungry."

"Here's the problem," Jem said, "as I see it, anyway. If you don't eat this Egg McMuffin, I'm going to eat it. And if I eat it, it's just going to spike my cholesterol even higher. And then I'm going to have a heart attack. And you won't be able to perform CPR because you'll be so upset about your best friend having a heart attack."

"Regular, normal-level friend." Tean looked like he wanted to stop there, but the hook was already set. "And it probably won't be a heart attack. It'll probably be choking. Because you swallow those sandwiches whole like a duck, and it'll get stuck in your throat, and I won't even be able to give you an emergency tracheotomy because you'll have aspirated your hash brown."

"God, yes, that's so bleak. And then?"

"And then you'll be dead. And I'll be publicly shamed for not having saved you. And I'll run away with that off-brand Mexican circus that comes through every year."

"And you'll start boning the lion tamer."

"And I'll—no, I won't. And I'll get caught up in some sort of cartel drug-running mule operation and I'll get my butt packed with heroin."

"Interesting. Tell me why your mind went immediately to getting your butt—"

"And then I'll probably mess it up somehow and the cartel will cut my face off and I'll have to wear a big floppy hat and a veil."

"Now bring it home."

"And I'll die alone, probably in the desert, and someone will find me a hundred years later and put me in a children's museum or something like that. Still wearing the floppy hat and veil."

"Wow. But honestly, not as dark as I was expecting—"

"And then the museum will burn down while several orphanages are visiting for a field trip. No fire exits. It's an old building."

"There it is."

"So that's my future," Tean said. He slumped back in the seat, looking incredibly satisfied with himself. "Ending my days as a mummy who gets incinerated on top of a pile of orphans. I hope you're happy."

When Jem offered the Egg McMuffin again, Tean accepted it and took a huge bite.

Progress, Jem thought.

After that, the stakeout passed relatively quietly. Because Mormon congregations were organized geographically, and because those geographic boundaries were so small in Utah, most of the families on Hannah's street walked to church. When Hannah and Caleb emerged from their home, holding hands and turning toward the sidewalk, Jem and Tean agreed to a division of labor. Tean slipped out of the Mercedes and followed Hannah on foot, while Jem stayed behind to watch the house. A typical Mormon worship service lasted three hours—divided into three hour-long parts—and by the time families started walking back home, Jem desperately needed to pee. He left Tean in the car, jogged south to the Sinclair, used the bathroom, and bought as many TastyKake snacks as he could carry at one time. When he got back to the car, Tean needed to pee, and Tean brought back a bag of unsalted, unseasoned sunflower seeds and a bottle of water.

"Good choice of snacks. They didn't have any raisins or prunes?" Jem said. "Or fresh fruit? Or unsweetened shredded coconut?"

"What?"

"Or, you know, like a box of instant corn mush?"

"What are you talking about?"

"Never mind. You're hopeless."

They passed the day that way. Like the day before, they saw nothing that might have constituted someone keeping watch on Hannah, and although her only trip had been to church, Tean was confident he would have spotted someone who didn't fit in. Jem thought that was another clue that whoever was following Hannah might be closer to home than she realized, but he didn't say this to Tean.

The spring day warmed up enough that they rolled down the windows, but after that it was perfect. Sometimes the air smelled like pine and sagebrush—Tean—and sometimes it smelled like roses and something else, another plant.

"Hyacinth," Tean finally said.

"What?"

"You're smelling the hyacinth in the flower bed right over there."

"How did you do that?"

Tean just smiled and shrugged.

On his next trip to the Sinclair, Jem bought a pack of cards, and they played War, Slap Jack, Speed, Nerts, and Egyptian Rat Screw. When they got hungry, Jem searched on his phone and walked the mile and a half to the Whole Foods, and he brought back chicken salad and crackers and a huge loaf of rye. When Tean started in on the likelihood of contaminated rye and death by ergotism, Jem threw crackers at his head until he shut up. All in all, Jem thought it was about a perfect day.

Dark fell over the valley. Porch lights came on, and a soft yellow glow glazed the inside of the windows. When the evening mountain breeze picked up, Jem got cold, and they rolled the windows up. Then the smell of Tean—that wild mixture of sagebrush and range grass, which had to be a cologne or an aftershave even though Jem couldn't imagine where Tean had gotten it—filled the small Mercedes, and Jem started losing: War, Speed, Slap Jack. It was getting too dark to see the cards, but mostly, he just couldn't keep his mind out of the gutter.

He was thinking about how the pink polo had slid askew across Tean's shoulders, about the hint of collarbone and chest hair, and he almost missed it.

On Hannah's street, half a block up, a light flashed in a car. It was there and then gone, and Jem immediately recognized the illumination from the screen of a cell phone. In that moment, though, Jem spotted two figures sitting in the car.

"Hey," he whispered.

Tean froze.

"Look," Jem said, indicating the car where he had seen the light. "I don't see—"

Then the light flashed again.

"Frick," Tean said.

"Does that car look green to you?"

"Maybe. It's hard to tell in the dark. Maybe it's blue."

"I think it's green."

They watched another five minutes, but the car remained dark.

"When did it get there?"

"Maybe when you had your nose buried in the bag of Cheetos, trying to lick up all the dust."

"Maybe when you were drawing that diagram of a seal's penis."

"That wasn't—it sounds bad when you take it out of context!"

The car up the street was still dark.

"I'm going to see who they are," Jem said.

"No way. We're just watching."

"I want to see."

"It's probably just a pair of kids—"

"Great. I like kids."

Before Tean could say anything else, Jem opened the door and slid out of the car. He jogged up the street, checking the pocket of his jacket for the paracord with the hex nut, the telescoping antenna, the barrette, and the folding slim jim. He settled on the barrette, tracing the sharpened tip with one finger as he approached the driver's window.

Behind him, Tean suddenly groaned, and the sound of the doc's footsteps slowed. "Hey, um, Jem. Remember how we thought maybe the people watching Hannah might have not been noticed or reported because people weren't worried about them?"

By that point, Jem was within five feet of the car. The driver's door popped open, and a tall, blond man got out. He was handsome, in his midthirties, an athlete well on his way to a dad bod. Jem knew him and, for one glorious heartbeat, thought about punching the tip of the barrette through his jugular. Then he decided that Tean wouldn't appreciate Jem murdering his former fuckboy.

"What the hell are you two doing here?" Detective Ammon Young of the Salt Lake City police department demanded.

9

Tean stepped forward, catching Jem's shirt before he could move any closer to Ammon. The residential street was quiet again, Ammon's question already carried away by the mountain breeze. Then the car's passenger door opened, and Ammon's partner got out. Kat—from Katsuki, her last name—rested her arms on the sedan's hood and watched.

The silence lasted another moment, and Ammon said, "Ok, fine. If you don't want to tell me, just get out of here. We'll talk about this later." The last half of the comment was directed to Tean, and in spite of everything that had changed over the last seven months, Tean felt his face heat.

"Why are you following Hannah?" Jem said.

"Turn around," Ammon said, "and go home before I arrest you for obstruction."

"Come on," Jem said, smiling, not taking his gaze away from Ammon as he reached down to loosen Tean's fingers from his shirt. Tean didn't miss the way Ammon's eyes darted down to where Jem's hand closed around Tean's. He didn't miss the way Jem held on a little longer than necessary. "We're buddies. We're old friends. We've been through some serious shit together, and that turned out all right."

"Get rid of him," Ammon said to Tean.

Seven months ago, Tean would have done it. Instead, though, he said, "Ammon, this is serious."

"You're damn right it's serious. You're blowing up this whole operation. Get the hell out of here, both of you."

"You're a homicide detective," Tean said. "You can't honestly tell me you've been following Hannah around for weeks because you think she killed someone."

"The only thing I'm telling you is that you have five seconds before I cuff you and have a squad car come pick you up."

"I call bullshit," Jem said, grinning as he inched closer to Tean, slinging an arm around him. Tean pushed him once, trying to dislodge him, and then gave up. "You're worried about us messing up your spot, so you're not going to call for backup. Not on your old friends."

"This is ridiculous," Kat said to no one in particular. Then, her gaze shifting to Ammon, she added, "Handle your shit." She got back into the car and shut the door.

Ammon set his jaw; it was an expression Tean knew from all the way back in high school, and for a long time — almost twenty years — Tean had reacted to that expression automatically. He'd learned to apologize when he saw that expression. He'd learned to back down. He'd learned to change course. But Jem was standing right there, his arm across Tean's shoulders, and Tean couldn't explain why that made a difference, but it did.

"Hannah asked us to—"

"Will you stop it?" Ammon snapped. The detective took two steps, grabbed Tean's arm, and dragged him down the sidewalk. Jem turned to follow. "Stay," Ammon said, pointing a finger at him.

"That one never works," Jem said with a big grin. "Except maybe with Scipio."

"Jem," Tean said, stumbling to keep up as Ammon towed him along, "just hang out there for a minute, please?"

Jem scratched his beard, but he stopped following. "A minute."

Tean and Ammon went another twenty yards before Ammon stopped. They were standing in front of a yard littered with toys — frisbees, jump ropes, the remote control for an RC car, an Elsa doll with most of her hair ripped out. Tean's eyes skated over Ammon, the set of his jaw, and settled on the lawn, the toys, the house with honey-colored light in the windows. Sometimes, when he was lost in his own thoughts, he would come up against a house like this, a husband, kids, things hoped for at the edges of consciousness and never fully put into words. He could smell Ammon's faded aftershave and his sweat.

"What are you doing?" Ammon asked.

"I'm not sure I can tell you."

Pressing the heels of his hands against his eyes, Ammon seemed to struggle to hold something back. "Ok."

"Do you want to tell me why you think Hannah committed a murder?"

"Come on, Tean." Ammon dropped his hands. He had blue eyes; tonight, they were shot through with red. "I'm working an active case. I'm not going to talk about it with you."

"It involves someone I care about."

"To some degree. That's all I'm going to say."

"Should I be worried?"

"Maybe. Have you noticed any changes in her behavior? Anything unusual?"

"Maybe. Who is she supposed to have killed?"

"Will you stop that? Jeez. Do you have any idea how you sound? Hanging out with that . . . with that asshole has made you just as much of a smart aleck. Why are you even with him? Please don't tell me you're dating."

"That's none of your business."

"Ok, ok. I know." Ammon held up both hands. Then he smiled, the old smile. "It's really good to see you. I like hearing your voice, but it only makes me miss you more."

The night breeze was colder now; goose bumps pebbled Tean's skin.

Ammon's hand, warm and solid, found his arm. His touch slid down until he caught Tean's fingers. "I know you're not happy with me—"

"Ammon, let's not do this right now."

"No, this is when we have to do it because you won't agree to meet in person, you won't answer the door when I come to the apartment, you won't write back when I email. Did you even read my emails?"

Of course Tean had. Pages and pages of them. Over and over again. Until he was sick, physically sick, with how much he hurt. And then reading them some more. But he had drawn a line in the sand the year before, after yet another broken promise, and he couldn't erase it now. He just pressed his lips together and looked past Ammon at the perfect house on the perfect street.

"I know you're not happy with me," Ammon said again, "but I want you to know that I care about you in a way I've never cared about anyone else."

"I can't," Tean said, trying to work his hand free. "Please let go."

"And I'm seeing a therapist. I'm figuring myself out."

"And you're married and have four kids. Please let go."

"If I let go, will you let me finish?"

"No."

Ammon tightened his grip, but he smiled a little. "Then I'm going to hold on a little bit longer. One of the things Chaz has helped me understand—"

"You're seeing a therapist named Chaz?"

"—is how unfairly I've treated you. That really upsets me. I want to make things right. I want to treat you the way you deserve to be treated."

"What about Lucy? How does your wife deserve to be treated?

Ammon's blue eyes widened like the words had been a slap. His lips parted, but he just took a few labored breaths. Then he managed to say, "I moved out. You're the most important person in my life; when you ended things, I realized I needed to show you that. So I moved out."

For a moment, Tean was frozen. Then he said, "I can't do this with you right now. I honestly can't. What do you want me to say to that? Why are you telling me now?" He shivered, and he didn't know if he was trying to pull away or not. "Let go, Ammon."

Ammon released him, but before Tean could take a step, he said, "I'll tell you about Hannah."

Tean rubbed his hand. "Why?"

"I'll tell you anything you want to know if it means you'll talk to me for a few more minutes."

"Don't do that. Don't make this about us. Jem and I are trying to help Hannah. You and I don't have anything else to talk about."

"She's not in trouble," Ammon said. "Not exactly."

"So why have you been following her?"

"We're looking for someone; this is a missing-person investigation. It seems like Hannah might know something. We got a tip that Hannah might go visit this person tonight; we're waiting to see if she does."

Tean blinked, trying to process this. "This is a missing-person investigation? Who's missing?"

"Her name is Joy Erickson."

It sounded vaguely familiar, but Tean shook his head. "I don't know who that is."

"Well, she was close to Hannah at one point. Some people have suggested that Hannah might know where Joy is."

"Who?"

"I can't tell you that. Please don't be mad at me; I really can't."

Tean forgot what he had been about to say. He'd never heard that note of desperate pleading in Ammon's voice before. He'd never heard Ammon beg him not to be angry before. He glanced at Ammon's face and saw unshed tears shining in the detective's eyes.

"Maybe you could talk to Hannah," Ammon said. "See if she'll tell you anything. We've called her, and she hangs up. We've tried to meet with her, and she avoids us. She's a brick wall. She knows something, and if you could get it out of her, it would mean a lot to me. I know I don't have any right to ask you —"

"I knew the homicide unit handled missing-person cases, but I thought they were pretty low priority."

"Unfortunately, that's true, especially with transient populations. A lot of people go missing, but it's hard to tell if they left town, if they just found a different crew, or if something really happened to them. In a case like this, with Joy, it's different. She's got a history of disappearing, which makes it more complicated, but she's been living in a stable situation for a long time. She's been missing for a few weeks. We found her phone in her condo, and there's been no activity on her financials." Ammon let out a breath. "It's possible that it's not a missing-person case anymore, honestly."

"And someone really thinks Hannah is involved?"

"She might know something — where Joy was last seen, if she was meeting with someone, if she had last-minute travel plans. That kind of thing. And she might be holding back because she doesn't want to get Joy in trouble; Joy has a colorful history. So maybe you could . . ."

"She's convinced someone has been stalking her. Is it you?"

"She might have seen us. Or it might be tied up with this Joy thing." A tentative smile crossed Ammon's lips. "Look at us. We're already a good team."

Off in the darkness, a poorwill was whistling its two-note song. Just two notes. Just two. Over and over again. And Ammon was singing his two-note song again. And Tean was singing his own too.

"I should get back to Jem."

"Let's get dinner," Ammon said. "To talk about what you learn from Hannah."

"If I learn something from Hannah."

"You will. You're the smartest, most determined person I know. The best person I know."

Tean's face was hot again; he took a step back. "If she shares something relevant, I'll pass it along."

"Great." Ammon grinned, and suddenly he was that same beautiful, sixteen-year-old boy Tean had fallen in love with over the cafeteria table. "You have no idea how much I've missed you."

"Good night, Ammon."

"It's really good to see you again, Tean. I want you to know I'm figuring myself out. And I'll always be waiting for you."

Tean didn't answer. He backed away, in case Ammon made another move, but Ammon just stood there in his cheap suit, his face washed out by the sodium lights, like an echo or a ghost or a lost soul. The poorwill was still whistling its two notes. Over and over again. The same two notes. Forever.

The touch of a hand startled him, and he whipped around. Jem had come up behind him, his face unreadable.

"Well?" Jem said.

Tean shook his head.

"What'd he say?"

In a few disconnected sentences, Tean managed to convey the basics about Hannah and the woman named Joy Erickson. He couldn't seem to put the pieces into a coherent order. As he stammered through the details, Jem's face darkened, a flush moving into his cheeks, his eyes cutting past Tean to fix on Ammon.

Tean finally trailed off. The poorwill had gone silent.

"Shake him off," Jem said. "Don't let him get in your head like that."

"It's not—that's not what happened."

"Yeah, it is. But you can just shake him off. I know—tell me something really horrifying. Like ants eating people alive or heat death or how the Electric Slide went out of style when kids started doing meth and dressing like Britney Spears in grade school. I ate a bunch of processed food today. Tell me about the evils of enriched flour."

"It's mostly about your blood sugar."

"Good, good. And how I'm probably going to get diabetes and fall into a diabetic coma and no one will find me and cockroaches will eat their way into my stomach and breed inside me while I'm still alive."

Tean nodded, but in his mind, he kept seeing Ammon, the windows glazed with warm light, the feeling of his hand. He'd never done heroin, but he thought this treacherous warmth, the unbearable need to believe that this time, finally, things would be different, that it must be something like this. What real addiction feels like.

Then Jem let out a single, hissing breath and muttered, "Fuck this."

"What?" Tean said.

Jem's mouth narrowed out into a thin smile and he just shook his head. "All of this. Every last fucking bit of it. Let's go; I want to go home."

10

But Jem couldn't go home. Instead, after leaving Tean at his apartment, Jem drove to the Apollonia again.

Jem didn't have a home. Not anymore. Maybe he never had, if he looked at things squarely. Was a shithole where you squatted a home? What about Decker—the dormitory rooms, the group showers, Blake and Antonio holding him down while Tanner forced his legs apart? What about LouElla's place, the antenna flaying open his back, cutting down to the bone, or the dog in the basement? What about the place before that, with the old diddler who had tried to force the lock while Jem was in the bathroom? What about before that, before that, before that? The closest he had come were the Jenkins, who used to let him and Benny stay the weekends so they could get away from LouElla. Certainly not his mother, Mary B. Berger, the cipher on his foster paperwork. Jem remembered her mostly in a series of impressions: a chemical smell that he associated with window cleaner—he still got the sweats when he picked up a bottle of Windex; her hand, chapped and rough, on the side of his face while they sat on the couch, her stoned out of her mind, him absorbed by *Darkwing Duck*; the burst of salty chicken flavor, what she called eggy-droppy, just an egg cracked into boiling ramen.

Jem picked up a guy at the Apollonia that night, a meal in exchange for a blow job, but that was as far as it went. He was a cardiac surgeon from Houston who had a framed picture of Jesus in his suitcase, propped up by a pile of dirty socks, the Good Shepherd watching while Jem went down on him. He refused to let Jem stay the night; his wife was coming back from a late dinner, he said, and she'd murder him if she caught him with Jem. Jem managed to squeeze an extra two hundred bucks out of the guy, but what he wanted was a bed and a warm body and not to feel so fucking awful about himself.

He rode the Kawasaki east, into the foothills near the University of Utah campus. The mountains were jagged black teeth taking bites out of the stars. The streets were wide and empty, the streetlights placed far apart. The cones of milky light made him think of bowling pins, like the universe was one big bowling alley, and he was just one more fucking bowling ball hurtling along: emptiness, emptiness, emptiness, and then, no matter what he did, one big mother-fucking crash at the end. He stopped at a red light, staring at the double lines on the road, seeing Ammon, seeing Tean, seeing how most of the conversation—all the important parts—happened without words because they'd known each other for so long. Because Ammon had mindfucked Tean for so long.

A horn startled him out of the black hole; the green light was so bright that he had to blink. He hit the gas too hard, braked too hard, overcompensated, and the bike slewed, spilling him into the gutter. The Kawasaki lay on its side, sputtering, and then the engine died. When a white van rolled up beside him, someone cranked the window down. A middle-aged man with bad teeth leaned out, adjusting his trucker cap.

"You all right?"

Jem stared up at the dome of stars, barely visible through the light pollution. For a moment, the anger, the hurt, the loneliness — they were overwhelming. In Decker, he had lashed out when he'd felt this way, and he had spent a lot of the time in isolation as a result. He had learned the hard way it was better to shut things down, better not to feel anything at all. He closed his eyes. After a moment, he was fine.

"Hey, buddy."

"Yep," Jem said, touching the wad of cash in his pocket, making sure it was still there. "I'm perfect."

He made it to Chaquille's without any more problems.

"Shit," Chaquille said when he answered the door. Tall, skinny, his hair in cornrows with a tight fade, Chaquille didn't look like what most people probably expected a grad student in aerospace engineering to look like. He was on fellowship and, from what Jem had pieced together, had turned down offers from Boeing and JPL before starting the program. He was wearing a tank printed with a huge marijuana leaf and the numbers 4/20 and boxer shorts with cartoon space shuttles. Behind him, strobe lights flashed inside the apartment, and a steady beat reverberated through the air. In his usual croaky voice, he asked, "What happened to you?"

Jem flashed the roll of cash.

"Fuck yeah," Chaquille said, pushing the door open wider.

After that, the night blurred for Jem. He smoked a couple of joints, tossed back shots of something that burned like hell and had an aftertaste like pineapple, and ended up making out with a guy wearing eyeliner and a skinny black tie. He didn't recognize a lot of the music—he thought they were EDM remixes of songs he'd never heard originally—but the thumping bass and the frenetic pace blended with the weed and the booze and the guy grinding on him. Eventually, the guy in the skinny black tie left to get a drink and didn't come back, and Jem found himself sprawled on a patched sofa next to Chaquille.

"What's so funny?" Chaquille shouted over the music.

That was when Jem realized he was laughing. He tried to rein it in, but it kept exploding out of him in huge, hysterical guffaws. Chaquille's eyes were flat and dull and unruffled, partly from his own blaze, partly from his natural personality. It was what made coming to Chaquille's easy.

"He's just such a selfish, self-absorbed bag of dicks," Jem managed to say between fits of laughter.

"Who?" Chaquille said.

"Both of them," Jem said, and then he was laughing too hard to stop.

Chaquille said something to a girl who was wearing nothing but an MIT t-shirt and a pair of black panties. She rolled her eyes, sauntered over to the kitchen, and came back with four shot glasses. Rolling her eyes again, in case Chaquille had missed it, she lined up the shots in front of Jem.

"Fuck 'em," Chaquille said too loudly into Jem's ear.

"Yeah," Jem said, grabbing the shot. "Fuck him."

These tasted like cinnamon, roaring to life at the back of Jem's throat. He finished all four and felt like he was breathing fire. His head sagged back on the couch. Just like Puff. Breathing fire just like Puff the Magic Dragon. What would Tean say about that? Probably something about how Puff was contributing to the irreversible effects of climate change by releasing more greenhouse gasses. Jem laughed so hard that he fell off the couch. Then he was gone.

When he woke, the apartment was painfully quiet, and his mouth tasted like dog shit. A needle of light came in through curtains that hadn't been closed properly, and Jem blinked, moaned, and squeezed his eyes shut. The headache that had been waiting at the back of his skull lunged forward, and he moaned again. He was pretty sure his two options were: a) die right there, right then, immediately; b) crawl into a hole and die there, maybe fifteen minutes from now. Option A sounded pretty good, but Option B wasn't bad either.

When a few minutes passed and he hadn't died, Jem got to his feet, wiping his eyes, wincing as the room rocked around him. The thunder in his head redoubled. The kitchen and living area of Chaquille's apartment were a continuum of the same space, and Jem spotted the girl in the MIT t-shirt curled up in an armchair, and the guy with the skinny black tie passed out on the floor. The guy had a Truman Capote-style hat covering his face, and Jem made the mistake of rolling his eyes. He paid for it with another groan.

Picking a path over sleeping bodies, Jem made his way to the door. He patted his pocket, found a single ten-dollar bill left from his score, and thanked God for McGriddles. When he slipped out of the apartment, Chaquille was in a webbed lawn chair on the stoop, poring over a page in a textbook. A packed bowl—rainbow-striped glass—sat on the facing page, and without looking up, Chaquille passed it over along with a lighter. Jem took the bowl, lit it, and took a long hit. When he exhaled, he started coughing and almost threw up, but then, by inches started feeling better. He passed the bowl back.

"Check-out service," Jem asked, his voice like gravel.

"Something like that," Chaquille said.

"God," Jem said, scrubbing his face, the head rush coming on like a train. "God."

"Yep," Chaquille said.

Jem leaned against the brick wall. The sun still made his head throb, but at least the morning was cool, the air smelling wet and clean, like new leaves. He checked his phone and saw that it was a little after nine, Monday morning.

"I don't think I said this," Chaquille said, ashing the bowl, "but I was really sorry to hear about Benny."

"Yeah," Jem said. "Me too."

"What's going on with you?"

Jem gave himself the once-over: the Super Mario t-shirt was stained with something he didn't recognize, but other than that, he was passable. "Just the same old shit," Jem said. "Different day."

"You need somewhere to stay," Chaquille said, shrugging, "you know you can crash here. For a few days, anyway."

"Thanks."

Chaquille just shrugged. He was already repacking the bowl.

Jem found his bike, the weed buoying him up like he was floating now, the headache shrinking, and made his way to the closest McDonald's. Over a McGriddle, a hash brown, and a coffee, he replayed as much of last night as he could remember: finding Ammon in the car, watching Tean and the detective touch each other, talk, the defensive lines of Tean's body relaxing, his posture opening up to the bigger man, until at the end Ammon said something that went through Tean like lightning, even if Tean wouldn't admit it. What had Ammon said? No fucking clue, Jem thought as he doused his hash brown with ketchup. And why did he have that kind of effect on Tean, no matter how badly he treated him? No fucking clue about that either.

But another part of Jem's brain was trying to track everything that had happened since he had met Tean in October. Tean was helping him learn how to read. Tean had helped him get his Social Security card and number. Tean talked — at length, whenever he saw the slightest opening — about GED programs, about community college and trade schools, about university. Tean said crazy things like 401k and Roth IRA and dental PPO. His latest mania was an apartment. So maybe that was it. Jem had assumed that, by lying to Tean when they first met, he had burned a bridge, ruining his chance to be anything more than friends. But maybe Tean's hang-up was really about HMOs and credit scores. Ammon had all that stuff, after all.

Before Jem had finished thinking about it, he was driving out to Tooele. The town sat in the valley on the western side of the Oquirrh Mountains, so Jem rode west, following I-80, passing the Great Salt Lake to the north, the water black and dimpled with sunlight, and the Oquirrh Mountains to the south. Ahead of him, the ground was flat, covered in scrubby brush that was all the same browns and dusty greens. Where nothing grew, the bare earth was pale, the color of bone when the sun hit at the right angle.

After a childhood of bouncing from foster home to foster home, Jem had ended up in Tooele with a woman named LouElla. In some ways, that had been a good thing: he had met Benny there, who had become a real brother to him; he had met the Jenkins, a lovely, older couple who had let their ranch be a refuge for LouElla's neglected foster children; he had become, if only in embryo, the person he was today. The scar on his back, where LouElla had lashed him with the RCA antenna. The scar on his arm, where Antony, the poor dog she kept chained up in the basement, had taken a piece of him. Here was where he had finally stood up for someone—for Benny—shoving LouElla when she continued to try to hit him. And, of course, that was how Jem had ended up in Decker Lake Youth Center, where he'd spent the remaining years until he turned eighteen.

He didn't need directions; he remembered the way to the 1970s split-level that sat at the edge of the foothills. It had a timber-and-stucco design, a boxy upper floor that protruded like a bad overbite, cheap windows that didn't keep out the cold. LouElla had painted the house—more accurately, she had probably made a troop of foster kids paint it—and the bluish-gray paint looked like a pathetic attempt to update the house's appearance. The basketball hoop—no net—was the same, though. The dinged-up garage door was the same. The steps where Jem had skinned his knees when an older girl had shoved him, those were the same. The Super Mario tee clung to his back when he climbed off the bike. The weed was messing him up; his head felt like an enormous wind chime, something rushing through him, a shrieking note coming back in answer.

He knocked. On the other side of the door, the house was silent. He tried to count to five, rocking from heel to heel, and then he jammed the doorbell and kept jamming it. The hammer of pulse in his ears was so loud that he didn't hear footsteps, and when the door swung open, he was still pressing the doorbell.

LouElla had always been thin, always prided herself on her looks. She was still thin, wearing a soft, clinging sweater, leggings, calfskin ankle boots. She had more jewelry than Jem remembered, a web of necklaces, rings glittering on every finger, but Jem thought that made sense: she'd had a lot of time, and a lot of kids churning through here, to build up her collection. She'd changed her hair—it was an artificial blond, short and feathery, probably expensive as hell and ugly as sin.

It took her only a moment to recognize him. Then she struck: a flurry of blows—open-handed slaps landing on Jem's face and the side of his head, driving him back, forcing him to crouch, arms up to ward off the blows. He didn't even think of the paracord or the antenna or the barrette. He was thirteen again, brain and body resetting the last fifteen years. When she had forced him to the edge of the porch, she kicked him once, hard, with a calfskin boot, and he fell off the porch and landed on his back.

She was breathing hard, but she composed herself, her hands floating around her feathery hair as though making sure nothing was out of place. Jem tasted blood. His cheek, his ear, his eye—they all felt hot and puffy.

"Well, well, well," she said. "Princess Jemma. I still owe you a broken tooth."

11

LouElla watched him for a moment and then headed back inside, leaving Jem on the ground. After a minute, he picked himself up and beat the dust out of his Super Mario tee as best he could. He spat blood from a cut on the inside of his cheek, and then he climbed back up onto the porch and went inside.

The home's interior hadn't changed much in its overall décor, although many of the details were different. LouElla had always liked expensive things that, to Jem anyway, still looked tacky: crystal figurines of angels, wooden carvings of children, enormous paintings of Jesus in thick gilt frames. Today, Jesus was walking on water, waving at people on shore with a kind of *Look, Ma!* expression. The wooden children were playing ring-around-the-rosy on the sideboard. This year's crystal angels were looking sad, wings drooping, squatting like they had the shits. Automatically, Jem toed off his sneakers in the entry hall. The shoe rack he remembered was gone, and the only shoes he saw were a pair of black flats that had to belong to LouElla.

He found her in the kitchen. She was pouring Diet Pepsi into a tumbler with ice, her attention fixed on making sure the fizz didn't escape the glass. The kitchen had been updated, definitely a gut job — Jem remembered drop-ceiling lights and acres of melamine countertop, and now he was looking at marble and stainless steel.

"This is breaking and entering," LouElla said, still eyeballing the Diet Pepsi. "Or at least trespassing. Jemma, sweetheart, I really thought you'd learned your lesson. I really thought you were on the strait and narrow." She looked up now. She had bitten her lip, an old gesture of excitement, and a bead of blood stood there. Neatly, she creased a paper napkin and blotted her lips. "I suppose I'll have to call the police. Sit down, darling. You might as well be comfortable your last few minutes as a free man."

"I want my money."

She threw her head back and laughed. When she finally settled down, she sipped the Diet Pepsi and shivered — the whole thing was a production, right down to the shiver, which she did by wrapping her arms around herself like she was on camera. "Princess, you always had such a sense of humor."

"I want my money, LouElla. You ruined my life. You ruined my whole fucking life. And I can't get most of it back, but I can get the money. I want it. Right now."

"I don't have any idea what you're talking about."

"I'll call the police."

"The DCFS money is long gone, and it wasn't ever yours. It's not like it was supposed to go into a piggy bank, darling. I spent it on food, clothes, haircuts, everything you needed. It's very expensive, raising a child."

"It's not expensive when you fed us those shitty one-dollar Banquet meals and had two deadbolts on the pantry and a lock on the fridge so we couldn't get anything you didn't want us to have."

"Many emotionally disturbed children have a hard time with self-control. They just eat and eat and eat." She oinked. "Of course, you know all about that. I heard that Benny was practically glued to you after you got out of Decker. How do you keep him fed? Oops. Did. I heard about his accident."

Something clicked on in the house — the AC, maybe, or an appliance — and a rush of white noise filled Jem's head. "Don't talk about Benny."

LouElla smiled; another drop of blood glowed on her lip.

"I want my money," Jem said. "The credit cards. Every fucking dollar you stole, you're going to pay me back. Otherwise, I'm going to take this to the police. I'm going to claim identity theft. And that'll be the end of you, LouElla. No more kids. No more cash cow."

The ice clinked as she set down the glass. "Do you see any kids, Jemma?"

"What happened? Did someone finally realize you're a heartless, money-grubbing bitch, and they took away the goose that lays the golden eggs?"

"Go away, dear heart." She touched her temples. "You're giving me a headache."

That was an old song—a headache, a headache, you're giving me a headache. Jem had a headache of his own, only it didn't hurt so much as it felt like his head was expanding, like he was floating, untethered, and just about anything felt possible right then.

"You'll go to prison. And then I'll file a civil suit and take everything you have."

Leaning across the marble, LouElla seemed to consider him for a moment. Then she laughed, and the drop of blood slid to the corner of her mouth, staining fine lines there that she had doubtless tried to plaster over with makeup. "Darling, you're serious. This is fantastic."

"I'm absolutely serious."

"Well, I have bad news for you: I didn't commit identify theft or whatever you were calling it. I've never taken out a credit card in a child's name. Really, I'd have to be pretty stupid to try something like that, wouldn't I?"

"Don't bullshit me. I'm a better bullshitter than you ever were."

"Jemma, the state would have been crawling all over me if I'd tried something like that. I was perfectly happy with my dear, dear children."

"Your address was on the credit report."

"That doesn't mean anything. Anyone could have applied for the cards. Another child, for example. Many people find it difficult to believe, but we do occasionally have a troubled child who can't tell right from wrong. Or someone else could have done it and stolen the cards out of the mail. It was all so long ago, darling. I have a hard time remembering last week."

"I know it was you."

"Prove it," she said, picking up the tumbler and rattling the ice.

"Fine," Jem said. "We'll do this the hard way."

LouElla smiled at him and sipped her Diet Pepsi.

"I'm not afraid of you," Jem said.

"Then come a little closer," LouElla said, her smile expanding, her fingertips white against the glass.

Jem's ear stung. The corner of his eyes stung. His lips stung. He tasted blood from the cut on the inside of his cheek. He was thirteen again, and no one would believe him, the way no one had believed him then. His throat was hot and prickly and tight. Shaking his head, he took a step toward the front of the house.

"I could," LouElla said, swirling the glass, the ice clattering, the sound the exact same from all the days and nights Jem had spent here. He'd forgotten how the bitch loved to swirl her ice. "I could hazard a guess, though. About who got those credit cards, I mean. If you're interested."

"Blow me," Jem said. And then, "Who?"

"I'll have to do a little digging. It was so long ago," her eyes ran up him, "and you're all grown up now. Really a man, now, Princess Jemma. Mmm. And those arms. Although I heard that your time in corrections gave you a taste for something else. Is that right? Such a waste."

"You're full of shit."

"If it's who I'm thinking of — if I'm right, I mean — you'll be able to recoup whatever you think is fair. And they'll pay a good bit on top, too, just to keep it out of the news, I'd bet."

Jem looked over his shoulder at the entry hall, the front door. And then his gaze moved back to LouElla.

"I just need," she said, rattling the ice, "a little favor first."

12

Sunday night, Tean didn't sleep. He kept thinking of Ammon. They had ended things—more accurately, Tean had ended things—months ago. He hadn't seen Ammon. He hadn't wanted to talk to him. He'd changed places he liked to go, convinced—hoping?—that Ammon would try to track him down. The changes had been easy because Jem had been there, a part of Tean's life, showing up one day to force Tean to watch 90s sitcoms and another day to make him go try a new taco place. And, of course, every day, without fail, showing up for reading lessons. And all of that had helped, made it bearable. He only ever thought about Ammon on long nights when the phone calls came, when the moon shone too brightly through the blinds and Tean considered, again and again, if he'd made a mistake.

And then Ammon had been there, tonight, back in Tean's life like a stroke of lightning.

Jem's face: the anger, the suspicion, and something that Tean wanted to call hurt.

Near dawn, he dragged himself out onto the balcony. Wrapped in an old camping blanket, he sat and watched the slow dissolve of night. A part of him bent, as always, toward the mountains. In the half-light of morning, they hung before him like clouds, like smoke, a blue haze that a strong wind could drive away.

After his tea and a walk with Scipio, he went to work. He settled in to look at the canine distemper reports again. Miguel, one of their conservation officers on the east side of the state, had sent an email to let Tean know about the increasing number of coyote deaths linked to distemper that were being reported on the Wasatch Back. The question written in invisible ink was: *What are you doing about this?* Tean went back to the research; he needed an answer to that himself.

A little past eight, Hannah came into his office, a whirlwind of Merrells and cargo pants and chestnut hair. "Phone," she said.

"What?"

"Give me your phone. Unlocked, please."

"Ok," Tean said, passing it over. "Hannah, we need to talk about last night. I think Jem and I might know what's been going on, and I don't think you're going to like it."

"Don't want to hear it," Hannah said. "Don't want to know about it. I'm done with that. I'm done fighting with Caleb. I'm forgetting anything happened. I'm forgetting we ever even talked about it." Her eyes were too bright. She was talking too high and too fast. "Did anything happen with you and Jem over the weekend?"

"What? No."

"You were in a car together for two days. You didn't accidentally grab a potato chip at the same time or bump heads when you leaned in for the same can of Dr. Pepper or both say the exact same answer to the same question at the exact same time?"

"No. And I have no idea what you're talking about. Why would I be drinking Dr. Pepper?"

"You didn't even kiss?"

"No. We're just friends. Normal, regular friends. Do you have any idea how much sugar Dr. Pepper has? And my teeth are already probably going to fall out just because that's how my great-grandmother was. I don't need any extra sugar."

"Fine. If you're not going to kiss him, and you're not even going to have a cute, rom-com close encounter with him, then it's time to get things moving."

"You seem really, um, up today, Hannah. What's going on?"

"We're getting you on a dating app. Smile."

"Absolutely not."

"Yes. It's time. Smile, please."

"Hannah—"

"I'm taking the picture whether you want me to or not, so you might as well make it a good one."

Tean stared at his phone, which was currently betraying him.

"Smile," Hannah prompted again.

"I am smiling."

"With your mouth."

Tean tried.

"A human smile. The way humans do. Like you're happy."

"I don't —"

"That's good enough," she said, lowering the phone and tapping madly at the screen. "Beach or mountains?"

"What? What is this app? What are you signing me up for? I don't want any weirdos —"

"For a vacation: beach or mountains?"

"If I want sandflies, heat stroke, and a third-degree sunburn that requires hospitalization and possibly skin grafts, the beach. If I want to break my ankle, drag myself around for days, slowly dying of dehydration, only to eventually be eaten by a mountain lion or a grizzly bear, the mountains."

"I'm putting mountains."

"Hannah!"

"It's called Prowler."

"Prowler? Are you kidding me?"

"I don't know. It's something like that."

"Prowler sounds like the guys are going to lure me into a sex trap and have their way with me."

"I don't even know what a sex trap is," Hannah said to herself.

"The guys on Prowler do!"

She lowered his phone long enough to look him in the face and say, "It's the hottest thing for gay guys right now. I was just reading about it in *Cosmo*."

"You don't read *Cosmo*."

"I didn't used to. Now I do. I'm tired of the old Hannah. I'm making some changes. And so are you. If you could donate a million dollars, who would you give it to?"

"Nope. We're stopping this right now. Give me my phone."

"Tell me, or I'll put down that charity that dresses cats like famous feminist figures."

Tean made a noise that sounded an awful lot like a scream. "There's this philosophy program that focuses exclusively on absurdism and existentialism, why life is meaningless and everything is a joke —"

"I'm going to put the World Wildlife Fund. That'll be a good opener for you to talk about your career."

Tean lurched out of his seat and grabbed the phone before she could pull it away. "Hannah, we've got to talk about last night." She opened her mouth, and he rushed to say, "Ammon was there. With his partner. I think the police are the ones who've been following you."

She had braced herself, as though expecting something terrible, but shock wiped her face blank. "What?"

"The police were at your house. They've been following you. They think you might know something about a missing-person investigation."

"That doesn't make sense. The person who was following me was a woman, right? We talked about that. The one on the trail. The one with the knife."

"The knife was just a guess," Tean said. "And Ammon's partner is a woman. Kat is about the right height. She might have been doing surveillance."

"Hold on, hold on. I'm still trying to catch up. I thought you weren't talking to Ammon. I thought you had a big fight with him last year."

Tean decided not to mention the phone calls. "Yeah, well, it's pretty hard to avoid someone when he's the point of the whole stakeout. Anyway, you're focusing on the wrong part. He said they've talked to you and you're stonewalling them, Hannah. What's going on?"

"Nothing."

"Why didn't you tell me the police were involved?"

"I didn't know! They called a couple of times. They tried to talk to me once at home. I don't want to get involved with . . . with what they're working on. I'm staying out of it. I had no idea they might be the ones following me."

Tean perched on the edge of his desk. Down the hall, he could hear Norbert, eighty-something, and Miguel, twenty-something, having a 'conversation' about state politics. It was Miguel, not Norbert, who sounded on the verge of having a stroke.

"It's really nothing," Hannah said, her eyes dropping to her lap. She played with a crease in her cargo pants. "And I can't help them."

"Ammon thinks you can. Why would he think that?"

"I don't know where Joy is," Hannah said, her voice rising just like Miguel's. Then, at a more subdued volume, she said, "I really don't. And I don't know why they care so much."

It was a lie. Tean wasn't sure Hannah had ever lied to him before this strange change in her life, whatever it was, had taken place. Worse, it was a bad lie.

"They think she's dead," Tean said.

"Oh my gosh," Hannah said. Tears filled her eyes, not spilling yet, and she used the heel of one hand to rub out the crease in her pants. "Well, she's not. Ok? She's fine. She's an activist, and she's probably just staying out of sight. She's used to the law looking for her. Anyway, she'd be furious if I got involved."

"So you do know where she is?"

"No. Will you quit it with that? I already told you I didn't."

But she wouldn't look at him.

"What if she got hurt?" Tean said. "What if she had an accident? What if she needs help?"

Hannah just shook her head.

"And what if it wasn't the police following you?" Tean asked. "What if it was someone else?"

She wiped her cheeks, which were still dry, and took a deep breath. "It's got to be connected to Joy. Maybe you could find her."

"No, that's not what I was suggesting."

"Maybe you and Jem could find her. That would solve everything. The police would leave me alone. And if—and if it's someone else following me, someone else looking for Joy, well, they'd leave me alone too. It's all tied together; it has to be. Doesn't it?"

"You need to talk to Ammon."

"This is not a police matter, Tean. If they're looking for her, it's because they want to get her in trouble for something."

"Get her in trouble for something? Can you hear yourself right now? This is Ammon we're talking about. Yes, I'm really mad at him, but you and I both know he wouldn't frame an innocent person."

"That's not what I meant."

"Then what do you mean? Help me out here, Hannah, because I don't understand what's going on."

"I want you to find her. You and Jem. Just to see that she's ok. And then things can go back to normal." The tears spilled now, and she slashed furiously at her cheeks.

"You need to talk to Ammon."

"Please?"

Sighing, Tean rummaged through a drawer until he found a wadded—and, he was fairly sure, clean—tissue. He handed it over to Hannah. She stared up at him with bloodshot eyes, unmoving, the tissue crumpled inside one fist.

"If we get even the slightest whiff that something is wrong—" Tean began.

"Thank you."

"Even the tiniest hint that this isn't above board—"

"Oh my gosh. Oh my gosh. Thank you, thank you, thank you."

"But you have to tell me what's really going on—"

"I love you." She flung herself at him, wrapping him in a hug, and—in a very un-Hannah-like display—kissing him on the cheek. "I know you only like boys—"

"Ok."

"—only California surfer boys like the ones in your Hollister calendars—"

"This is enough affection, please."

"—but I just love you so much."

Tean squirmed and wriggled until he was free. "You can thank me by never kissing me or hugging me or touching me or setting me up on a sex-predator app again. Maybe not necessarily in that order."

"No deal," Hannah said, dropping back into her seat. "Give me some paper. I'll write down some places you can check, and I'll text you a few pictures of her."

13

After work, Tean called Jem. No answer, so he left a message. He walked Scipio—a good, long walk—and called Jem again, this time while he was pouring kibble into Scipio's bowl. Still no answer. He looked through his cabinets, checked the fridge, and decided on stroganoff. He didn't have sour cream, but he thought he could just double up on cream of chicken soup, and he only had zoodles instead of real pasta, and he had jerky instead of ground beef, but he figured it was probably going to be pretty much the same. He was slicing the jerky—well, trying to; it was splintering more than slicing—when he had another idea. He grabbed his phone to send a text to Jem.

Normally, he and Jem communicated by phone calls and voicemails. Tean was just old enough that it was a form of communication he'd grown up with, and Jem had lived so much of his life unable to read that, for years and years, texts hadn't even been an option. Now, though, Jem was evolving into some sort of millennial-tween hybrid, texting constantly, and although the written content of the texts remained relatively low, Jem was a fiend for GIFs and emojis. Pushing his glasses back up his nose with one hand, Tean found a telephone emoji and then browsed GIFs until he found a black-and-white Hollywood starlet sitting by a phone, staring at it longingly. He sent the message.

Nothing.

He went back to the stroganoff. He was stirring the globs of cream of chicken soup together with the crumbled jerky, wondering if maybe this needed a can of mushrooms, when he heard steps. The door opened—it wasn't the kind of neighborhood where Tean felt the need to lock the door every minute of the day. Scipio leaped to his feet, barking wildly for ten seconds before ending in a confused *whuff.* Jem stood there, studying the kitchen, sniffing the air, and then bumped the door shut with his hip. When Scipio came over to lick his hands, he still tensed up, the way he always did, but not as much as he had at the beginning. He ruffled the Lab's ears. He hadn't moved from the door. His eyes looked hollow.

"Are you ok?" Tean asked.

"You should lock your door."

Tean opened his mouth, shut it, and tapped the wooden spoon on the pot's rim. He tried again. "How was your day?"

"You realize that somebody's going to try one day, just to see if it's open, and they'll walk in. And you'll be here, and then—and then somebody will do something stupid."

"Maybe they'll just run away when they see Scipio," Tean said. "He's so fierce."

Scipio was on the floor, one leg hooked behind his head as he took care of his downstairs business.

"Right," Jem said with a laugh, but it wasn't a nice laugh.

"Or maybe he'll have a knife, you know, like, a switchblade. And he'll stab me. Three or four times in the belly, but the one that'll really do me in will get me here," Tean indicated a spot on his chest, directly over his heart. "Or maybe I'll get lucky and he'll just perforate my lungs."

"Great. This is a joke."

"And while I'm dying, I'll just be confronted with the complete and utter meaningless of my existence. You know, just, the reality that we're all ants pushing grains of sand around on a desolate cosmic beach, spending our whole lives on things that mean absolutely nothing in the end before something bigger than us comes along and crushes us out."

Jem took a few deep breaths. Then, peeling off the Super Mario shirt, he said, "I can't do this with you right now. I'm going to take a shower."

"It's my shower," Tean said. "Should I put a lock on that door too?"

Digging around in the duffel, the scar on his back—running diagonally from shoulder to hip—on full display, Jem said, "It already has a lock, dumbass. Don't be snarky." Then he headed into the bathroom.

Scipio looked up when the door closed, gave another experimental *whuff* in Jem's direction, and went back to cleaning the undercarriage.

"I agree," Tean said, "he's being a real ball-muncher."

The bathroom door opened. "I heard that."

Tean's face heated.

"Put a nickel in the swear jar, Doc."

Then the door closed and the shower started, and Tean finished cooking dinner. He served himself a plate, left the burner on low in case Jem was hungry, and ate at the dinette table. He barely tasted the food; he was replaying the whole conversation again and again.

When Jem emerged from the bathroom, he was in knit shorts and a Dungeons & Dragons ringer tee. It was hard not to give him a second look: huge biceps, solid chest and shoulders, killer calves. He wasn't pretty, but he was handsome, and cute when he wasn't being such a jerk. Cute when he smiled, exposing the slightly crooked front teeth. Cute when he watched TV with one arm behind his head. Cute when he worried about his hair, teasing the part with the comb until the hard side part—he had drilled the words into Tean's memory — was exactly right. Cute when he worried about his beard, going after it obsessively with the trimmer. Cute when he leaned into Tean, in what he insisted were platonic snuggles, best-friend snuggles, when they crashed on the couch to watch a movie.

"Is it too late to apologize?" Jem said as he passed Tean and headed into the kitchen.

"It's never too late to apologize."

"I'm sorry I didn't immediately agree that Scipio is fierce. He's the fiercest."

Scipio, who was now zonked out on the dog bed and snoring loudly, was in no condition to accept the apology, so Tean said, "I think he'll let it slide."

"And I'm sorry I was a total ball-muncher."

Tean's face heated again, but he was grinning a little too. When Jem glanced over his shoulder from where he was serving himself stroganoff out of the pot, he smirked. "Busted," Jem said. "I knew you felt like a bad boy for using naughty words."

"I don't—that's not what I—"

Jem was still laughing when he came back to the table with his food. He had nice hands. And nice feet. Tean tried to reboot his brain to friend mode, but these days, that was getting harder and harder.

"I really am sorry about being a ball-muncher," Jem said, stirring the stroganoff with a fork. "I had a shit day. I went to see LouElla."

"What?"

Jem took a bite, and his face went totally blank. After a moment, he chewed and swallowed, and then he put down his fork. "This is good."

"I know you hate it. I don't care right now; tell me about LouElla. Are you ok?" Now that they were closer, Tean could see the faint bruising on one side of Jem's face. He reached out before he could stop himself, adjusting the angle of Jem's head, inspecting. "Did she do this to you?"

Jem was silent.

"I'm calling the police," Tean said. "That's assault and battery."

When he reached for his phone, though, Jem reached across the table and caught his arm. He shook his head. After a moment, Tean sighed and nodded, holding up both hands to show they were empty.

Then Jem told him: the conversation with LouElla, her claim that someone else had committed the fraud, and her offer of a trade.

"Do you believe her?"

Jem stirred the stroganoff; he still hadn't taken another bite. "I think she's telling the truth about this. She's been very smart about how she's played the system. She's greedy, but she's not stupid."

"She abuses children. She gave you that huge scar."

"But only when she knew she could get away with it."

"I think she's lying."

"She might be."

"What does she want you to do?" Tean asked.

"She's actually in the middle of being relicensed as a foster parent. There was an incident; she got suspended. Now she wants me to be there for the home visit." A hard smile creased Jem's face. "A success story, you know."

"You don't have to do this," Tean said. "I've been doing some research on how to rebuild your credit, and —"

Jem shook his head, and Tean stopped; he recognized that gesture, knew he'd hit a dead end. Jem took a few more bites and set his fork down.

"Let's go pick up a burger for you," Tean said.

"Thanks, but I'm really not hungry."

Tean tried not to let his eyes fall out of his head. He managed to say, "I think you've got some more work if you want it."

"What?"

So Tean told him about Hannah, and he showed him the pictures that Hannah had emailed him. When he'd finished, he added, "She gave me phone numbers for Joy Erickson and her wife, Zalie, and two addresses: their condo here in the city, and a farm they have near Heber. And I did a little research. Joy is an environmental activist, blogger, and speaker, all of which sounds like a lot of unpaid labor. Zalie, her wife, has her online stuff locked down, but my guess is that she must make the money. Or Joy has family money. Anyway, I said you'd be willing to look into it without involving the police."

"What do you think?"

"I think it's good money, and it's something you're good at."

"No, about Hannah and all this mess."

"I don't know. She's lying, but I don't know why. I can't even understand why."

"But you want to find out."

Tean had to think about that. "I want to help Hannah. I think this is the best way right now."

Jem nodded. "Looks like I'll be a gainfully employed, upstanding citizen for a few more days. I guess I should get going; you probably want to call it a night. Thanks for letting me crash your dinner like this."

As Jem carried his plate into the kitchen and scraped the rest of his dinner into the trash, Tean said, "Hey, would you do me a favor?"

The scrape of the fork's tines across ceramic paused. "You know I will. What?"

"Would you stay here for a few nights? I know you're still getting everything set up at your new place, and I'm excited to see it when you're ready. But I—I don't like the thought of you being in limbo. I was up a lot last night, worrying about you."

"You don't have to worry about me."

"I know I don't have to. But that's just what worrying is. You do it when you care about someone, whether you want to or not."

When Jem came back to the table, his face was unreadable.

"On the couch," Tean said, "just so we're clear."

"I think you told me that last time I stayed here, and you remember how that turned out."

"Well, I mean it this time. I care about you a lot, but I don't think we're right for each other as romantic partners, and —"

"Ok, ok, ok," Jem said. "I know. You've given me the speech like eight times. I didn't forget; I was just teasing."

"Please?" Tean said. "So I can sleep at night. Until you've got everything set up at your new place, I mean."

"I'm really fine."

"I know."

Jem scratched his beard. "If it'll help you sleep, I guess."

"Yeah, it will. Thanks."

"God, you're adorable when you think you're manipulating me."

"What? I wasn't —"

Tean's denial was cut off by a sound from his phone: a roar. He had no idea what it was.

Apparently, Jem did because his eyes got huge and he said, "You're on Prowler?"

"Hannah made me!" The words burst out before Tean could stop them.

"Holy shit," Jem said, a grin slowly growing.

"You don't have to look so happy about it."

"I am happy about it. This might be the best thing of my entire life. Let me see your profile. Did you say anything about philosophy or existentialism or the universe spinning farther and farther out into nothingness until all life is inevitably extinguished?"

Tean just stared and finally managed, "No. Of course not."

"This is the best thing of my entire life," Jem mumbled as he took out his phone.

"Come on," Tean said. "We don't have time for that. Let's start looking for Joy tonight; the faster we get this resolved, the faster Hannah will get back to normal."

"Ok," Jem said, laughing as he let Tean wrangle him toward the door. "Just one teeny, tiny question."

"No. If it's about Prowler or dating or the increasing likelihood of an asteroid hitting the Earth and wiping out humanity, I don't want to talk about it."

"Right, got it. But can we just swing by McDonald's?"

14

They drove north on 700 East, heading toward a wealthy part of the city known as The Avenues: multimillion-dollar homes sitting in the foothills of the Wasatch Mountains. The streets were wide here—avenues, Jem thought as he pounded down the first Big Mac—and patched with tar, showing their age. This part of the city wore the years well. Most of the homes sat on huge lots that were no longer the norm in most of Utah, and where tear-downs and new construction hadn't replaced the original structures with stucco McMansions, the original buildings were red brick with midcentury elements that were still appealing. And beautiful lawns, of course. It wouldn't be the perfect, pristine Salt Lake Valley if the Mormons didn't coax lush lawns out of the mountain steppes.

Holding out a really stellar fry specimen—long, with lots of salt and oil—Jem waved the fry at Tean until the doc took it and ate it. He didn't even seem to think about it, which was a good thing. For the most part, Tean seemed to subsist on air and some sort of grass tea that he brewed himself. Jem was determined to fix that, so he held out another of the really prime fries. Tean took that one too.

"Has anybody stalked you on Prowler yet?"

"We're not talking about this. End of conversation."

"What about clawing you? Has anybody clawed you?"

Tean was silent, pretending to focus on the road.

"That's one of the features," Jem said. "It's an invitation for you to send them a pic with one piece of clothing removed. You know, like they clawed it off you."

"You're making that up," Tean said. Then, shifting in his seat, he glanced over and asked, "Aren't you?"

Jem knew his grin probably looked insane, so he shoved fries into his mouth.

"I hate you," Tean said as he slumped forward onto the steering wheel.

Tean stopped the truck in front of a brick condominium building. It was clearly an expensive place to live: the lawn and the building itself were well maintained, flower beds exploding with color, the windows large with freshly painted trim, large balconies attached to each unit with privacy screens. At the main entrance, a porte cochere offered a safe loading/unloading zone for Utah's occasional rain and much more frequent snow. Jem pointed through the windshield at the valet.

"I see him," Tean said.

"Let me guess: we don't have an invitation."

"Well, Joy isn't answering her phone. And neither is her wife, Zalie."

"So why are we here?"

"Because what if something happened to her? What if Joy was here and fell or had an accident?"

"You don't think that Ammon already checked her condo?"

"I think I want to check for myself."

"So we're breaking and entering?"

"For a good cause."

Jem considered this and said, "Ok. I like lesbians. Let's do it."

Tean blinked. "I like lesbians too. I mean. I guess."

"And lesbians like me. Because I'm butch."

Suddenly Tean had to scratch his nose, his whole hand covering his mouth.

"What?" Jem said.

"No, I'm sure they do. Should I drive up there?"

"No, let's pretend we're visiting Great Aunt Mimi. I think there's a parking garage at the back. Why do you think it's funny that lesbians like me?"

"I don't think it's funny," Tean said, steering the truck toward the parking structure Jem had indicated. "It's kind of a sweeping statement. I mean, I'm sure not all lesbians like you."

"You're sure? Did one of them say something?"

"And, I mean, you do kind of go on and on with your hair. I don't know how butch that is."

Jem froze while clutching more fries. One by one, he let them trickle back into the cardboard container. Then he wiped his fingers on his leg, where the oil and salt wouldn't stain the knit shorts.

"Excuse me?"

"And you really love that comb. I caught you talking to it one day."

"I wasn't talking to—" Jem blew out a huge breath. "Wow."

Shrugging, Tean pulled into a visitor parking space.

"Your hair is a fucking mess."

"I know."

"It looks like a haystack."

"Probably."

"After a bunch of cows got at it."

"A herd. A bunch of cows is called a herd."

Jem wasn't sure what to call the noise he was making.

When Tean slid out of the car, Jem jammed a few more fries in his mouth, grabbed the second Big Mac, and trotted after him.

"Ok, what now?" Tean said, staring up and down the aisle of the parking garage.

"What do you mean? It was your idea to come out here."

"They live in Unit 5C. They're not answering the phone, and I'm not scaling the building, so use your criminal mind and figure out how we're going to get inside."

"Why are you being so mean to me? I gave you the two best fries in the whole sleeve."

"Prowler," Tean said, as though that explained anything. "Now think."

Grimacing, Jem jogged up the aisle, checking the cars on either side of him. He didn't have anything specific he was looking for, not yet. He was riffing. It was one of the things he did best. Halfway down the aisle, he stopped next to an ivory-colored Crown Victoria that looked almost as old as he was. He peered in the window, examining the spread of birthday cards on top of what looked like a stack of mail, and called, "Doc."

When Tean arrived, Jem pointed through the window. "I can't read that."

"That is some seriously bad cursive," Tean said. "I don't know if I can read it either." Squinting, he leaned closer to the glass. "'Happy

Birthday, Edna. Love, Dick and Linda and the pork boys.' No, wait. 'Pool boys. PS – Next year, easy on the tanning oil.'"

"Pork boys?"

"Shut up."

"Can you see her last name anywhere?"

"No."

"Ok, back to the truck."

When they got to the Ford, Jem rummaged through the cab. After a moment of digging through the junk—rubber boots, coveralls, miscellaneous tools, he found something he could use. He let out a little crow of triumph and squirmed backward out of the truck.

"That's a Whirl-Pak bag," Tean said. "I use those when I'm collecting specimens."

"Knife," Jem said. "And stick these gloves in your pocket for when we get a little more criminalish."

Tean handed over his pocketknife, and Jem trimmed away the yellow seal from the top of the transparent bag. "Come on."

"What are we doing?"

"Something devious and criminal."

"I know. But what exactly?"

Jem led him out of the parking garage. Flower beds ran along the side of the garage that faced the main road, so Jem pointed to the flowers and said, "Time to make a lovely birthday present for third-cousin twice-removed Edna."

He went to work, using Tean's knife to trim tulips and early roses. No one had come outside since they'd arrived, and no new cars had come toward the garage. The transparent sleeve of the Whirl-Pak bag worked to wrap the bouquet, and in under five minutes, Jem had a decent flower arrangement to deliver.

"So we just walk up to the front door and tell them we've got flowers for Aunt Edna?"

"Third-cousin Edna," Jem said, working his phone out of his pocket again.

"But they're going to say, 'Edna who?' And I'm just going to immediately confess everything."

"This would be a lot easier," Jem said, placing a call, "if you were even remotely disposed to sneakiness." Into the phone, he said, "Yeah. Yeah, you can help me. You can help me get that bitch's car out of my fucking parking spot. And you can help me by doing it fucking yesterday so I didn't have to come home to deal with her fucking shit again."

Tean was staring; Jem almost broke, biting the inside of his cheek to keep from laughing.

"Sir, I'm sorry, I don't—"

"That bitch Edna. Her fucking Crown Vic is halfway into my goddamn parking spot!"

Frantic typing came on the other side of the call. "If I could just get your name—"

"Right now. Call that bitch right now and get her to move her ancient piece of shit out of my spot!"

"We'll have someone move Mrs. Partridge's car right away. And sir, we really ask our residents not to use that kind of language—"

Jem disconnected the call. Tean's eyes were still enormous.

"Partridge," Jem said.

"That really worked?" Tean said.

"People believe what they want to be true," Jem said. "Or what they're afraid is true. And you'd be surprised how many people are afraid someone is yelling at them for a justified reason. Come on."

Rolling his eyes, Tean kept pace with Jem to the front door.

"Hello, gentlemen," the valet said. He was obviously doing double duty as the bouncer because he stood as they approached and hedged their path to the door. He was probably in his thirties, round-cheeked, sweating in a red polyester suit that looked kind of like a bellhop's uniform and kind of like an old movie theater usher. "How can I help you today?"

"We're delivering a bouquet for Edna Partridge. Um, let me see," Jem checked his phone, "a birthday bouquet. We've tried three or four times and she's been gone; we called ahead this time, and the girl at the desk told us she was back from her vacation."

The valet's gaze lingered on the improvised bouquet.

"You ever use BioFlora before?" Jem asked, shoving the bouquet at the valet. "We're a local startup. Biodegradable bouquet sleeves that actually keep the flowers fresh for an extra four business days. It's this patented polymer—"

"Yeah," the valet said, grabbing the door, his face already slack with uninterest.

"Hold on. I've got a QR code you can scan—"

"Not when I'm on duty," the valet said, although it sounded more like, not in my entire fucking life.

Smiling, Jem nodded, said, "Thanks," and headed inside.

Tean was staring at him as they climbed the fire stairs.

"Crypsis," Jem said with a grin. "See? I remembered a new word."

Tean was still staring.

"What?"

"Business days?"

"Huh?"

"Why would the patented polymer only keep them alive extra business days?"

Jem laughed. "I throw in bullshit like that just to keep myself entertained."

Tean just kept studying him.

"Cut it out," Jem said.

"Do you know how smart you are?"

"Come on. You're going to make me blush."

"I'm serious. You came up with all of that on the spot. And it sounded really convincing."

"Um, yeah. That's the whole point." Jem pointed at himself. "Liar, remember?"

Tean looked like he might say something else, shook his head, and then opened his mouth again.

"You'd better just say it," Jem said, "or you're going to choke on your tongue."

"I really think you should consider college."

"Pass."

"Jem, you might be the smartest person I know. You could do anything you wanted."

Jem rolled his eyes as they reached the fifth floor. "Pledge a fraternity, play beer pong, listen to twenty-year-olds whine about getting cockblocked? I'll just stick my head in a paper shredder instead, thanks."

Based on the brief glimpse Jem had caught of the lobby, the fifth-floor hallway kept to the same style: buttercup-colored paint, gingerbread crown molding, tables spaced at regular intervals for residents who might need to steady themselves. Tiny ceramic figurines adorned the tables—children, dogs, cats. But mostly children. A heavy perfume of artificial lavender hung in the air. The whole place made Jem want to double down on the paper shredder.

The door to 5C didn't look any different from the other doors along the hall: it had ornate wooden trim, a peephole, and a brass doorknob and deadbolt. Jem jerked his head at the door, and Tean knocked. After a ten count, Tean knocked again. They waited a full minute, and when nobody answered the door, Jem produced his picks. He knelt on the rose-print carpet and went to work.

"Is this a new skill?"

"I knew the basics, but I've been practicing."

Tean didn't make another noise, but he didn't need to; Jem could feel the waves of disapproval radiating off him.

"I'm thinking of taking up burglary," Jem said as he worked the picks. "Larceny. Petty theft. Grand theft. Grand theft auto."

Still Tean said nothing, but he relaxed a little, and when Jem glanced up, Tean rolled his eyes.

"You're too easy," Jem said.

"Says the guy who got on his knees for me and I didn't have to say a word."

The door popped open, and Jem let the picks fall to the ground in shock. "Dr. Leon, did you just make a naughty joke?"

"I hate you," Tean said, pushing past him into the condo.

"Gloves," Jem reminded him. "And don't say hate," Jem said, scooping up the picks. "That's a bad word."

He shut the door behind him. Tean had already turned on a few lights, and Jem followed a short hall past a closet—coats, umbrellas, and a lot of black flats—and a wall of framed pictures. He recognized Joy as the woman with the shock of orange, curly hair. She appeared in most of the pictures, ranging in age from a teenager to a woman on the cusp of middle age. He didn't see her wife in any of the images, though, and a second glance confirmed that several of the frames were empty or had pictures that had been severely trimmed.

Tean was standing in a living room that smelled like a resale shop. The furniture, in Jem's opinion, explained the smell: an orange mohair sofa, a pair of dining chairs with ripped upholstery, and a chunky pair of bookshelves that looked straight out of the 70s. The shelves were empty, and cardboard boxes of books sat on the floor.

"I bet you guys shop at the same place," Jem said.

Tean glared at him, passed him a pair of disposable gloves, and stalked into the bedroom.

"You could ask about getting a group discount," Jem called after him.

"We're breaking and entering," Tean shouted back. "So be quiet!"

Jem moved through the room quickly, noticing the indentations in the carpet, the nail marks on the walls, the scuffs and scrapes to the paint. He moved into the kitchen and saw a stack of Corel plates taped into a bundle, with $2.99 scrawled on the tape in an unsteady hand. The cabinets were empty except for a single, battered pot with the Teflon coating flaking away inside. In the sink, he found a spoon. At the fridge, he took an extra two minutes to really carefully examine the contents and sound out the words on the packaging to himself so he could say them without looking like a moron.

"No beer," Jem called over his shoulder, narrating the contents of the fridge, "but she's got moldy imitation cottage cheese, a jar of jalapeno-and-quince jelly, and a one-pound tub of vegan anchovy paste. Maybe you guys can go grocery shopping together too."

"Stop talking," Tean yelled from the other room.

Jem had never heard of imitation cottage cheese, which was apparently a—he had no idea what the word was, so he didn't even try—product, or vegan anchovy paste, so he hunkered down and examined the containers. Both of them were produced by the same co-op, Heavenly Helpers Organic Farms, which had a PO box address in Heber. He grabbed the cottage cheese and carried it to the bedroom.

Tean was shuffling papers; a stack of documents sat at the foot of an unmade twin bed, and he was obviously working his way through them. The only other furniture in the room was a three-drawer chest painted Big-Bird yellow; judging by the Dora the Explorer stickers that had been only partially scraped away from the side, Jem figured it had previously been in a child's room.

"What's this word?" Jem asked, holding out the cottage cheese container.

"Huh? Seitan."

"I would have said saitan. Like Seinfeld."

Tean mumbled something.

"Hey, it kind of sounds like Satan," Jem said.

Tean finally looked up. "What?"

"Seitan. It sounds like Satan. And it's made by the Heavenly Helpers Farm, which is kind of funny, right?"

"A pun," Tean said, smiling. "When one word sounds like another, and you're supposed to hear the other meaning and find it funny."

"I made a pun."

"Well, actually you just noticed a possible pun. You didn't make one."

Jem tried. He really tried. But he might have done a little stomping on his way back to the fridge.

"Look at this stuff," Tean said when he came back, passing over a stack of pages. "What do you think about that?"

The printouts were Facebook posts, tweets, and emails. It was too much text for Jem to process in a reasonable amount of time, so he glanced at the Facebook posts first, many of which included pictures of a large man with military-cut hair, often standing next to dead dogs—some hanging from trees by their back legs, some curled up, looking like they'd died in agony, and once just a picture of a severed leg still caught in a trap.

"Why'd he kill all those dogs?"

"They're coyotes," Tean said. "Look at the tweets."

"'That bitch deserves to die,'" Jem read, painfully aware of how slowly he did so. "'Somebody kill that bitch, please.' 'Somebody get this cunt off my property.' 'Wish they made traps for noisy dykes.' Who the hell is this guy?"

"John Sievers," Tean said. When Jem glanced at him, Tean shook his head and said, "I don't know him, but it's on some of the Facebook and Twitter stuff, and his email address is johnsievers at some personalized domain."

Jem frowned. "There's no way Ammon and Kat didn't come check out her condo when they started looking for her. They had to have seen this stuff."

"I'll ask him," Tean said.

Jem tried again. He tried really, really hard. But he said, "You'll ask him?"

Tean just frowned and said, "Even if I'm still mad at Ammon, we could use his help."

"Right."

"Excuse me?"

Tossing the pages back on the bed, Jem shook his head.

"If you want to say something, just say it," Tean said.

"I'm trying to be cool about this," Jem said. "You're making it really goddamn hard."

"Why do you need to be cool? I don't understand. Ammon is the detective investigating her disappearance. We're trying to help Hannah find her. It makes perfect sense that I'd talk to Ammon and see if we can help each other."

"Of course it does."

"You can be a real jerk sometimes."

"Everybody's got a talent."

Tean stared at him, glasses sliding to the end of his nose, his chest rising and falling.

"Glasses," Jem said quietly.

Tean shoved them back into place and then turned and marched out of the room.

For the next minute, Jem tried to remember Saturday mornings as a kid: *Darkwing Duck,* Lucky Charms — extra marshmallows picked out of the box, a swimming pool's amount of milk — and a few quiet hours when he could just hang with Benny, without LouElla breathing down his neck. Then he went after Tean.

"Did you find anything in the kitchen?" Tean said. "Can we go?"

"Nothing in the kitchen, but take a look at this. Here, here, over here."

"She moved her furniture."

"No, it's not the right size. None of the pieces in here fit this spot, for example. These are new pieces. Well, new for this room, anyway."

"Ok," Tean said, some of the heat ebbing from his voice.

"And look at these pictures near the front door," Jem said.

"She cut somebody out."

"She cut somebody out of a lot of them," Jem said.

"And there's only a twin bed and that little dresser in the bedroom," Tean said. "She and Zalie split up."

"Looks like it."

"Maybe we should talk to Zalie."

"Good idea. Where would Zalie be living now?"

Tean frowned. "Hannah gave me an address for a farm in Heber."

Jem thought about this and pulled out his phone. He went back, checked the containers in the refrigerator, and searched for Heavenly Helpers Organic Farms. He got a webpage for the co-op. The main page included a few pictures of unplowed fields and then a wall of text. Holding out the phone, Jem said, "I know you're mad at me, and I know I should be able to do this, but it's going to take me too long."

"I'm not mad at you," Tean said grumpily as he took the phone.

"Gee," Jem said. "It's hard to tell sometimes."

The doc was pretending to stare at the screen, but a small smile broke free. "Ok, I hear how that sounded. Now be quiet and let me read." After he'd scanned the page, he opened a new tab and typed in another search. He clicked through several things until the maps app launched, and then he passed the phone back to Jem. The app was currently trying to navigate them to an address in the Heber Valley.

"Good guess," Tean said. "They own a pig farm that's part of the co-op."

"It wasn't a guess. It was detective work."

Tean made a throwing-up face. "Want to go out there tonight?"

"Sure. Unless you've got your first Prowler date."

The sun was setting as they drove east, and the last daylight crashed against the Wasatch Mountains, washing the slopes, cresting in blinding flashes at the snow line. Everything was golden — the valley, the young leaves of the scrub oak, the Russian olives, the bird circling overhead, thinning as it turned until it was nothing but a sliver. Everything was bright.

"An eagle," Tean said when Jem glanced over. "I think."

Then they hit the canyons and drove into a wall of blue and purple shadows. They followed I-80 through Parleys Canyon, climbing toward Summit County and Park City. Instead of heading into Park City, though, they turned south, following the back of the Wasatch Mountains. Jem and Tean had made this trip together once before, at the beginning of their friendship, when Jem had brought Tean out here to see a sunrise. Jem still couldn't explain to himself why he had done it, why he had thought it might work. But it had worked. It had changed something between them, that frozen morning, daylight flooding the valley like it was spilling out of a cup. He thought about it now, as they drove through bruised shadows, as he heard in his mind the note of excitement that Tean hadn't been able to suppress when he'd said, *I'll ask him*. He shivered and leaned his head against the glass; it might as well have been a sheet of ice.

Tean fiddled with the heat and angled the vents toward Jem.

"I'm ok," Jem said.

"It's freezing up here," Tean said. "The canyons are always a lot colder."

They drove south on US 189, passing the Jordanelle Reservoir, which was black and sleek in the nightfall, no ripples, no reflected stars. Darkness had fallen almost completely when Tean turned onto a frontage road and then turned again, guiding them east into an emptiness of scrub and brush. They almost missed the farm. The maps app blurted out a warning, and Tean hit the brakes. Then he had to back up to turn onto the narrow dirt drive. The Ford rocked and bounced over the ruts and folds baked into the ground.

"Phew," Jem said when the smell hit him.

"Yep," Tean said. "Smells like a pig farm."

"Shouldn't it be called something, you know, else?" Jem said.

"Like what?"

"I don't know. A ranch. A slop. A porkery."

The faint glow from the dash left most of Tean's face in shadow, but Jem could hear the smile in his voice. "I'm pretty sure it's just called a pig farm."

The house at the end of the drive was small and dark; no lights showed in the windows, and Jem could only identify it because its low roofline broke the emptiness of the valley.

"Doesn't seem like anyone's home," Jem said.

"Let's have a look," Tean said.

"I've corrupted you. I've made you a criminal mastermind."

"Don't flatter yourself," Tean said. "When I was fourteen, I stole a library copy of *Bop* because it had a shirtless picture of Freddie Prinze, Jr."

"What the hell is *Bop*?"

Tean just shook his head and slid out of the truck. The smell of dung and, well, pigs, rushed into the truck, and Jem opened his door, pulled his shirt up over his nose, and got out too.

"And who's Freddie Prinze, Jr.?"

"He was, I don't know. Freddie Prinze, Jr."

"Was he hot?"

"I committed a felony for him."

"I don't think stealing a library's copy of *Bop,* whatever the hell that is, is a felony. On the other hand, if you—"

Before Jem could finish, the door to the house flew open. A small figure stood outlined against a weak patch of light, and then a voice rang out.

"Get off my property. That's the only warning you're going to get."

"Ms. Maynes?" Tean said. "Zalie Maynes? My name is Tean Leon, and I'm looking for Joy—"

The figure in the doorway moved. Something exploded: a flash of light, a blast of sound. Jem was already wrapped around Tean, bearing him to the ground, as his brain processed what had happened. She had fired at them. A shotgun, he thought.

When a second shot didn't come, Jem scrambled up, dragging Tean toward the truck.

"You come back," she shouted, "and the next one won't be a warning."

15

On Tuesday morning, Tean was sitting in his office, staring at the poster opposite him that showed a sea turtle with a plastic straw stuck in its nose and the words YES, YOU PROBABLY DID NEED A STRAW TO DRINK THAT DIET COKE. I HOPE YOU ENJOYED IT. His phone buzzed. It was a message from his sister Sara.

You still haven't RSVP'd for Sunday. We'd love to see you.

He dismissed the message. Almost immediately the phone buzzed again, and Tean readied himself to dismiss another sibling text—or, worse, phone call—when Ammon's name flashed on the screen. The last five months had conditioned Tean to dismiss the call automatically, but then he thought about Hannah's situation and answered.

"Hi," Ammon said, with that fresh edge of uncertainty that had never been in his voice before. "How are you?"

"I don't want to do small talk, Ammon. What do you want?"

"Thank you for telling me how you feel right now. I really appreciate when you do that because it makes me feel like you value me enough to be honest."

Tean squinted at the sea turtle, who was squinting back, and then Tean glanced around the room, looked at the phone, and tried, generally, to see the trap. He settled for saying, "What do you want?"

"I had a phone call last night—"

Tean groaned.

"And I've been thinking about something that I would like to talk to you about. I'd really like to hear your thoughts about it too."

"Ok, just—can you talk normally to me, please? What's going on with you?"

Silence on the other end of the call. Tean visualized Ammon reading off a page, which probably wasn't too far off. "I understand that you went and saw Zalie Maynes last night. Is that right?"

"Yes. I mean, if you call being shot at and almost killed a visit."

"I want to share with you that when you put yourself in danger like that, it makes me feel really, really vulnerable — not just because I can't help you but also because I don't know how I would keep going without you."

"Ammon, enough already. I can't stand this. Just yell at me or shout or slam the phone or swear or something."

He paused, and when he spoke again, his voice sounded almost like the real Ammon, the one Tean had sat across the table from in the high school cafeteria. "It's that bad?"

"Well, no. But I keep waiting for the other shoe to drop."

"I'm really trying, Tean. I'm really trying right now."

"I know." And, oddly enough, Tean did. "Ok, I'm sorry I made you feel that way. I honestly didn't think I'd be in any danger. We were just poking around, and it seemed logical to check out the farm that Joy and Zalie own — "

"We?"

"Come on. We've been doing so good."

"No, Tean. No, we haven't been doing so good. You've been fucking around again, getting involved in a police investigation — "

"You asked me to!"

"I asked you to talk to Hannah! I didn't ask you to . . . to snoop around with a criminal who you like to fuck just to make me angry. Jesus fucking Christ, I cannot believe you!"

"Ok," Tean said, "this is the other shoe dropping. Goodbye."

"Stay out of this case, God damn it. Do you hear me? This is not going to be a repeat of last year."

Tean disconnected the call. The phone buzzed again almost immediately, Ammon's name on the screen again, and Tean dismissed it. Then he turned his phone off. When his desk phone rang, he gathered up the maps and paperwork he needed for the canine distemper containment project, and he headed for his truck.

It was a long, frustrating day. He met up with Miguel, the conservation officer who worked the Heber Valley, and Miguel took him to several different spots in the valley where people had reported seeing feral dogs and coyotes that looked sick. Reports like that were hit or miss, though, and they only managed to collect a single coyote specimen. The coyote was thin, with crusty deposits around its eyes and nose—typical of the discharge produced by canine distemper, but not definitive. They had to gear up with disposable coveralls, disposable gloves, and rubber boots, and then they had to document the specimen *in situ*, transfer the specimen to a plastic bag, seal it, and haul it back to the truck.

"I think it's time to start looking for a few to euthanize," Tean said, "to supplement the diagnostic evaluation. We need to find a pack that's infected."

"That's a pretty generous use of 'we,'" Miguel said. His long hair came to the nape, glossy and smooth, and when Hannah was around, he'd take off his Jazz hat and shake out his hair like he was in a Head & Shoulders commercial.

"I'll see if I can send Maddie or Jamal to help."

"Are you signing overtime?"

"Not if I can help it."

"Ok, then send Maddie."

"Why? Is there some kind of problem with Jamal?"

"Are you kidding? He's great. But I kind of got a spark from Maddie, you know."

Tean sighed. "I'm sending Jamal."

Miguel expressed his disappointment while Tean double bagged his personal protective equipment and disinfected his boots. He was still expressing his disappointment when Tean drove away.

After delivering the coyote specimen to the DWR building and storing it in the refrigerator in the lab, Tean cleaned up in the locker room and headed home. Scipio bowled into him, desperately trying not to jump—they'd been working on that—but licking Tean in a frenzy and checking him with his shoulder whenever Tean looked like he might try to do something negligent and forgetful like take a single step away from the dog.

They walked, and as Tean was scooping kibble into Scipio's bowl, the door rattled. It opened, and Jem stepped inside. He looked better today, his color normal, his blue-gray eyes brightening when they landed on Tean.

"You really should lock your door."

"We're tough," Tean said, stroking Scipio's flank. Scipio took the gesture as an invitation to slam his butt into Tean's knees, still chomping kibble the whole time. "We've made it this long."

"Especially now that you're on Prowler," Jem said.

Tean pressed the heels of his hands to his eyes.

"One of your crazy one-night stands could walk right in."

"Why would he do that?"

"I told you: he's crazy."

"I don't have one-night stands," Tean said, dropping his hands. "And even if I did, I'm sure none of my one-night stands would want a second round."

Jem's face contracted as he leaned against the door, folding his arms. "I'm hurt."

"Ok."

"No, really. As your first—"

"You were not my first," Tean said, his face heating.

"As your first good sex, I mean," Jem said with a smirk, "I'm really offended that you think I've taught you nothing."

"Goodbye, Jem. Go tease someone else tonight."

"Nah," Jem said, the smirk softening into a smile. "Nobody else is nearly as fun."

"Want to earn some more money?"

"Why? Are you paying?" Jem's eyebrows went up. "Sex lessons? Yes. Definitely. Let me check my schedule. I offer a three-week intensive course—"

"I will buy you Rancherito's if you will be quiet for the entire car ride."

Jem cocked his head. "If you'd said McDonald's . . ."

Tean grabbed his keys. Scipio was just finishing dinner—licking the bowl now, just in case any kibbley goodness had escaped him— and so Tean got the harness and helped the Lab into it. He held out the leash to Jem.

"Um, changed my mind," Jem said. "I don't need money that bad, and besides, Scipio and I kind of have our own arrangement when it comes to walks."

"I believe you called it a gentleman's agreement."

"That's right."

"And it consists of you letting him out of the apartment and then chasing after him and shouting his name until he comes back."

"Well, when you say it like that—"

"Leash, Jem."

Jem groaned and took the leash.

They went downstairs, and all three of them piled into the Ford's cab. Scipio sat on the narrow bench at the back, which was the perfect spot for him to lick Jem's neck, the side of his face, and his hair.

"Good doggie," Jem kept saying as Tean eased the truck out into the street. Jem patted the air, not quite willing to touch Scipio. "Ok, but don't eat my hair. Good boy. Good boy. Bleh. Pfeh. Tean, his tongue got in my mouth."

"That's another advantage to being quiet," Tean said. "You won't get a dog's tongue in your mouth."

"Ok, but can you—you know, just—Scipio, sleep. Sleep, boy! Sleep! Why haven't you taught him any commands?"

Reaching back, Tean found the Lab's head and pushed. "Leave him alone."

Scipio gave Tean a few desultory licks and then settled down onto the bench.

Jem flipped the visor and checked himself in the mirror.

Flicking a glance over, Tean said, "Your hair is fine. It's still got that line in it."

"It's a part. It's called a part. And you are absolutely the last person I'd trust to tell me if it looks all right."

Tean had to hear all about hair—specifically, Jem's hair, and how the dog had ruined it—as they drove south. They stopped at Rancherito's long enough for Tean to order each of them a bacon breakfast burrito, and then they continued south. They took I-15 to Sandy, a suburb at the far end of the Salt Lake Valley, and then they headed east on 10600 South toward the mountains. At that point, Tean activated the maps app, and it navigated them past a retirement community—Desert Sunset, which sounded more like a Western with a lot of sun-bleached bones—and past a Mormon church, and past another Mormon church, and past a Jamba Juice. When they passed an Arctic Circle, Jem made an appreciative noise.

"You just ate," Tean said.

"They have really good ice cream."

"Oh my gosh."

"And it was one burrito, Tean. Not all of us live on air and, if we're really indulging, a crisp frond from a fern, lightly seasoned with tap water."

Tean turned on the next street, which was residential.

"Oh, and if it's a holiday, maybe we'll have a single corn flake that somebody with peanut-butter breath has breathed on."

"Are you done?"

"For now. I've been saving the peanut-butter breath one for like two months, so I need time to come up with something else."

The homes here were a mix of construction from the late 70s and early 80s: ranch and two-story frame homes, some with brick-and-siding combinations, some painted in colors — robin's egg blue — that probably dated back to when they'd been built. The lawns were well-kept, which made sense because this was another Utah suburb, and the streets were wide and well-maintained. A family, mom and dad included, was playing tag on their front lawn on the next block. Two houses later, Tean saw a banner that said WE ARE ALL MOMS – CELEBRATING A WEEK OF MOMS! – THANK YOU MOMS FOR ALL THAT YOU DO.

"Is Mother's Day this weekend?" Jem said.

"Don't remind me." When Jem glanced over, Tean shrugged and said, "My family is already hassling me."

"Why?"

"Because they think I need to be at every family function."

"Huh."

"I'll probably go."

Jem was just looking at him. "You sound like it's a firing squad."

"No. It'll be fine." Tean braced himself against the steering wheel, elbows locked, knuckles white. "I'll just think about hamsters the whole time."

"Ok, I'll bite: why?"

"Because hamsters are straightforward. Hamsters don't spend almost forty years sucking the life out of their young. Hamster mothers just chow down on the pups when they need extra protein because they're lactating."

"If it's that bad, don't go."

"No, it'll really be fine."

"Uh huh."

"Anyway, I have to go."

"You don't have to do anything."

"It's Mother's Day."

"So?"

"Never mind."

"I just don't get the big deal. I thought you got along with your family."

"I do."

"They didn't cut you off or anything when you came out."

"They didn't."

"And they want you to be there."

"Judging by the number of texts and reminders and calls and nudges, I guess so."

"I mean, tell me if I'm missing something, but that sounds kind of awesome. People who want you to be there. People who care about you. People who are making sure you know you're welcome. People who love you."

"Yep," Tean said.

Out of the corner of his eye, he saw emotions flit across Jem's face too quickly to process. Then Jem smiled, squeezed Tean's shoulder, and said, "If it helps, you can spend the whole time imagining party disasters. Like when that deck collapsed in the middle of a big graduation party, and people fell and got skewered on the joists, and the bodies hung there for days, *Game of Thrones* style, with the birds pecking out their eyes."

"That never happened."

"But you can imagine it."

The maps app announced they were arriving at their destination.

"And you can add your own gory statistics about the number of people who die annually from choking on boiled hot dogs at birthday parties thrown by their grandmothers or something like that."

Hemming, Tean parked at the curb and killed the engine. "It's not a terrible idea," he finally said. "I'd have to do some research."

"And you can take me," Jem said, "and tell everyone I've got brain-eating bacteria from sucking on live snails."

"Why would I do that?"

"Sometimes I think you need a little backup," Jem said, smiling as he unbuckled himself and hopped out of the truck.

Tean followed, shaking his head. They had stopped in front of the worst house on the block: patchy lawn, weeds growing through cracks in the driveway, paint peeling from the trim around the windows. On the front door's jambs, someone had pasted stickers for Greenpeace, PETA, SPCA, and WWF. Many of the stickers were sun bleached and faded, but it looked like whoever had put them there preferred to just layer on new ones rather than removing any of the old. As they headed up the drive, Tean said, "This is Joy's father's house. His name is Leroy Erickson. I found him through Joy's social media; it looks like he's some kind of activist too."

"Crazy runs in the family," Jem said.

"In all families," Tean said, "obviously, but who better to help Joy lie low for a while than a family member who supports the same kind of causes?"

Jem nodded and knocked. A dog immediately started barking, and Scipio answered from the truck. Shuffling steps came toward them inside the house, and a man shouted, "Roger, shut up," and then the barking grew more distant as the steps moved away again. A few moments later, the deadbolt clicked back. When the door opened, Tean noticed that Jem had his hands in the pockets of his denim jacket, probably holding on to one of those improvised weapons he carried. Tean's first glance at the man he assumed was Leroy Erickson made him glad, for many reasons, he had Jem along with him.

Leroy looked like he was in his late fifties, maybe early sixties, with a thick beard going to gray and his head completely shaved. He wore overalls without a shirt under them, and he was a very big man — taller than Jem and built with a lot more mass. At some point, most of it had probably been muscle, although age had given him sagging shoulders and a belly. On his neck, a black-ink tattoo of Fozzie Bear stared back at Tean.

"Can I help you?"

"Mr. Erickson?" Jem said. "My name is Jem. This is Tean. We were hoping we could have a few minutes of your time."

"You're having them, and they're going fast."

"Leroy — can I call you Leroy?"

"Son, you can call me anything but late for dinner, but you're about out of time."

"Leroy, I think you're the only person who can help us at this point. I wanted to say that right at the beginning so you know how important this is. Hannah Prince is in trouble, Leroy. Pretty serious trouble, actually. Do you know Hannah, Leroy?"

Leroy crossed his arms.

"Her maiden name is Lackey," Tean said.

"Maybe you knew her as Hannah Lackey," Jem said. "Does that sound familiar, Leroy?"

"I think you'd better talk a little faster," Leroy said. "My dinner's about to burn."

"The police are trying to get Hannah into trouble. They're making her life miserable. Hannah asked us to help her find Joy. Leroy, that's why we need your help. You are seriously the only person who can help us. Anything, we'll take absolutely anything at this point."

Leroy just stood there, the fingers of one hand coming up to tease his beard.

"Zalie fired a shotgun at us when we tried to ask her the same question," Jem said. "What does that tell you, Leroy?"

"Nothing new," he muttered. Something beeped behind him. "You boys better come in. Shoes off, please." He turned and headed into the house without looking back at them.

"Why'd you bring up Zalie?" Tean whispered.

"His daughter is either getting divorced or really pissed off at her wife," Jem whispered back. "Parents like to take sides too."

They took their shoes off in the foyer, and Tean tried to breathe through his mouth as they moved into the living room. The air was a composite of dog, body odor, and what Tean's grandfather had called 'plastic food,' meaning anything boxed, canned, or frozen—a smell that Tean associated with microwave dinners. The sofa was the only place to sit. The upholstery had originally been cream colored, with what looked like old-fashioned drawings of plants printed on the fabric; now, stains marked the cushions, and body oil had darkened the sofa after years of use. A CRT television the size of a buffet table took up one wall. An opening at the back connected to the kitchen, where Tean could hear Leroy moving around, and a hallway led to the rest of the house. The dog—Roger, presumably— was still barking in one of the back bedrooms.

"Look," Jem said, grinning over his shoulder at Tean. "Captain Hook's crocodile."

The blond man was standing in front of a wall of photographs: dogs, cats, birds, lizards, snakes, rodents, fish. The only human featured in any of the pictures was Leroy Erickson, and the photos must have represented much of Leroy's life: in some of them, he was young, still tall and big, but his skin tight and shiny, his eyes bright; in a few of them, he was older, his head shaved, his beard already long and bristly.

"That's an alligator," Tean said.

"Same thing. He even dressed up like Captain Hook."

"They're not the same thing, although they look a lot alike."

"I'm going to ask him if it's a crocodile. Why would he dress up like Captain Hook if it wasn't a crocodile? Captain Hook wasn't afraid of an alligator."

"You don't need to ask him," Tean said. "You can tell by the teeth. Alligators usually don't have visible lower teeth when the jaw is closed. Crocodiles do—especially the fourth tooth on each side. No lower teeth visible, so it's not a crocodile."

Jem narrowed his eyes.

"Sorry," Tean said. "I know I'm annoying."

"Do it again."

"Do what again?"

Jem put his hands on his hips. "Do it again."

"I don't—"

"Whale," Jem said, whipping out a finger to point at a porpoise; Leroy was floating in what looked like a tank inside a building—not ideal conditions for a porpoise, and Tean wondered, for a moment, where it was.

"You know that's not a whale."

"Dolphin."

Tean clamped his jaw shut.

"This dolphin," Jem said, "was born in 1949, and it was the first dolphin to kiss President Harry S. Truman—"

"It's not a dolphin. Dolphins usually have long, prominent beaks, and they have a curved dorsal fin. That's a porpoise." Tean tried to hold back. "I mean, just look at the teeth!"

The blue-gray squall of Jem's eyes was unreadable, and he murmured, "God, those boys on Prowler are going to go into a feeding frenzy when they get wind of you."

As though on cue, Tean's phone made another of those growling noises.

"You met the family," Leroy said as he came back into the living room. "That's Tessa. Met her down in Florida. You wouldn't believe what those bozos were making her do, the kinds of tricks. Filthy, disgusting things. Bunch of perverts, the whole state. You don't want to sit down?"

"We were just waiting for you."

"I've got to sit these days," Leroy said. He was carrying a bowl of painfully orange macaroni and cheese, and he eased himself down onto the sofa with a grunt. "I don't know where Joy is. Haven't seen her in weeks. Doesn't talk to me. Doesn't want anything to do with me. I can't say it much plainer than that."

"Thank you —" Tean said, but he cut off when Jem's hand lighted on his back, and Jem gave a tiny shake of his head.

"I'm sorry to hear that," Jem said. "I don't have much of a relationship with my parents; that's not easy for anybody."

Shoveling noodles into his mouth, Leroy just grunted.

"Who's this lucky guy?" Jem asked, thumbing at a cluster of pictures featuring a Goldendoodle. In each of the pictures, Leroy and the dog were together, with the dog climbing on Leroy, kissing Leroy, or just stretched out alongside him. It took Tean a moment to realize that the tattoo on Leroy's neck wasn't Fozzie Bear — it was a very poor rendition of the Goldendoodle.

"That's Bo," Leroy said.

"He's beautiful," Tean said.

"Looks like a sweetheart," Jem said.

Leroy ate for another minute without saying something, just a mixture of snuffles and grunts as he worked on the mac and cheese. Then he said, "Cancer. Got him young."

"I'm so sorry," Tean said, hating how empty it sounded.

Jem moved over to the sofa, taking the seat at the other end, and put his hand on Leroy's shoulder. Leroy froze, and Jem waited for the first punch, for the shouts, for the demand that they leave. Then Leroy's shoulders heaved, and he ran a thick wrist over his eyes. Jem didn't say anything. Leroy didn't say anything. But after a moment, Leroy coughed and cleared his throat and wiped his eyes again.

"Like I said, they're my family now." Leroy waved at the wall of pictures. "I taught Joy everything she knows. Taught her what matters in life. She took it and ran with it, took it way past what any decent person ought to do. That girl is out of her mind. Crazy. If you find her, I don't want anything to do with her."

"Trouble?" Jem said. He still had his hand on Leroy's shoulder, and Tean suddenly remembered, as though seeing himself from the outside, how Jem did the same thing to him. He knew how it felt. Knew how effective it was, just to be touched, just to feel like someone cared about you.

"That girl's whole life is trouble. Girl. She's a grown woman, but she acts like a girl. Can't keep one thing in her life from falling apart because she's so dang crazy."

"Like this thing with Zalie?" Jem said.

"Like that, sure. But that's just ordinary stuff. People divorce all the time. People have affairs all the time. Nothing new under the sun. But the rest of the stuff—bombs, guns, hurting people. I'm supposed to believe some dumb son of a gun driving a delivery truck deserves to die because she doesn't like how that company keeps their chickens? That's bullspit to me." Leroy eased his weight forward on the cushion, gesturing at Jem with the spoon. "I told her we've all got to make a difference. I taught her that. I said, 'Look what I'm doing, sweetheart. Taking these poor animals in. Giving them a better life.' But that's not what she wanted. She always had to feel important, and somebody else always had to pay for it."

"These are rescues?" Tean said, glancing at the array of animals featured in the photographs. "That's really impressive."

"I've got nothing better to do with my time. I was a fireman, hurt my back, and it was either a few years of daytime TV before I dragged myself out back and put a bullet in my brain, or find something important to do with my life."

"What organizations do you work with?" Tean asked.

"You know what I think?" Leroy said, stabbing the spoon at Jem. "It might be trouble, sure. Joy loves trouble, and she loves the drama of it, the hiding, the running, as much as she loves actually doing something. But it might be that wife."

"Zalie?"

"Lot of money. Lot of money. People kill for less than that."

"Kill?" Jem said.

"You bet your butt. That pig farm's got to be worth a few million. They're already in that co-op, they're fully organic, they own the land outright. Zalie built it up from just about nothing, but Joy's going after it with both hands in the divorce. I know she is. She wasn't ever one to let something she loved slip away from her."

"You think someone killed your daughter?" Jem said. "You think she's dead?"

Leroy flushed, and with some difficulty, he got to his feet. "I don't know where she is. I don't know what she's up to. If she's in trouble, leave me out of it. But I'll tell you one thing: if Zalie touched a hair on her head, I'll put that woman in the ground myself. Now, you boys ought to leave. Tell Hannah hello for me."

He ushered them out of the house, refusing to answer any more questions, and Tean and Jem made their way to the truck. Scipio went wild sniffing them. Jem seemed to have a similar idea: as they drove back to the highway, Jem pulled his shirt up to his nose and made a face.

"Thank God your apartment doesn't smell like that."

"Roger probably needs a bath."

"Yeah: it's fucking disgusting. I'm probably going to have to wash my jacket and shoes just so I don't smell like dog."

"I'm more worried about those rescue animals. A lot of them — maybe most of them — are prohibited. You can't own them, rescue them, transport them. I wonder if he still has any of them."

"Uh oh. The big bad DWR wolf just got your scent, Leroy. Watch out!"

Tean stretched, reaching across Jem for the handle on the passenger door.

"What are you doing?" Jem said, laughing as he wrestled Tean away from the door. "Will you pay attention to the road, please?"

"Sure. I just need to kick your butt to the curb first."

Jem laughed some more, grappling with Tean until Tean had to merge onto the highway and really focus on driving. They drove north, the valley spread out ahead of them, a blaze of amber and blue-white lights, the dark bulk of the mountains like the end of the world.

"What about that shit about blowing up a delivery driver?" Jem asked, his hand resting on Tean's shoulder again, his index finger playing with Tean's collar, the flat of his nail pleasant against Tean's nape. "Do you think that's for real?"

"I don't know," Tean said, "but Hannah didn't tell us everything. She's got more of a history there, and I want to know what it is."

16

They drove to Hannah's house in Wasatch Hollow. It was almost nine, and the streetlights revealed a suburban landscape of abandoned toys and overturned bikes, minivans and crossover SUVs, neatly weeded flower beds, lawns that got aerated and seeded and fertilized like Jesus Christ himself might do a surprise inspection. In many of the Craftsman bungalows, dormer windows glowed.

Tean was already slowing the truck, looking for a place to park on the crowded street, and Jem had a better look at the houses they were passing. In one, through a large picture window on the main floor, he could see a family kneeling in a circle: mom in wrinkled cotton pajamas, dad in a BYU hoodie, Billy and Bobby and Susy and Sally in shorts and t-shirts that obviously served as sleepwear. They were praying, and when the prayer finished, Bobby said something to Billy, and they immediately started fighting, both boys going to the ground, rolling across the carpet as they struggled with each other. Sally and Susy skipped upstairs, completely unconcerned. Dad was yelling. Mom was tired. Was she thinking about Mother's Day coming up, Jem wondered. Was she worried she wasn't a good mom? Or was she thinking she'd made a mistake, that she should have moved to California and tried her luck as a character actor? Then the fight broke up, and Dad scooped up Billy, who was sobbing into Dad's shoulder while Dad walked him around the house and patted his back.

And then the truck had driven on, and Jem couldn't see them anymore. Couldn't see anything. He was startled, the world rushing back in, when Tean said something.

"What?"

Tean's face was strange; his hand lay lightly on top of Jem's, where Jem was holding the doc's shoulder. "I said you're hurting me."

Then Jem felt the ache in his fingers, and his face flooded with heat as he pried his grip loose. "God, I'm so sorry. I was—I don't even know what I was doing. My brain was totally somewhere else."

The doc just watched him. He didn't massage his shoulder, although he probably wanted to. He just stared at Jem, his dark eyes like they always were: warm, soft, frighteningly open.

"Do you want to handle this?" Jem said. "I don't think Hannah likes me."

Tean grabbed the keys, but he didn't pull them from the ignition. He was still watching. Scipio snored softly in the back seat. Jem ran his fingers over the vinyl upholstery, his fingers bumping over the stitching.

"You're the one who's good at talking to people," was all Tean said. "I can't believe you got Leroy to talk to us. Gosh, I can't believe you got him to cry."

Jem shrugged, glued on a smile, and slid out of the truck. Behind him, the doc's steps hurried across the pavement.

"Are you ok? What's going on?"

"Yeah, of course. Just—my stomach. I think that breakfast burrito might have been wonky."

They were almost to the porch when Tean pinched him. Hard.

"Ow," Jem roared. "What the hell?"

"You don't have to tell me what's bothering you," Tean said, staring up at him, the glasses halfway down his nose. "You're always entitled to tell me it's none of my business, or just not say anything at all, or tell me you want to talk about it later. But don't you ever, ever speak ill of a Rancherito's breakfast burrito again. Not in my hearing."

Rubbing the aching spot on his arm, Jem stared at Tean.

"You're insane."

"I know."

"You're out of your goddamn mind."

"Duh."

"I can't believe you pinched me."

Tean shrugged and headed for the porch. "Believe it, sweet cheeks."

Jem watched him go. "Sweet cheeks? What the hell has gotten into you?"

"I don't know," Tean mumbled without looking back. "I might be having a stroke."

Jem was smiling. Grinning, actually. And when he realized that, he forced the expression away and clomped up onto the porch next to the doc.

When Tean knocked again, the door opened immediately. Caleb stood there, his hair mussed, stubble on his chin and cheeks. He was still in work clothes: collar undone, shirt half untucked, trousers sagging like they were about to slide right off his nonexistent ass. His expression, in that first instant, was painfully hopeful. When he saw them, it evaporated.

"Tean, I don't want to be rude, but I've got too much going on to do this with you right now."

"We just have a few questions for Hannah. We ran into some strange stuff, and we just need to clear it up."

"No."

"What the hell do you mean, no?" Jem said. "Go wake her up if you have to. This is important. It's her butt that's in the frying pan."

"You need to go." He raised one hand; he was shaking. "Get off my property." In his other hand, Caleb held a phone. A voice rumbled, and Jem would have put money on the voice belonging to Howard Lackey. Hannah's father was saying something that sounded like "Get rid of them." And then Jem realized no Divorcee. No barking.

"Is that Howard?" Jem said. "Let me talk to him."

"Don't answer any of their questions," Howard was shouting. "Lock the door and wait until I get there."

"Caleb," Tean said, "where's Hannah?"

Caleb started to cry, putting one shaking hand over his eyes. He disconnected the call. Through the tears, he managed to stammer, "I don't know."

"Come on," Tean said, "let's sit down and talk about this."

As always, Tean was a different person in emergencies. He ushered Caleb into the living room, got him seated, and then headed straight for the kitchen. He came back with a glass of water and sat on the sofa next to the sobbing man. When he put his arm around Caleb, Caleb just cried harder, and Tean talked to him quietly. Jem had seen Tean talk to Scipio the same way during thunderstorms. He didn't need to imagine him talking this way to wild things; Tean had talked to Jem this way after Benny died, and there were few things in the world more feral than Jem. The Tean who burned toast and wore all-khaki ensembles, the guy who squirmed away from casual touch and practically ran out of the room when the topic turned to sex, the guy whose glasses were always on the edge of sliding off his nose — that guy was still there, but somehow he was calm, in control. Even in control of his glasses.

Jem took the opportunity to excuse himself to the bathroom. He checked the vanity — combs, brushes, scrunchies, an empty box of condoms, pregnancy tests, disposable razors, dentist-sized cartridges of floss, toothpaste. He checked the mirrored cabinet. Bingo, bongo. A nice row of scrips. Jem took out his phone and snapped pictures. Then he scanned the vials. Most of the drug names he gave up on automatically — there was no time to work on each one — but as Tean liked to point out, one of Jem's crutches with reading was scanning for words he already knew. He spotted one right away: Valium. He emptied half the vial and put the pills in his pocket. He figured he was doing Caleb a favor; the guy looked like he was doped to the gills on the stuff already. More interesting was the vial hidden inside a half-empty box of tissues; the drug name was too hard for him to read, but he put some of those pills in another pocket.

Next, Jem hurried to the master bedroom. He didn't want to risk the overhead lights, so he used the flashlight on his phone, doing a quick sweep: dresser, nightstands, bed, closet. He tried to hit all the regular hiding spots too, but he didn't have time to be thorough. He found more or less what he'd expected: clothing, a dog-eared copy of *The Secret*, two empty glasses on Hannah's nightstand, some sort of collapsible home-gym equipment under the bed. Nothing quite as useful as a print-out travel itinerary, unfortunately.

When he got back to the living room, Caleb's crying had subsided, and Tean offered the water again. After a drink, Caleb said, "We had a huge fight. Huge. It's been going on for days."

"Since we came over?"

"Well, before that it was kind of . . . underground. She went to work early. I stayed at work late. But yeah, after you came, it blew up."

"What have you been fighting about?"

The glass of water shook in his hand.

"We're not going to say anything to anyone," Tean told him.

"I don't even know. I mean, she's been so different lately. You've noticed, right? Her parents certainly have. She's angry. She's closed off. She shouts. Honestly—this is me being a hundred-percent honest—I don't think I'd ever heard her shout before a few weeks ago."

"Do you know why things changed?"

"No." Then, without pausing, he added, "She might be having an affair."

"Hannah?" Jem said.

Tean shot him a glance, and Jem decided he probably needed to watch his tone.

"What makes you say that?" Tean said.

"It started a few months ago. She'd tell me things that seemed perfectly logical at the time, but then they started to add up. She'd claim she forgot to pick up the dry cleaning. Or she'd tell me she was having dinner with friends. Or she had to work late. I just believed her. Why wouldn't I believe her? I mean, she's Hannah."

"Did something happen? Why did you start thinking she wasn't telling the truth?"

"Because I stopped by the DWR building one night when she was supposed to be working, and she wasn't there. I had picked up some Thai, and I wanted to surprise her. When they told me she wasn't there, I thought maybe she was doing field work. But . . . but there was this part of me that didn't believe that. So when she got home that night, late, I asked her about work. Probably a little too much, actually, because I think she got suspicious. But she told me she'd been in the office doing paperwork." He shook his head, as though he still couldn't quite believe his own words. "She lied to me. Right to my face. And after that, I started thinking. She said she was picking up the dry cleaning, but I never saw any clothes come back from the cleaners. She said she was meeting friends for dinner, but I couldn't find a charge on the credit card statements. I feel like such an idiot. I believed all of it."

"You trusted her," Tean said. "You shouldn't feel dumb for trusting her."

"And it's human nature," Jem said. "People will believe anything if they want it to be true, or if they're afraid it's true—or if they expect it to be true, in this case."

Caleb's hands went to his forehead, massaging, and he groaned. "When did she leave?"

"I don't know. I came home from work. She wasn't here. I waited. She didn't come home. I texted. Nothing. I called. She didn't answer."

"Do you know the police are looking at Hannah for a missing-person case?"

"What? What does that mean?"

"It means they think she's holding back information about someone who's gone missing."

Shaking his head, Caleb looked like he was struggling to find words. Finally he managed, "Who?"

"Joy Erickson."

"You're kidding."

"No. Do you know Joy?"

"I know—I mean, I know Hannah used to know her. A long time ago. But that's over. And she hasn't done anything like that for a long time."

"Anything like what?" Jem asked.

Caleb glared at him.

"Like what?" Tean asked.

"The stuff that Joy does. Did. The ecoterrorism stuff. You know about her, right? And Hannah never did anything bad, nothing really bad. She swore she hadn't."

Jem was thinking about what Leroy had said: bombs, gun, a murdered delivery-truck driver.

"When were they friends? Are they still friends?"

"No, they are not still friends. Don't you know Hannah at all? She wouldn't have anything to do with someone like that. This was a long time ago. A long, long time ago. Hannah was just back from her mission. She was struggling, ok? She's always been, I don't know, liberal." He said it like she'd been kicked in the head by a horse as a child—tragic, but not her fault. "And she was having a hard time trying to figure out, you know, how these different parts of her life were going to fit. She wasn't active in the church for a while, I know that. And she was friends with Joy. But that's as far as it went. Just friends."

Jem's first thought was of Hannah in her Merrells, all the outdoor work she did, her love of camping and hiking and fishing. Stereotypes were just stereotypes; he knew that better than most. But stereotypes also existed for a reason. And Joy Erickson had a wife. And Hannah's husband was using the word *friends* a lot. And Leroy Erickson had said something about people having affairs.

"What kind of stuff did Joy get involved with?"

"I don't know."

"Her dad mentioned —"

"I don't know. I'm not — I don't even want to know." Caleb got up from the sofa and stalked to the other side of the living room. "She did bad stuff, ok? She's a bad person. But that's not Hannah. Hannah never did that stuff. She never would do anything like that. They were friends, and then Hannah got her head on straight —"

Interesting choice of words, Jem thought.

" — and she hasn't had anything to do with Joy in a long time. So I don't even want to talk about it, ok? I shouldn't have brought it up."

"You didn't bring it up," Tean said. "I brought it up. I told you the police think she's withholding information."

"She's not," Caleb snapped. "She's a good person. She's kept her covenants."

"That's not really the point right now," Tean said.

"Of course you'd say that. Of course someone like you would say that."

Tean let out a slow breath, his gaze settling on the floor. The house creaked and settled. Rocking back and forth, Caleb wiped his face. His breathing sounded like he was on the verge of tears again.

Jem had one hand in his pocket, coiling paracord around his fingers, imagining what it would sound like when the hex nut whacked the side of Caleb's head.

"But the police think she's hiding something," Jem said. "That's what matters. It doesn't matter if you think she walks on water. Why do the police think that?"

"I don't know."

"Sure you do."

"I don't know!"

"Come on, buddy. You're out of practice. You probably haven't told a decent lie since you spied on Aunt Suzy getting out of the shower. Try one more time. Tell me you don't know why the police think Hannah's hiding something. It'll be more convincing if you look me in the eyes when you say it."

"Get out! Get out of my house! I'm calling the police right now."

"Good energy," Jem said. "Good projection. A little heavy-handed with the volume."

"That's enough," Tean said. "Let's go."

"Sure. As soon as he apologizes to you."

Tean stood, made his way to where Jem stood, and caught his arm. "I want to go."

Jem jerked his arm free. "Go outside. I'll join you in a couple of minutes."

"Fine," Caleb said, pulling out his phone. "I really will call the police."

"I won't break anything," Jem said to Tean. "Maybe his nose. But I won't break anything else."

"Jem."

Jem glanced at his friend.

"Can we please go?"

When they left, Caleb was shouting into the phone, demanding a patrol car at his house as soon as possible.

17

On Wednesday morning, Tean went to work. Hannah wasn't there. He conducted the necropsy on the coyote specimen from Heber Valley and found signs of pneumonia, which was nonspecific — neither confirming nor refuting a diagnosis for canine distemper. He took samples from the lungs, mucous membranes, stomach, intestines, bladder, and brain — fresh samples as well as samples fixed in formalin — all of which needed to be tested. He packed and labeled the samples to be sent off to a specialized lab. Then he cleaned up the lab, cleaned up himself, and went back up to his office.

Still no Hannah.

He pulled up the DWR database and plugged in Zalie Maynes, hoping he could get a line on Joy's wife — or ex-wife. He got nothing. He tried again, this time with just the last name, limiting the search to the Heber Valley. This time, he got Azalea Maynes, with address, phone number, and hunting licenses issued for upland game and, two years ago, a turkey. He tried the phone number and got a robotic voice asking him to leave a message. He disconnected and tried again.

"Ms. Maynes, my name is Tean Leon. I'm calling because I need to talk to you about Joy Erickson and Hannah Prince. Please call me as soon as you have a minute." He left his number and disconnected.

He tried Hannah. No answer. He left her a message too.

Dead end, dead end, dead end. The condo had been a dead end. The pig farm too. And Leroy Erickson. And even Hannah herself had been a dead end. Tean made himself work through it all again. He thought about Hannah's story when she had first hired Jem. He thought about Joy's condo in The Avenues. He thought about the threatening emails and messages he'd found from the man named

John Sievers. Tean plugged that name into the DWR database and got a hit: phone number, address, and a list of related documents — hunting and fishing licenses, citations, and bounties paid to Sievers.

He called Jem. "What are you doing?"

"Honestly?"

"Why would I want you to lie? Why would I ever want you to lie?"

"Um, right. Never mind. Scratch that. I take it back."

Tean waited. "So?"

"Well, since I'm being honest — always, completely, totally, never the slightest shadow of change — I am watching *Visionaries* re-runs and eating chips and queso." He cleared his throat. "In my underwear."

"Ok."

"You're not mad?"

"That sounds like how you spend every Saturday."

"But now I'm doing it on your couch."

"You always do it on my couch."

"And I might have dripped some queso and —" Jem suddenly giggled, high pitched, and said, "No. Stop it!" He was obviously trying to make his voice normal when he spoke again. "And Scipio keeps licking where I spilled it. And obviously that tickles."

"Remember when you didn't like dogs?"

"I don't like dogs. I'm scared as fuck of dogs. But Scipio —" Another of those giggles. "I said stop!"

"Ok, well, if you two can stop licking each other for five minutes, I thought we might run out to Heber again."

"We're not licking each other, although Scipio did get a little queso on his fur, so maybe —"

"I'll pick you up in fifteen minutes."

As Tean drove back to Central City, his phone buzzed, and Ammon's name appeared on the screen. Tean considered letting it go to voicemail, but something pulled tight in his gut, the old breathlessness, and he answered.

"I got a call from Caleb Prince this morning," Ammon said. Tean could hear the strain in his voice as he tried to sound calm.

"Are you going to yell at me right now," Tean asked, "or do I have to wait a few minutes while you pretend to be nice?"

"I'm sorry about last time. I'm sorry I let my emotions get out of control like that. I take responsibility for how I spoke to you, and I apologize."

"How long have you been seeing a therapist?"

He laughed, and for a moment, he sounded like the real Ammon. "Since you dumped my sorry ass."

"I didn't dump you," Tean said gently. "We weren't dating."

"I miss you so much."

"Ammon."

"I know. I know. I want you to know that I've figured out some stuff about myself. I'm a sex addict, and I'm going to a twelve-step program."

"Wow."

"I'm going to make myself a better person, Tean. You deserve the best person in the whole world. I don't know if I'll make it that far, but I'm going to try my hardest." Ammon cleared his throat and said, "I need to express something to you, and I hope you'll hear me out and validate what I'm saying."

"Ok."

"This is a police investigation. Your . . . friend is dragging you into something that you shouldn't be involved in."

"Jem isn't dragging me into anything."

"What you're doing, talking to people, you're jeopardizing my investigation. This is my career, Tean. I have professional responsibilities. I'm not going to look the other way while you compromise an important case."

"Hannah is missing too."

"Hannah is an adult who has chosen to walk away from her husband. She's not a missing person." Ammon didn't say *yet*, but the word was a ghost at the end of the sentence.

"You didn't tell me Joy Erickson was an ecoterrorist. You just said you were worried about finding her."

"There was no need to tell you. We're not looking for her to arrest her; this is a missing-person case. And Hannah knows something. She and Joy go way back. Did you know that?"

"It came up."

"Well, you should think about what that tells you. Hannah might not be doing this to protect Joy. She might be trying to protect herself."

"What do you mean?"

"She and Joy weren't exactly traveling the country planting daisies, Tean. They did some bad stuff. People got killed."

"No, she didn't have anything to do with that."

"Very funny," Ammon said. "Tell me another. Come down here one day and I'll show you what they have in the file on Hannah Lackey from the mid-2000s."

"This is a misunderstanding," Tean said.

"I want you to stay away from this investigation. You're putting me in a difficult situation where I'm going to have to choose between my feelings for you and my profession. That's not fair."

And, Tean realized, it wasn't fair. Not at all. "Jem and I just need to find—"

He cut off when he heard the shift in Ammon's breathing. Then Ammon said, "Can we go five minutes without you bringing him up?"

"I wasn't—"

"We're talking about us right now. You and me. Why are you even saying his name?"

"I'm trying to tell you—"

"I know perfectly fucking well what you're trying to tell me. You're trying to tell me to go fuck myself, you and your boyfriend are going to do whatever you want."

"He's not—"

But Ammon was shouting, and then a series of thunderous claps came across the call. It took Tean a moment to realize what he was hearing: Ammon pounding the receiver of his office phone against the desk.

Tean disconnected and threw his phone on the dash. It buzzed a moment later, Ammon's name on the screen. Tean ignored it.

At the apartment building, Tean hurried past the bulletin board and took the stairs two at a time. He stopped on the second-floor landing and jogged back down to the main floor. This time, he read the notices more carefully. He grabbed one and ripped it free from its tack, and then he hurried upstairs.

As he got through the door, Scipio bounded off the couch. The Lab crashed into him at the knees, whining and dancing with excitement, and Tean scratched his ears and greeted him and then said, "He's got nacho cheese on his muzzle."

"It's not nacho cheese," Jem said. "It's queso." The blond man had obviously showered after Tean's phone call, and he was dressed in acid-washed jeans and what he was currently claiming was his favorite t-shirt: purple cotton embroidered with three old ladies wearing giant hats and the words THE BIGGER THE HAT, THE BETTER IT GETS. He grabbed his windbreaker, checked the pockets, and said, "Ready."

"Remind me to talk to you about this when we get back," Tean said, dropping the flyer on the counter.

"What is it?"

Tean locked up the apartment, and they headed for the truck. "They've got apartments to rent."

"Where?"

"Here."

Jem didn't say anything.

"I know you just got your new place," Tean said. "But I thought maybe you'd still have some flexibility."

"Yeah," Jem said slowly, and Tean could sense Jem studying him. "Maybe. That wouldn't be weird for you?"

"Why would it be? We're friends."

"We're best friends."

"We're ordinary, get-pizza-once-a-week friends."

"We're soulmate-level friends, the kind who can't live without each other, so we'll probably die within fifteen minutes of each other."

"You smell a little skunky," Tean said as he climbed into the driver's seat.

Jem looked like he was trying to smother a huge grin. "I just took a shower."

"It's not BO. Well, it kind of is. But it's worse."

"Noted."

"You might need to get that windbreaker cleaned."

"I'll put it in my day planner."

"And change soaps."

Jem was biting the corner of his mouth to stop a smile, shaking his head.

"What?" Tean said.

"It's nice to know that if I ever get cocky —"

"If?"

" —I've got you around to bring me down a few pegs."

Tean cut over to I-80, and he followed it east again, cutting up Parleys Canyon toward the Wasatch Back. Jem fiddled with the music on his phone, and after a few minutes, a familiar song came over the stereo.

"What is this?" Tean said.

"Music."

"I've heard it before."

"It's Nirvana. 'Smells Like Teen Spirit.'"

"Huh."

"Do you like it?"

"I don't know."

Jem sighed, but he was smiling as he sprawled in the seat. "Add it to the list. We'll figure out what you like."

"Maybe you should do some reading practice."

"I didn't bring my stuff."

"On your phone. Why don't you look up some articles about Joy, Zalie, and Hannah?"

The tires thrummed. When Tean glanced over, Jem's cheeks were red, and he said, "Tean, come on. I'm reading at the *Everybody Poops* level."

"Give it a try. We're not in any rush, and there's no harm if it's as hard as you think. Besides, we've been slacking the last week because of all this stuff with Hannah."

"Maybe I should just be the DJ. Do you think you'd like—"

"No. I don't like anything. And I want you to do some practice."

Jem muttered something.

"What was that?"

"I said I know one thing you like. When we used to—"

"Phone, Jem. Right now."

But Tean's face was hot, and he kept his eyes on the road winding up through the canyon.

When they turned south toward Heber, they left behind the cool shadows of the high rock walls, and the sun enameled everything with gold. The junegrass rippled, its blue-green stalks like waves. Where Indian ricegrass grew in clumps along the highway, it was already flowering. A cottontail, bold enough to venture onto the gravelly stretch, ripped a blade free as Tean and Jem drove past. Everywhere the valley was coming alive: the Russian sage blossoming in purple clusters, a shelterbelt of poplars with pale trunks the same color as the sunlight, ferns growing wild on the shady bank of a creek. It was the kind of day where the world opened up. The sky seemed impossibly big. Everything was light, everything floating like the world had jettisoned its anchor. Ten heartbeats, twenty, a hundred. He was part of it too: the light, the junegrass, the glowing poplars. And then the highway jagged around a spur of stone, and the Indian ricegrass was just grass, its flowering heads bobbing in the wake of a tractor trailer, and the world dropped anchor again.

Tean's phone buzzed, and he answered without looking.

"Why haven't you RSVP'd?" his sister Miriam asked. "It's Mother's Day. Mom really wants you to be there."

"I might have a conflict."

"No, you don't."

"I said I might."

"Teancum Leon, you're doing what you always do: you're putting off the decision because you're hoping someone else will make it for you or something will come up so that you don't have to make a decision."

"I don't—" Tean was suddenly aware of Jem listening intently, although the blond man was pretending to be reading. "Mir, this isn't a good time."

"I'm telling Mom you'll be there."

"Don't you dare."

"She's going to be so happy."

"Mir, I honestly don't know if I can—"

The call disconnected.

Tean threw the phone on the dash for the second time. He was thinking maybe he should just leave it up there.

"Was that your dentist?" Jem asked.

"Can you not, please?" Tean said, the double yellow lines blurring in his vision. "Why couldn't I have been a black-tailed prairie dog?"

Jem nodded. "I knew you wanted a tail like Scipio's."

"They're not really dogs; that's just a name. They're harem-polygynous squirrels. And infanticide runs rampant. And if I'd been a black-tailed prairie dog—"

"With a tail."

"—I could have just been killed and cannibalized by my black-tailed prairie dog family—"

"Harem."

"—instead of being slowly murdered by disingenuous kindness from these people I have nothing in common with except being mixed from the same genetic slurry."

"Maybe you should shout about it."

"I am going to shout about it. I'm so tired of this. This is what they do every time. Every time, they pretend like I have a choice. Every time, they pretend like nothing's wrong, like everything's just perfect. Every time, they leave me an out because they want me to be the one who ruins things. They can't stand the idea of not inviting me, because then they wouldn't be perfect, but God help them if I actually show up. That's even worse because then all the in-laws have to face the ugly reality that I'm a huge, raging fag."

The echoes of his shouting faded slowly from the cab.

"That didn't sound like an unvitation."

"What the hell is an unvitation?"

"Oh doc. That's a nickel in the swear jar. An unvitation is when you invite someone to something in a way that means they're not really invited. Or in a way that will make them not want to come."

"That is . . ." Tean struggled. "The stupidest thing I've ever heard."

"It sounded like she really wants you to be there."

"You don't understand. You don't know them. And you don't know how this works."

"Why would anybody care if you're gay? You came out like twenty years ago, right?"

"Eighteen," Tean yelled.

Jem put a hand over his mouth.

"And it wouldn't matter if it had been a hundred years ago. They're still embarrassed. They still hate having to admit they've got someone like me in the family. They still hate the fact that their husbands and wives and kids have to interact with a homo. They hate how upset I make my mom and dad."

"Ok," Jem said, and he put his hand on the back of Tean's neck and began to massage lightly. "God, you've got so much tension up here. Stop squirming. I said stop! I know you don't like being touched, but you're going to steer us off the road if you keep that up."

Tean managed to stop trying to get away from Jem's fingers.

"And can you try to relax? You can keep shouting, but it feels like you've got steel cables in your neck and shoulders. I'm going to break my thumb doing this."

One deep breath. Then another.

"That's better," Jem said. "Now do a little more yelling."

"I just hate this so much. I hate how they don't want me there, and I hate how they make it my fault if I don't go. I'm tired of everything in that family being my fault."

"Outsider's perspective?"

Tean grunted.

"I know I don't know the whole thing, but it genuinely sounded like she wanted you there. Maybe a lot of this is in your head. Is that a possibility?"

They drove another mile past fields of alfalfa, the tiny green sprouts just getting started. A fat chukar was picking around the edge of the field and, in fits of excitement, flapping its wings.

"Maybe," Tean finally said. "Some of it."

The alfalfa fields transitioned to a run-down apple orchard, the trees gnarled and scraggly, the rail fence toppled over for twenty or thirty yards before starting up again.

"You think I should go to the party."

"I think you should do whatever's going to make you happy," Jem said, his fingers still working their magic on Tean's neck and shoulders. It was surprising—always surprising—to Tean how good it felt to be touched. Just like this. Just by a friend. Once he got past the initial urge to shrink away, of course. "But if you want to go, I'll go with you, and I'll beat the shit out of anybody who gives you the side eye."

"You can't beat the crap out of my family."

"Beat the shit. Say it, Doc."

"I'll have to think about it."

"It's only a dime in the swear jar. Just do it. Be wild."

"I'm talking about the party."

Jem just squeezed his neck and laughed.

The maps app on Tean's phone took them toward John Sievers's home, which was only half a mile past Zalie's pig farm, marked only by a gravel turnoff. Ten minutes later, they reached a gate, and Tean stopped the truck.

Jem jumped down, jogged to the gate, and spent a few minutes fiddling with it. When he came back, his cheeks had little red circles, and his eyes were bright. Tean had to be very careful about his thoughts, very careful to think only friend thoughts.

"Locked," Jem said. "I can pick it, though."

"Let me try calling him."

So Tean called the number he'd gotten from the DWR database, but he didn't get an answer—not even a voicemail. He tried again and got nothing. Then he tried Miguel, and the conservation officer answered on the first ring.

"How's it hanging, Dr. Leon?" Miguel asked.

"Low and nice-sized," Jem shouted.

"What?" Miguel said with a nervous laugh.

"Nothing. That was someone else in the truck." Tean glared at Jem. "He's got cat-scratch disease."

Miguel did some more nervous laughing.

"What's the update on the coyotes? Did you find a sick pack?"

"I think so. I put out some live traps—that's what you wanted, right?"

"That works. If you find one or two that are sick and euthanize them yourself, that's fine too."

"I'm on it."

"Have you seen any affected kit foxes? That's what we want to prevent."

"Not yet."

Tean nodded. "Miguel, what do you know about John Sievers?"

"Come on," Miguel said. "I told him to let this go. I'm sorry he's bothering you."

"Why don't you start from the beginning?" Tean said, raising an eyebrow at Jem. Jem shrugged and shook his head. "Let's hear your side of it."

"He's always been a pain in the butt, Dr. Leon. For the most part, though, he just does his own thing. You know the last few years, he's had the record for the most coyote scalps turned in? The money probably helps, sure. I mean, fifty bucks a pop doesn't sound like a lot, but this guy lives off the grid as much as possible, and he's getting a lot of them. But I think he really just likes trapping and killing and skinning. I told him he needed to take down those videos. He can pretend all he wants that they're educational, but anybody who watches them can tell he enjoys it."

"That's part of our work, Miguel. We support hunters and fishermen."

In Miguel's silence, Tean could hear the wind pushing on the truck, the truck's suspension whining.

"You haven't seen those videos, have you?"

"I saw some tweets, messages. He was threatening Joy Erickson."

"Oh yeah. They're always going at it. But that's not what I'm talking about. I'll send you some links." He paused, and this time, a note of curiosity entered his voice. "Sievers has been moaning for years about how I don't have any right to tell him what he does on his own land. I figured that's why you were calling—he'd finally run this up the ladder to you. But that's not it, is it? Is it something to do with Erickson?"

"I'm not really sure yet," Tean said. "I'll probably need to talk to you again when I have a better idea what I'm looking for."

"You know me," Miguel said. "At your command. You can't see it but I'm snapping a salute."

"Goodbye, Miguel."

In a military cadence, Miguel barked, "Goodbye, sir!"

Tean disconnected the call. "Why do I have so many smart alecks in my life?"

"You're a cosmic magnet," Jem said. "It's because of your bright, shining optimism. People are just drawn to you. Yin and yang. Light and dark."

Covering his face, Tean said, "Exhibit A. What did you learn about Joy, Zalie, and Hannah?"

"I learned that I'm still a fucking imbecile who can't read a newspaper article."

Tean dropped his hands. Jem was staring out the window, his phone in a white-knuckled grip. The shift in his tone and posture had been immediate.

"Want to try that again?" Tean said.

"A fucking fourth-grader could read this shit."

"We talked about this. This was one of the first things we talked about, and you agreed."

"Well, fuck our agreement. And fuck those articles. Here. You read them." He tossed the phone at Tean.

Tean caught it. He was surprised to see a picture of him and Jem on the lock screen. He remembered Jem asking someone to take the picture when they'd gone to the Museum of Natural History. A fossilized raptor skeleton loomed over them, and Jem was replicating the raptor's pose. Tean was staring straight ahead at the camera. Tean didn't know if it was just his memory or if he could actually see it in the picture, but he'd been trying desperately not to smile. He couldn't remember why that had seemed so important at the time.

"I thought we might wait for Sievers," Tean said. "For a little while, at least. That gives us some time to practice."

"Great. Did you bring *Jane Falls Down a Well* or whatever fucking board book I'm supposed to be working on?"

Tean ran through possible responses. He settled on Jem's own words: "Maybe you should shout about it."

"Yeah," Jem said, pinching his brow. "Great idea." Then he shook himself, looking a little like Scipio when he got in from the rain, and said, "Ok. I'm ok. I'm back. Sorry about that."

Tean wanted to tell Jem he could shout if he wanted to. He wanted to tell him he could cry if it would help—he knew that many times Jem had done so, out of the sheer rage and helplessness and embarrassment and frustration he felt as he struggled with reading and writing, but always out of sight, always when he thought Tean wouldn't find out. Instead, he passed the phone back and said, "Let's work on one of them together."

Jem shook his head, but he unlocked his phone and set it where they could both look at it, and they started from the beginning.

It was slow going, made slower by the fact that the angrier Jem got, the more he tried to bottle up his anger, and the more energy he spent on controlling his rage, the less he could spend on focusing. They limped through a short article that the *Deseret News* had run in 2005. It didn't add much to the portrait that Leroy and Caleb had painted of Joy, but it did confirm many important points: Joy had a long history as an environmental activist, and although the paper shied away from the term ecoterrorist, it mentioned several violent incidents in which Joy had been implicated. She and Zalie— described euphemistically as a close friend in the paper—had links to groups responsible for destroying agricultural equipment with explosives, tearing down fencing in order to herd cattle away from ranches, and trying to blow up a bioengineering lab at Brigham Young University. The article's main focus, though, was the death of a delivery truck driver who had worked for a poultry farm outside of Ogden. The article didn't say that Joy and Zalie had caused the explosion that had destroyed the delivery truck and killed the driver, but it came right up to the line, laying out their history and establishing their connection with times, dates, and locations, all to suggest their responsibility.

When they finished, Jem ran his arm over his forehead and said, "Ok. Beer now. Lots of beer. And then burgers. And fries."

"You did really well."

Jem rolled his eyes. "Burgers, Tean. I need lots of protein after that shitshow."

"When we get back to Salt Lake—"

"Now, Tean. I need to drown my humiliation. Maybe I should go straight to whiskey."

"Let me call Mrs. Wish and see if she can walk Scipio."

Mrs. Wish still hadn't forgiven Tean for suggesting that Senator George H. Moses had eaten one of her kittens, and she spoke in clipped, pseudo-polite tones, but she agreed to make sure Scipio got a walk and dinner. When Tean disconnected, he saw that he had missed several messages from Miguel. He checked them and saw that they were links to various YouTube videos.

They were all variations on a theme: John Sievers, the big man with the military hair cut whom Tean had spotted in the pictures in Joy's condo, killing and skinning and then, sometimes, gutting and quartering coyotes. Miguel had been right: Sievers clearly enjoyed what he was doing, and although he talked through each process as though he were instructing the viewer, Tean didn't have any trouble spotting the perverse amount of pleasure Sievers took in the acts.

"It's like porn," Jem said. "Hunter porn."

And he was right, Tean realized. There was something gratuitous about Sievers's performance. Something about the relish he took in the most savage parts of the videos. When he peeled the hide away from muscle and bone in long, savage jerks, he was grinning, micro-droplets of blood beading on his nose and cheeks and lips.

The last video, though, was unlike the others. Sievers was ranting about Joy — that dyke, he called her — building himself up into a hysterical rage. The camera wasn't quite at the right angle, but Tean could glimpse something, what he thought was a coyote, struggling on the ground. Its leg was caught in a trap, he guessed, and heat and prickling sickness washed through him.

"And this is what I'll do to that dyke if she comes on my property again," Sievers screamed, and then he grabbed something off camera and spun toward the coyote. The action was blurred and messy, but Tean could make out a hatchet in Sievers's hand, and he heard two pained howls as Sievers hacked at the trapped coyote. Then the coyote was dead, but blood continued to fountain up as Sievers hacked at the dead animal. And hacked. And hacked.

18

"They have to have a McDonald's," Jem said. "Look, down that street. I think I see one."

Tean looked, but too late. "Dang," he said. "Missed it."

"Just flip around."

"Let's try this place instead."

"McDonald's will be faster."

"We're not in a rush."

"McDonald's will be cheaper."

"It's my treat."

"McDonald's—"

"Jem," Tean said, his dark eyes soft, "let's try something new."

So Jem flopped back in his seat as they pulled into the parking lot for a building marked with big white plastic numbers: 1-8-9. He'd never been to Heber before this week, but it reminded him of the few times he'd been to other rural Utah communities, almost all of them founded by Mormon pioneers. It had a main street lined with small brick and frame homes, strip malls with Beto's and Wendy's, a grocery store—in this case, Lee's, with a brick-and-timber façade— and, of course, a Walmart Supercenter. The restaurant Tean had picked, 1-8-9, was in yet another strip mall, with a grassy berm separating it from an O'Reilly's.

"In case you need to pick up a spark plug after you get your burger," Jem said.

"What was that?"

"Nothing," he said as Tean pulled into the parking stall. "Let's just try this place."

Inside, 1-8-9's décor made Tean think he was ordering burgers in a ski lodge: a high, open ceiling; lots of exposed pine; the smell of searing meat and caramelized onions. A hostess who looked barely sixteen, her hair in pigtails, flashed braces at them and led them to a booth at the back. It was barely five o'clock, but the restaurant was already filling up—lots of families, lots of shrieking kids. A red-cheeked toddler shot toward Jem like a heat-seeking missile, and Jem slid out of the way. A woman, presumably the toddler's mother, was chasing after him, her own cheeks red, her ankle-length dress billowing behind her. Laughing, Tean caught the toddler under the arms and spun the heat-seeking missile back toward his mother. She smiled, thanked him, and walked the boy back to their table.

As they were sitting down, though, something wiped the laughter from Tean's face.

"Don't think about it right now," Jem said. "Unless—did it ruin your appetite?"

"Oh. No, not really. I've seen worse, and, I mean, we have to eat. Did it ruin your appetite?"

"Does it make me psycho if I say no? I mean, it was disgusting and horrifying, but if I let that stop me, I wouldn't have eaten anything until I was eighteen."

Tean's dark eyes shone, and he blinked and looked away.

"Stop," Jem said. "It was just a joke."

"I know."

"That's all over and done with. That's why I can joke about it."

"Right," Tean said, and then he cleared his throat as their waiter, who barely looked older than the hostess, came over.

The waiter set down menus, introduced himself as Jonah, and asked for their drink orders.

"Oh, I'm so sorry," he said. "We don't have beer."

He said it like maybe they didn't have any hardcore pornography or crack cocaine in the restaurant either.

"This is what I was saying," Jem said across the table.

"You didn't say anything," Tean said, still studying the menu. "And McDonald's doesn't have beer either."

"Cokes," Jem said.

The boy glanced at Tean.

"He's going to ask for water, so just ignore him and bring him a Coke."

With a hesitant smile, the boy trotted away. Judging by the wires on his teeth, Jem figured he and the hostess were seeing the same orthodontist. They might have been brother and sister: the same straw-colored hair, the same shape to their mouths. Or cousins. In a place like this, Jem thought, maybe everyone was cousins.

Then Tean got another prowl on his phone. The sound was unmistakable: the roar of a wild animal — a bear, probably, which Tean thought was a little too on the nose. Tean flinched, a dusky color moving under the light brown of his cheeks, and pretended he was still reading the menu.

"Check it," Jem said.

"I don't want to check it."

"Why not?"

"Because it's stupid. Do you like onion rings? I thought maybe I'd try one."

"You'd try one? Wait, does that mean you've never had an onion ring? No, stop, you're trying to sidetrack me. Let's see who just prowled you."

"Eh."

"Maybe he's cute."

Tean picked up his menu and held it in front of his face.

"Maybe he's cute and smart."

"What about cheese fries? Is cheese really good on fries?"

Jem yanked the menu out of his hand and jabbed a finger at Tean. The doc flinched.

"First of all, I'm tired of having to witness firsthand the absolute, total injustice of your life, at least as far as food goes. Yes, obviously cheese is good on fries. Second, maybe he's cute and smart and rescued a million puppies from getting turned into coats."

Tean frowned. "Like *101 Dalmatians*?"

"Exactly, but more awesome because it's a million instead of a hundred and one. Now check your phone."

Their waiter came back with the Cokes.

"He wants a single leaf of lettuce," Jem said. "Hold the salt. And if you could squeeze it to get all the water out of the lettuce, that would be perfect."

Tean snatched the menu back and threw a murderous look at Jem. "I want the chili burger with fries —"

"Cheese fries," Jem said.

"Fine, with cheese fries."

"And an order of onion rings," Jem said.

The poor waiter's eyes were huge, ping-ponging back and forth.

"And an order of onion rings," Tean said, his voice betraying his effort to control himself.

"And for you, sir?"

"Well, I don't want to look like a pig," Jem said.

Tean was making a noise like a kettle about to boil.

"What's your best burger?"

"Well, if you look at this page of the menu —"

"No, what's the best one? Your favorite?"

That was a stumper, and the waiter had to think about it, chewing the tip of his pencil. "I guess the Red, White, and Bleu."

"Do you like bleu cheese?" Tean said.

"I'll try that," Jem said.

"Have you ever had it before?" Tean said. "It's kind of strong."

"I'm sure I'll like it," Jem said to the waiter. "And don't forget the onion rings. He's never had an onion ring, and this is one of those make-a-wish kind of things where he's about to die of a terminal illness and he just wants to eat onion rings before he croaks."

The poor kid backed away, holding his order pad to his chest.

"You can't tell people —"

"Tean, why don't you want to check Prowler?"

"Because it's got a stupid name."

Jem waited. Speakers tucked in the corners of the ceiling were playing Dolly, barely audible over the low roar of conversation. She was pouring herself a cup of ambition.

"And because I never wanted to be on it," Tean said, staring at a point somewhere to one side of Jem, "and Hannah did it without even asking me, and — and the guys on there are crap."

"Five cents in the swear jar," Jem said.

Tean shook his head and grabbed a wad of napkins from the dispenser, and then he just sat there, staring at them, obviously not knowing why he had grabbed them.

"Ok, let's start from the beginning," Jem said. "I know you didn't want to be on there. Fine. But you aren't seeing Ammon, and you aren't going on dates. What's the harm in trying?"

More color flooded Tean's cheeks. "It's embarrassing."

Jem burst out laughing. He covered his mouth, and then he dropped his hand and said, "Sorry. I just — it's not embarrassing. Millions of people do it, right? And it's particularly important for gay guys. It's not like it's easy to meet people once you're in a job and out of school."

Tean rolled his eyes. He was playing with the edge of one napkin now, folding it back and forth.

"So what's the harm in trying?"

"The possibility of being murdered, skinned, tanned, and turned into a rug."

"You've got no imagination at all. At least say they'd use your skin to make wallpaper. Or they'd use your intestines for haggis. Or they'd put your eyes in the taxidermied head of a moose, and then your ghost would spend the rest of its life stuck inside a moose head."

"'My ghost would spend the rest of its life stuck inside a moose head.' Do you even hear yourself sometimes?"

Nudging Tean's leg under the table, Jem smiled and said, "Why are the guys crap?"

"They just are."

"I think you want it to be a bad experience so you can just write it off."

"Fine. You want an example? Here. Here's Robert, who's fifty-seven—"

"Too old for you."

"—and for his favorite memory put, 'eating ur ass.' U-r, Jem. Not y-o-u-r. And he's almost sixty."

"I think you should be flattered that he enjoyed your ass so much."

"And here's—really creative pseudonym, by the way— BigGuy69, and look at these pictures." Tean held out his phone.

"He's not that big."

"He's with his mom! In every single one of them."

Jem swiped through the pictures and then he grabbed the phone. "Hey!"

"I just want to see your profile."

"Absolutely not."

Jem ignored him and tapped over to Tean's page. Tean was reaching across the table, trying to get the phone back, but Jem absently batted his hands away. "Not bad," he said.

"If it's horrible, it's not my fault. Hannah made it."

"I said not bad. You're way cuter than you look in this picture though."

"It's my face. That's my face. It doesn't change."

But it did, Jem thought. Tean's face when he walked in the door and saw Scipio. Tean's face when he was reading. Tean's face in the blue-black shadows of morning twilight, when he searched the mountains for something he'd never been able to name for Jem. Tean's face when he laughed, really laughed, and the lines around his mouth and his eyes opened, like the time Jem had tried to fix the light switch in the bathroom. Tean's face when he was grumpy from lack of sleep. Tean's face in the morning, before he'd even attempted to tame the wild mane of hair. Tean's face asleep, the only time the poor guy seemed to relax. Tean's face when they went hiking, when something seemed to open inside the doc, every inch of him alive and vibrant. Like today, when they'd driven into the valley, and for a moment he'd been so beautiful that it had shattered Jem.

"You know what?" Jem said. "We should get a picture of you out in nature. Somewhere you really like. I'll take one when you're not expecting it."

"That sounds like assault."

"Then I'm describing it correctly. Is World Wildlife Fund really who you'd give a million dollars to?"

Tean rolled his eyes.

"I thought you'd at least cut me in on some of it," Jem said. "Or, if not me, that absurdist philosophy program you're always talking about."

Dolly wasn't getting enough credit; she was singing to them all about it. In the next booth, an older man in a Stetson was trying to explain to two grade-school children—his grandkids, Jem guessed—how to properly castrate a steer. Tean's face was full of some emotion that Jem couldn't read.

"What?" Jem said.

"Nothing," Tean said. "Life's just funny sometimes."

"We'll doctor up that profile. It'll be irresistible gay bait by the time we're done."

"I don't want to be gay bait on an app called Prowler," Tean began to say, cutting off when another growl from the phone interrupted him. He tapped the screen.

"How bad is it?" Jem said.

"He's ok. I mean, ears, nose. You know."

"Great, he's passably human."

"He says he likes dogs."

"Check."

"He's a coder for a startup in Lehi."

"Oh, man. Money, money. Check."

"Not necessarily. Some startups—"

"Nope, no getting sidetracked," Jem said.

Tean lowered the phone. His eyes were huge. "He sent me a message."

"Did he ask you to take your shirt off? Maybe wait until we get out to the truck."

Tean just stared at him.

"What did he say?"

"It starts, 'hey,' and he says, 'how's your day going?'" Tean's eyes, if anything, had gotten bigger.

"Damn, he's not going to make this easy for you, is he?"

"What do I say?"

"Well, how's your day going?"

Tean shook his head. His mouth was slightly open, and his eyes were glazed. Cartoon characters usually had little birdies dancing around their heads, but Jem couldn't see any sign of that.

"I mean," Jem said, "do you want to say something? Because you can just ignore him if you're not interested."

"Should I?"

"Do you want to?"

"He's not horrifying."

Jem bit his lip. When he trusted himself again, he said, "Ok. He passes the first test. Why don't you tell him how your day is going?"

That opened a floodgate. Tean messaged. The phone growled. Tean messaged. The phone growled. Dolly had already punched out, and now Reba was asking does he love you, does he think of you. The grandpa in the next booth had decided words weren't enough, and now he was illustrating the process with a steak knife and a pair of dinner rolls. Grandma, who was wearing a lace dickey, was completely focused on separating the green beans and carrots on Grandchild #1's plate. And Tean was still messaging.

When the food came, Jem said, "You don't have beer?"

The waiter shook his head.

"Whiskey?"

"I just need you to cut into your burger, sir, and let me know if it's ok."

"Cough syrup? The kiddie kind, grape flavored if you have it."

"If you could just check—"

"Rubbing alcohol. Does that make you go blind? You know what? It doesn't matter. A double shot of rubbing alcohol."

"His burger is fine," Tean said without looking up from his phone. "Thanks."

The kid beamed at them as though he'd really accomplished his life's purpose, but he was a little too fast for Jem to catch his sleeve.

"What about those little things of jet fuel they use for camping stoves?" he shouted after the waiter.

"What is going on with you?" Tean asked, his gaze still locked on his phone. Then he giggled. Honest-to-God giggled. "Orion is kind of funny."

"His name is Orion? Gag."

Tean just giggled again.

"What kind of restaurant doesn't have beer? I really don't think that's too much to ask."

Tean was tapping madly.

"Maybe you should let him wait a while," Jem said. "So he doesn't think you're too eager."

If Tean heard him, he gave no sign.

"I heard some families make everybody put their phones away during dinner."

"You literally beat some sort of fruit-slicing game last week during dinner and had to dance around the room shouting and celebrating."

"I didn't beat it," Jem said. "I got past a hard level and—you know what? I'm not even going to get involved. I'm just going to eat my burger."

But he took one bite and set it back down.

"What's wrong?" Tean asked half-looking up.

"Nothing."

"You don't like bleu cheese."

"No, it's great."

"It's really strong. Not everybody likes it. That's what I tried to say."

"You've never had an onion ring. You've never had cheese fries."

Without shifting his gaze from the phone, Tean grabbed an onion ring and took one bite. "They're ok, I guess." Then he wiped his fingers and went back to typing.

"They're ok," Jem repeated.

Reba was still asking. Reba really wanted to know.

"I bet Orion likes bleu cheese."

"That's funny," Tean said, and Jem guessed he would have said the exact same words, in the exact same tone, if Jem had told him the restaurant was on fire. "I'll ask him."

"I need to use the bathroom," Jem said.

He lucked out. It was a single-user facility, so he locked the door and stared at himself in the mirror. Then he turned his back on the guy in the glass. You're just friends, he told a paper-towel dispenser. Good friends. Best friends. And tonight, after you drop off your best friend, you can drive around Salt Lake until you find somebody named Orion and then you can disembowel him. Hell, maybe you can take a page out of John Sievers's book and just chop the motherfucker to bits. Then he washed his hands and went back to the table.

While he'd been gone, Tean had switched burgers. He'd put away his phone too.

"You didn't have to do that," Jem said.

"I like bleu cheese. And you like chili burgers."

"How'd you know that?"

"You like chili dogs. And you love hamburgers. And you made a moaning noise when that Carl's Jr. ad with the chili burger came on. The one with the girl who probably needs a back brace."

Jem smiled in spite of himself. "You got me."

"You're a really good friend, Jem," Tean said.

"What brought that on?"

"I just wanted to tell you."

Jem just nodded and took a bite of the chili burger. He couldn't taste a damn thing. Then a thought struck him.

"Jealousy."

"Huh?"

"Leroy said that Joy was having affairs. If something bad happened to her, maybe that's connected somehow."

"I don't think Zalie is going to talk to us, and even if she did, she probably wouldn't confess to hurting or killing her wife out of jealousy."

"Zalie might not tell us," Jem said, wiping chili from his face with a napkin—the burger was messier than he expected. "But I bet those girls Joy was fooling around with, I bet they will. Especially if we put the fear of God into them. How do you feel about trying to hack some dating apps?"

"You look unbearably pleased with yourself."

"It's a great idea," Jem said, puffing up a little. "Sue me for being proud of it."

"You've got chili in your nose hairs."

19

They struck gold on their third try, and the dating app — Playmates — recognized Joy's email. The password was a combination of her first dog and date of birth; to Tean, it felt like more impossibly good luck on a night that had already been perfectly lucky already. It had been Jem's idea to try that app, which was notorious for same-sex couples having affairs or conducting open relationships. It had been Jem's idea, too, to extract the relevant information from Joy's Facebook page. As usual, he had been right.

Inside the Ford, the only light came from the dash; when Tean turned to Jem, he was surprised to see his friend looking washed out, almost ghostly.

"She definitely found what she was looking for," Jem said.

Joy's inbox was full of messages from women. Tean had only sampled them, but the content was surprisingly banal: hi, how are you, what are you doing this weekend, you've got a nice smile. Several of the messages included arrangements to meet in person, and the locations for those meets ran the length of Utah: from St. George all way to Logan. On April 18, though, something changed.

"She stopped responding," Tean said, waving at the unanswered messages. "Why?"

"Because she didn't want to," Jem said, "because something changed in her personal life, or because she couldn't."

"Because she's dead."

"Or hurt," Jem said gently. "If she was in an accident, she might not be conscious."

Tean shook his head. "Her last Playmates date was on April 17 with night_rabbit2000."

"That sounds like a sex toy."

"There's a phone number," Tean said. "And in one of the messages she says her first name is Becca."

"You should order your own personal night_rabbit2000 before your date with Orion."

Tean copied the phone number and placed the call. It rang four times before a woman picked up. "Hello?"

"Yes, I'm trying to get in touch with Becca."

The call disconnected.

"Of course," Jem said, "maybe Orion already sent you a picture of his night_rabbit. Maybe you won't need to order the night_rabbit2000."

"What is going on with you?"

"So he did send you a dick pic?"

"No. What are you—wait is that a real thing? Or are you just making it up like you did with that swipe thing?"

"It's called a claw. Somebody claws you. Did Orion claw you?"

"I honestly don't even know if we're speaking the same language."

"Give me that," Jem said, taking Tean's phone. He placed another call to the same number. This time, it rang and rang until voicemail picked up. Jem said, "Yes, this message is for a woman named Becca who communicated with Joy Erickson and met with her on April 17. I'm calling pursuant to an ongoing police investigation. Please return this call immediately. Thank you."

When Jem handed back the phone, Tean said, "Pursuant?"

"I heard it on *Dragnet*."

"You can't pretend to be a police officer. You could get in trouble."

"I didn't pretend to be a police officer. I implied I was a police officer, but I just stated the facts. She can interpret them however she wants."

The phone remained dark.

"Did they agree on a place to meet?" Jem said.

"Yes. The Kneaders—it's just south of here, the other end of Heber."

"Let's go take a look."

The Kneaders looked like every other Kneaders in the state: a brick and stucco exterior, plate-glass windows, a dining area with vinyl-covered seats and melamine tabletops. A bell jingled when they stepped inside; the smells of yeast and cinnamon hung in the air. It was half past six, and the dinner rush had slowed, but the dining room was still open: a pair of teenage girls who were probably sisters, wearing identical tracksuits and both bent over their phones; a family of eight, grandpa presiding at the head of the table, all of them shouting to be heard as they exchanged opinions on Aunt Claire; an elderly man who turned the pages of an *Auto Trader* with visible trembling. What little space in the restaurant hadn't been taken up by display cases was filled with baskets. Baskets, baskets, baskets. Most of them were filled with plastic fruit and loaves of bread with little price tags, in case — like any normal person — you were suddenly seized by the need to do some home decorating while you were ordering a grilled cheese sandwich.

Six people waited ahead of them, and Jem rolled his eyes when Tean took a place at the end of the line.

"What?" Tean said.

"Just wait here."

Jem walked past the waiting people, several of whom shot him dirty looks, and approached a girl who was wiping down a table. He spoke to her quietly, and the girl nodded and hurried back into the kitchen. Jem came back, caught Tean's arm, and moved him to stand in a quiet corner of the dining room.

"We could have just waited."

Jem snorted.

"That's the whole point of a line."

"Did you want to order a turkey bacon club?"

"No."

"Did you want to order an éclair?"

"No."

"Were you going to buy me a peanut-butter-chocolate-chip cookie?"

"Maybe," Tean said. "Your eyes get really big when I give you sugar. It's cute."

Jem actually blushed, but then he grinned and said, "Ok, smoothie. Save some of that for Orion."

The woman who emerged from the kitchen had dark hair in a ponytail, lines webbing the corners of her eyes and mouth, and skin the color of Tean's Keens. Her name tag said Kristine and, underneath, Manager. She gave them a big smile and shook hands with both of them.

"You must be Dr. Leon," she said, pumping his hand.

"Yes."

"Well, anything we can do for the animals, we're just really thrilled we can help."

"Right. For the animals. Well, we're looking into some strange activity, and we're wondering if you've seen this woman." He pulled up Joy's picture on his phone.

"Miss Joy? Sure. She's in here pretty regularly. Likes to bring her dates here. I went with a guy like that once. Every girl, the first time they went out, he took her to the same Applebee's. I know because I was waitressing. I finally worked up the nerve to talk to him one night. Want to guess where he took me on our first date?"

"At least you got the employee discount," Jem said.

Kristine laughed. "I never thought about it like that."

"When was the last time you saw Joy in here?" Tean asked.

"Oh, I don't know."

"What about a rough guess?"

"Not this week. I know that for sure. And—well, honestly, I don't think I saw her last week either. It all runs together. Is she back in trouble?"

"Has she been in trouble before?"

Kristine flushed. "Oh, no. I just meant—nothing recent. But everybody's got a past."

"Is there something in particular you're thinking of?"

"No."

"Did she mention travel, friends, plans? Did she give you any clue that she might not be coming back here?"

"We only knew each other to say hi," Kristine said. "Honestly, I thought she was just mad about the car."

"What about her car?"

"We had to have it towed. Say, is it true you aren't ever supposed to pick up a cat by the tail?"

"What?" Tean asked. "You definitely shouldn't pick up a cat by the tail."

"Where did you have it towed?" Jem asked.

"Perkins. It's the only one in the valley, and we didn't do it out of meanness. Company policy. If it's in the lot more than twenty-four hours, we've got to have it towed. I don't like it, but I'm the manager, and that means doing the stuff nobody else wants to do."

"He knows all about that," Jem said, clapping Tean on the shoulder. "He's kind of a manager too."

"Not really," Tean said, trying to shrink out from under Jem's touch.

"He's hell on those people. Pure hell. You should see him go after them if he thinks they're slacking."

Kristine's eyes had narrowed as she reconsidered Tean.

"Don't even get him started about bathroom breaks."

"I don't—I'm not—they can use the bathroom whenever they want."

"Sure," Jem said. "That's what he's legally required to say."

"Huh," Kristine said, like she'd turned over a rock and found something slimy.

"Thanks for your time," Tean said.

Kristine didn't shake his hand when they left.

"I'm not anybody's manager," Tean said, jerking away from Jem as soon as they were out in the chilly May evening. "And I'm not—"

"God, just chill. I'll be right back."

He sprinted back into the Kneaders, catching Kristine at the counter. Jem was smiling, touching her arm, touching her shoulder, laughing, throwing worried looks at the door. Then the smiles faded. He hunched his shoulders. He tried again, whatever he was asking, and Kristine apologized profusely—Tean couldn't hear her, but he could read the pantomime.

When Jem emerged, he said, "Damn. I thought she'd help me out because I have such an ass munch for a boss."

"I'm not your boss. And I'm not an ass munch!"

"It's a no on the security footage. She cited company policy: only with a warrant. Let's try the tow yard."

A quick search brought up Perkins Towing and Impound, which appeared to be the only tow yard in the valley, as Kristine had claimed. They drove south out of Heber, following US 40, and then they cut east past fields of scruffy alfalfa and acres of vines under floating row covers. Tean was pretty sure they were watermelons. Then the watermelons ended, and a wall of corrugated sheet metal began. When they got to the gate, PERKINS had been spray painted on rusting tin shingles. The gate stood open, and Tean guided the Ford into the tow yard.

Night had settled in, and the security floodlights illuminated the tow yard in patches. It looked like an impound lot had grown up around a small, 1960s home. Board-and-batten siding was painted canary yellow, the windows were trimmed in flaking white, and the whole structure was low and long, with only a slight bump to mark the gabled roof. Scraggly cheatgrass grew in clumps around the house, and someone had obviously tried, at one point, to plant roses, although now the bushes were dead and skeletal. In every direction, cars and trucks and minivans were parked. Some were obviously fresh victims, waiting for owners to come and claim them, but most of the collection spanned thirty years of design and manufacture. It wasn't just cars, either. Among the trucks and vans stood electric ranges, refrigerators, even a six-foot plastic replica of Apollo 11, with the words BUZZ OFF hand painted on the command module. Tean wasn't sure what the long-term plan was for Perkins Towing and Impound, but it seemed to involve stockpiling rusted heaps of junk.

The home's front door opened as Tean parked at the edge of the asphalt pad, and by the time he and Jem had gotten out of the truck, a woman was approaching them. From inside the house, a hound howled. At the curtained window, a doggy shape moved frantically back and forth, obviously desperate to be part of the action. As the woman got closer, Tean could make out more details in the bright flood from the security lights. The woman's white hair was clipped shorter than Jem's, her face held a million wrinkles, and she was eating some sort of mush out of a bowl. "Wanda Perkins," she said, gripping Tean's hand so hard that he felt a knuckle pop. "Wanda Perkins," she said, repeating the gesture with Jem. "What can I do for you?"

"We're looking for a car that was towed from the Kneaders," Jem said. "Probably on . . ." He glanced at Tean.

"The eighteenth," Tean said, massaging his hand.

"All right. Make, model, and license plate. I'll need a copy of the vehicle registration and a valid driver's license. The eighteenth?" She whistled. "Yard fees add up, boys. I hope you've got cash because we don't take cards, and I only take checks from my granny."

"Actually," Jem said with a smile, "we're not looking to retrieve the car. We just want to take a look at it."

Wanda dug some more mush out of her bowl. Around a mouthful, she said, "Take a look at it?"

"That's right. Pursuant to an ongoing police investigation."

"Oh. That's all right then. I'll just take a look at your warrant."

"Wanda," Jem said, "you're not really going to make us drive all the way back to Salt Lake, are you?"

"Is that where you're going to get a warrant?" Wanda said.

"If we have to."

"Then I guess you're going to be making a drive. Be careful in the canyon, boys."

The howling inside the house had only gotten louder — judging by the baying noise, Tean was pretty sure he was listening to a Basset. The doggy silhouette behind the curtain was still racing back and forth, and then all of the sudden the dog yelped and tumbled out of sight. Wanda's expression tightened, and she turned back to the house.

Help me, Tean mouthed at Jem. Then, to Wanda's retreating form, he said, "Is it arthritis?"

Wanda kept walking.

"Elbow dysplasia is very common in Basset hounds, and it makes most of them suffer from some degree of arthritis as they get older."

This time, Wanda stopped. She turned to face them, almost invisible in a pool of shadow that the security lights didn't touch.

Jem squeezed Tean's nape once, the blond man's excitement electric in his touch, and then he moved forward, already talking, already back in the game. "Wanda, my friend here is probably the best vet you'll find this side of the Mississippi. He's not hard on the eyes, either, am I right? Why don't you tell us about your dog? What's her name?"

"Toby Keith. He's a boy."

"How old's Toby?"

"Twelve."

Jem whistled. "I had a dog named Antony. He was pure mutt, but he had a lot of pit bull. He only made it to eleven. God, I've never cried so hard in my life. I was a kid, but Jesus, it still gets me sometimes. Have you had Toby long?"

"Only since the day he was born," Wanda said. She stirred the mush with her spoon and then let it clink back against the bowl. "He just gets too excited when somebody new comes around. He starts running. He shouldn't be doing that at his age."

"But I bet you know how to take care of him, right? What do you do? Antony got really sick, stomach stuff, so sometimes we'd just make a game out of letting him chase ice cubes, and he loved that. What do you do for Toby?"

"I don't know. Nothing really helps. I put him on my lap and rub his little legs, I guess."

"Wow," Jem said, beckoning for Tean to come forward. "Wow. You really love him, don't you?"

Wanda didn't answer; her eyes were lost in the darkness.

Tean grabbed his gear bag from the truck and moved to join Jem.

"This guy here," Jem said, slinging an arm around Tean, "this stud, even if he won't brag about himself, he's a genius with animals. And he's a softie, too. There's no way he's going to let us leave until he at least takes a look at Toby. Would that be all right with you? I mean, please, Wanda, do me a favor here, or this guy's going to be crying on my shoulder the whole ride home."

"Have you tried anti-inflammatory supplements?" Tean said.

"Course," Wanda snapped. Then, more softly, "Just glucosamine."

"Well, that sounds like a good place to start. I'd like to take a look at him, but I could recommend some foods you could include in his diet, and I could prescribe something for pain and inflammation. It's a generic, the one I'm thinking of, so it won't break the bank."

"Let's go inside and take a look," Jem said. "How about that?"

Wanda was silent.

"Here we go," Jem said, dragging Tean forward. "Let's meet Toby."

Toby Keith was perhaps the fattest Basset hound that Tean had ever seen. He was also perhaps the most adorable. He howled for a while, just pure excitement, and then the howling turned to pleased groans and moans as Tean sat down in the cramped living room and petted the dog. He got Toby settled and began an abbreviated examination, checking the joints, speaking quietly to Toby—just nonsense, the kinds of things that sounded soothing, things you picked up after doing the job long enough. When Tean looked up, he was surprised to see Jem staring at him, those blue-gray eyes unreadable.

"My main concern is his weight," Tean said. "He's certainly suffering from a degree of arthritis, but I think he'd be more comfortable if he were at his ideal weight. I bet this guy loves treats. Is that right?"

"Lord," Wanda said. "You should see Toby when I get the Cheez Whiz."

Tean laughed. "Ok, well, I'll write down some healthier alternatives you can use as treats, and then I'll make a list of some dog food brands that are a good choice for this breed and for joint problems. Unless—do you make his food?"

"Sometimes. It's a lot of work."

"Well, I'll put down some options, things you can mix into dry food, that might help with the inflammation. The main thing is going to be portion control, treats, and then starting him on Novox." Tean took the pad out of his bag, wrote out a scrip, and handed the piece of paper to Wanda. She was still staring at them. In the harsh indoor lighting, the crags and wrinkles looked even deeper; her eyes were black and shining.

"You boys aren't police," she said.

Jem glanced at Tean.

"No," Tean said. "We're not. We're looking for someone who went missing. We're afraid she's hurt."

"Joy Erickson."

"You knew she was missing?" Jem asked.

"I know her car. I wondered why she hadn't come to pick it up." Wanda hesitated. Then, with what looked like some difficulty, she got down on her knees and stroked Toby's head. "Head toward the gate like you're leaving, and then turn right, keeping up against the wall. It's a powder-blue Plymouth. Can't miss it."

"Thank you," Jem said. "Thank you, Wanda. Thank you."

"And you got your days wrong; it came in the seventeenth, not the eighteenth. Don't go breaking the windows or messing with anything."

"Of course not."

"He's going to go pretty soon, isn't he?" she said quietly, stroking Toby's head. The Basset was crooning with pleasure.

"I hate to make any promises without a more thorough exam," Tean said, "but aside from the arthritis, he seems healthy and happy."

"I haven't taken him to a vet since he was a year old. The damn fool did something with the needle — giving him a shot — and Toby yelped like you wouldn't believe. The poor thing trembled the whole way home. I cried for hours." Wanda's hand slowed on Toby's head, the strokes gentle now. "Never took him back. I thought I was doing him a favor, keeping him away from a dry drunk with shaky hands. But I wasn't, was I? I could have kept an eye on his weight. I could have given him that medicine a long time ago."

"We all try to protect the things that we love," Tean said. "Sometimes, like with the shot, they get hurt and don't understand why we're doing it."

"And sometimes we do the wrong thing," Wanda said, "because we want so bad to keep them safe."

"Yes," Tean said, "I guess sometimes we do."

They left her and headed out into the night. As they paced along the corrugated metal wall, the smell of rust and gravel and antifreeze followed them. The moon had risen, a waning sickle balanced on the valley's rim. The sky was dark except where a narrow gash of stars opened to the east.

The powder-blue Plymouth was exactly where Wanda had told them. They walked around it once. The tires were decent, but the wheel wells were full of rust. The front and back bumpers both showed the dings and dents accumulated over the years. Inside, the pleather upholstery had peeled away in places, exposing the foam padding underneath. A beaded cover hung over the driver's seat.

Jem pulled a folding slim jim out of his pocket, extended it, and worked on the driver's door for a couple of minutes. Then he let out a smooth breath, pulled up, and the lock disengaged. He opened the door, leaned on it with one elbow, and flourished the slim jim. Tean tried to smile and handed him the disposable gloves he'd brought from the truck. Jem squeezed his arm, holding on a little too long for Tean's comfort, his eyes unreadable the way they'd been in Wanda's home.

In the glove box, they found a packet of Clorox wipes, travel-sized tissues, insurance and registration, and the Plymouth's original manual — someone had stuck chewing gum between two pages. Tean popped the trunk and moved around to the back. Jem crawled into the back seat.

"Jem."

"I found a quarter and, oh God, a diaphragm. And I touched it with my bare hands!"

"Jem."

Inside the trunk lay a shoulder bag and a bulging business-size envelope. Tean took the shoulder bag, opened it, and began laying out the contents: wallet, sanitary napkins, spearmint Tic Tacs, two blue Bic roller ball pens, an eyeglasses case that held a pair of cheaters, and more tissues in plastic packaging that was thin and dingy with age. The wallet held twelve dollars in cash, Joy Erickson's driver's license, several credit cards in her name, and a blank check drawing on a Wells Fargo account shared by Joy Erickson and Azalea Maynes. When Tean nudged aside the Wells Fargo check, he saw a Kneaders receipt. At first glance, he thought it must have been from the last time Joy had eaten at Kneaders, when she had left her car there. But instead, he saw that it was dated for April 16—the day before Joy had arranged to meet Becca.

"Holy shit," Jem said, displaying the envelope for Tean. Cash was stuffed inside. "It's mostly twenties, a few fifties. I bet there's a thousand dollars in here. Maybe more."

"I'm going to call Ammon."

They put everything back the way they had found it and returned to the truck. Tean placed the call to Ammon. Ammon didn't yell, which was worse, but several times he must have pulled the phone away because their conversation was interrupted by dead patches, and when Ammon's voice came back, it had that brittle, artificial calm that was starting to make Tean want to smash things. When it was over, he shook his head without looking over at Jem.

"Don't say anything."

Jem just sighed and squeezed Tean's shoulder, his hand warm and pleasantly heavy, his blunt fingers teasing the muscles there.

Tean called Hannah next. She didn't answer, but he let her know they'd found Joy's car. Disconnecting, he shifted the truck into gear and guided the Ford out of Perkins Towing and Impound. They headed north. It wasn't even eight yet, but Heber had slowed to a stop. The wide main street was brightly lit and empty, the orange glow and the ashy shadows uncanny in the total absence of life.

Then Tean's phone rang. He didn't recognize the number, but he answered anyway.

"Dr. Leon," the voice was rough with emotion, but under other circumstances, Tean thought it would have been light and musical. "This is Zalie Maynes."

Tean switched the phone to speaker and thumped Jem's leg because Jem was playing some fruit-slicing game on his phone again.

"Yes, hello, Ms. Maynes. Thank you for returning my call."

"Hannah just contacted me. She said you found Joy's car."

"We think so."

"A piece of trash Plymouth?"

"That sums it up."

"Oh God," Zalie said, the word on the edge of a sob. "I'd like to talk to you."

"Of course—"

"Right now if you can."

Tean glanced at Jem, who screwed up his face to show how dumb he thought Tean was and mouthed, *Duh.*

"We'll be there in ten minutes," Tean said, and he pegged Jem in the leg as hard as he could when he disconnected.

20

On their second trip to the pig farm, the gravel drive and the farm itself were both swaddled in the same impenetrable darkness. The Ford's headlights cut papery holes in the night, but otherwise it was like they'd drifted out of the real world and into some sort of nightmare place—kind of like that show with the kids that Jem made him watch. All Tean could do was follow the gravel track and park where the drive ended in a circle.

"What are the odds we're going to get blasted in the face by a shotgun?" Tean said.

"Fifty-fifty," Jem said, popping open his door and dropping out.

The smell of pig dung, mud, and animal bodies rolled into the truck. Tean grimaced, got out of the truck, and followed Jem toward the door. The automatic lights clicked off behind them, and Tean stumbled. Jem's hand found his in the darkness, and for some reason it was so comforting that Tean squeezed it once in gratitude. Jem squeezed back.

Lights switched on, blinding Tean: first, porch lights; then high-powered security floods that illuminated the gravel circle. Tean blinked, trying to hurry his vision as it adjusted. Jem was swearing softly next to him. The sound of a door opening carried through the stillness, and then the same rough voice said, "Dr. Leon?"

"That's right. And this is Jem. Hannah hired him to help find Joy."

Tean still couldn't see much, and Zalie was hidden behind the powerful lights. If she had a shotgun, he couldn't tell. If she was sighting down the length of it, trying to decide if he and Jem had stuck their noses in too deep, he couldn't tell. He realized he was clutching Jem's hand, and Jem was clutching back.

"Come on in," Zalie said. "Mind the second step; it's loose."

Then her footsteps moved back into the house.

"I'm going to hug you like a crazy motherfucker later," Jem said, his hand still tight around Tean's. "Remind me."

"Let's not and say we did."

"Never mind. I'll just make a note in my phone." As they climbed onto the porch, Jem took out his phone and said to the virtual assistant, "Remind me to hug Tean like a crazy motherfucker."

"No," Tean said to the phone. "Cancel. Abort. Order rescinded."

"Got it," the virtual assistant said. "I will remind you to hug beans like a crazy mother fork cancel abort order rescinded."

"Perfect," Jem said. "Thank you."

"You're welcome. Is there anything else I can help you with?"

"Yes," Tean said. "I told you to abort. Belay that order. How do you make this thing obey you?"

"Quiet, Beans," Jem said.

When they stepped inside, Tean only got a glimpse of the space because he was trying to find Zalie, trying to make sure she hadn't decided to lure them into the house before eliminating them. He had an impression of exposed joists, peeling wallpaper, and floors badly in need of stripping and refinishing. His gaze settled on Zalie. She was black, tall, thin, with wiry muscles. Her salt-and-pepper hair was buzzed. She was leaning heavily on a cane, and one foot was wrapped in bandages.

No shotgun. Tean spotted it a moment later — it was propped by the front door next to an equally ancient-looking rifle, both weapons dark with gun oil, the stocks scratched from wear and polished from all the hands that had held them over the years.

She must have recognized something in Tean's expression because she said, "I'm sorry about last time. Things have been strange around here. I heard a car, and I wasn't expecting anyone, and, well, I reacted."

Tean wanted to know how strange things had been if her go-to response was firing a shotgun.

"Sit down," she said, indicating a worn sofa covered by a quilt. She lowered herself into a rocking chair next to a potbellied stove, where a small fire was burning. As Jem and Tean sat, Tean had a moment to study the room more carefully. Half the space was clearly a living room, while the other half was given over to a galley kitchen and a table and chairs. In the living-room portion, aside from the sofa and rocking chair and stove, the only furniture was a record player in a teak cabinet, a pair of overloaded bookshelves, and a basket with knitting needles and several balls of yarn. Tean took a longer look at the bookshelves—he could see a copy of *The Anarchist's Cookbook* that had obviously been produced in a home office: printed on standard inkjet printer and paper, with a DIY spiral binding. Two doors opened off the front room. One clearly led to a bathroom, while the other, Tean guessed, was the bedroom. He thought about Leroy Erickson saying the pig farm was worth several million dollars.

"This is cozy," Jem said, bouncing on the sofa as though demonstrating it for a potential customer. "Have you been here a long time?"

"Twenty years or so. The land was cheap, and we built up the farm slowly."

"Do you like it?"

Zalie cocked her head, seeming to consider the question and Jem at the same time. "I did," she finally said.

"What changed?"

"Just about everything, I'm afraid. You said Hannah hired you?"

"Sort of," Tean said. "I'm just a friend. She hired Jem, though. Hannah's worried something might have happened to Joy. An accident. Something like that."

"That's rich."

"What?" Jem said.

"Coming from her," Zalie said, "that's rich. She's the whole reason Joy ran off in the first place."

"Were they—" Tean said.

"Having an affair? That was my first guess. No, I don't think so. You have to understand, though, that we all go back a long way. I was never very involved in Joy's . . . group. I knew Joy. I was attracted to her. We'd seen each other on and off. But I was never interested in being an activist, and I certainly wasn't going to do some of the things that she did."

"But they didn't bother you enough to cut things off," Jem said.

"No, they didn't. Maybe the opposite, actually. There's something potent about being attracted to someone different from you. And, of course, we all think that we'll be the one who can make them change. We believe we're doing it for their own good, of course."

Tean thought of the flyer, the apartment applications, the Social Security card. He felt hot, sweat prickling in a line down his chest.

"And I thought Joy would mellow with time. She didn't, of course. And that's why we're getting divorced."

"You were saying something about Hannah?" Jem said.

"Right, well, back then, Hannah was more than happy to go along with whatever Joy wanted her to do. She's fifteen years younger than Joy—maybe a little more—and Joy was her idol. They were involved romantically as well, and that complicates everything. And then one day, Hannah left, and things were over."

"Not quite over," Tean said. "Were they?"

"I guess not," Zalie said, running her thumb down the cane's dark wood. "A few weeks ago, Hannah started calling. Joy was still here some of the time; we were trying to work things out, although I think we both knew things were over. At first, I thought Hannah was just back in the rotation, another of Joy's girls; there have been a lot over the years, no matter how many times we tried therapy, no matter how many times I threatened to leave. But then I realized it was something else. Joy would be very quiet, and usually they'd only exchange a few words before they ended the call. Joy would dink around for fifteen minutes and then make up an excuse to leave. I don't know how stupid that woman thinks I am, but it wasn't flattering. When Joy came back, she was always angry. I realized it wasn't just an old flame."

"So what was it?"

"Do you know Hannah's parents?"

"We've met," Tean said.

"And you know her dad is a bigwig in the Mormon church?"

"He was a bishop. Maybe a stake president."

"Right, right. But those are local positions. He's being considered for something bigger."

"How'd you know that?" Jem asked.

"Joy told me. She was laughing about it. 'How would people feel if they learned his daughter was a carpet muncher and had blown up a guy for delivering chicken eggs? How would they feel if they knew even ten percent of what that closet dyke thought?' That was what she said, more or less. She always thought she sounded so tough when she said things like that—carpet muncher, dyke. Ugly, ugly words that she said she was reclaiming."

Jem threw a quick glance at Tean, and Tean knew what the blond man was thinking: the envelope of cash in Joy's car. A payoff? Hush money? Something to keep Joy quiet? Tean immediately felt guilty for suspecting Hannah of something like that, but he looked again at Zalie, and he saw a woman who was tired and hurt and, as far as he could tell, wasn't lying.

"You think Hannah had something to do with this?" Jem asked.

Zalie tapped the cane against the floor and didn't look up.

"Is there anything else you can tell us?" Tean asked. "Anything strange in Joy's behavior over the last few weeks? Anything she said or did that might give you a hint where she might be now?"

"Everything she did was strange. She was moving out. She was stringing along young girls she met online. She wanted the farm—I'm not going to lie about that; I know how it looks, but it's the truth—and I didn't want her to get a red cent out of my hard work. She'd gone vegan, and that stupid woman wanted to own a pig farm. How does that make any sense? And half the time she was talking about getting back to the good old days, how she was really going to start shaking things up. It was a relief when she finally moved into the condo permanently; I didn't want to be involved in whatever she was planning."

"When did she make the move?"

"Middle of April, I guess. Maybe a little after that."

"Do you think she's still alive?"

"I think so. I think she likes the drama of hiding. I think she likes the attention. Lord, it makes me tired just thinking about it."

"Why'd you call us? You said Hannah told you about the car—isn't it strange that she'd call you?"

"I suppose so. She and I never were friends. The poor girl is scared out of her mind, probably worried that Joy is going to work her over for more money, that this disappearing act is all part of some way to air all that dirty laundry."

"But why would she call you?"

"I don't read minds."

"And why did you call us?"

"Because I know how these things go. When someone goes missing, they look at the spouse. I wanted to tell you what I knew about Hannah. I've already told the police the same thing, but if you're digging around, you ought to know too."

Which meant Ammon knew about Hannah, the phone calls, the possibility of blackmail. And Ammon hadn't said anything. He'd lied to Tean. Again. Tean took a deep breath and looked over at Jem, ready to announce their departure, but his friend's face was fixed with thought. Then Jem said, "You told us things had been strange around here."

"That's right. I've heard someone skulking around the farm at night. We're pretty far out, and sometimes kids from town like to make trouble. This is something else. I can't go out and look because I cut my foot pretty bad when I was chopping firewood. Scares me out of my mind to hear them."

"Every night?" Jem said.

"No."

"How many times?"

"Twice. I was going to say three times, but the third time was you boys."

"Who do you think it is?" Tean asked.

"Joy's friends. I bet she told them they could come out and help themselves to whatever we've got. She might have hidden stuff on the property. Or it might be Joy herself. She wouldn't be above sneaking around, trying to make things worse—wreck things up a little so she can claim in the divorce proceedings that I can't keep the place up, that I don't do half the work I claim to do."

"Have you seen anything like that?"

She gestured to her foot. "I can barely keep up with the daily chores. I'm not going to tromp around looking for whatever nonsense they've been up to. I don't know what goes through that woman's head. I wouldn't put it past her to—"

"You think she might try to kill you?" Jem said.

"Of course not," Zalie said, her eyes on her hands.

A coyote howled out in the night.

"Do you mind if we take a look around?" Jem said.

Tean's eyes cut towards his friend, but Jem didn't look at him.

"Pigs are put in for the night," Zalie said. "I don't want you riling them."

"If Joy's been coming back here—"

"I shouldn't have said that. There's no need for you to go poking around."

"Are you going to shoot me if I do?"

Zalie threw him a hard look.

"What if we take some pictures?" Jem said. "If we find damage, tire tracks, footprints, that kind of thing, you might be able to use them in the divorce proceedings."

With a grunt, Zalie rocked in the chair.

"We'll be fast," Tean said, "and if we find anything, we'll make sure to get pictures for you."

"Don't mess with the pigs. Don't even go near the barn."

Jem gave a huge, gameshow smile and held up three fingers, Scout's honor. Tean wondered if it would look unprofessional to slap him upside the head.

Leaning heavily on the cane, Zalie escorted them to the door. She hit a bank of switches, and outside, more floodlights came on, illuminating a series of pens with rail-and-wire fencing, churned earth, troughs, industrial-sized plastic water tanks, and three-sided sheds. All of the pens backed up to a barn which looked like much older construction, the red paint and white trim bleached and ghostly in the security lights.

Something glinted; golden eyes caught the light.

"What's that?" Jem said.

"A coyote," Tean said.

"Goddamn nuisances," Zalie said. "Hold this." She shoved her cane into Tean's hand and grabbed the rifle next to the door. Taking unsteady steps, she made her way out onto the porch. The coyote was busy worrying something at the base of a pile of gravel. A rabbit, maybe. Or a fox. Whatever it was, it was too small to be a pig. Zalie lined up the shot and fired. The gunshot made Tean's ears ring, and the smell of gunpowder overpowered the reek of dung and livestock. The bullet sparked against the gravel, and the coyote spun and sprinted off into the darkness. Zalie fired again, and then she swore under her breath and lowered the rifle. "Damn things don't give me a moment's peace. They're why the pigs are in the barn every night."

Jem squeezed Tean's shoulder. "Is that thing going to come back and eat us?"

"Coyote attacks against humans are uncommon," Tean said.

"Uh huh," Jem said.

"But they are happening more frequently than they used to."

"I knew it. You looked so happy I knew it had to be something terrifying."

"They don't often hunt together—never as a pack, more often singly or in pairs, which makes them different from wolves. The attacks, when they have happened, are usually a lone coyote attacking a child."

Jem groaned. "And what's the rest? You're thrilled. You're thrilled about this. You're going to tell me that they rip out a man's throat in fifteen seconds flat. This is why people built cities. You understand that, right? So we didn't have to worry about wild animals ripping out our throats when we went to take a leak. Just spit out your next natural horror fact."

"Well, when they do attack adults, they usually do it in pairs. Those attacks are frequently fatal because the wounds are so severe."

"This is like your birthday and Christmas wrapped up together." To Zalie, he said, "He does this just to torture me. He's saving the worst for last. Look how he's smiling."

"I'm not smiling."

"You are on the inside!"

"I just was thinking about coywolves."

"Are those what they sound like?"

"Do they sound like hybrids of coyotes and wolves that are way scarier than either species on its own?"

Jem just groaned and started shoving Tean toward the steps. "Tell me when we're back in the truck. Safe. And driving to a city where coywolves is just the next weird gay tribe, like maybe they only have hairy backs or something."

"No, coywolves have normal pelts—ok, ok, you're going to push me down the stairs."

As they moved away from the house, Tean was surprised to feel Jem's hand slip into his again. Tean glanced over.

"It's your fault," Jem said. "You got me thinking about coywolves and insects that lay eggs in your eyes and snakes that crawl up your butt when you take a dump in the woods."

Tean blinked. "I don't remember saying anything about a snake. I don't even know what kind of snake you're talking about."

"Well," Jem said, gesturing vigorously at the darkness around them. "It's out there. Guaranteed. So just hold my hand and be the butch doctor who will chop a coywolf in half with a machete before it can rip out my throat."

"Huh," Tean said.

"And don't do that either. Don't start plotting more terrifying things to tell me."

"I was just thinking it would be fun if we go camping."

"Sure," Jem said. "Just kill all the bugs and plants and animals and make sure the ground is perfectly flat and then build a four-star hotel. Then I'll go camping. Where do you want to start?"

"Where we saw the coyote," Tean said, gesturing to the pile of gravel.

Jem groaned. "Do you at least have a syringe full of whatever they use to put down bears with rabies?"

"It would be a little hard to get the coyote with that. They're pretty fast."

"It's for me."

Tean tugged on Jem's hand, dragging him forward.

The security floodlights illuminated one side of the mound of gravel, but the other side, where the coyote had been, was hidden in shadow. Tean turned on the flashlight on his phone, and Jem followed his example.

"What are you looking for?"

Tean was kicking aside small stones. "Whatever the coyote smelled. Most canids will scavenge, and coyotes aren't an exception. They're opportunists. The easier the meal, the better."

Glancing around, Jem said, "This is a strange place to dump gravel."

"It's a pile of gravel. Why does it matter where it goes?"

"Look around," Jem said. He used their joined hands to point out patches of disturbed earth. "You can see where they've pulled out fence posts. And look at the ground. No grass, not like the rest of the area."

"So this area used to be a pen, but they're changing it over to something else. A parking lot, maybe, for delivery trucks."

"I guess," Jem said.

Then Tean kicked aside some more gravel.

"Holy shit," Jem said. "That's a head."

21

Tean was at work the next morning when the call came.

"Please hold for Dr. Castorena," a nasally young man said.

Tean didn't mind holding. His brain was fried. He and Jem had been at Zalie's for over an hour waiting for the Heber City police, the Wasatch County sheriff, the Salt Lake City police, and the state Office of the Medical Examiner to get their collective butts out of bed. Then there was the tangled nightmare of jurisdiction. The sheriff, a balding, shrunken man who had to be close to seventy, had put Tean and Jem in the back of his Wrangler. Then Ammon had given him ten kinds of hell until the sheriff finally turned Jem and Tean over to the SLCPD, at which point, Ammon had sent them to headquarters with a patrol officer following Tean's truck the whole way. They'd spent the rest of the early morning hours in an interview room, telling their story over and over again to Ammon's partner, Kat, until she'd finally let them go.

After that, they'd driven home to find an ecstatic Scipio who had needed breakfast and a walk—not in that order—and then Tean had showered and changed, ignoring Jem's suggestions that he take the day off. When he'd left the apartment, Jem and Scipio had been tangled together on the couch, one of the Lab's legs resting on Jem's head. Jem had been snoring.

A husky woman's voice came on the line. "Dr. Leon?"

"Yes."

"Elvira Castorena. Sorry. That is some pretentious nonsense, the 'please hold' business, but I can't get Jeremy to do it any other way."

"It's no problem."

"I'm not sure if you know this, but I'm the new state medical examiner. Dr. Seamount took early retirement, and I've stepped into the role."

Tean was silent.

"I understand you and Dr. Seamount did not see eye to eye on a case," Castorena said.

"I'm not sure what I'm supposed to say at this point. It sounds like you already know what happened."

She laughed. "You don't need to say anything. The first part of the call was just to tell you that we won't have that problem going forward. I look forward to collaborating with you on appropriate investigations; that's all I wanted to say. The second part of the call is about one such investigation."

"Joy Erickson."

"Yes. We have a positive ID, and we're moving forward with the investigation into cause and manner of death. I was hoping you could consult."

"Absolutely."

"Today?"

"Things are moving fast at the ME's office now, it sounds like."

That same deep laugh. "You know where we are?"

"I do."

"Eleven?"

"Perfect time to work up an appetite."

Castorena was still laughing when she hung up.

Tean gave the email on his computer screen one last glance. It was from Hannah, and it had been sent to both Tean and HR, informing them that at the direction of her doctor, Hannah was taking unpaid FMLA leave. The accompanying medical certification only specified traumatic stress, and it was signed by a Salt Lake psychiatrist—Rowen Kates—whom Tean had never heard Hannah mention before. HR had sent a separate email to Tean confirming that Hannah would be out of the office for two weeks, with a re-evaluation at the end of that period.

He still had an hour and a half before he needed to leave for the ME's office, so he took out his phone. Tean placed a call to Hannah first. She didn't answer. He tried Caleb, hoping he might be able to tell Tean more about what was going on, but the call was dismissed and sent to voicemail. Then he tried Miguel, the conservation officer tracking the canine distemper outbreak in Heber Valley, but he got voicemail there too. He called the lab where he had sent the samples from the coyote specimen; they were still processing the samples, so Tean thanked them and buried himself in paperwork for the rest of the time.

At half past ten, he drove south to the relatively new facility that housed the Office of the Medical Examiner. The building included labs for forensic pathology, the state crime labs, and offices for the ME and her deputies and investigators. It was in Taylorsville just off the I-215 beltway, almost due south of the DWR offices, and Tean made the drive in twenty minutes. The structure was tan brick and glass and steel, and it could have passed for a twenty-four-hour gym or a dentist's office in a strip mall. He checked in at the front desk, and the receptionist sent him toward the labs.

Tean had just turned down the next hall when he saw a large woman in scrubs emerge from what he thought he remembered was a locker room. Her dark hair was in a neat bun, and she had tortoiseshell glasses with huge lenses.

"I was going to meet you," she said, offering him a hand. "I recognized you from all the news stories. Elvira Castorena. I know I should use a nickname, but my parents got the full version stuck in my head."

"Tean," he said as they shook. "I do use a nickname because I'd go crazy if I didn't."

Elvira smiled. "Let's get to it, shall we? Locker room connects to the autopsy lab. You'll find disposable PPE for observers."

They both geared up with PPE equipment—coveralls, mask, face shield, apron, gloves, boots—and met in the autopsy room. The body on the table was already in a state of active decay: blackened flesh at the extremities and around the orifices, ruptured where gases had escaped, and in places the degloving process had begun, with skin detaching and sliding away from muscle. Tean had only glimpsed part of Joy Erickson's head buried in the rubble. He was shocked now to see what they had recovered.

"Our best estimate for time of death is approximately three weeks ago."

"Where's the rest of the remains?"

"Good question," Elvira said. "They're still tearing up that pig farm, but the honest answer is, nobody knows. We recovered the torso and the head, as you can see. All four limbs are missing."

"Pigs can eat and digest bone," Tean said, considering the dismembered body. "The trope about people using pig farms to dispose of bodies didn't come from nowhere. Jem—the investigator hired to find Joy—he believed that the area where the body was found had recently been in use as a pig pen. It's possible the body was placed there in hopes that the pigs would consume it and eliminate the remains."

"I understand the police are talking to the man who delivered the gravel. It'll be interesting to hear why he didn't report the dead body he buried under a pile of loose stone."

"That seems strange," Tean said. "Why bury the body under stone if you want the pigs to eat it and eliminate it?"

"A very good question. Take a look at this, will you? One thing that's interesting is that the amputations all occurred postmortem; that's completely clear based on the histopathology. In a body at this stage of decomposition, we look for hemorrhaging in the remaining soft tissue, any evidence of clotting, histamines. Some of these abrasions and lacerations to the head and face were antemortem injuries, as well as bruising on the back and shoulders, but the amputations are definitively postmortem."

"Cutting off her arms and legs after she died might make sense if the goal was to destroy the remains; if the limbs were scattered in other pens, it might speed up the process."

"That seems likely. Unfortunately, none of the antemortem injuries explains how she died. I already mentioned the lacerations, abrasions, and bruising. There's no indication of asphyxiation, strangulation, or drowning. We're waiting for a more complete toxicology report, but the preliminary panels don't show any evidence of drugs or toxins."

"You don't know how she died?"

"The mechanism was exsanguination. The problem is that I don't know the proximate cause—where is the injury that produced this massive blood loss? Amputation should be the obvious answer, except these injuries were all inflicted after she died."

"Damage to the brachial or femoral artery seems like the most likely answer. Then the limbs were amputated to conceal the nature of the injury."

"That was my thought too."

Tean leaned closer, inspecting the body through the face shield. "All of these other injuries are antemortem? These bite marks, for example. And the teeth marks on the bone. I can see pits, punctures, and scoring on the intercostal ribs."

Elvira shook her head. "I'm not sure. My best guess is perimortem. I can't definitively say."

"It's entirely possible an animal attacked her," Tean said, moving to consider the amputation sites, "although this damage could have been caused by scavenging—not the pigs, because the marks aren't consistent with pig teeth, but coyotes are a possibility. Actually, just to double back, coyotes also have been reported to eat bones, and we did see a coyote trying to scavenge the body. That might explain where the limbs went." Tean paused, turning this over in his mind before continuing. "It's entirely possible that, during an animal attack, a limb was amputated. But no animal purposefully amputates all four limbs and scatters them, and no animal attack would leave these tool marks on bone. Someone used a hatchet or an axe to dismember the body." He glanced up and saw the look of surprise on Elvira's face. "After that last case," he explained, "I decided I ought to do some reading about forensics."

"Don't tell anybody," Elvira said, "or they'll give you my job. Here's the real question: do you think this was an animal attack?"

"An animal clearly inflicted some of this damage. And if the bite pattern or the teeth marks are distinctive, we might even be able to match it to a particular animal, assuming we have a suspect. But if the wounds are perimortem, as you say, and none of them is the proximate cause of death, then my answer is no. This was not an animal attack."

"But someone wanted it to look like one. You see why I wanted your opinion. I don't want a repeat of last year."

She was talking about the last murder that Tean had gotten tangled up in, when Jem's foster brother had been killed. The killer had left the body for scavengers, hoping that animal predation would hide the killing wound.

"This is similar," Tean said. "But whoever amputated those limbs made a mistake. My guess is that the killer had two safety mechanisms, if that's how we want to describe them: first, hoping that the pigs would consume and destroy the remains; second, if they didn't, hoping that the amputations and the bite marks would suggest some sort of animal attack."

Elvira nodded, still considering Joy's body. Then she looked at Tean. "Thank you. If we recover any more of the remains, I'll need your expertise again."

"You already knew everything I told you," Tean said with a small smile, "but I appreciate the sentiment."

"I didn't know all of it, and I needed to hear some of it from an expert."

"Of course. If the pigs — or the coyotes — did consume the limbs," Tean hesitated, "it's possible that key evidence has been destroyed."

Elvira sighed and nodded. "I know."

22

Jem woke that morning with a paw over his eyes. For a moment, the old fear was there, paralyzing Jem, the thought of Antony lunging at him in LouElla's basement, teeth closing around his arm. Then Scipio did a huge doggy snore, and the knot between Jem's shoulder blades loosened. He tried to tell Scipio to move, but another paw was over his mouth.

Worming free, Jem saw that it was late morning, the light spilling in through the sliding glass door that led onto the balcony. He vaguely remembered Tean leaving for work. Scipio had rolled onto his back, apparently untroubled by the fact that Jem was trying to get up, and the Lab was now sleeping with all four paws in the air and looking incredibly comfortable.

In the kitchen, he poured himself a bowl of Trix with two-percent milk — breakfast staples that, at some point, Tean had started stocking just for Jem. The doc had left something on the counter, and Jem studied it between slurps of sweetened cereal milk. It was the rental application for Tean's apartment complex. Tean had filled out the forms in blue ballpoint ink. He knew Jem's full name, his date of birth, and his Social. At the end of the form, Tean had filled in his own information as a cosigner. On top of the form, on a yellow sticky note, Tean had written, *Better act fast*. All Jem needed to do was sign, carry the application down to the manager's office, and voila. Tean had even left the blue ballpoint pen, capped, next to the form.

But Jem didn't grab the paperwork, and he didn't take it downstairs. He sauntered through the apartment in the plaid boxer shorts he was wearing, examining the landscape paintings. The images mostly showed the Wasatch and Oquirrh Mountains from different places in the valley, at different times of the day and year.

The same mountains, the same valley, but jog a few miles north, or wait until sunset, or spring instead of autumn, and they were totally new. You could spend your whole life being surprised by something, no matter how well you thought you knew it, and Jem realized that was one of the things people meant when they said beautiful. He thought about Tean's face when they'd driven into the Heber Valley, the way he'd lit up, how he'd smiled without knowing he was smiling. And then Jem thought, slurping down the last of the milk, that when you had your own apartment and you had your own job, nice people probably didn't let you sleep on their couch, and they definitely didn't buy milk and breakfast cereal just because they knew you liked it, even though you'd never said it, even though you'd never asked.

As he was rinsing the bowl in the sink, his phone buzzed. He padded over to the couch and dug it out of his jeans. Scipio snorted violently and then flopped onto his side, his head coming up to stare at Jem reproachfully.

"Sorry," Jem whispered.

We're still on? LouElla's message read; Jem was proud that he read it almost immediately.

Jem had forgotten that today was the day, but he typed out, *Yes,* and sent the message.

Toyota Camry, silver, and then a license plate number followed. *Noon.*

Jem checked the clock; it was ten to eleven.

Swearing, he stumbled into the bathroom, washed his face, scrubbed under his arms with a towel, and spent five frantic minutes with a comb making sure the part in his hair looked good and cursing himself for letting his hair get so long. Then he rushed to the duffel and found a clean pair of chinos and a blue-and-white striped Ralph Lauren polo, complete with the little polo player doing his thing. He got socks and his sneakers. Scipio watched the whole thing, his tail thumping on the couch.

"Oh shit," Jem said. "Come on; I can't let you explode."

He didn't even pretend with the harness this morning, although most of the time he liked to do a whole production out of trying to get the harness on and Scipio making it too difficult. It spared his ego, a little, and let him keep up the act of not being quite as terrified. This morning, though, there wasn't time, and Jem just opened the door.

He spent the next ten minutes chasing Scipio along the sidewalk, calling the dog's name, sprinting to get ahead of the Lab and then trying to herd him back to Tean's place. Scipio was mostly interested in a half-eaten bagel he found near a bus bench; after that, he was happy to let Jem take him back to the apartment. Jem grabbed his windbreaker, checked to make sure his tools were in place, and then, in a last rush, folded up the application and shoved it in his back pocket.

He drove the Kawasaki into West Valley, toward Your Friend Towing and Auto Mechanic. The business consisted of a two-room building, its stucco broken and flaking the ground around it like dander, with a single-bay garage attached. The rest of the lot was fenced with an eight-foot privacy screen, which did a decent job of blocking the view from the street—in case a stolen car was sitting back there, or in case a different kind of deal was going down. When Jem went inside, he waved to Marcy, who was playing World of Warcraft on an ancient monitor, and walked past her to the inner office.

When he rapped on the door, Toro glanced up from his phone and said, "Business is good, and I don't need to play your kiddy games."

"Morning."

"Fuck off."

"I need to borrow a car."

Toro laughed and went back to his phone. He'd cut his hair since Jem had seen him last, and there was more gray in the stubble on his jowls. His belly was straining the button on the blue work shirt he was wearing. The nice thing about Toro was that he had a real sense of style that he imparted to everything he touched. He'd done a great job coordinating the Playboy centerfolds that blanketed the walls, for example.

"Three hours tops," Jem said. "I'm in a hurry. A trooper with light bars."

Toro hesitated. He almost looked up. Then the chair squeaked as he settled his weight, and he said, "Fuck off."

"Do it because we're old friends."

"You screw me every chance you get—you'd do it twice if you thought you could get your little dick hard again."

"Fine. I'll go ask Anjelo."

"Oh fuck you," Toro said, the chair rocking forward as he tossed the phone onto the desk. "I don't lend people cars. I rent cars. Sometimes. To people I like."

"You owe me from when I took you those rubbers. You know, from when you were at that motel in Santaquin."

"That doesn't even come close."

"Three hours."

"You're a fucking mooch."

"I'll treat her like a princess."

"God damn it," Toro said, grabbing his phone. "Keys with the red tag."

"You're my brother," Jem said, grabbing the keys.

"If you bring that trooper back with a single fucking scratch, I will take it out of your ass."

"Kinky," Jem said, "but I'm spoken for."

He was already sprinting past Marcy as Toro roared his response.

The trooper was a white Dodge Charger hidden at the back of the lot, behind a box truck that had been sitting in place so long that the tires had gone flat and the panels were covered in mildew. The sides of the Dodge held the iconic beehive, and STATE TROOPER was printed above the front wheel wells. Red-and-blue lights on the roof were what really sold it. Jem got behind the wheel, started it up, and headed west.

He followed I-80 out of the Salt Lake Valley, and once he was past the Oquirrh Mountains, he headed south on Route 36 toward Tooele. A few minutes later, he pulled into the lot of a Holiday gas station, parked with his nose pointed at Route 36, and waited. He thought about pulling out the rental application and looking at it again. He liked Tean's handwriting, liked the neat cursive, and he'd taken to imitating it sometimes just because his own letters still looked like he'd peaked in third grade. The doc had this way of adding little tails to letters. Jem wondered if he had a whole menagerie for the alphabet, if the doc envisioned B is for grizzly bear when he drew a little curlicue tail onto a B. Instead, though, he stayed focused on the road.

At 11:44am, a silver Camry rolled past the Holiday, and Jem caught the first three letters of the license plate. They were a match, so he pulled onto Route 36. The rest of the license plate was also a match—it never hurt to be sure—and so he hung back and followed the Camry through Tooele and east, into the foothills, where LouElla lived.

When they were still ten minutes out, he flashed his lights and sped up. The Camry hesitated, drifting to the left as though uncertain what Jem wanted. He kept right behind her, and then the driver got the message and pulled across the rumble strip and onto the shoulder. Jem copied her. He sat in the car for a few minutes, letting her stew, letting the panic build. Any kind of strong emotion made people willing to believe bullshit they wouldn't usually swallow, and flashing lights and police car were a stir-and-serve mix for fear.

When he got out of the car, he kept his pace slow and measured as he approached. The Camry's window buzzed down. Jem got his first look at the driver in the side mirror; she was still young, but she wasn't a kid. Midthirties, he guessed. She had a lot of brown hair that she didn't seem to know what to do with, and she kept looking at him in the mirror and looking away.

"Good morning, miss," Jem said as he reached the window. "Could you put your hands where I can see them, please?"

"Oh my gosh," she whispered, her hands blanching as she clutched the wheel. "Was I speeding? What's wrong . . . officer?" The hesitation hit when she finally took a full look and realized he was wearing a polo and chinos and not a uniform.

"Off duty," Jem said with a smile. "I'd like you to open your glovebox and find the vehicle's manual, please. Do you have a tire pressure gauge?"

"I'm sorry," she said, her eyebrows shooting up. "What?"

"Please find the vehicle's manual, miss. If you have a tire pressure gauge, that would be a help."

When she gave a helpless twist of her hands and bent toward the glovebox, Jem moved to the back of the car and squatted near the rear driver's tire. He put his back to the front of the car—not a move a real officer would have made, but Jem needed to use the bulk of his body to hide what he was doing. He unscrewed the plastic cover on the tire's air valve stem, produced a penny from his pocket, and used the penny's edge to depress the metal pin inside the valve. Air hissed out.

"Officer? I found it."

The tire wasn't flat, but it was obviously low, and Jem figured that was good enough. He got to his feet, dusted his hands, and moved back to the driver's window.

"No gauge?"

"I'm sorry. I don't even know what one looks like."

"Then you probably don't have one," Jem said with another smile. He accepted the manual, flipped pages, and found the section on tires. Half a year before, this would have been the trickiest part of the game he was running. Now he could read *tire* because half the middle grade books Tean bought him were about cars. Tire, fire, wire. "I'm going to fold this page. You'll need it. 35 PSI—if you don't remember that, just look at this page again."

"I'm sorry, Officer, but what is going on?"

"Come take a look."

She got out of the car, and he walked her to the rear tire.

"But I didn't even feel anything," she said. "It was driving just fine."

"Well, it's not a blowout, miss. It's just got a steady leak. But I really don't think you should be driving on it. You might limp around for a while and it'll seem all right, but you'll be doing a lot of damage to the suspension and the frame. Do you have AAA?"

"I have—" She glanced at her watch. "I have something like that, yes, but I've got to get to this appointment."

"Is it far?"

"Just a few miles."

"Well, you'll make it all right. I'll follow you over there in case you do have a blowout, and just make sure you get that tire inflated before you go any farther."

"You really don't have to follow me."

"I'm off duty, and I've got nothing waiting for me," Jem said with a self-deprecating smile. The woman blushed and smiled back. "And it's not far, you said."

"It's really not."

"Then let's get hopping."

When they got to LouElla's, she parked on the street, and he pulled into the driveway. He could see the surprise on her face when she got out of the car. Jem opened the door, laughing, and beat her to the punch, "You're joking, right?"

She stared at him.

He laughed a little more. "You can call those people back. You don't need anybody to come out and fill that tire for you."

"I'm sorry?"

"I'm pretty sure Mom has an air compressor in the garage. Gosh, talk about coincidence. She told me somebody was coming out today, but I never thought it would be you. I was picturing one of those matronly types, really fierce, face like a bulldog." Jem covered his grin. "Oops."

She laughed, touching her hair, and Jem knew he'd sold it.

"Lily," she said, holding out her hand as she met him on the driveway. "Lily Pederson."

"Jem Berger. Gosh, you've got Mom shaking in her boots. She's convinced she's not going to pass whatever test you're giving her."

"It's not a test," Lily said, but she was smiling. When she shifted her weight, Jem shifted his. When she touched her clothes, Jem touched his. When her smile widened, Jem was grinning like a loon. "This is just a safety inspection, you know. And a few follow-up questions." She blushed and added, "We're obligated to ask, even if the reports we get don't seem reliable. Sometimes people don't understand what they're seeing."

Jem shrugged. "I'd rather have somebody who's overly concerned and makes a report. We need more people like that in the world. Anyway, let me walk you inside."

After that, everything ran smoothly. LouElla was charming. Jem was charming. Foster mom and foster son, with their enduring affection and relationship. Lily smiled as Jem and LouElla hugged. Lily asked about how long they'd known each other. Lily asked about life after foster care.

"She put me through college," Jem said, "and the only reason I graduated is because she said she'd taken out a second mortgage on the house to pay the tuition."

"Jeremiah," LouElla snapped in mock anger. "You know you weren't supposed to tell anyone that."

Jem grinned guiltily and rolled a shoulder.

At the end of the safety inspection, Lily said, "There are a few things that we need to talk about. Otherwise, everything looks in order except — well, the bathroom door doesn't lock. I won't be able to approve the home until that's fixed, so we'll need to arrange a second visit. It'll be much shorter than this one, I promise."

"Tell you what," Jem said. "I keep some tools in Mom's garage. Let me fix that door for you, and you can check it off right now."

"I have another appointment," Lily said.

"Nope, don't worry about it. I'll be done in five minutes. You ask your questions, and then I'm going to snooze on Mom's couch while she makes me chocolate-chip-and-banana pancakes."

"They've been his favorite food since he was twelve," LouElla said with a gentle roll of her eyes. "I keep telling him protein, protein, protein."

The mommy-and-son shtick was so good, so easy, that Jem was starting to wonder why he hadn't run a game like this before. Not with LouElla, of course. But with someone the right age, someone who could hit the right notes the way LouElla did.

"All right," Lily said. "If you really think you can fix it quickly. Mrs. Arnold, I'm afraid this next set of questions won't be pleasant. Although the child involved in this alleged incident denies that anything happened, a neighbor reported seeing you strike the child—"

Jem missed the rest of it when he went into the garage, but he didn't need to hear it. He could have written the script himself. Strike the child with a belt, with the sole of one of the black flats you're always wearing, with a rolled-up towel, with the collapsible antenna from an RCA TV. The scar that ran from shoulder to hip on his back had healed almost fifteen years ago, but he could feel it now, the red-hot line she'd opened across his back. He stood in front of the pegboard full of tools, his hands curled into fists, blind. Maybe not tomorrow, maybe not even next week, but pretty soon kids would be back here. He picked up a screwdriver. What the fuck, he wanted to ask himself, was he doing?

When he passed Lily and LouElla—she was crying now, just the right amount, touching the corners of her eyes with a tissue—he offered a sad smile, as though he wanted to check in on his mom but was too polite to interrupt. Any doubts Lily might have had about the answers, any reservations about LouElla, were buried under the performance Jem and LouElla had put on: the devoted foster son, a college graduate, a state trooper, the kind of guy who helped people even when he was off duty. Those stories about LouElla—whatever they were, whatever she'd done—couldn't be true. Not with a foster son who still came to check on her and zonk out on her couch for a few hours. Not with banana fucking pancakes.

The bathroom door was an easy fix: loosen the strike plate, move it down a quarter inch, screw it into place. The door shut. The thumb lock worked. Presto chango.

He was using the air compressor from the garage to fill Lily's tire when she and LouElla emerged from the house.

"This is what we want to see," Lily told them, clutching a clipboard to her chest. "If we can't help families stay together, this is what we want. Thank you both for what you've shown me today. I just—I just needed to know that the system works, I guess."

They waved—just a friendly, mom-and-son wave to see off a favorite guest. When the Camry turned out of sight, LouElla said, "Help me pull down the bunk beds. I can still return those to IKEA."

"You are one cheap bitch."

She still had her arm around him. Someone walking past might have smiled, might have thought what a pretty picture. LouElla could be very elegant when she wanted to be.

"If you want that name, Princess Jemma, you'll do what I say."

And he did. He wanted it bad enough to do this, to put kids back into this house, to put them where LouElla Arnold could lash them down to the bone with an old RCA antenna. He wanted it for reasons he couldn't even say to himself. Because something had been stolen from him, yes. Because he wanted to be able to rent an apartment without a cosigner. But really, it was about something he couldn't even put into words. Something he saw in everybody else's life, just not in his own.

When they'd finished pulling down the furniture and boxing up the parts, LouElla handed him a slip of paper with a name and an address.

"Who's Brigitte Fitzpatrick?"

LouElla's smile could have opened a can of cat food. "Why don't you go find out?"

23

Jem was halfway back to Toro's, still turning over the name Brigitte Fitzpatrick, wondering why he didn't recognize it and how the bitch could have stolen his identity, when his phone rang. He answered it without checking the screen.

"Hannah's been arrested."

It took him a moment to place Caleb's voice.

"Ok," Jem said. "I'll be right over."

"No," Caleb said. "I've got to—I don't know. I'm going down to the station, and I'm going to see what we do next."

"What you do next is get a lawyer," Jem said. "A good one."

"I know that!" Caleb drew a broken breath. "I'll pay you whatever Hannah agreed to pay you. I just want you to prove she didn't have anything to do with this."

"What was the charge when they arrested her?"

"Murdering that woman."

"Joy Erickson?"

"Yes." Someone spoke in the background, and Caleb said, "I know, I know." Then, to Jem, he said, "I've got to go."

The call disconnected before Jem could answer.

As he drove the rest of the way to Toro's, he called Tean and told him what had happened.

"You've got to be freaking kidding me," Tean said.

"Just say it. Just one time. Fuck."

"Should we go down there?"

"Just once. You can whisper it if you want."

"I mean, would they even let us talk to her?"

"I won't even make you put a dollar in the swear jar."

"Jem!"

Jem turned into Toro's lot and guided the Charger to the back of the lot. As he parked it behind the mildewed box truck, he said, "I think one option is to go to the station. But you know how these things go."

"Not really."

"The whole process takes time, and that means we'll just sit around waiting. Probably better to wait until we know where Hannah is going to be held until the arraignment and try the normal visiting hours."

"Or I could call Ammon."

Jem turned off the car, rested one elbow on the steering wheel, his palm pressed to his forehead.

"It's worth a shot," Tean said.

"You know what?" Jem said. "Do whatever you want." And he disconnected the call.

He went inside Your Friend Towing and Auto Mechanic, where Marcy looked like she was having a competition with herself for the biggest bubble she could blow with her gum. Toro was on the phone, so Jem just hung the keys where he'd gotten them, waved, and headed out.

His phone buzzed as he approached the motorcycle.

"I'm going over to the station," Tean said. "I can't get Ammon on the phone."

"Like I said: do whatever you want."

"Will you please go with me? And before you say no because you're mad, remember that you're working for Hannah and Caleb and you can count this as billable time."

"I never say no just because I'm mad."

"So you are mad?"

"I've had a weird day."

For a full second, the call was silent, and then Tean said, "Maybe you should tell me about it."

"I'd hate to keep your phone busy. Ammon might call."

"That's not fair. You really don't sound good. What happened? Are you ok?"

"I'll meet you at the police station, but I'm telling you, we're going to be sitting around with our dicks in our hands for the rest of the day."

"Hey, will you please tell me what—"

Jem disconnected again. The phone was buzzing when he got on the Kawasaki, but the nice thing about a motorcycle was that you had a great excuse not to answer any calls. By the time he was on I-215, he couldn't even tell if the phone was still vibrating.

The May afternoon was warm. His windbreaker rustled and snapped as the bike hit sixty. The valley looked like a bowl of shit: the brown slopes of the Wasatch Mountains, the brown stucco of homes and businesses, the bleached brown of empty lots and dead weeds. Sure, the peach trees were in bloom, and the lawns were green, and everybody and their mother had roses these days, but that was the thing about shit — it made a hell of a fertilizer.

The Salt Lake Police Department's main facility was in the heart of the city, relatively new construction that looked like a glass-and-steel amoeba. Jem found a parking spot in the lot, and he locked the windbreaker and his tools in the under-seat storage. Then he made his way to the entrance and sat on a bench. A pair of guys in their twenties were talking quietly to an older woman who was crying — she had a daisy in her hair, and Jem couldn't tell if the flower was real or fake. Then, after a while, he couldn't tell if the crying was fake either. At first he'd thought the guys were her sons — they were young, and he guessed they were Latino. One of them had light brown skin the exact same shade as Tean's. Both of the guys had neck tattoos. Mom — if she was Mom — was white. She had a neck tattoo too. Then one of the guys gave her a kiss that was sixty percent tongue, and Jem figured she probably wasn't their mom after all.

"You beat me," Tean said. The doc's wild hair was pushed straight back again, looking a little bit like a mushroom cloud. The poor guy was worried. It was easy to tell with him; all the signs were right on the surface. Good, Jem thought. Let him worry.

"Glasses," Jem said.

Tean caught them right before they fell off his face.

Standing, Jem said, "I guess we'd better get in there."

"Hold on. I want to know what happened today. You said it was a weird day. You don't . . ."

"I don't what?"

"I don't know," Tean said. "You're giving me a weird vibe. I know you're mad at me, but it's more than that."

"I'm not mad at you."

"Of course you are, but you also seem like you're upset or hurt or sad about something else, and I—"

"I think I'd know if I was mad at you. Don't you think? If one of us would know, don't you think it'd be me?"

The doc pushed his hair back with both hands.

Jem turned and went inside, and Tean followed. They gave their names to a woman and explained that they were there to see Detective Ammon Young. She nodded and promised to let him know. Then there wasn't anything else for them to do. The lobby continued the glass-and-steel amoeba theme, and it was full of echoes. A pair of kids—a boy who was probably four, and a girl who was probably six—were playing tag, their shoes squeaking on the concrete floor. A young guy, probably not yet twenty, was sitting in a molded-plastic chair and holding an ice pack to his face. Down a small corridor, a middle-aged woman was having an argument on a payphone.

"I know that, Dad. I understand that, Dad. Oh my God, you never even listen to me."

Jem dropped onto an empty bench, and Tean sat at the other end. Then, after a minute, Tean slid along the bench until his hip bumped against Jem's. Jem scooted away. Another minute passed. Then Tean set his jaw and slid along the bench again. Jem scooted a few more inches. Tean started to slide.

"Just stop," Jem said. "Jesus Christ, I'm half-cheeking it as it is."

"Well, quit trying to get away."

"I don't want to sit next to you. You're the one who hates being touched and always squirms away. Give me a few fucking inches."

"No."

"Excuse me?"

Tean shoved his glasses back up; the gesture looked reckless and almost made Jem smile. "You heard me."

"What the hell has gotten into you?"

"Get back on this bench, mister. Right now."

From the short hallway came the sound of the middle-aged woman's voice: "Jeez, Dad. You're so unfair! You're ruining my life!"

"Mister?" Jem said.

"I think she got in my head," Tean said, waving at the hallway, "you know, channeling her inner sixteen-year-old. I'm literally hearing echoes of my dad right now. Is it too late for me to retract that?"

Jem scooted back onto the bench until his hip and thigh and knee were pressed against Tean's. After a moment, the doc screwed up his face and put an arm around Jem.

Burying his face in his hands, Jem laughed.

"What?" Tean sounded both outraged and embarrassed. "Am I doing it wrong?"

"No."

"I am."

"No, you're doing fine."

"Then what?"

"Nothing," Jem said. "Maybe just don't make a face like you're about to kiss a cobra the next time you put your arm around a guy."

"Oh."

"Definitely don't do it on your date with Orion."

"Ok."

"You hate this. I know you hate this. You don't have to do it."

"I don't hate it," Tean said. He gave a little pull, and Jem leaned into him, his head resting on Tean's shoulder. "I'm just not very good at it."

"You're doing all right," Jem said. He barely heard himself. He was focused on the warmth of Tean's body, the smell of range grass and pine, the feather-light uncertainty of the doc's arm around his shoulders.

"What happened?" Tean asked quietly.

"I don't know. I don't want to talk about it. I just—I did something I'm not happy about, and I don't even know why I did it."

"I bet you had a good reason."

"I don't know. That's the whole problem: I don't even know."

The kids were still playing tag, the boy chasing after the girl, both of them shrieking with laughter that echoed back from the high ceiling and the concrete floor. A door opened, and a man called out a name. The kid with the ice pack shambled out of the lobby. When the door swung shut, stale air with the smell of microwave popcorn gusted through the lobby.

"I think for a long time, I told myself I didn't want to be like all the sheep around me because it was a way of feeling better than everyone, when I've never really felt better than anyone. I mean, I know what I am."

"You're Jem Berger," Tean said. "That's pretty amazing."

"Yeah. And I'm a fucking idiot who can't read. And I didn't graduate high school, and I didn't go to college, and I don't know how to fill out a job application or look for an apartment on my own. I didn't know my Social Security number until you—"

"Jem, what happened?"

He shook his head.

After a moment, Tean said, "You can read."

"I can't read like an adult."

"You're getting better."

Jem just shook his head again. They'd gone round and round like this too many times, and somehow he'd said it all wrong anyway. What he wanted to say was that he'd never wanted a normal life until he'd met Tean. And even that was a lie because he'd always wanted a normal life; he'd just never been willing to take risks for it until Tean. And it wasn't just reading, it wasn't just his ruined credit, it wasn't just jobs and apartments and whatever the hell Tean meant when he talked about IRAs. It was the fact that there was something fundamentally screwed up inside Jem, something that made him not normal, and there weren't any workbooks or GED classes that could fix that. He'd proven it today with the game he'd played with LouElla, the way it had gotten in his head and made him realize all over again how different he was from everybody around him.

"Beep beep boop?" Tean said.

"Boop," Jem said. "Fucking boop."

Across the room, the same door opened again, and another eddy of stale popcorn air rushed into the lobby. Ammon stood there in another of his cheap suits, trying hard to look unreadable when he was obviously excited. A little of that excitement faded when he took in how they were sitting: Tean's arm around Jem, Jem's head on the doc's shoulder. Ammon came across the room toward them, the heels of his wingtips clicking.

"I don't have time to talk," he said. "I'm sorry, but today's crazy."

"You arrested Hannah," Tean said, his arm sliding away from Jem as he stood.

"I can't talk about that."

"Without talking to me? Without even telling me?"

"This is a police investigation," Ammon said. "I couldn't tell you something like that even if I wanted to."

"How did you find her?"

"She came in on her own."

"Why did you arrest her?"

Ammon shook his head. "Are you not listening to me?"

"No, I want to know. I deserve to know. On what grounds? What's the evidence?"

"I only came out here to let you know that you should go home. The best thing you can do for Hannah right now is make sure Caleb is ok, support him while they go through this. You can check her visiting hours—"

"Fuck visiting hours," Tean said.

"That's a dollar in the jar," Jem said.

"You lied to me," Tean said. "You used me. You told me you just wanted information from Hannah, and then you sat back and waited for us to drop the whole case in your lap."

Tean turned to go, but Ammon gripped his arm and yanked him back. "First of all," Ammon said in a furious whisper, "I begged you not to get involved again. I ordered you not to get involved again. Yes, I asked you to see if you could get Hannah to give up some information. At the time, I thought I was just looking for a missing person."

"You're an awful liar," Tean said.

"I thought, at the time, I was doing the best thing for everyone. But don't pretend I wound you up and let you loose and just waited for you to assemble all the evidence that your work wife is a murderer. I tried to stop you, and as usual, you ignored me and did whatever the fuck you wanted." Ammon was still clutching Tean's arm, and now he shook him. "Don't you dare act like this is somehow my fault."

"Let go of him." Jem didn't remember standing, but he was on his feet, and he was patting his sides, trying to find his tools. A part of his brain distantly remembered locking them in the under-seat storage. "Take your hand off him, or I'll fuck you up."

Ammon dropped Tean's arm.

"Get lost," Jem said.

Instead, Ammon turned, squaring up with Jem.

"No," Tean said, trying to move between them. Ammon used one hand to shove Tean to the side. "No, absolutely not."

"Why not?" Ammon said. "This has been coming since October. He thinks he's your boyfriend. Let's get this out of the way."

Jem didn't say anything. Talking in a fight was only good if it got the other guy to do something stupid, and Ammon already looked plenty stupid, thanks very fucking much.

"Here?" Tean whispered. "Are you out of your mind? You'll be fired. And you'll both get charged. Ammon, come on." He caught Ammon's shirt, and Ammon's gaze broke away from Jem and slid to Tean. "Come on. I want to talk to you for a minute. Come on."

Slowly, by inches, Ammon let Tean usher him to the other side of the lobby.

Jem watched them go. He rolled his shoulders, bounced on his toes, cracked his neck. He thought the best plan was to start with a big, telegraphed roundhouse, the kind of punch that Ammon would see coming from a mile off. Then, while the detective was watching the roundhouse, he'd knee him in the balls so hard they went up into his stomach.

But after a few minutes of conversation, Ammon turned and left, passing through the same door he'd come out of. Tean made his way over to Jem and said, "Let's call Caleb and see if we can get some more information from him."

"What did he say?"

"Nothing."

"No lies. That goes both ways with best friends."

"All he'd say was that they had enough evidence to arrest Hannah, and they only do that when the prosecutor is convinced they'll get a conviction."

"That's not all he said."

"No, he said a lot of bad things about you too. Big surprise. Come on. And quit flexing your muscles."

"I'm not flexing my muscles."

Tean just stared at him, and after a moment, Jem felt his face heat. He tried to even it out with a grin, but the doc just rolled his eyes and walked out of the lobby.

When Jem got outside, the day smelled like warm asphalt and diesel exhaust. Tean was on the phone, but he pulled it away from his ear and shook his head. "Caleb's not answering. You try."

Jem placed a call. It went to voicemail, and he left a brief message. Then, to Tean, he said, "Caleb told me he'd continue to pay me to investigate. He wants us to clear Hannah."

"Which is perfect because that's what we were going to do anyway."

Jem's phone buzzed with a call from an unknown number. He answered.

"This is Lynn Ellen Lytle," a woman said in a clipped, professional tone. "I'm providing legal counsel and representation to Hannah Prince."

"Oh," Jem said. "Great, I just—"

"Per Mr. Prince's instructions, I am canceling your outstanding contract with him."

"Wait, what?"

"Your services are no longer needed, Mr. Berger. Please do not contact my client or his family. If you need anything, you can reach me at this number. Please send a finalized invoice for your services to my firm. I understand that you were paid a retainer; if you have not earned the full amount, Mrs. Prince wants you to keep the balance as a bonus. If you are owed money, I will see that you're paid."

"Hold on," Jem said.

"Goodbye, Mr. Berger."

The call disconnected.

"What was that?" Tean asked.

"I just got fired," Jem said.

24

When they got back to Tean's apartment, Scipio pranced around them, licking Jem's hand, oblivious to Jem's flinches. Jem walked straight to the couch and collapsed face-first onto it.

"Leave him alone," Tean whispered. He grabbed a rubber bone and squeaked it a few times. Scipio charged him, got his teeth into the bone, and began growling and whipping his head back and forth in an impromptu game of tug of war. That went on for a while, with Tean moving around the kitchen, checking the fridge, noticing that Jem probably needed more milk, and all the while getting his arm ripped off as Scipio yanked on the toy.

Then Tean walked over to the couch and grabbed Jem's ankle.

"Ungh," Jem groaned.

"Come on."

"I got fired. That lawyer fired me."

"You don't even like having a job. You told me, your exact words were, 'Jobs are for suckers.' You told me that while I was trying to get ready to go to my job."

"Yes, and I stand by that statement, but I like having money."

"You know plenty of ways to get money."

"Yeah, but I kind of liked earning it. Is that weird?"

Tean laughed and pulled on his ankle again. "Up. We're going for a walk."

"Go without me."

"I'll put this bone under your shirt if you don't get up in the next five seconds."

"Is that a sex thing?" Jem said, rolling onto his back and smirking up at Tean. "Let me see that big bone."

"Up, or you're going to have eighty pounds of slobbering Lab trying to rip your shirt off."

"Just try it a little bit differently. Try telling me you're going to throw me your bone."

"Ok," Tean said, grabbing the hem of Jem's shirt, "you asked for it."

It turned into wrestling, with Tean trying to get Jem's shirt and Jem trying to force him away, Jem's eyes bright and his grin manic, and Scipio lunging in to try to be part of the game — and to try to get the rubber bone out of Tean's hand. Tean threw the bone in Jem's lap, and Scipio charged toward it.

"Fine, fine, fine," Jem shouted, laughing as he twisted away from Scipio. "I'll go on the walk. You're a fucking cheater."

When Tean had Scipio in his harness, they headed out of the apartment. The spring day was perfect: the sun warm on the back of Tean's neck, the sky clear and blue, a grove of apple trees on the edge of Liberty Park in bloom. Midafternoon, the park was busy. A pair of girls, one black and one white, was chalking out a hopscotch game. A half dozen Latino kids were playing a pickup game of soccer on a grassy stretch, using the trees as goal posts. Two women — one with her hair cut high and tight, wearing boots covered in gunmetal rivets, the other in an honest-to-God poodle skirt, her hair styled like she'd just had it done with Mrs. Cleaver under the dryer next to her — were walking a Goldendoodle, and the doodle and Scipio had to stop to sniff and meet each other.

"You realize they fired you because they're terrified Hannah's going to be convicted," Tean said once they were walking again. "It's not a comment on you personally."

"A little bit it is."

"No, they just don't want to leave anything to chance. The defense attorney probably has her own private investigators that she uses." Tean hesitated. "So you liked the job?"

Jem looked at him.

"I'm just asking," Tean said, raising his free hand.

"That was a moment of weakness."

"Understood."

"Working is for chumps."

"Got it."

"And don't get any ideas about making me work in a Walmart spraying down the toy department or helping old ladies try on pantyhose or chopping up horses for the meat case."

"Have you never been to a Walmart?"

"I just liked, you know, having these skills and being kind of good at something."

"Do you even know what a retail employee does? Why would you spray down toys?"

"Because kids get their grubby hands on everything. Will you please focus?"

"What if I paid you?"

"What?"

"I'll pay you to help prove that Hannah's innocent."

"I'm not taking your money. I only accept trade in the form of sexual favors."

"Jem, I'm serious. You're good at this, and it could be a really great launching-off point for you to do this professionally. We'd have to see about getting you licensed, but if you could say that you saved an innocent woman from conviction, then you'd have people pounding down your door to get you to work for them."

They cut across a grassy swath toward the pond. Ahead of them, a black boy was sitting against a tree, knees to his chest, eyes glued to a book; two younger boys who might have been his brothers were throwing rocks into the water.

"You can't afford me," Jem said.

"Don't worry about that part."

"I'm not dumb, Tean. I know you're kind of, you know, strapped."

"I said don't worry about that. I don't want to talk about money with you. I just want you to say yes or no."

"No."

"Jem!"

"We'll do this together. You're my friend; I'm not going to take your money. The rest of it, like a job down the road — I'll think about it."

Tean pushed his glasses up his nose. He was struggling with something on the tip of his tongue.

Jem glanced over. "Spit it out."

"Best friend."

An instant of shock, and then Jem's face was smooth, and he shrugged. "Obviously."

When they got back to the apartment, Tean got out half of a Walla Walla onion, a box of Eggos, ground turkey that looked a little green, and a serrano pepper that had shriveled up.

"What do you think you're doing?"

"Oh, you can make these waffle tacos—"

"No."

"They're actually really—"

"No goddamn way," Jem said, reaching past Tean to grab the Eggos. He shoved them in the freezer. "You can defile Eggos on your own time. And throw that turkey away; you're going to get sick."

"I think most of it's still good."

"Why did Ammon arrest Hannah?"

"I told you: he said the prosecutor thinks they have a case they're going to win."

"Based on what evidence?"

Tean frowned. "He didn't say."

"That doesn't matter. We did most of the legwork on the case." Jem leaned on the counter. The blue-and-white polo he was wearing rode up, exposing pale skin and a trail of golden hairs. "Whatever they've got, it's because we led them to it. So what do they have?"

"The body," Tean said. "But the ME told me she couldn't determine cause of death. She must at least have decided it was a homicide, or they wouldn't have arrested Hannah, but unless they recovered more of the body, the cause of death is probably still undetermined."

Jem made a face. "Ok, they've got part of a body. What else?"

"Zalie told us about those phone calls between Hannah and Joy. I'm sure they've got Hannah's phone records, and they can show communication between the two of them. Zalie will testify. According to her, Hannah saw Joy as a threat—Joy might reveal details about Hannah's past that would either incriminate Hannah or ruin her father's upward trajectory in the church."

"Those details being: a) Hannah might have been involved in an ecoterrorist bomb that killed a delivery driver, and b) she's a total lez."

"More or less," Tean said, trying to keep his eyes from drifting as Jem got a hand under his polo and scratched absently.

"Possible blackmail. That's a motive. But we don't know anything about means or opportunity."

"We can't really say anything about means yet," Tean said, "because we don't know what actually caused Joy's death. Opportunity, though—I think it comes back to phone records. They can probably track where Hannah's phone was, and it must show her near Joy around the time Joy disappeared."

Jem's blue-gray eyes narrowed, and he stopped scratching his stomach. "Pen and paper."

Tean grabbed them from his desk.

"Write this down: two Quarter Pounders, a large fry—ow!" Jem ran his thumb over the spot where the pen had hit his cheek. "I'm bleeding."

"That's ink. Don't be an—"

"Say it. Say a bad word."

"Don't be a pest."

Laughing, Jem pushed the pen back to Tean and said, "Ok, let's make a timeline."

"You can make a timeline."

"You know I can't."

"Yes, you can. And you need to practice."

"It'll be faster if you do it."

"Then abbreviate."

"This is why I hated school," Jem growled, grabbing the pen and paper. "Bunch of smartass teachers who think they have all the answers." He wrote S-M-T-W-T-F-S at the top, and then he made four rows of boxes. He filled in the bottommost Thursday with *H arest*.

"Two r's."

He scribbled in an extra r.

They worked backward, filling in the stages of their investigation day by day, until they got to a Saturday in April. *H creek stragner.*

"Switch the n and the g."

"Will you please just do this?"

"You're doing great."

Jem growled some more, scratched out the word, and wrote it again correctly.

"Who was this person that Hannah saw following her?"

Tean paused to ruffle Scipio's ears. "If you're the police, then you say it's a lie—she made the whole thing up."

"And if you're not the police?"

"Maybe it was the real killer."

"Maybe," Jem said. "That was April 21." He moved back a few more days. "On April 17, Joy meets her Playmates date at Kneaders."

"Kneaders has a K at the beginning. And it's e-a, not e-e. K-n-e-a-d-e-r-s."

The pen tore through the paper this time as Jem rewrote the word. "As far as we know, that's the last time anyone saw her alive." Jem made a face. "Could Joy have been the person that Hannah saw following her?"

"No; the ME told me that they estimated Joy had been dead for three weeks. Whoever was following Hannah, Joy had to be dead by then."

"So the last time Joy was alive, as far as we know, was Tuesday the seventeenth."

"And that's consistent with what Elvira told me. The ME, I mean."

"Ok." Jem made a face. "Come on, there's something else."

"The car."

"Damn it. Ok, a bunch of cash—that sounds like hush money. And Joy's purse."

"And the Kneaders receipt."

Jem hesitated. "But it was a different date, right?"

"Monday. The sixteenth."

"So she was at Kneaders two days in a row?"

"That's what the manager told us—it was her first-date spot."

"Oh shit."

"What?"

Jem shook his head and took out his phone. When he started speaking, his voice was harsh and deeper than usual. "Get Kristine on the phone!" He waited, and then he wrote *e mal* on the paper and tapped it. "This is Bill Frederickson from corporate legal. Do you want to tell me why I have the prosecutor's attorney excavating my asshole because you didn't send them the security video they requested?" Another silent moment passed. "I don't care what you did. If they say they don't have it, they don't have it. You're going to do it right now. Right fucking now, before we get slapped with obstruction. Do you have something to write with?" Jem nodded at Tean, and as Tean recited an email address, Jem repeated it into the phone. "I don't care if it doesn't sound like the same email they told you. Right fucking now, Kristine. Don't make me call you again." He disconnected.

"You're a little bit scary sometimes."

"That's not even my mean voice."

"I'm not talking about your voice."

Scipio rammed his head into Jem's leg, and Jem flinched and, after taking a breath, stroked the dog's ears once. "Yeah, well, just don't give me any dog-related work."

Tean's phone buzzed. "Got it. She sent two files. The sixteenth and the seventeenth."

"Let's take a look."

At the desk, Tean opened his laptop and navigated to his email. He was sitting in the chair. Jem, instead of pulling over one of the dinette chairs, rested his chin on Tean's shoulder, his arms in a loose hug. Tean tried not to squirm.

"Play the seventeenth first," Jem said.

"Why?"

"I've got a hunch."

Tean clicked the video and said, "It's really annoying when you do that, you know."

"What?"

"Pretty much everything."

"I know. That's why I do it."

After double-checking the time that Joy had arranged to meet her date on the Playmates app, Tean scrubbed forward and then they watched the sped-up video.

"She didn't show?" Tean said.

"One more time."

They watched it again, more slowly.

"I knew it," Jem said.

"But if she didn't show up for that date, why did the woman, Becca, act so scared when we contacted her?"

"Because Becca had just gotten a phone call from strange men asking about a date she had arranged on a hookup app."

Tean grimaced. "Hannah's not even on this video. Why would the police request it?" Then it hit. "Oh."

"Yep," Jem said. "Because it's proof that Joy had plans and she didn't show up, didn't respond to messages, didn't cancel her date."

"Because she'd been killed."

Jem let out a soft breath. His cheek was warm where it grazed Tean's, and his arms tightened slightly, a kind of ghost hug, probably because he knew that Tean would have scrambled away if he'd tried anything more.

"I guess we need to watch the video from the sixteenth."

Tean opened it and scrubbed forward in bursts, guessing that Joy would have picked approximately the same time for her rendezvous on the sixteenth as she had for the seventeenth. He was wrong, so then he had to scrub back. At 14:41:09, based on the timestamp in the corner of the feed, Joy Erickson walked into Kneaders. She was moving quickly, her head down, but even on the low-quality black-and-white footage, Tean recognized her. He let the video play at normal speed. Joy went straight toward a table and sat. She kept her head down. Her shoulders were curved in. Her hands were hidden below the table, but judging by the way she sat, Tean guessed that she was clasping them in her lap.

"She's scared," Jem whispered, and it sounded like he was talking to himself.

Then the door to the Kneaders opened, and Hannah came in. She moved across the dining room in jerky steps. She didn't look well— her eyes were fixed straight ahead, her face rigid, and if Tean hadn't known her better, he would have thought she was high or drunk and on a serious tear. When she got to the table, she jabbed a finger at Joy. She was saying something. The security video didn't have audio, but the message was clearly a threat or a warning.

"Oh fuck," Jem whispered.

Then Hannah pulled out an envelope and threw it at Joy. It hit the table, skidded, and fell to the floor. The envelope opened, spilling cash across the floor.

Hannah turned and left.

"Fuck, fuck, fuck," Jem whispered.

"Well," Tean said, trying to make his voice normal. "I guess now we know why they think Hannah did it."

25

Jem was resting his chin on the doc's shoulder, his arms loose around his chest. He could feel Tean struggling to breathe normally. He could feel Tean's desire to break out of Jem's arms and get away. The doc's gaze was still fixed on the screen, frozen in the moment Hannah exited the Kneaders.

Tean tapped Jem's arm.

Jem ignored him.

Tean pulled on Jem's wrist.

Jem settled his chin and tightened his arms a little.

"Jem."

"I know, but you're not going anywhere right now. Sorry."

"Jem, come on."

"I'm really comfortable."

"Ok. Enough. It's not funny right now." The doc tried to wiggle free. "Get off me. I'm angry and I'm hurting and I'm scared for my friend, and it freaks me out when people touch me, so just get off me."

"Ten seconds."

"No, right now."

"Sometimes you need to know people care about you. Especially when you're hurting. And it's not about words. Nine seconds."

Tean's shoulders dropped, and he slumped in the chair. It was like the nonviolent resistance approach to enemy hugs. Jem thought it was adorable.

"Eight, seven, six—get ready to do some really good shouting—five, four, three—try to yell in my left ear, because I already have some hearing damage in that one—two, one, zero. And you're free."

Jem released the doc and stepped back.

Tean shot to his feet. "What the hell was she doing?"

"Something stupid."

"You're right it was stupid." Tean's volume was rising. "She could have handled that situation a million different ways. A million better ways."

"Yep."

"She made herself look like a criminal. This is why she's under arrest—because she tried to handle things on her own. I knew something was wrong. I tried to help. I asked what I could do."

"This is not your fault. She made her own choices, and she had her own reasons. It's not about you."

"Well, it's affecting me. It feels like it's about me."

Jem raised an eyebrow. "Hannah getting arrested for murder is really about you?"

"Of course not! I'm just angry, so I'm shouting and saying things I don't mean!"

Covering his mouth, Jem nodded.

"And you! When I tell you I don't want to be touched, you need to listen to me."

"Noted."

"Don't bully me into feeling better."

"So you do feel better?"

Tean's crazy dark eyebrows drew together, and he put his hands on his hips.

"God, yes," Jem whispered. "Tell me about how every time I hug someone against their will, a teddy bear dies."

"Teddy bears aren't even alive."

"Tell me about how involuntary hugging is a sign of aggression in water penguins."

"There's no such thing as a water penguin. They're all water penguins."

"Tell me about how a sneak-attack hug is America's silent killer, the highest cause—we're speaking statistically here—of death in the United States."

A tiny smile pulled at Tean's mouth. He still had his hands on his hips.

"Don't do that," Tean finally said.

Jem just shrugged. "What now? If you're done yelling, I mean."

"I guess so." Tean rubbed his face. "Can I sleep? I feel awful, and I just want to sleep until this is all over."

"You could," Jem said, "but since it's only three in the afternoon, maybe you could wait a few more hours."

Tean just shook his head.

"Shake it off," Jem said, "because we've got to work. How do you prove Hannah didn't kill Joy?"

"If she had an alibi—"

"We know she doesn't; they wouldn't have arrested her if she had an alibi. How do you prove Hannah didn't kill Joy?"

"You prove someone else did."

Jem gave him double finger pistols.

"I hate you sometimes," Tean said.

"It's ok," Jem said, "our epic, everlasting, bromance-for-the-ages can survive your bouts of pissiness."

Grabbing a blank piece of paper, Tean sat at the dinette table and said, "Who are our suspects?"

"Zalie and Sievers."

"Motives?"

"A multimillion dollar pig farm for Zalie, plus revenge or jealousy. For Sievers, pure hatred."

"If I were investigating—"

"And you are," Jem said.

"—I would have done a lot more digging, figuratively and literally, around both of them. Why was Ammon so quick to settle on Hannah?"

"You're not seeing it the same way he does. From Ammon's point of view, Hannah has just as strong a motive as the other two. And he's got her on video in a violent confrontation with Joy the day that she goes missing. They probably have more stuff we haven't figured out yet. Glasses."

Tean caught them on the bridge of his nose and slid them back up. "Did you just take Ammon's side?"

"Ugh. It was an accident. Do you have any special veterinary acid I can take a shower in?"

"Jem, this is pointless. How am I supposed to prove someone else did this?"

"Use that big brain full of book knowledge." Something cold and wet pressed against Jem's arm, and he flinched. Scipio was shoving the rubber bone into his hands. Jem's heartbeat climbed, and he had to take a breath and smile before putting his hands on the table, out of reach. "All three of them have motive. That doesn't mean she did it."

Tean was staring at Scipio.

"He's fine," Jem said. "He's not bothering me."

"Sure he is," Tean said absently. "I'm starting to figure out when you're lying, which is going to be very useful. The bone."

"Yeah, well, tug-of-war isn't my favorite game. Too much growling. And his teeth are too close to me. I'll throw him a ball if you want."

"No, Jem. The bone. Whoever killed Joy also amputated her limbs to hide the cause of death."

"Ok."

"So we find the limbs, find the cause of death, and prove someone else killed Joy."

"Ok."

"Don't look at me like that."

"I'm not trying to give you a look, I just don't know how we're going to find the limbs. Oh God, I can't even believe that sentence came out of my mouth."

"Coyotes," Tean said. He sprinted to the desk, with Scipio bounding after him in case Tean had suddenly remembered a treat- or toy-related emergency, and came back with his laptop. Pulling his chair next to Jem, he said, "I've been reading about them nonstop because of this outbreak. Coyotes are omnivores, which means they'll eat anything—kind of like you."

"I wouldn't eat that weird two-layer dip you made that was just sour cream and navy beans."

"It was seven-layer dip. I just made alterations."

"It's only seven-layer dip if it has seven layers."

"And they'll travel over a hundred miles to find food if they can't find it in their current territory. Kind of like you finding a McDonald's."

"Jesus Christ. Does the doc have jokes?"

And coyotes always hang around farms and ranches. Not just because they want to eat the animals, but also because there are a lot of animal byproducts—afterbirth, sometimes even the droppings of newborn animals—that they love to eat. That explains why they hang around the pig farm. And they're not above scavenging, which is why we saw one of them trying to dig Joy's body out of the gravel."

"Is your brain like a giant Wikipedia?"

"Isn't everyone's brain kind of like a giant Wikipedia?"

"Yeah, but mine only has the parts on sex stuff and the 90s."

"I'm not even sure about the 90s."

"Jesus Christ! When did you decide you've got jokes?"

"Here's the important thing about coyotes: they carry food away from humans, so they can eat without being disturbed, and they're well known for caching food. Storing it for later. Usually they'll loosely bury it and then mark it with urine."

"You know what? This is good material. This is grade-A material. You should talk about this with Orion."

The doc was a sneaky little bastard, and he got Jem in the gut with his elbow.

While Jem doubled over and gasped for air — making a big show of it, and enjoying the huge grin on Tean's face — Tean clicked and typed, navigating to a satellite mapping program.

"Uh, I hate to break it to you," Jem said, "but those images can be years old. There's no way you're going to be able to see where a coyote has been digging recently. Unless you're hacking into a military satellite? Are you hacking into a military satellite?"

"I cannot believe I told Hannah she should pay you for this." Tean zoomed in on a small home with several outbuildings. Farther out, a quilt of pasture and crops — he couldn't tell what they were from the image — were broken up by dirt roads and two small creeks. "Look familiar?" Tean asked.

"That's the pig farm."

"Yep."

"And, like I said, the picture is old."

"Right. This is definitely not current. But it's relatively current, which should be all we need."

"Time-traveling coyotes."

"What?"

"Like the Terminator."

"Sometimes it's like a horrible game of Mad Libs with you."

"I'll be back."

"From where?"

"Oh my God," Jem groaned, dropping his face onto the dinette table. "I don't know if I can even help you at this point. We might just have to put you down."

"Do you know how to trap a coyote?"

"Yes. And then I skin it, make a hat out of it, and wear it while I'm in a log-splitting contest against Abraham Lincoln."

"The best way to trap a coyote is to figure out its travel corridors. Normally, you're only trapping on your own land, so you'd already have a good idea of where they travel. We're taking a shortcut because we don't have a lot of time." He paused, his face screwing up. "Dang. I hadn't thought of that."

"Sievers was trapping on their land," Jem said.

"What? How did you do that?"

"I just figured that's what the whole problem was from the beginning: Joy wasn't just angry about him killing animals, she was angry about him doing it on her property. Then you said that thing about coyotes hanging around farms and ranches, and we know he was the top bounty collector in the state. Boom. It all made sense."

"Boom?"

"Pretty much, yeah: boom."

"Were you going to tell me?"

"I thought you had figured it out too." Jem shrugged. "Sometimes I overestimate you."

Tean stared at him.

Scipio snuffled.

In the hallway, Mrs. Wish said, "Senator Henry Cabot Lodge, get back here this instant."

Tean was still staring.

"You were just so busy with the computer, though," Jem said. "All that typing and clicking."

"Uh huh."

"Your mind was elsewhere."

"Uh huh."

"It could have happened to anyone."

"Thank you."

"Coyotes? Travel corridors?" Jem asked with his best smile.

"Coyotes tend to follow borders and junction areas. Creeks and rivers, for example. The edges of crop fields. Fence lines. Roads. Hedgerows."

"Love me a hedgerow."

"What is going on with you?" Tean asked, scrubbing his hands backward through his hair.

Jem grinned. "I'm excited. This is exciting stuff. We work really well together."

"We'll print out this map," Tean said, "and we'll mark possible travel corridors. Then we'll look for tracks. Then we'll do some hiking."

"Hiking?"

"Only a few dozen miles."

"You know, we've been leaving Scipio alone a lot lately. Maybe I should stay and keep him company."

"No."

"He looks so sad."

Scipio was lying on his back, all four paws in the air, sound asleep.

"He's fine. Fill up some canteens. I'll get bear spray and bells. No point in getting too close to the coyotes if we can help it."

"Bear spray? Will that work on coyotes?"

Tean walked away, shoulders slumped.

"What?" Jem called after him.

The drive out to the Heber Valley went quickly, and they parked on the gravel drive in front of Zalie's small home. Tean went up to the porch, knocked, and spoke briefly with Zalie when she answered the door. As he came back down from the porch, Zalie shut the door.

"She says we can look around," Tean said, checking the can of bear spray that was hanging from his belt. He handed Jem an identical can and showed him how to hang it from a belt loop. Then he produced a small bell that he attached to a separate loop on Jem's pants, and then he hung one on himself. Last, he grabbed a daypack and slung it over his shoulders. "She also told me that the gravel got delivered early Tuesday morning, and she knows the guy, and he was probably still drunk when he got here. That narrows our timeline down even further, and it also explains why the guy wasn't bothered about dumping the gravel on top of a dead woman. Zalie doubts he even got out of his truck—he just backed it up and dumped his load. What? Why are you looking at me like that?"

"Say that again."

"What?"

"Dumped his load. And with your thumbs in your belt, the way you were just standing."

"I hate you."

"It was so butch."

Tean stalked away.

"It's the bear spray," Jem called after him. "And the bell. And the boots. It's really doing something for me."

Tean kept going, and Jem sprinted after him, laughing.

The first travel corridor they checked was the gravel driveway, and they took opposite sides of the drive to cover more ground. They were halfway to the road when Jem shouted, "I got one!"

Tean crossed the gravel, studied the impression in the dried mud, and shook his head. "Dog."

"Yeah, of course it's a dog. That's what I'm saying."

"No, a dog isn't a coyote. Or a wolf. Their tracks look different. That's a dog. See how round it is? A coyote's print is elongated."

"Well, I still found the first track."

"You did," Tean said with a small smile. "Very good job. Wolf tracks are much larger, just so you know."

"Great. That's great. Much larger. That's perfect."

In the late afternoon, the light in the valley was golden, dusting fields of alfalfa that were just starting to grow, throwing long shadows from a line of stunted apricot trees, infusing an old, rotting haystack so that it seemed to glow. The smell of pig shit was pretty bad, in Jem's opinion, but when they were past the fields, he could smell dust from the haystack, and he could smell the last of the apricot blossoms, and when they backtracked and walked shoulder to shoulder, he could smell sage and resin on the doc.

They checked each possible travel corridor, with Tean marking them off on his map as they went. Jem did find the first coyote track, and he whooped with excitement and picked Tean up in a bear hug, ignoring how Tean whapped him on the head with the map, the bell at his waist ringing wildly. But it was a solitary track, and after another half hour of searching, they tried another travel corridor. The sun dropped farther, the bottom edge of its disc slipping behind the Wasatch Mountains, and the shadows got longer. The cool, humid air from the creek carried the smell of mud. Jem jumped when he thought he saw a snake, stumbled, and landed with one foot in the creek.

"These are original Air Jordans," Jem growled as he shook his foot, flinging drops of water everywhere. "You wouldn't believe what I had to do to get these."

"I would actually probably believe it."

"Very funny."

Tean's expression was a little too carefully neutral.

"You know people invented these things called roads and sidewalks and bridges and—and dry land!"

"People invented dry land?"

"Don't start with me!"

Face solemn, Tean mimed zipping his lips.

"I'm going to murder this coyote when we find it," Jem muttered.

"They can run up to forty miles per hour," Tean said as they continued their search.

"Then I'll shoot it. A bullet is faster than forty miles per hour."

"They're one of the most resilient and adaptable creatures in North America. They've managed to survive and thrive even as humans have moved into their territories and disrupted the ecosystem around them."

Jem's foot was squishing on every step. He fixed Tean with a glare. "You sound like you like them."

"They can create patchwork territories out of green spaces in urban environments, and they can be an important part of an urban ecosystem. One coyote pack was found denning in the parking lot of Soldier Field Stadium."

Jem grunted. "They'd better be Cubs fans. If those dogs are White Sox fans, I swear to God I will kill myself. We might as well just reboot the whole fucking universe."

"They're not dogs. They're coyotes. They mate for life and they're a hundred-percent faithful to that mate, but they're also incredibly effective at surviving on their own. Unlike wolves, who struggle to hunt successfully without a pack, coyotes almost always hunt alone or, at most, in pairs."

"Oh my God. You like them. You like these dumb dogs, and you don't have anything bad to say about them."

"And our taxes—well, not yours, because I don't think you've ever paid taxes—but everybody else's taxes have paid around $30 million dollars to have over 500,000 coyotes killed."

"There it is," Jem said with a sigh.

It was almost an hour later when things started to turn around. They were following the border of a hayfield, the tender green stalks barely ankle high, when Jem spotted the next track. More whooping, more bear hugs, more spinning Tean around while their bells chimed. Tean was trying to look mad, and Jem was grinning because he'd already seen the next one. Twenty yards later, they found a trap.

It was bigger than Jem had expected from what he'd seen in cartoons, cruder, just thick metal designed to snap tight on a leg. Tean's face was bleak as he backtracked, collected a stick, and used it to set off the trap. The metal jaws snapped shut, breaking the stick in half. Tean dropped the part that he still held and dusted his hands.

"I understand that coyotes are a problem. I know why the DWR has the bounty in place, and I support it. But these fucking things." Tean just shook his head and started walking again.

They followed the tracks. They were moving into the foothills on the eastern side of the valley. Their shadows swooped ahead of them, great black birds, and a purple fringe darkened the edge of the sky. Neither man spoke. There was the wind, their steps, the jingling bells. Tean's jaw was set, his bushy eyebrows drawn down. Jem thought what he always thought: what it would be like to feel so much, to feel so sincerely, without all the layers, without irony, without trying to wad it up to block the mouse holes in your brain? What would it be like to just be able to feel it and show it and then be done with it?

He was so caught up in the thoughts that he didn't stop until Tean caught his arm.

Jem didn't know why they had stopped, and he opened his mouth, but Tean gave a tight shake of his head. Then the doc's eyes cut up, and Jem followed his line of sight. On a hill almost directly in front of them, a gray dog was stretching. But it wasn't a dog, Jem realized. It was a coyote. The old panic was there, building inside Jem at the thought of getting too close to those teeth. He thought of Antony because he always thought of Antony around dogs.

But there was more to the moment than just the panic. The mountain breeze carried the smell of day-warm stone, and the sun hung at the right angle to pick out the tufts and contours of the coyote's fur, lighting it up like it was on stage. Then the coyote finished its stretch, and it trotted down the side of the hill, gathering itself at the bottom to bound forward, and Jem had the wild thought that it was enjoying itself, having fun, jumping the way kids jump just to feel their muscles do something different. The coyote stopped at a puddle, lapped water, and then splashed forward. Its head swiveled. Its yellow eyes passed over Jem. And then the coyote's gaze came back, and the two of them were staring at each other.

Jem didn't have words for the experience. Part of it was being eye to eye with another living creature, with all its unknowableness, all its difference. Part of it was the opposite: feeling himself alive, electrified, and connected to this thing because they were both alive, because they had both run and swum and jumped, because to be alive was to share in the same vital force. Part of it was the frozen moment itself: the motes of dust in the air, the coyote's lean muscle under gray fur, the rippled water in the puddle, Jem's skin prickling and drawn tight, the coiled energy in his chest. It was a fire without any heat, turning him into light as it burned through him. Then the coyote looked forward again, and it loped off into the gathering shadows.

Jem was trembling. "Holy God," he said. "Did you feel that?"

When he looked over, Tean was smiling.

"Did you feel that?" Jem repeated, louder than he meant. He grabbed Tean in a one-armed hug, laughing, unable to stop his own shaking. "Jesus Christ, have you ever felt anything like that?"

"Once or twice," Tean said, still with that small smile.

Jem ran his hand through Tean's hair, squeezed his neck, pulled him into another one-armed hug. "Jesus fucking Christ, if I live a hundred years, I don't know if I'll ever feel that again. I can't even — I don't even know — I mean, what was that?"

Tean shrugged. Then his smile got a little bigger. "What were you saying about cities?"

Just for that, Jem dragged him into another bear hug and swung him around for a while.

Laughing, Tean straightened his clothes when Jem finally released him. "We're not done yet. We haven't found anything, and we've got to be careful now that we know we're near a pack."

"Get your coyote spray ready."

"It's not—" Tean sighed. "Never mind."

They began a spiral search, moving out from where they stood, calling out loudly and shaking the bells. Tean was the one who found it. He called Jem over, pointed to the dark splashes marking the disturbed earth.

"I didn't bring a shovel," Jem said. "Why didn't I bring a shovel? I guess I'll find a stick."

Tean had already dropped his daypack to the ground and was pawing through it. He pulled out a small orange aluminum trowel and handed it to Jem.

"You always carry a mini shovel with you?" Jem said.

"Well, normally that's for digging latrines when I'm backpacking."

Jem held it back toward him with two fingers.

"What?" Tean said.

"I don't want your poop shovel."

"It's not like I, you know, did my business on it."

"Don't want it. Won't hold it. You'd better take it or I'm going to drop it."

Tean snatched the trowel back.

It only took a few minutes of digging, and then Jem swore and pulled his shirt up over his nose and mouth. "Fuh. That's awful."

"That," Tean said, dropping back on his heels, "is a human arm."

26

Friday morning at eight o'clock, Tean was waiting in the lobby of the medical examiner's office. People were arriving for work, some of them stopping to mingle, others moving with brisk strides. A young woman who looked barely old enough to have graduated college was lugging a briefcase almost as big as she was. Two guys in t-shirts and shorts were laughing, the sound echoing against the poured concrete and glass.

Once again, Tean and Jem had lost most of the previous night to questioning: first by the Heber City police, then the Wasatch County sheriff, and then, when Ammon and Kat had finally gotten there, to Kat.

The third time Kat had asked Tean to tell her step by step how he had come to find the arm, Tean had said, "Why isn't Ammon doing this?"

"Detective Young is examining the scene. Let's start at the beginning again: what prompted you to come back looking for the victim's remains?"

So Tean told her for the third time.

"And it didn't occur to you that your expertise might be valuable to the police, and you could have offered this same theory to me and Detective Young, and we could have come out here and searched properly?"

"Properly? I found the arm, didn't I? And anyway, the two of you are too busy fitting Hannah for a prison uniform."

Kat was short, but she had big, ropey muscles that even her baggy suit couldn't hide. She fixed Tean with a look while she redid her ponytail.

"I realize that didn't come out the way I intended it to," Tean said.

"And this is why I'm in here," Kat said as she worked a scrunchie into place.

Now, standing in the lobby, Tean's eyes were gritty from another sleepless night, and a headache made his head feel hollow. When he'd crept out of the apartment that morning, Jem and Scipio had been tangled together on the couch again—Tean couldn't decide which one had been snoring louder.

"Dr. Leon?"

Elvira Castorena came toward him, her dark skin a little ashy this morning, her hair frizzy in its bun. She tried to say something, put the heel of her hand to her mouth, and waved for Tean to come back with her. Like last time, Tean pulled on disposable PPE and met her in an autopsy lab. Joy's torso was on a table again, and now the recovered arm had been set in place.

"I'm sorry to do this so early," Elvira said after another huge yawn, "but by the time I got back from Heber, I was too amped up to sleep, so I stayed and got some work done. I wanted your professional opinion on this before I went any further."

"They only recovered one limb?" Tean said.

"So far. Right now, I believe they're getting a warrant to search the rest of the property."

"Zalie didn't want them to search?"

"No, you'd left her land. The arm was recovered on adjacent property."

It took Tean a moment because he was so tired. "John Sievers's land?"

Elvira mimed zipping her lips. It was a strange gesture because of the face shield, and it took Tean a moment to realize what she was doing.

Tean nodded slowly.

"How likely is it that a coyote would scavenge this limb," Elvira asked, "carry it approximately half a mile, and bury it?"

"It's certainly possible," Tean said. He explained the same points he had communicated to Jem. "It might not be common, but it's well within the range of possibility."

"But it's spring," Elvira said. "The Heber Valley has plenty of wildlife. Why not just get a few pet dogs and cats from the city if it was really hungry instead of eating a corpse?"

"Well, I'm not sure the coyote would make much of a distinction between a pet or a corpse or any other convenient source of food — not if it was hungry, anyway. Although, just so you know, in the studies I've seen, pets actually seem to be a rare exception in a coyote's diet. The bigger issue is competition. If cougars or wolves are taking prey, or if cougars are threatening the coyotes — they're a coyote's natural predator — then it's even more likely the coyote would have seized any opportunity at an easy meal. Another source of pressure on that pack would have been Sievers, of course. He's been taking a lot of coyotes in that valley."

"What would the coyote have done with the other limbs?"

"It's hard to say. Anecdotally, coyotes can break down and eat bone, so it's entirely possible the other limbs have already been destroyed."

"Well," Elvira said, gesturing him closer, "take a look at this. How much of a look did you get at the scene?"

"I didn't see much. I didn't want to disturb it any further."

"This is the proximate cause of death: amputation of the arm. It's an antemortem wound severing the brachial artery. She would have been unconscious within fifteen seconds, dead in under two minutes."

"Antemortem?" Tean said, bending closer to look. Much of the soft tissue had been torn away by scavenging, exposing bone. He pointed to a portable magnifying glass and microscope combination, and Elvira nodded. He looked first through the magnifying glass, examining the bone and the marks on it.

"Definitely," Elvira said. "It looks like an animal bite to me, but I was also thinking about those big ugly traps that Sievers has on his land."

"No," Tean said, switching to the microscope, "it's definitely an animal. Is it just the soft tissue damage that's antemortem, or is the fracture antemortem too?"

"That is a very good question. It's incredibly difficult to tell with bone, so we actually make the decision based on other data. Why did you think to ask that?"

"It seems like the most important question," Tean said, lifting his head from the microscope to consider the remains. "You told me that all four of the limbs were amputated postmortem. But the amputation site on the arm is antemortem. And I can tell from how you've positioned it that a piece is missing. A few inches."

"Based on average ratios and her height," Elvira said, her dark eyes sharp as she considered him, "we believe approximately three inches of her arm are missing. That portion was not recovered."

"So an animal attacks her. It amputates the arm above the elbow. She dies from exsanguination. Then someone comes along and uses a tool to amputate the remaining limbs and to amputate what remains of the damaged arm."

"Why would someone do that, Tean?"

"To hide the nature of the injury that killed her."

"But it was an animal."

"That doesn't exempt the owner from liability or criminal charges. More importantly, there are certainly cases where people have used animals to kill people. In this case, it seems like this was clearly a homicide, and one that was planned." Then Tean's face heated. "Sorry. That's your job. I just got a little carried away."

"No, it's . . . refreshing. Even if we leave aside intent and premeditation, I think your basic idea is the right one: someone amputated the limbs to hide the nature of the attack. They then disposed of the remains in a place where they hoped they would be destroyed. They might have done this out of a misguided attempt at self-preservation as they tried to cover up a terrible accident, or they might have done what you suggested: planned and executed a homicide."

"Or something in between," Tean said, and he felt a guilty flush at the treacherous thought of Hannah. "In an argument, a heated exchange, maybe some pushing, an animal might have misunderstood the seriousness of things and become defensive."

Elvira nodded slowly. "Is there any chance of identifying the type of animal that caused the fatal injury?"

Tean shook his head. "Unfortunately, it's not that simple. I might be able to narrow it down if more of the soft tissue were available and if a complete bite mark were present, but even then it would be a bit of a guessing game. Many mammals share a relatively similar arrangement of teeth: incisors, canines, premolars, molars. The shape of the mouth and how the teeth are used can tell us something, but as it is, with only some soft tissue and mostly bone, the best I can do is tell you that this animal has some kind of dental defect."

"It has a broken tooth?"

"Possibly." Tean pulled the microscope into place and scanned the bone as he spoke. "Or a chipped tooth. Something like that. Most of the teeth marks on the bone are punctures, pits, and furrows. What you'd expect, in other words, from an animal that bit down hard a few times and shook its head back and forth. But here you can see a partial bite pattern. Clear pitting and punctures, no furrows—it bit down hard and locked its jaw."

Elvira took Tean's place at the microscope. After a moment, she said, "And there's a gap in the pattern."

"Exactly. So, as you said, either the animal is missing a tooth, or it's chipped just enough to prevent it from closing on the bone at the same height as the other teeth."

Stepping back from the microscope, Elvira shook her head. "So we're not any closer to figuring out what killed her or who might be responsible for the damage to the body."

"No," Tean said, "but once we have a suspect, we can take dental impressions from specific animals and compare them against the bite mark. This is how we prove who killed her."

27

Jem woke with a paw on his face. Again. And the same cold flare of panic in his chest, the same disorientation, the tightness that made it difficult to breathe. He tamped it down, pushed the paw aside, and began the process of disentangling himself from Scipio. Scipio woke up and realized this was the best game anyone had ever played with him, so he decided to participate by biting the hem of Jem's polo and making growling noises as he yanked on the fabric.

By the time Jem got free and stumbled into the bathroom, his heart was pounding, and he was covered in flop sweat. It's dumb, he told himself in the mirror. It's stupid. That dog is crazy about you. That dog wants to sleep with you even when Tean's here. He doesn't want to bite you; the only thing he wants to do is eat peanuts when you accidentally crack the shell too hard and the nut shoots across the room.

He ran the water, showered, and found his *XXX Files* t-shirt that featured a shirtless Fox Mulder on the front and, on the back, *Scully? Who's Scully?* He pulled on clean jeans, realized he needed to do laundry, and got himself a bowl of Lucky Charms. There was a new container of milk in the fridge, and as he stood on the balcony, the morning air cool against his bare arms, the boards rough under his bare feet, he thought about fresh milk. When had Tean gone out to buy some? It had to have been this morning, which meant that Tean had gone and done it sometime after he and Jem had stumbled into the apartment and before he'd gone to work a couple of hours later. After finishing the cereal, Jem went back to his pile of dirty clothes and rifled the chinos until he found the slip of paper that LouElla had given him, the one with a name and address. He also found the rental application that Tean had cosigned. He let himself think, for a few minutes, scratching Scipio's ears when the Lab laid his head in Jem's lap. Saturday mornings, he could stumble down here earlier than he wanted to be up, and he and Tean could go on a hike. And weeknights, when Tean got home from work and was tired, he could just go straight to Jem's apartment, and Jem would have an actual, edible, human dinner waiting. Scipio pawed at his arm, and Jem said, "Yeah, you can hang out there too, but the first time you pee on the rug I'm going to taxidermy you." And when Tean got busy with work—he worked too much—Jem could pick up groceries for Tean, instead of the other way around, so the doc didn't have to sacrifice sleep for a jug of two-percent milk.

He finished the cereal, drank the milk from the bowl, and rinsed the bowl at the sink. Scipio followed him into the kitchen.

"And how am I supposed to pay for it?" he asked the dog.

Scipio cocked his head.

"Am I supposed to work minimum wage at Snow's with Mr. Kroll eye-fucking me for the rest of my life? Am I supposed to spend my whole life doing jerkoff work for absolutely no money, while Tean goes on dates with guys named Orion and Kismet and Buffalo and they all earn a million dollars a year and they've got great teeth and Roth IRAs, whatever the fuck those are?"

Scipio butted him gently with his head.

"And don't get me started on college. If I hear one more fucking word about college, I'm going to cut my own throat."

Scipio shoulder-checked him, his whole weight slamming into Jem's thigh, and Jem reached to pet the Lab's flank.

"It'd be different if I could read. It'd be different if I weren't such a fucking moron."

Scipio whuffed.

"Exactly," Jem said. "That's exactly right. I don't have any other choice."

Borrowing Tean's laptop, Jem pulled up a browser and pecked out the address for a search engine. He typed in the name Brigitte Fitzpatrick. According to LouElla, she was the bitch who had stolen Jem's identity and ruined his credit. He got millions of results, some of them for Bridget Fitzpatrick, some of them for a CEO's account on LinkedIn, some of them for Facebook. The wall of text stopped him cold, so he did what he always did. He gave up and tried something else.

"Oh," Tinajas said when she answered. They'd been in some of the same foster homes at different points, and although Tinajas had managed to make a real life for herself — she even had a sweet job at the DMV — they still stayed in touch. "You're alive."

"I'm alive."

"Too bad. I figured some rentboy had finally cut you open from balls to butt and let you bleed out in an alley."

"That's kind of poetic. You've been working on that one."

"Not that I'd know if you were dead. Not that I'd have any idea."

"Ah. That's what this is about."

"Not that I'd have any idea if you're alive and happy and cuddling a million puppies or hooked up to a ventilator in an ICU and waiting for a butt transplant after that rentboy opened up your stern."

"Have you been watching those gay pirate movies again?"

"Where the hell have you been?"

"Busy."

"I've been calling you. I've been worried about you. Kike went by a few days ago, and the Latus told him you got kicked out. Where have you been staying? Are you ok? Do you want to crash on my couch?"

Kike was Tinajas's coworker and Jem's semi-regular hookup. Friends with benefits might have been another term, but Jem and Kike had never been friends. So maybe just human with benefits. Acquaintance with benefits. Sexy but also stuck-up lifer government bureaucrat with benefits might have been closest.

"I'm ok. And I'm sorry. I've just been really, really busy."

"Where have you been sleeping?"

"I know it's shitty to call just to ask for a favor — "

"Bitch," Tinajas said, "all you ever do is call me to ask for favors. If that bothered me, we wouldn't be friends. Why are you avoiding my question?"

"The name is Brigitte Fitzpatrick, and I need to know where she lived back — "

"Oh no. Don't you dare tell me you're playing bunkmates with that emotional black hole who fucked up your entire life last time you started dicking him."

Through the open sliding door came the smell of fresh-cut grass; a string trimmer was whining in the distance.

"First," Jem said, "I want to know what a respectable pencil-pusher like you is doing saying words like 'dicking.'"

"Do not test me right now. I am pregnant and I am uncomfortable and I am really seriously considering driving over there and rearranging that guy's pretty face."

"He is pretty, isn't he?"

"Jem!"

"I know you don't like him."

"I don't like him," Tinajas said in a tone that was clearly meant to be a mocking imitation of Jem's, "because he tore your heart out and stomped all over it."

"That went both ways."

"Yes, but you're the one I care about. I don't give a shit what happens to him. Come stay with me, please."

"Wait. You're pregnant?"

"God, yes. Tony. Again. And he proposed. Again. If I have to see his grandmother's ring one more time, I'm going to lose my fabulous, fabled cool."

"Congratulations! Boy or girl?"

"Do not try to change the subject."

"Look, he's—I don't know how to say it. We're just a good fit. And I like being here. And I honestly think I might get another job. You know. I don't know. I mean. It kind of seems like it's time to grow up."

"Whoa."

"Very funny."

"Next thing, you'll be talking about getting a checking account. And then you'll learn how to stitch samplers. And then you'll be canning peaches and wrangling a herd of tiny veterinary doctor babies."

"Goodbye. I'll call you in nine months."

"For fuck's sake, what do you need?"

"Brigitte Fitzpatrick. Previous address."

"There are six women with that name who have vehicles currently registered to them."

"I've got a current address." He read it out to her. "Does that match anything?"

"Yes. She had vehicles registered previously in Sandy and West Jordan. Do you want one of those addresses?"

"Not in Tooele?"

"No, I don't have anything for her in Tooele. Is she married? Maybe she changed her name."

"I don't know. Ok. Do you have like flags on her account or anything?"

"No. What's this about?"

"Honestly, I don't even know anymore."

Scipio gave an enormous sneeze.

"What was that?"

"His dog."

"Oh Christ. Will you please come stay at my place? You won't have to play mind games, and you won't have to deal with a dog."

"Thanks for the offer. I've got to go."

"I'm not picking up the pieces when this goes to hell."

"Thanks, Tinajas."

"You can get high and pass out on somebody else's couch and tell her all about existentialism or whatever you were trying to tell me last time."

"I'm hanging up now."

"And I'm not bailing you out—"

Jem disconnected the call. He let Scipio out of the apartment, and this time he managed to herd the Lab toward the strip of grass at the back of the apartment building. Scipio pranced around for a while, peeing on everything he could reach, snuffling patches of clover for minutes at a time.

His phone buzzed, and Tean's name showed on the screen.

"I just finished up with the ME," Tean said.

"Oh. Shit. Ok."

Tean told him about the injury that had ended Joy's life, the animal attack, and the attempt to cover up how she had died.

"But it doesn't really get us any closer to a suspect, does it?" Jem said. "I mean, if the bite can't tell us if it was a coyote or a dog or a cougar, you know?"

"Well, it won't be that specific, but we can eliminate some types of animals. The teeth marks on the bone weren't perfect, but I could at least see the partial shape of the mouth. It's not a pig, and I don't think it's a coyote. I think in both cases, their mouths are too small."

"Hannah has a dog, doesn't she?"

Tean was silent for a moment. "Hannah didn't do this."

"I know, but that's not what I'm asking."

"Yes, she has a teacup Yorkie. I've never read of a teacup Yorkie biting through someone's arm and amputating it."

"Maybe it's like that rabbit from Monty Python."

Another silence. "Oh my gosh. I actually think it's worse when I understand what you're talking about."

"So," Jem said, "we're not any closer."

"We know how she died, and we know someone wanted to cover it up."

"Not necessarily. We know how she died, but we've always known someone wanted the body destroyed so there wouldn't be any evidence. Chopping it up might not have been to hide the manner of death. It might have just been to speed the process along." Jem paused. "I also want to say I'm not a psycho, because I'm saying a lot of stuff I never thought I'd say."

"Ok," Tean said. "Ok, I guess that's true. We got a little carried away because we finally had the cause of death."

"Covering it up doesn't make any sense," Jem said. "It was an animal attack. If it really was a murder, that's the perfect way to do it because you've already got your alibi: my Yorkie did it."

"But there's liability, criminal charges—"

"I know, I know. I'm just saying, a cover-up doesn't feel right."

"I'm not even sure it matters. Unless we find a specific animal and get a match with dental impressions, this is all moot."

"We're getting closer," Jem said. "We just have to keep working."

Scipio barked.

"It sounds like you're outside." Tean said. "Was that Scipio?"

"Um."

"Wow, you got him into his harness?"

"You know what? I've got to go."

Jem disconnected while Tean was trying to ask another question. Scipio was still inspecting every square inch of grass. Jem followed him, quietly suggesting they go back upstairs, reminding Scipio he had other things to do, and wondering if Scipio had forgotten their gentleman's agreement. Eventually, though, Scipio let Jem coax him back upstairs, and Jem locked the apartment.

After pulling up the maps app on his phone and plugging in the address LouElla had given him, he got on his bike and headed north and west into the part of the city known as Capitol Hill. He passed the Marmalade District, one of Salt Lake's gayborhoods, and zagged east again down two side streets. Some of the homes here had been extensively renovated, while others were obviously teardowns, but many of the original homes still stood: brick Victorian, Craftsman-style bungalows, many of the squat, boxy, 1950s-era homes with aluminum carports and bleak, industrial lines.

He stopped in front of a home that was relatively new construction. Two stories sprawled to the edge of the lot, with gray stucco that had been popular ten years before, a strip of perfect, thick green lawn, and flowerbeds popping with color—he recognized marigolds and petunias. Tean would have known all of them, he was sure. The trees were older in this part of the city, big and already thatched with leaves, so Jem parked in the shade and continued to study the house. The garage door was down, but through one of the house's front windows he could see an immaculate living room, expensive-looking furniture, and a grand piano. The other front window opened onto a dining room with a table and chairs for twelve and a built-in china hutch that took up an entire wall. A breeze carried the smell of chlorine and fresh mulch and, from the trash cans lining the street, garbage warming in the sun. Children's laughter came from the back yard.

Jem made his way down the sidewalk, trying to see into Brigitte's backyard. The privacy fence blocked him. He walked the other direction and found the same problem. Instead of turning back, this time he kept going, following the sidewalk around the block. The ground sloped up. He turned on the next street and counted houses until he was pretty sure he was in the right spot, and then he did a quick double check: nobody else was on the street. He jogged between two of the homes. From the one on the right came the sudden burst of a vacuum coming to life and then shutting off again.

At the back of the lot, he could see down the hill and into Brigitte's yard. Two towheaded kids were splashing in a huge inflatable pool, the kind Jem would have killed for as a kid. A woman was watching them from a patch of shade. She was blond, and Jem guessed she was in her forties, although it was hard to tell. Hard to tell much of her features, in fact, because she was wearing big sunglasses, but she was thin and well dressed, and she made him think of every other rich Mormon mommy in the valley. She looked familiar, but it might have been the perfect Mormon mommy getup; they all started to look alike after a while.

Jem jogged back to the sidewalk, went back around the block, and considered Brigitte's house from the front. Half a dozen riffs were already starting—he could pretend his bike had broken down, could I please use your phone? Or he could simply risk entering the house by himself and hoping nobody else was inside—but then Jem dialed it all back and made himself take a deep breath. This bitch had stolen his life. There was no point in moving forward without more information, and she'd offered him plenty of it without even meaning to.

He flipped open the trash can in front of the house and ripped open the top bag. Kitchen trash and diapers. He gagged, wished he had a pair of the doc's disposable gloves, and used the plastic bag to jostle the contents until he was pretty sure he hadn't missed anything good. After removing that bag from the can, he pulled out the one that had been beneath it. When he glanced up, a woman in a housedress and curlers was standing at her mailbox, watching him.

Jem ripped the bag—a smaller opening this time—and was pleased to see a mixture of papers, Q-tips with orange smears of earwax, used razor cartridges, a pair of kid's socks with holes in the heels, and plastic shrink wrap. Someone—the maid, Jem guessed—had collected all the upstairs trash in one bag. Bathroom, office, kids' room. He tied a second knot to re-seal the torn part of the bag. When he looked up again, the woman in the housedress and curlers was gone. Jem tossed the other bag back in the can and hurried to the bike.

Balancing the bag across his lap, Jem drove down the block. He glanced back once, just to check, and swore under his breath. The blond woman had come outside and was staring at the trash can, her gaze moving to him. Her neighbor must have called to warn her about the prowler going through her trash. Jem whipped his head forward, turned at the end of the block, and sped up.

For lack of anywhere better to go, Jem returned to Tean's apartment. A pair of picnic tables, the wood white from the sun and the benches sagging ominously, offered the only outdoor seating at the apartment building, but Jem didn't think Tean would appreciate having his apartment filled with trash. Jem perched on what looked like the safest stretch of one bench and dumped the bag out across the picnic table. Then, grimacing, he ran upstairs, managed to survive

Scipio's onslaught of love and kisses, and found a pair of disposable gloves in the doc's bathroom.

"Can you be good?" Jem asked.

Scipio was still nuzzling into him.

"Fine," Jem said, "but remember our agreement."

They went downstairs together, and after some initial frolicking and peeing and sniffing, Scipio lay on his side, chewing grass while Jem picked through the garbage. The bathroom junk went back into the bag, and so did the socks, the cardboard box from a LOL Doll, whatever that was, and miles and miles of shrink wrap and plastic packaging. Behind Jem, cars came and went in the parking lot, the sound of tires on asphalt and worn brakes providing a background music as he worked.

The only thing left on the table was paperwork. Most of the documents he didn't read completely; reading still took him too long, and it was frustrating. He relied instead on the habits Tean was trying so hard to break: skimming, inferring, and best-guessing. Jem sorted the papers into three stacks. In the first stack, he placed anything that looked personal. It was a small pile: just a torn corner of a takeout menu that had $37.95 written in the corner, and a handwritten grocery list on a piece of stationery that was printed *From Brigitte with love . . .*, because apparently the bitch spent a lot of time sitting at her desk thinking loving thoughts and scribbling them on stationery. In the next stack, Jem placed all the documents that looked like they were from businesses. Either Brigitte or her husband obviously owned a shredder because none of the documents contained sensitive information. Most of them were junk mail, one was an official notice to Brigitte B Fitzpatrick that the fees and service charges structure for her Wells Fargo account had been updated, and one was a postcard warning YOUR FREE TRIAL IS ABOUT TO EXPIRE – DON'T LET YOUR SUBSCRIPTION TO *LDS MOMS* EXPIRE! Jem snorted so hard he almost hurt himself; the Mormon mommy mafia hard at work. In the third pile he placed the unopened mail, junk that Brigitte or her husband had tossed without even opening it.

The first stack told him one piece of information: the stationery meant that he could be fairly sure that Brigitte really did live at that house, and this wasn't some elaborate ruse pulled by LouElla. The second stack told him that Brigitte had a Wells Fargo account and, possibly, that she was a practicing Mormon. It was always useful to know where people stashed their money, and religion could be a nice pressure point if Brigitte got obstinate.

He worked his way through the unopened mail piece by piece. Most of them were credit card offers targeted to Brigitte and Gerald Fitzpatrick. Two were life insurance policy scams. One was from a mortgage refinancing company. The next one he opened looked so similar to the others that he almost tossed it. Only habit made him take a second look.

This notice is for cardholder BRIGITTE BERGER FITZPATRICK. The name was in capital letters.

Jem couldn't read the rest of it. His mom's name, Mary B. Berger. And now this, Brigitte Berger Fitzpatrick. The words exploded into individual letters he couldn't assemble, buzzing black swarms that wouldn't settle into place long enough to make sense. He thought of the blond woman in her nice outfit, with her beautiful home, with two towheaded kids swimming in an inflatable pool. He'd looked right at her and hadn't recognized her. His brain kept coming back to the pool. He wasn't sure what a pool like that cost. Probably not that much in the big picture. But kids loved a pool like that. Two blond kids splashing and giggling. And that big home. And the perfect Mormon mommy hair and skin and clothes. And that pool.

He wasn't sure how long he sat there, staring at the page, when he finally realized Scipio was growling. Jem managed to look up, instinct and old habit making him fold shut the paper he was holding.

Ammon was standing there, wearing another cheap suit, his tie loosened and flapping in the breeze. Red with a blue stripe. A power tie. He'd gotten a new haircut—almost a skin fade, the top short to hide where it was thinning. He'd lost some weight, and although it probably hadn't happened overnight, Jem was noticing it now.

"Playing with trash?" Ammon said.

Scipio was still growling, his legs locked, his whole body aimed like a missile at Ammon. Without even thinking about it, Jem put his hand on the Lab's back, and the dog leaned hard into his leg. The growl vibrated up into Jem.

"What?" Ammon said. "No jokes? No little jabs?"

Jem couldn't swallow. His throat was too dry.

Two young guys—brothers, by the look of them—emerged from a ground-floor apartment, laughing, and then one pushed the other and took off in a run. The other stumbled, recovered, and sprinted after him, screaming, "I'm going to put a Super Soaker up your asshole!"

"Come on," Ammon said. "This is where you get to be the tough guy. Be macho. Piss all over everything like a dumb dog. Tell me this is your turf. Tell me to back off."

When Jem spoke, it sounded like someone else was talking. "Tean's not here."

"I know he's not here." Ammon shifted his weight. "Come on. Say something."

The world came down to the paper crinkling as Jem's hand tightened around it, Scipio's silky fur, the thrum of the growl passing into Jem's body, the warmth of the sun, the laughter fading in the distance.

"Damn, you really are stupid, aren't you?" Ammon said. "I mean, I knew you were an illiterate, drugged-up punk, but I always thought you were street smart. You don't see the way things are going? You don't see how it's all changing?"

Jem stood up so abruptly that Scipio let out a startled noise, and the dog backed away from him.

"That's right," Ammon said. "I'll give you the first one free. Take a swing."

Be smart, a tiny voice was saying inside Jem's head. Be smart, because he wants you to be stupid. He wants you to hit him because then you're going to jail, and by the time things get straightened out—if they get straightened out—it'll be too late.

Too late for what? Jem wanted to ask.

But he thought he knew.

"Pussy," Ammon said.

"You need to go. Get out of here."

To Jem's surprise, Ammon grinned. Then he laughed. "You have no idea how funny that is."

"Goodbye, Ammon."

"I'll be back. He's mine. You get that, right? All the work I put into him, all the years, all the things we've shared. You can be his little fuckboy distraction. That's all right. He needs to get it out of his system. But he's mine, and when I say the game is over, the game's over."

"You're psycho. You know that, right?" Jem finally managed to work some saliva into his mouth, and he swallowed. "That's a crazy way to talk about another person."

"I'll see you around," Ammon said, still smiling. He sauntered off to an unmarked car, and when he pulled away, he waved at Jem.

Jem dropped onto the bench; it creaked, and for a moment, he thought the wood might split. It didn't matter. He was shaking too hard to get up again. After a minute, Scipio pressed against him, his nose cold against Jem's hands, and Jem let out a shaky breath and patted Scipio's flank. He was still holding the paper with the name Brigitte Berger Fitzpatrick. He folded it and placed it in his back pocket with the rental agreement that Tean had cosigned. Then he gathered up the rest of the trash, returned it to the bag, and tossed it all in the dumpster.

Scipio followed him upstairs, and Jem paused outside Tean's apartment. A note had been slipped between the door and the frame. When Jem tugged it loose, a key fell onto the mat. Jem scooped it up and opened the note.

Hi, neighbor,
Can I borrow a cup of sugar?
Ammon, 4D

Jem bounced the key on his palm. He let Scipio into Tean's apartment and pulled the door shut. Then he went up to the fourth floor and let himself into 4D. The kitchen counters were empty. The living room was empty. In the bedroom, he found an inflatable air mattress and an electric pump, a pillow, and a gym bag. Jem went back to the kitchen and opened the cabinets until he found the bottle of Everclear.

He left, locked 4D, and went downstairs. He put the key onto his keyring, considered Ammon's note, and then tore it into tiny pieces. He pushed the pieces down the disposal, ran the water, and flicked the switch. He let it run for almost a full minute, turned it off, and crawled onto the couch. He lay there with Scipio squeezing into the curve of his body as a narrow ray of sunlight crossed the room, thinned, and vanished.

28

Jem woke to darkness, and a paw on his ear, and the sound of a key in the lock. Then Scipio thrashed with excitement, managing to smack Jem in the face several times before getting off the couch. The door opened, and a ribbon of light fell in from the doorway. Jem blinked. Then Tean hit the switches, and Jem had to squeeze his eyes shut.

"Didn't you get my messages? Hi, hello, Skip. Yes, I saw, you were being very good as his nap buddy." When Tean spoke again, his voice had changed. "Are you sick? You really don't look good."

Jem shook his head.

Footsteps crossed the room, and then a cool hand touched Jem's face. He flinched, but another hand cupped the back of his head, and then Tean touched his face again. "I don't think you have a fever, but I'll get a thermometer."

"Rectal, please," Jem croaked.

"Open your eyes."

After a few blinking attempts, Jem managed to comply.

As always, when it came to moments like this, Tean's normal hesitancy and discomfort evaporated, and he seemed calm and in control. His bushy eyebrows were drawn together, and his hair looked like the Bride of Frankenstein had tried to get a chop.

"Have you been throwing up?"

"Just twenty times. Don't worry. It was mostly blood."

"Are you in pain?"

Jem found the doc's hand. He guided it to his elbow and marked a spot with Tean's index finger.

"That's where it hurts?" Tean asked.

"No, that's the only part that doesn't hurt."

"Jem, what happened?"

"I played in the trash." Jem sat up slowly. His head was throbbing, his eyes were itchy and grainy, and he ached all over. "What messages?"

"I left you—never mind, it doesn't matter. You need to take some Tylenol, eat something light, and go to bed. I'll make you some chicken soup."

"No," Jem said. "Uh, I mean, you don't need to do that. I'm fine. Really. I'll just go vomit some more blood and I'll be right as rain."

"Are you really vomiting blood?" Tean asked. "Because if you are—"

Jem stumbled into the bathroom and shut the door before Tean could finish. He leaned on the sink. Then he opened the mirrored cabinet and shook out one of the doc's generic Xanax. He held it under his tongue and watched himself in the mirror until the world took a couple of steps back. Just for kicks, he put a second Xanax under his tongue. It was like the air got a little thicker. The light gelled. Try getting through that, motherfucker.

When he went back to the living room, Tean was coming back in from outside, Scipio pulling on his harness.

"He barely stayed down there long enough to go the bathroom," Tean said, undoing the harness while the Lab pranced in place. "He was desperate to get back up here."

"Maybe he wants dinner."

"Oh," Tean said, looking at the clock. It was half past seven. "I thought you'd fed him."

"Sorry. I was asleep."

"Are you—"

"Why were you at work so late?"

"I had to catch up on some stuff, and then I was waiting for a call."

"About what?"

Tean hesitated. "Let's just get you something to eat. I'll go grab you a Big Mac." He offered a scraped-bare smile. "I won't even try to cook."

"I'm not sick," Jem said. "I just fell asleep." He pulled out his phone and looked at the messages from Tean. "You found where they're doing a celebration of life for Joy. That was the call you were waiting for?"

"I did something dumb. I talked to Zalie earlier, just trying to see if I could find any of Joy's friends, and she said she'd call me back. I told her to call the office. Then I was stuck waiting because I hadn't thought far enough ahead and I couldn't get through to her. When she finally called, she told me about the celebration of life and gave me the details."

"Not dumb. You got us a good lead. Let's go see who shows up to Joy's celebration of life."

"I really think—"

But Jem was already grabbing his windbreaker and heading toward the door. "Better give him his dinner."

Tean sighed behind him, and then Jem was out of the apartment, the sound of kibble hitting the bowl following him down the stairs.

He was waiting by the truck when Tean finally came down, and they drove east. The sunset was fading, the orange and ochre stripes sliding down the flanks of the Wasatch Mountains. The canyon was darker, full of thick shadows that shifted when they went around corners and the steep rock walls closed behind them. Tean seemed to want to talk, so Jem buzzed down his window, and air whipped through the truck. It was cool and slightly humid, and it smelled like stone. Glassed under by two Xanax, Jem played with the door's latch, wondering what Tean would do if he pushed it open.

Instead of turning south and heading toward Heber, Tean followed I-80 east a few more miles and then exited and turned north. The sun had dropped behind the mountains now, and a weak, crushed-red light flickered along the crests, brighter where a saddle opened the ridge, extinguished where a spur extended. Some of the land they passed was pasture, with barbed-wire fencing along the road, and some was hayfields with tender young stalks that were colorless in the night.

Tean slowed and turned, crossing a cattle guard and passing under a ranch sign that was suspended on two posts. It was too dark to read the name of the ranch, but the gate was open, and in the distance, a bonfire flickered among trees. Tean followed the drive until they reached the cars parked on the shoulder, and then he guided the Ford off the gravel and onto the grass. Jem was surprised to realize they hadn't spoken during the drive.

"Are we looking for anything in particular?" Jem asked.

"I don't know. Someone who shouldn't be here. Someone who's not acting normally."

"What's normal at a celebration of life for an ecoterrorist?"

"I don't know," Tean said again.

Jem opened the door and dropped out of the truck. Gravel crunched underfoot as he headed toward the fire, and behind him, the Ford's door opened and shut, and steps moved after him. The breeze carried the smell of woodsmoke, and someone was blasting music: what sounded like bluegrass, with a fiddle calling out wildly. Even over the volume of the music, Jem could hear people shouting and laughing. The dark outline of a house was off to the right, and the party was off to the left. Jem followed the drive past the house and toward the party.

When he got closer, he could see people—just shadows against the flames—dancing, some of them tangled up in each other, some of them kissing, almost all of them holding cups. Beer kegs made a line at the edge of the party, and a card table held red plastic cups and a mason jar stuffed with cash. Jem headed straight for the beer. A girl in a leather skirt and a red bikini top was standing there, swaying to the music, sipping from a plastic cup. She seemed impervious to the chill. As Jem got closer, she caught his eye, smiled, and did a little more swaying.

Jem filled two cups from the keg; Tean put some cash in the mason jar, which made Jem smile even under those glassy bricks of Xanax stacked on top of his brain. The girl must have thought it was for her. With one hand, she tugged on her top, and with the other, she waved the cup in Jem's direction. She smiled again.

"If you try to drink that," Tean said, "I'm going to take it away from you. I don't know what you're on, and I'm not going to let you mix it."

"I'm not—"

"Don't. You're freaking me out, and I don't want to hear any more lies."

The blaze of the bonfire flickered and twisted. The smell of woodsmoke mixed with the cool air off the mountains, the pine, the wet grass of the trampled field.

"I'm just holding it," Jem said, passing the second cup to Tean. "To blend in."

"Great. So long as we're on the same page." Then Tean put his head back and chugged the beer. He made a face when he pulled the cup away, but he shoved it into Jem's hand without missing a beat and took the full one. "Now you're blending in."

"Hey," the girl called, swishing her hips.

Tean didn't exactly growl, but he did bare his teeth a little, and he grabbed Jem's arm and pulled it across his shoulders.

"What in the world is going on with you?" Jem asked, but he liked the feel of those thin shoulders, he liked the way Tean fit against his body.

"I'm cold."

Jem opened his mouth.

"Not tonight," Tean snapped.

"Ok," Jem said. "You're cold. We'll go with that."

The girl's smile had slipped. Jem shrugged a wordless apology, winked, and let Tean lead him away from the beer.

After a few minutes of observation, Jem guessed that the celebration of life had drawn over a hundred people. He wasn't sure if that was a lot or not; he'd never been to a funeral. But with only the light of the fire painting the scene, sudden tongues of illumination lapping up the darkness and then retreating, human faces bright and crisp one instant and then gone, it seemed like a lot. A lot of people to drive out to a ranch in Summit County, with minimal planning, to drink and dance by a bonfire, supposedly while mourning Joy Erickson.

Tean's arm was around his waist, and he squeezed Jem now and nodded at the other side of the fire. "I just saw Zalie."

Through the dancing flames, Jem could make out a dark-skinned woman seated on a log. He let Tean guide him around the bonfire, and when they were closer, he could see that Tean had been right. Zalie's long frame was stretched out, her legs extended in front of her. Tiny red stains marred the bandage that still wrapped one foot, and her bare toes stuck out toward the fire, probably to ward off the cold. She gripped her cane with both hands. Her gaze was fixed on the burning logs.

"Ms. Maynes?" Tean said.

She stirred and looked over at them. It seemed to take a moment for her to recognize them, then she nodded. "I thought you two might be—" She waved at them, standing together, with her cane. "I wasn't sure."

"We're not—" Tean began.

"We're not always public about it," Jem said over him. Then, not letting himself stop to think, he kissed the side of Tean's neck and bumped him affectionately with his head. The doc's whole body went rigid. "Play along," Jem whispered before kissing his neck a few more times. To Zalie, he added, "It's new, and things are complicated."

"It's very new," Tean said flatly.

"He won't even kiss me in public yet," Jem said, hugging Tean to him and peppering more kisses on his cheek, his ear, the crazy brushed-back hair. "But at least he wanted me to put my arm around him. It's little steps, you know?"

"You're about to take a little step back into the fire," Tean whispered.

Zalie stared at them.

"Mind if we sit?" Jem asked.

She waved to a couple of empty stumps, and Tean tried to use the opportunity to break away. Jem let him slide free, but then he rolled his stump next to Tean's and put his arm around the doc. He only grunted a little when Tean elbowed him in the ribs.

Over the blaze's crackle, Jem almost missed Zalie's words. "Joy was like that."

"Like what?" Jem asked.

"Like you. You should've seen me the first time we went out in public. Black and queer with a pretty little ginger on my arm. I thought I'd be lucky if all they did was crucify me. But Joy didn't miss a beat. She was always very affectionate. Demonstrative. Kisses and handholding in public, no matter how people looked at us. It took me a long time to realize that she loved people the same way she hated them—it was always all or nothing with her, never anything in between. Being loved like that, it's like a drug. Have you ever felt like someone loved you, the real you? Knew who you were, really knew, and loved you for it? That's powerful stuff."

Jem thought about how Tean laughed when Jem insisted on fixing the blinds. Jem thought about how Tean ordered an extra hash brown because he knew Jem would want a second. Jem thought about how Tean knew when Jem was frustrated with reading, knew when to push him to work through the frustration, knew when to pull back and let him rest. He thought about how Tean had asked Jem to stay at his apartment, turning it into a favor, making it possible for Jem to say yes without sacrificing his pride. Jem felt like he was seeing all of it happen again from the bottom of the ocean, the light refracted, everything on the other side of a barrier.

"Yes," Tean said. "It is."

And then Jem thought of Ammon, thought of Tean thinking about Ammon.

Zalie leaned forward, poking the fire with her cane. "It makes it hard to see her for the bitch that she was."

"What do you mean?" Jem said, clearing his throat when he heard the roughness in his voice.

"She was a bitch. She was a selfish, spoiled, entitled, privileged, egocentric bitch." Zalie shook her head. "I knew she was fooling around. I knew she wasn't interested in me anymore. I knew it was over, and I was ready to fight her for the farm. She could have the rest of it, but the farm was mine, and I wasn't going to let her take it." She raised her head to stare at Jem. "So why does it hurt so much?"

Jem was looking at Zalie, meeting her dark eyes, considering the heaviness in them. But he was also still underwater, looking up through something like glass, something like an ocean, at Tean. Tean and Ammon. "Maybe we never stop loving some people," Jem said. "Maybe we keep loving them, but we pile all the hurt and pain on top, and we have to carry it around forever."

Zalie didn't blink. She didn't even seem to breathe.

A raucous laugh broke out, and Jem glanced over to see an old man in a tank top and jean shorts, grinding against a younger girl, his belly flattened between them.

"At least I'm not making a fool out of myself," Zalie said. "Just like his daughter, doesn't have the sense to know when he's too old for a girl."

Jem did a double take and realized that the old man in the tank top was Leroy Erickson. His shaved head looked flushed in the flare and fall of the firelight. He was laughing again, the tattoo on his neck — Bo? Was that the dog's name? — stretched out when he threw his head back.

"He doesn't seem too upset," Jem said.

"He didn't look too good earlier," Zalie said, "but then somebody offered him a bump. The horny old goat probably thinks he's going to get laid. Just like his damn daughter."

Tean touched Jem's leg.

"I'm sorry for your loss," Jem said, leaning in so he wouldn't have to shout over the bluegrass. "Thanks for taking the time to talk to us."

"I don't even know why I'm here," Zalie said, looking around as though surprised to find herself in the midst of the dancing and shouting and drinking. "I don't know what I'm doing half the time anymore."

"You're grieving," Jem said.

Zalie nodded slowly, her gaze already drifting into the flames again.

"He's moving," Tean said, tugging on Jem's arm, and then the doc was sliding through the crowd of grinding bodies. The wild rhythm of the bluegrass had gotten inside Jem's blood, and now he felt himself bouncing with it, wanting to grab Tean, wanting to spin him along in some sort of foot-stomping, hell-raising jig — never mind that Jem didn't know anything about dancing to bluegrass.

They emerged from the press of bodies, and the night air was cool on Jem's face, making him aware of the sweat on his chest and back, the heat of Tean's shoulder under his arm. The smell of beer was a whisper, and the smell of pine resin, and the smell of sweating bodies. Leroy was pumping one of the kegs. He had lost a boot, and his bare foot was dirty from dancing.

"Mr. Erickson," Tean said. "My name is Tean Leon. We met a few days ago."

"Damn thing," Leroy said, still trying to pump the keg.

"Here you go," Jem said, bumping Tean, and the doc stepped forward and offered the second cup of beer.

"God bless you, son," Leroy said. He put his head back and drained the cup in one go, some of the beer escaping to trickle down into his beard, down his neck, staining the tank top. When the firelight brightened, Jem could see where the white cotton had been stained before.

"God damn," Leroy shouted, throwing the cup down and stomping on it with his remaining boot. "God damn, that's good."

"Mr. Erickson, we just wanted to extend our condolences," Tean said. "We're so sorry for your loss."

"My loss?" He blinked at them, wavering on his feet. Through the denim shorts, the outline of a partial erection was visible. He scratched one armpit.

Jem waited. He knew Tean would do the next part without any prompting.

"Joy," Tean said. "We're so sorry about Joy."

The transformation was so sudden that it was almost funny. Leroy's face seemed to collapse, and he wailed, "My baby girl. They took her. They took my baby."

Tean shifted under Jem's arm, offering a quick, sidelong glance.

"Oh God," Leroy sobbed. "She was my baby. She was the only thing I ever loved."

A pair of girls—even if you added them together, Jem thought, you probably still wouldn't get someone age appropriate for Leroy— emerged from the crowd. One of them took Leroy by the elbow, pulling him away from the table. His hand came to rest on her butt, squeezing a few times. The other girl glared at Jem and Tean and said, "You should be ashamed of yourselves. Hasn't he suffered enough?"

She hurried to join Leroy, passing him another cup full of beer. The girls were taking turns pressing Leroy's head against their breasts, obviously in some weirdly eroticized fantasy of mothering him. Leroy, for his part, was squeezing their asses hard enough that the poor girls probably wouldn't sit down for a week. A third girl with dark red hair was watching the whole thing with a weird smile.

"Hey," Jem said, studying the third girl more closely. He indicated her with a nod of his head and said, "Hey, is that who I think it is?"

"That looks like the girl from the Playmates app. Becca?"

"Yeah. That looks like fucking Becca. What's she doing here?"

Leroy's laugh cut through the music again. He was dancing again, grinding against a twiggy blonde, beer slopping out of the cup to run across the back of his hand, dripping off his wrist. And Jem thought about the piece of mail, the name, the woman with a beautiful home and beautiful children and an inflatable swimming pool.

Tean was saying something.

"She was his daughter," Jem said.

Tean was saying something else, tugging on Jem's arm.

"She was his daughter. Doesn't he even care that she's dead? Don't you even care that your daughter's dead, motherfucker? She was your daughter. You were supposed to keep her safe!"

The last half had been directed toward Leroy, Jem moving into the crowd of swaying bodies, getting closer and closer to the old man with each word. He was vaguely aware of resistance, something dragging on him. A woman bumped into him, and her beer went down his front. A young guy, shirtless, still trying to get his locs started, stumbled and fell into Jem's path. Jem stepped over him. Leroy seemed to have realized something was wrong; he turned, his eyes wide and blank as he stared at Jem. The blonde scampered off. An opening formed in the crowd. On the portable speakers, the banjos played faster and faster.

"She was your daughter," Jem said again. "You had one job. The only thing you were supposed to do was keep her safe."

"Wha—"

Jem got the first punch in, landing it hard and fast, his knuckles cracking against Leroy's teeth.

"You were supposed to make sure she was ok."

The older man stumbled, twisting away, his hand coming to his mouth. Jem followed. He threw another punch, aiming for the side of Leroy's head, but this time the man had his arm up. Jem's punch glanced off.

"You were supposed to watch out for her."

Jem swung again, but this time, Leroy moved in toward Jem. Jem's punch caught him on the shoulder, and then Jem was wide open. Leroy got him in the solar plexus. The air whooshed out of Jem's lungs, and then he was falling. Someone caught him and laid him down, and then Jem couldn't see anything because a body was in his way, interposed between him and Leroy. More shouting. Jem rolled onto his side, trying to pull in air, his eyes burning, his lungs on fire. Then he managed a breath, then another. Firelight swelled in his vision and then shrank down to embers. Woodsmoke scorched the back of his throat.

Then someone was pulling him upright, and he smelled pine resin and sagebrush as he was maneuvered away from the fire, into the cool darkness. He stumbled the first ten yards, still trying to catch his breath, and then he got his balance and started thinking again. Tean had him in a wrist lock.

"Ok," Jem said. "I'm ok."

Tean kept marching him toward the truck, a blur of white farther down the drive.

"Ow," Jem tried.

"Be quiet."

When they got to the truck, Tean released him with a half-shove that sent Jem stumbling into the Ford, one side panel flexing under his weight. Massaging his wrist, Jem turned around. He reached out.

Tean slapped his hand away.

"I was just trying to—"

"Be quiet."

"Your glasses."

The internal struggle flashed in Tean's face, and then he shoved the glasses back up his nose. "What the heck was that?"

Jem shook his head, his eyes dropping to his arm, and he pretended to study his wrist as he rubbed it.

"What were you thinking?"

"That didn't seem suspicious to you? He's laughing and drinking and rutting with teenage girls at his daughter's funeral? When he gets called out, he turns on the crocodile tears and then goes out and does it again. Does that sound like he's mourning his daughter? I think we've got a new suspect."

"You're unbelievable."

"That's what we're trying to do, right? Clear Hannah? And now we've got another suspect—"

"He's not a suspect. And don't pretend that was about Hannah."

"I'm telling you, he's not acting normally—"

"Do you want me to tell you what that was about? Do you want me to say it?"

Jem finally looked up, and he was surprised to see tears in Tean's eyes.

"You don't know what that was about," Jem said.

Tean just shook his head. "Just get in the truck."

"I think we should talk to Becca."

"She ran off when you picked a fight at a funeral, Jem. Nobody's going to talk to us anymore, not after you attacked the dead woman's father. Let's go."

The music had settled into something slower, softer. A fiddle wailed in the background. When the breeze shifted, it carried the smell of the fire away, and in its place came the smell of gravel dust and crushed grass.

On the highway, lights flashed, a horn blared, and someone screamed. It wasn't a cry for help. It was a ululating, exultant cry, competing with the horn and the strobing lights to break the quiet darkness along the road. Jem looked at Tean, and they both set off at a jog toward the highway. Behind them, shouts and angry questions came from the people around the fire.

When they got to the cattle guard, Jem had to cover his eyes for a moment as the lights came on again. An engine rumbled, and diesel exhaust pooled around a big truck. The vehicle was parked perpendicular across the highway, pointed at the bonfire and the celebration. Someone was standing by the driver's door, turning the lights on and off. Then glass shattered, and the peaty notes of whiskey mixed with the exhaust. Shards of the broken bottle spun across the blacktop, glittering when the lights came on again.

"Could you cut it out?" Jem said. "You're giving me a migraine."

The man's laugh was deep, and it was followed by another of those long, victorious howls. Nudging Tean with his elbow, Jem guided both of them out of the path of the headlights, and then he blinked to clear his vision.

"You two stay over there," the man said. Even with his night vision ruined, Jem could make out his general shape: big, with a military-style haircut. Then Jem noticed the shape of a rifle slung over his shoulder and what might have been a handgun at his waist. "We don't want any misunderstandings tonight."

"John Sievers?" Tean said.

"That's right." Another series of excited shouts. "The bitch is dead, the bitch is dead. Thank God that bitch is dead."

"You need to go," Jem said.

"It's a free country, isn't it? Besides, I'm here to celebrate. Aren't we all here to celebrate?"

"You need to go," Jem said. "Right now."

Men and women from the celebration of life were approaching the road now, some of them staggering from drink, some of them already shouting insults and threats at Sievers. They seemed to recognize him in spite of the truck's headlights, and—this was more interesting to Jem—they didn't seem particularly surprised to see him.

"This is about to get ugly," Jem said. "Nobody wants that. You did what you came here to do. You pissed on everything. You made your point. Just get in your truck and go."

As though to underscore the point, a rock whistled out of the darkness. It hit the side of the truck with a metallic thump.

Sievers's response was automatic. He unlimbered the rifle from his shoulder and fired. Men and women screamed, and the crowd broke up, racing back toward the fire in an uneven line. One man kept screaming, "I'm shot, I'm shot, he killed me!"

"Pussy," Sievers said. He produced something from inside a jacket, and the movement of his hands suggested unscrewing a cap. He tossed his head back, and then he threw something. Glass shattered again—a miniature bottle, the kind they sold at Sinclairs and Conocos. Judging by the blast of cinnamon-infused booze, Jem thought it had probably been a Fireball. "No way I hit him," Sievers said, almost conversational now. "At least the dead cunt had a backbone. This lot isn't worth a wet fart."

"Someone will have called the sheriff," Tean said. "You ought to go before he gets here."

"Yeah, yeah," Sievers said. He took his time settling the rifle in the rack at the back of the truck, adjusting himself in his seat, leaning out the window to consider the distant, red-gold flicker of the bonfire. Someone had turned up the music, and to judge by the shadows, they were dancing again. "You know," Sievers said, "it's really a shame the pigs didn't finish her. I thought the eco-dyke would have appreciated being shat out by her own fucking herd."

Then he hit the gas, and the truck leaped forward, tires slewing as he turned hard. The tailgate barely missed Jem, and he had to drag Tean back a step to keep him from being hit.

"Asshole," Jem shouted after the winking red taillights. "Motherfucker!"

"Did you hear what he said?" Tean asked.

"I heard."

"Did the police tell anyone where they found the body?"

"What?"

"Was it in any of the news stories? How would Sievers know that someone had tried to destroy the remains by feeding them to the pigs?"

Jem just shook his head. The day was catching up to him—Brigitte Fitzpatrick, the smell of her household garbage on him, Ammon, the key to apartment 4D, the fire, the music, the fight, the Fireball smell of whiskey and cinnamon, the tailgate whipping past Tean, almost hitting him. It all churned together into a white roar.

Tean looked at him, frowned, and said, "We need to get you home."

They were halfway up the drive when they saw a man lying in the grass, one hand over his thigh, moaning. A woman knelt next to him. It was the girl in the bikini top. When Jem looked at her, she smiled and rolled her eyes.

"He got me right in the leg," the man kept saying. "Right in the leg."

"You're not shot," the girl said in the tone of someone who has already said something a hundred times. "Get up, Uncle Hiram. Another beer will help."

"Is he really ok?" Tean asked.

"He's fine," the girl said. "He's just a hysterical old drama queen." The girl shivered, and Jem could see her skin dimpled from the cold as she wrapped her arms around herself. "Although, I guess to be fair, a run-in with John Sievers is enough to make anybody act like a drama queen."

"He shot me," Uncle Hiram said.

"Nobody shot you." To Jem and Tean, she said, "You can't blame them for thinking he'd do it, though. Those videos he puts out, damn. He's got to be psycho to do that stuff."

"Pretty ugly stuff," Tean said. "The traps. The way he goes after that coyote."

"What? Oh. Not that one. I'm talking about the things he does to that poor bear."

29

At eleven o'clock the next morning, they were sitting in an interview room at the SLCPD main station. PROCEEDINGS ARE ALWAYS MONITORED AND RECORDED was taped to the two-way glass, and someone had doodled penises around all the vowels. Tean had a cup of coffee, eight sugars and four creams, that he was spinning in slow circles. Jem had a cup of coffee, two sugars and two creams. The coffee almost masked the lingering smell of vomit that filled the room. Jem kept touching his head. Tean had already asked him three times if he was all right. The first two times, Jem had mumbled something. The third time he had ignored Tean completely.

"Thank you for bringing this to us," Ammon said. He'd just about worn the phrase out during the meeting. Then he rubbed his eyes. Dark circles ringed them, and they were bloodshot. "I promise we'll take this information into consideration."

Kat had been silent most of the time, sitting with her arms folded, grinding her teeth so hard that Tean thought once or twice he could hear her.

"It's all there," Tean said. His throat hurt from talking, and he could feel a headache of his own coming on. He'd been up all night, first watching the videos that the girl had mentioned, and then compiling everything he'd learned. He wasn't sure when he'd last slept a full night. Two days ago? Three? "He's got that bear somewhere on his property, and that's how he killed Joy. That bear is sick and hurt, and he's tortured it until it's crazy. It ripped Joy's arm off. Then he dumped the body in the pig pen. It's only his bad luck that they had the gravel delivered the next morning and ripped out the pen; otherwise, Joy would be gone completely, and nobody would have ever found her."

"Thank you for—"

"It's all there. What aren't you seeing? Means, motive, and opportunity. Means—I just told you, he's got the bear. Motive, that's easy. He'd been trapping near the pig farm because coyotes are drawn to places like that. His conflicts with Joy were escalating. He hated her with an insane level of hatred, and he's obviously unbalanced, sadistic, probably psychopathic. Opportunity, easy. His property adjoins theirs, and Joy had a habit of trying to free coyotes from his traps. All he had to do was wait until she was alone and take her at gunpoint."

"Yes, Mr. Leon. You've made those points very clearly. Thank you—"

"This is bullshit," Kat said, standing, and stalked out of the room. She slammed the door shut behind her, and Ammon flinched. In the silence that followed, Tean could hear the hiss of the HVAC system. Then the door opened, and Kat stuck her head in long enough to say, "Wrap it up," before slamming the door again.

"What's her problem—"

"Her problem," Ammon said, his voice rising with each word, "is that you've been going at us hammer and tongs like we're a couple of morons. Jeez, Tean. Have you even been listening to yourself? We're not stupid, ok? Did you even consider that there might be a reason we're not following your breadcrumb trail?"

Tean opened his mouth and hesitated. He thought about Kat's short absence. He glanced at PROCEEDINGS ARE ALWAYS MONITORED AND RECORDED. Then he looked at Ammon.

"Yeah, dummy," Ammon said, but he softened the word by touching Tean's hand. "When this goes to court, we don't want Hannah's defense claiming that we were influenced by her friend and co-worker, who also happens to be my longtime friend." Ammon bit his lip. "Maybe, hopefully, if you'll reconsider, more than friend."

"Now's not the time—"

"I know. I'm just telling you why we've only got a minute or two, and then I've got to walk you out of here, with Kat right there with us, so there's not even a shadow of suspicion."

"Ammon, I know Hannah didn't do this. I know she didn't. And I'm giving you, right now, the guy who did. It's all there."

"It's all there if you're playing cops and robbers, Tean. In court, what do you have? You have an anonymously posted YouTube video that shows an injured, captive bear. You don't have Sievers's face on the video. You don't have his voice. You have someone, and it could have been anyone, torturing a black bear on camera. You've got Sievers making a really awful comment about the body being eaten by pigs—"

"That nobody else could have known!"

"Please be realistic about this. Almost anybody could have known that. There were three jurisdictions present at that crime scene, not to mention techs and investigators from the MEs office. Do you really think nobody said anything about the body dumped in a pig pen? Half of Heber Valley probably knows what someone wanted to happen to Joy's body."

"But I could say the same thing about Hannah. All you've got is weird phone calls and a video showing her throwing money at Joy. That could have been anything."

"It wasn't anything, sweetheart. It was blackmail. You know it, and I know it. Joy needed the money; the divorce was expensive, and she was facing the possibility of losing everything. Hannah needed silence." When Tean opened his mouth, Ammon held up a hand. "She has no alibi after that meeting with Joy at the Kneaders on Monday. She claims she was at home, and her cell records make it look like that, but we've got her car on an HOV camera on I-15. She won't tell us where she was going or what she was doing. What am I supposed to think?"

"You're supposed to give her the benefit of the doubt."

"She's your friend, Tean. Not mine. And I've got a job to do."

"I cannot believe you're doing this. I know you. I know you're a good person. Why aren't you listening to what I'm telling you? You're punishing me. Is that it? You're doing this because you're mad at me, because I wanted to slow things down."

"I'm mad at you? I'm punishing you? What was yesterday? What the hell do you think that was all about?"

"Yesterday?"

"And you could give me a little credit, Tean. You and your boy toy want to play cops and robbers, fine, but at least do me the courtesy of pretending you believe I'm a professional and that I'm good at my job."

"You're not—"

"We found the hatchet in her garage," Ammon shouted over him. "Right in Hannah's garage. And someone had tried to clean the blood and the prints off it, but you can't ever get rid of all the blood. It's Joy's. We already matched it. So there's your means, motive, and opportunity. And I did it with warrants and by the book, Tean. Don't whine about how mean I am just because the truth hurts. And the truth is that your friend is a murderer. I'm sorry. I know that hurts you," Ammon's voice dropped now, "and I'm sorry. I really am. I would never hurt you, not ever, if there were any other way."

Tean squeezed his eyes shut. When he opened them, he looked at Jem. The blond man's head was down, and he was staring into his coffee.

"You're not going to say anything?" Tean asked.

Jem didn't even move.

"Fine," Tean said. "Let's go."

"I'll walk you out," Ammon said.

"Don't bother."

"Tean, I have to walk you out. Please don't make this harder than it has to be."

When Ammon reached for the doorknob, Tean said, "The bite marks won't match. You won't be able to match them to any animal Hannah's ever owned."

"She's a biologist who works for the Division of Wildlife Resources. She could have planned a dozen different ways to stage that attack."

"You can't prove that."

Ammon scrubbed his face with both hands. "Yeah, well, that's for a jury to decide."

Kat was waiting for them, and she took up position next to Jem, with Ammon at Tean's side, as though the detectives were escorting a pair of prisoners back to their cells. They moved through the homicide unit's offices, past cubicles, past messy desks, past a coffee station where a drip machine was spitting and hissing. Someone had put out a Nutpods creamer and taped a note to it: *Do not touch – Ammon's nut cream.*

Tean glanced at him.

Shaking his head, Ammon said, "It's fine."

"Why didn't you tell me?"

"During which conversation? At what point was I supposed to interrupt you shouting at me and tell you how things are going now that people at work know I'm a great big honking cocksucker?"

Kat snorted.

"Ammon, why didn't you tell me?"

They were approaching the lobby door now, and Ammon just shook his head. "Get some sleep. Get something to eat. What comes next isn't going to be easy for anyone."

Tean studied his friend, the first boy he had ever loved, the man he still loved: the bloodshot eyes, the slight hint of blond scruff, the hollow weariness.

"Go on," Ammon said with a quiet laugh, pushing Tean toward the door. "Before I do something dumb like kiss you."

Kat snorted again, this time adding an eye roll.

Tean let himself be hustled out into the lobby, Jem stumbling behind him, and then the door shut. He glanced back. If Ammon came through that door. If Ammon said he was sorry for all the years they'd wasted. If Ammon asked him, in that moment, to forgive him. Tean could hear his own heartbeat pounding in his ears.

Then he saw Jem, his face waxy, wobbling as though he could barely stay on his feet.

"Jem?"

Jem shook his head.

"Jem, what's wrong? What's going on? Are you ok?"

His blue-gray eyes, the color of deep ocean squalls, were glassy. "I don't know," Jem mumbled. "Tired." And then his knees folded, and he went down.

30

The blackness only lasted a moment — or so it seemed, anyway — and then Jem was blinking his eyes against harsh fluorescents. His head ached, as did his shoulder and hip, and he realized he was lying on the floor. The smell of cleaner adhered faintly to the cement: lemony, chemical. He still felt like he was underwater, those glass bricks on his chest. Somewhere above him, Tean was saying, "I don't know what's wrong with him; that's what I keep trying to tell you, he just collapsed."

"I'm ok," Jem said.

"Oh my gosh," Tean said, dropping down next to him.

Jem pushed the glasses back up his nose.

"Lie down," Tean said. "You need to lie down. We're getting an ambulance."

"No," Jem said. The look of shock on Tean's face made him laugh. "Nope, no way." He was sitting. When he went to stand, exhaustion kept him pinned to the ground. "Give me a hand, would you?"

"You passed out," Tean said. Behind the doc, a dour young woman in a blue uniform was watching. She looked more worried that Jem might try to make off with one of those chained-down pens than that he was actually ill. A middle-aged man holding a sheaf of parking tickets was also standing there, clearly hoping that this new distraction might somehow help him resolve his own problem. And, of course, Ammon was there, bending down to touch Tean's shoulder. "There's absolutely no way you're not going to a hospital," Tean added. "Right now."

"No insurance," Jem said.

A flicker of genuine panic ran through Tean's face.

"I just stood up too fast," Jem said. "And I haven't eaten today."

"Sure," Ammon said. "Happens to pregnant women all the time."

"Do you think this is funny?" Tean said to Ammon.

Ammon winced and held up both hands in surrender.

"Help me up," Jem said.

This time, Tean grabbed his hands and got him standing. Tean put Jem's arm around his shoulders, and Jem thought of the heat of the bonfire, the smell of wood smoke, bending to kiss Tean's neck. Pretend. He was just so good at pretending.

"Maybe I should do that," Ammon said. "He's a little big for you."

"I'm doing it," Tean said.

Ammon held up his hands again, but he followed them out to the truck. It was noon, the May day hot, and Jem was surprised to see that traffic was light and that the station's parking lot was mostly empty. Then he realized—remembered?—it was a Saturday. Somewhere on the next block, a horn blatted. Skateboard wheels clicked and whirred as a girl shot past them, crouched low, Tony Hawkette as she picked up speed on the sidewalk. Once, Jem made the mistake of glancing over. Ammon was staring at him, his face hard, and he mouthed two words: *Watch out.*

Once Tean had loaded Jem into the truck, he shut the door. Jem leaned against the glass. Tean was still standing there, turned toward Ammon, and Jem shut his eyes. You could only watch Romeo and Juliet eye fuck each other for so long before you needed intermission.

"I'm sorry I got upset in there," Tean said to the detective. "And I understand why you feel the way you do. But I know Hannah, and I know she didn't do this."

"Maybe we shouldn't talk about it anymore. Maybe you should talk about it with her lawyer."

"I want to talk about things with you."

"Really? Because you haven't said a word about yesterday. I was starting to think I made a mistake. Never mind. We can talk later."

Jem opened his eyes in time to see Ammon duck in, peck Tean on the cheek, and hurry away. Tean stood there, his hand to his face, watching him until he disappeared inside the station. Then he came around the front of the truck and got in. His expression was distant, and Jem felt twice as many of those glass blocks on his chest.

"Please don't look at me like that," Tean said as they headed out of the lot.

Jem slumped against the door, trying to keep his eyes open. The doc shrank and swelled in his vision.

"Why didn't he tell me?" Tean said. "Why can't he tell me anything?"

"It might have something to do," Jem paused to swallow, his throat dry, "with the fact that he's a major prick."

"You don't understand. I've told you that you don't understand."

"Maybe you don't understand."

The light at the next intersection must have changed because Tean slammed on the brakes. The truck jerked to a stop. Jem's head rocked against the glass. A sugary smell came through the vents; on the other side of the street, the door to a bakery stood open.

"His dad is a cop. That's how he grew up. His whole life is doing this, being police. And that culture is toxic. It's horrible. Most of those men are deeply afraid. They're afraid of the people they're supposed to protect. They're afraid of each other. They're afraid they'll answer a call and a citizen will shoot them in the back of the head. They're afraid they'll be blackballed by their brother cops and abandoned when they need them most. And all that fear manifests as anger. They're brutal because being brutal is better than feeling scared. His days revolve around violence—what he sees, what he tries to stop, what he does himself. It's this cycle of fear and adrenaline and self-defense that makes them do terrible things because they'd rather do something terrible than die. For most of those guys, their fellow cops are the only ones they can rely on, and now Ammon doesn't even have that because he came out. And he didn't tell me. I thought—I thought he trusted me. I thought he needed me."

The light changed. They accelerated again. Jem was having trouble keeping his head up, so he nuzzled against the seat, which smelled like his hair product. "Do you need that? Need him to need you?"

Tean answered as though he hadn't heard. "And he's Mormon, or he was, and Mormons are supposed to talk about their feelings. They're always talking about their feelings. So he calls, and I have to hear about his feelings. And now I find out he's been talking and talking and talking and he hasn't told me shit. Not anything that matters, anyway. He didn't tell me he'd moved out until he had to. He didn't tell me he'd come out until he had to. He looks sick and tired, and why the fuck can't he just talk to me?"

It might have been a mile. Maybe two. Jem's eyes closed, dark washed in, and after a while he managed to open them again. Tean was staring fixedly out the windshield as he drove.

"Poor Ammon," Jem said; he sounded drunk even to himself. "It's never his fault, is it?"

Tean shook his head, his shoulders drawn up tight.

When they got home, Scipio was ecstatic, jumping and licking and once whipping himself in the head with his own tail. This sent him spinning in a circle, trying to bite the tail, probably to teach it a lesson. It all would have bothered Jem another day, sent him bursting into panic, if only for a moment. Today, though, he was buried so deep that it didn't matter. He stumbled to the couch, kicking off his sneakers.

"No," Tean said, catching his arm and steering him down the hall. "Bed. And take off your clothes."

"Sexy times."

"No. Real sleep. Not whatever you've been doing."

"I like the couch."

"Great."

"It's comfortable."

"RC Willey's will be ecstatic to hear that."

"Maybe I should—"

Tean gave him a half-hearted shove into the bedroom—the doc really wasn't any good at being a bully—and said, "Pants. Now."

After undoing the waistband, Jem did a little shimmy, and the denim slid down to his ankles.

"Are you sure about sexy times?"

"I'm sure. If I want 'sexy times,'" he made the words sound like the bubonic plague, "with a heavily tranqued blond, I'm sure I can find someone on Prowler."

"I'm not tranqued."

Tean shook his head and pointed to the bed. Jem climbed under the sheets, still wearing his purple grandma shirt—THE BIGGER THE HAT, THE BETTER IT GETS. He patted the mattress next to him.

"What are you on?" Tean said.

"Come over here and I'll whisper it in your ear."

"If you die in my bed, I'm going to go crazy. I'll probably become one of those people who are homeless in San Diego, and I'll pass out from sunstroke in La Jolla and get eaten by a seal, and then it'll poop me out, and whatever's left of me will get processed by mollusks, and I'll end up being a bunch of low-luster, misshapen pearls that they'll put in a cheap silver setting and sell out of a Fred Meyer's jewelry display case."

"Because I died in your bed."

"Exactly."

"I thought pearls came from oysters."

"An oyster is a mollusk. Now go to sleep."

"I won't die in your bed. Because I don't want you to be a Fred Meyer's discount pearl jockstrap or whatever you were saying."

Tean said something else, but the bed was just as comfortable as Jem remembered, and the pillow smelled like Tean's hair, and all the chemicals he'd piled on top of his brain forced him down, down, down, and he disappeared for a while.

He woke, he ate a Big Mac and fries that Tean had kept warm in the oven, and then he slept again. When he woke the next time, the light was different. Morning. And not even early morning. His head was relatively clear, although he was dehydrated and all the shit he'd tried to bury was climbing up to the front of his brain again. The air that came through the open window smelled clean, like spring, and cool. But Jem wasn't cold; a warm body was pressed against him. Then he heard Tean in the other room, his voice pitched low and angry. Jem glanced over at Scipio, who was taking up most of the bed and watching him through half-closed eyes.

"I guess I should deal with that," Jem croaked.

Scipio responded by stretching out all four legs as far as he could and, in the process, shoving Jem out of the bed.

Jem didn't bother with pants; he just stumbled out into the living room.

"I understand that it's Mother's Day, Amos. What I don't understand is why I have to have this conversation again. I already went through the whole thing with Miriam. I've got some personal stuff that came up. I'm not coming to brunch. Mom will be fine; she'll understand." Tean listened, and then his whole body stiffened, and he shoved his hair back with his free hand. "Just because I don't have children doesn't mean I don't have personal stuff—"

"We're going," Jem said. It was more of a cough, so he cleared his throat again and said, "We're going."

Tean glanced over and shook his head. He waved for Jem to go back in the bedroom.

Instead, Jem stripped out of his grandma t-shirt and knelt in front of the duffel. "Tell them we're going," he said as he dug out fresh clothes.

"No," Tean whispered. Then, into the phone, "I'm hanging up now, Amos. I've already explained myself twice. Don't you dare tell Dad—"

"Teanthony Maharajah Leon," Jem said. Holding his *DuckTales* tee in one hand, a fresh pair of boxer briefs in the other, he said, "Tell them we're going, or I'll rip that phone out of your hand and tell them I'm hanging up so I can give you a blow job."

"You're not well," Tean whispered.

"Well enough to give a blow job."

"You wouldn't dare." Then, into the phone, "I don't have to explain why a single man is so busy he can't honor his mother the one day of the—"

Jem reached for the phone. Tean planted a hand on his chest and forced him away. Jem reached again. He had longer arms.

"Fine," Tean shouted, and it wasn't clear if it was meant for Jem or for Amos. "Fine. We're coming. I'm bringing a friend. Goodbye."

He disconnected the call and dropped the phone on the rug. His other hand was still warm against Jem's bare chest.

"There," Jem said, "that wasn't so hard, was it?"

"You are a pain in my butt," Tean said, forcing Jem out of his path. "And your beard is gross and still has fry salt in it."

When Jem checked in the bathroom mirror, he realized Tean was right.

By the time they'd both showered and gotten ready, it was time to leave for brunch—with Scipio along for the ride. Jem was swimming under a couple more Xanax again, and Tean kept throwing him looks as they drove south on I-15. It was Sunday, which meant traffic was light. The sky was a vibrant blue, empty of clouds, and the valley's bowl was full of spring sunlight. Tean's parents lived in South Jordan; Jem thought he remembered that the

Mormon temple was visible from the freeway, but now glass-sided office buildings and a redbrick hotel stood in the way. Progress. The sacred valley getting plowed under and built over with Gentile money. At least they had Starbucks now.

Like so many areas in suburban Utah, South Jordan was a mix of incomes and styles. One street might have half-million-dollar homes with immaculately groomed lawns; the next might have matchbox constructions from the 1950s, with asbestos siding and a patchy mix of dirt and weeds for the yard. Tean's parents lived in one of those houses. Wire fencing enclosed a lawn that was mostly weeds. The tiny house had vinyl siding that sagged in places and, in others, was chipped and broken. The windows were probably original; they looked thin enough to shatter if Jem sneezed on them. Six cars were parked in front of the house: four were squeezed into the driveway, bumper to bumper, and two more were on the street. Tean parked, and then he said, "This is a bad idea."

"It's fine."

"No, it's not."

"Are they going to burn me for being a fag?"

"No."

"Are they going to ask me if I'm the one who turned you queer?"

"No."

"Are they going to ignore me?"

"Unfortunately, no."

"So what are they going to do?"

Tean sighed. "They're going to be nice."

As soon as they were inside the fenced yard, Tean undid Scipio's harness, and the Lab shot around to the back of the house. Tean headed for the front door. He didn't knock; he just walked into the house, beckoning Jem after him, and it was like walking into a hurricane. Children were everywhere. Twin boys were jumping on the back of an expensive-looking leather sectional, while a third boy tried to join them, but they kept pushing him back down. A girl ran through the room screaming, while a slightly older girl chased her. A chunky toddler sat near an end table, one pudgy fist wrapped around an electrical cord that led to a lamp. He kept yanking on the cord while he wailed, and the lamp skittered closer and closer. Maybe it would be like a cartoon, Jem thought from deep inside his bubble. In cartoons, characters were always getting lamps broken on their heads.

"Jeez," Tean said. "Grab Ricky before he brains himself." He waved at the toddler without waiting for a response and circled around the sectional, shouting, "Aiden, Liam, get your butts off that couch right now, and quit being mean to Lucas. I don't care if he's younger. Nope, get down before I swat you. Uh uh, absolutely no twin talk. You heard me. Backyard. Now. And take Lucas."

Jem observed all of this while bending to get the toddler. He slowly loosened the pudgy fingers from around the cord, and then he picked up the kid and held him with his arms straight out.

"Look," Jem said. "You don't bite me, and I won't bite you."

The toddler's gaze focused on Jem, and he shrieked even louder.

Tean, meanwhile, had turned his attention to the girls. "Izzy, Emma, no running in Grandma and Grandpa's house. Where are the adults? Ok. Then go outside. Yes, right now. Yes, I brought Scipio." The girls shrieked with excitement, reversed course, and disappeared.

The toddler was screaming even louder.

"Um, Tean?"

"Well, don't hold him like he's a watermelon you're thinking about buying," Tean said. He went to one of the doors, pushed it open, and said, "No jumping on the beds. You know that. Tyslie, help Afton get down safely. No, no, no. Turn around and help her like I told you to. Ok. Outside. Right now."

"Tean?" Jem said a little louder.

But the doc was moving to check the next room. "Glade, put down that knife. Right now! You know you aren't supposed to touch Grandpa's stuff. Where did you put his fly rod? Nope, put it back where it goes. Come here, I have to pat you down." Tean squatted, patting down an eleven-year-old and producing a stainless-steel lighter and a folding knife. "Ok, now you can go tell everyone how mean I am."

The toddler was shrieking and kicking his pudgy legs.

"What are you doing to him?" Tean said.

"My arms are about to give out."

"Well, why are you holding him straight out from your body? Here, give him to me." Tean took the toddler and tucked him up against his shoulder. He whispered something in the boy's ear, stroked his back, and the boy settled into a steady, whining cry, obviously telling Tean how he'd been mistreated. Tean just kept rubbing his back. "Haven't you ever held a kid before?"

"No."

"But you were in foster care. I know you took care of the other kids."

"Never a kid that young. And all I did was make sure they had food. Sometimes clothes, I guess. It's not like—well, it wasn't like this."

"Nothing's like this," Tean said, glancing around the now silent room. "Except maybe hell."

Ricky gave an offended little warble.

"I know," Tean said. "I'm sorry. Come on, you might as well meet the rest of them. Believe it or not, that was the easy part."

Jem examined the house as they moved through it. The two doors that Tean had opened led into small rooms. One was a craft room with twin beds jammed up against the walls. The other looked like a den: an armchair, a flat-screen TV, trophy fish mounted on the walls, and various types of hunting, fishing, and camping gear in varying states of organization. They passed a bathroom and headed into the kitchen, which was galley style and barely big enough for the eat-in table that was pushed to one side. A woman was standing at the sink, drying her hands. Next to her rested a big bowl of fruit salad. An older man with lightly salted dark hair sat at the table, checking something on his phone. He was a big man, muscular, and he'd kept fit even as age advanced. He looked up and flashed a huge grin.

"Teancum," he roared, surging out of his seat to wrap Tean in a huge hug. Tean's whole body went stiff, and at first Jem thought maybe he was trying to save Ricky. The longer the hug went on, though, the more Tean's discomfort magnified. If the man hugging him noticed, he didn't give any sign of it.

"And who's this?" the man asked, releasing Tean and grabbing Jem's hand. "You must be the new boyfriend we've heard about."

"That's right," Jem said.

"No, it's not right," Tean said. "He's just a friend. His name's Jem."

"I am super gay, though," Jem said.

The man laughed. "Well, that's Linda, and I'm Robert. I'm this guy's dad." He grabbed Tean's shoulder and shook him with a good-natured excess of energy that made Tean's head wobble. "Look at this guy, already with the kids. He loves kids. Just like his sisters, this one."

Jem couldn't help it; his eyebrows shot up, but when he looked at Tean, Tean just shook his head.

"Do you need any help, Mom?" Tean said.

She offered a smile over her shoulder. "No, sweetheart."

"That's one thing this guy can't do." Robert bellowed a laugh as he clapped Tean on the shoulder again. "He can do anything his sisters can do except cook."

"What about his brothers?" Jem said.

"Leave it," Tean whispered.

Robert didn't seem to have heard. "How'd you guys meet?"

"Boy," Jem said. "That's a story."

"Come on, let's introduce you to the whole gang."

"Hold on, Robert," Linda said, drying her hands and turning to face them. "I want to say hi before you drag him off. It's very nice to meet you, Jem. Let me get a look at you."

It was easy to see how Tean had inherited a mix of his parents' features. He had gotten his Latino coloring from his father, the dark hair, the thick eyebrows, the brown skin. But he had his mother's thin build, her full lips, the delicate bones in his face and hands. Linda was still beautiful, even more so when she smiled and hugged her son and kissed his cheek. Then she took Jem's hand and shook it once.

"Pleased to meet you both," Jem said.

"Oh, he has such nice manners," Linda said to Tean. "He must have been raised right."

"He wasn't," Tean said.

Both his parents laughed.

"Come on," Robert said. "I want you to meet everybody." And before Jem could object, he had an arm around him, dragging him toward the aluminum storm door at the back of the house.

"I'll be right out," Tean said.

Behind him, Jem heard mother and son lower their voices.

"It's not as much," Tean was saying, "because I had some extra expenses."

"Oh, sweetheart," Linda said, "I promise it's just this month. They're going to turn off the gas if we don't pay."

"I know," Tean said.

"Things are really picking up for your father."

"I know."

Jem glanced back once before they reached the storm door, and he saw Linda standing with a check in her hand. And then Jem thought about when he had first met Tean, about the check register with monthly checks written out to cash in large sums, about the crappy apartment when Tean should have been able to afford better, about the crooked glasses that wouldn't stay on Tean's face, about the clearance-rack clothes, about the way Tean had shouted— shouted, when he almost never raised his voice—when Jem said something about money. And Jem knew how this game worked, knew the rules. Things were always *really picking up*. Things were always right on the edge of getting better. But this month, it was the gas. Or the water. Or the electric. Or an emergency repair for the car, because otherwise, your father won't be able to go to work. On and on and on.

Then they hit the storm door and went out into the yard.

Then the introductions. Amos, Corom, Timothy, Seth. The four brothers had more of their father's build, although Seth was closer to Tean in size. They had the same bushy eyebrows, and although they kept their hair buzzed short like their father, Jem would have bet money that it was just as wild as Tean's when it grew out. The sisters, Sara and Miriam, were night and day. Sara looked like Linda, and she'd inherited her mother's fair skin, her slender frame, and her large, sensitive eyes. Miriam was stout, with a cloud of frizzy dark hair, and out of the six siblings, she was the only one who ever laughed or smiled. There were in-laws too—wives and husbands, all safely heteronormative—and they introduced themselves as well, but something was buzzing in Jem's brain, the sound like a band saw.

Jem shook hands with everyone, and after a few awkward attempts at conversation—What do you do? Retail—the family seemed to silently decide to ignore him, and they went back to their normal rhythm. Robert talked over everyone. Sara said something about her youngest's school; Robert knew all about preschool. Timothy mentioned the deck he was rebuilding. Robert was a whiz at decks, it turned out. Amos offered an opinion on tariffs with China, and that got Robert going for almost a full five minutes. International trade? Just ask Robert. The pecking order emerged pretty clearly. Amos interrupted Corom when Corom tried to talk about electric cars. Corom interrupted Seth when Seth talked about an episode of *Ancient Aliens*. Jem watched it all from where he was swimming under the Xanax and tried to figure out why people who were born into families didn't kill themselves just to avoid this shit.

"Are you ok?" Tean asked quietly. He still had Ricky on his shoulder, and the little boy had fallen asleep.

Jem smiled and nodded. "Your dad is explaining how Chinese pork tariffs are ruining the world."

"Oh gosh."

The backyard was better kept up than the front, although the lawn was mostly weeds. A single, scrubby pine offered some shade, and window boxes with vincas gave splashes of color. The kids Tean had evicted from the house were running wild out here, and Scipio was in the middle of all of it, racing alongside the children when they ran, occasionally pausing, his whole body locking up with intense focus when one of the boys offered to throw him a ball.

On the other side of the group of adults, one of the in-laws was whispering into Sara's ear. Lou? Hugh? He was long-faced, extremely white, with straw-colored hair that lay flat over his forehead. Sara shook her head; red blotched her complexion. Then the man grabbed her arm and whispered again. She sighed, shook him off, and came around the group. Robert and Timothy were bellowing about a construction job that apparently both men had been fired from. Nobody acknowledged Sara, but everyone tracked her with guilty glances as she moved around the outside of the group until she was standing next to Tean. She gave him a quick kiss on the cheek and said, "You don't have to hold Ricky. I'll take him."

Tean's smile was sad as he passed the sleeping boy to his sister. Ricky stirred as he got comfortable against his mom.

"Sara," Hugh/Lou stage-whispered from across the group.

Sara gave an apologetic shake of her head and moved back to stand next to her husband.

"What was that?" Jem asked.

"Nothing."

"Bullshit."

"Excuse me," a mousy in-law said. She'd told Jem her name, but it was completely gone, so now he was thinking of her as Tanya from *An American Tail*. "We really don't use that kind of language. Especially around the children."

"Right," Jem said, his face heating. "Sorry."

"It's ok," Tean said. "I'm sure they hear worse at school and on TV."

"Well," said another in-law, this one with a platinum bouffant like she had just stepped out of a 70s beauty pageant, "Corom and I don't even have a TV anymore. We really feel like it's brought a better spirit into our home."

"We only use VidAngel," offered another in-law, this one with a kind of slack-eyed expression like she'd been kicked in the head by some barnyard animal. "I read the full description of the bad parts, and then we decide as a family what's appropriate and what isn't. Seth and I really believe in teaching our children correct principles so they can decide for themselves."

"What the fu—" Jem caught himself. "What's VidAngel?"

"Don't get me started," Tean said.

"If you read the description of the bad parts," Jem said, "isn't that the same as watching them?"

Slack-eye stared at him. "Um, no." She didn't add *obviously*, but it hung in the air anyway.

The group's rhythm had been broken, and now they were looking at each other, restless. Two of the little girls ran up—Jem thought they were Izzy and Emma—and they each grabbed one of Tean's hands.

"Uncle Tean, come play with us."

"Come make Scipio do a trick."

"I'm not sure—" Tean said with a glance at Hugh/Lou.

"Don't bother Uncle Tean," Hugh/Lou said. "If you want to play with him, you can do it here."

"But Scipio is in the front yard!"

"Then bring the dang dog back here. You don't need to go anywhere with Uncle Tean."

Jem kept himself from looking at Tean's face, but it was hard; his own cheeks were hot, and he found himself staring at his sneakers.

"So," said a heavyset brother-in-law with sideburns to the middle of his cheeks, "you guys are boyfriends." He looked incredibly pleased with himself and mildly surprised at his own daring. Probably thrilled he hadn't been struck down by a lightning bolt.

"No," Tean said. "Just friends."

"Best friends," Jem said, slinging an arm around Tean. The doc's shoulders were tight with tension.

"So did you, like, meet in a club?"

"Kevin!" Miriam whispered.

"Or on an app or something? I'm just asking, Mir. That's how gay guys meet these days."

"Oh my gosh," Tean said, covering his eyes.

"Definitely an app," Jem said.

"No," Tean said.

"It's called Prowler."

"Ok," Tean said, slipping out from under Tean's arm. "We're going to check on Scipio."

The dog and the children had disappeared around the house, and sounds of playing and barking were coming from the front yard now. Jem gave everyone a big gameshow smile as he followed Tean. Two of the boys—the ones who had been jumping on the couch—were tossing a ball back and forth, and Scipio was having a great time racing back and forth and scooping up the ball when one of them dropped it. Two of the older girls were trying to climb the wire fence, which sagged backward under their weight before they fell. Tean moved over to the front door and retrieved Scipio's harness from where he'd dropped it. Then he called the dog over. For the first time that Jem could remember, Scipio hesitated, as though considering a refusal.

"Hey, what are you doing?"

Tean's hands were shaking as he tried to get the harness in place. "I think we should go."

"No way. I'll be quiet, I promise. I won't make any jokes. I won't say anything dumb. Well, anything stupider than I usually say. And I won't even use bad words."

Scipio was twisting around, trying to keep his eyes on the boys, obviously desperate to sprint back to the game. Tean couldn't get the harness in place. "Damn it," he swore. "Scipio, hold still."

"Ok," Jem said, folding one of his hands around Tean's. "Don't take it out on him. Here, I'll put on the harness. Just sit back and take a few breaths."

"Really? You'll put it on?"

"Um. No, that was kind of an empty promise. But I was serious about taking a few breaths. If you still want to go in five minutes, we can go. But don't do it right now because I embarrassed you and you're upset."

"You didn't embarrass me."

"Sure I did. That's ok, though. I'll figure out how to do better."

"No," Tean said. He dropped the harness, and after a moment, Scipio bolted back to the game. "It's me. I can't even believe—"

"Come on, kids," Hugh/Lou said, waving toward the back of the house. "You don't need to be out here right now."

"Dad," one of the girls protested.

"Everybody in the backyard."

Jem shook his head.

"Where we can keep an eye on things," Hugh/Lou finished. And then, just so there wasn't any chance of missing the point, his gaze slid to Tean and Jem.

"What the actual fuck?" Jem said.

"Hugh has always been like that. Don't let it get under your skin."

"He's always been like what? Afraid the queers are going to sodomize his children in the front yard? Afraid we're going to gay them up?"

Tean shook his head. He dropped down onto the stoop, pushing his hair back with both hands. His glasses slid off his nose and landed in his lap.

"Is that why you weren't allowed to hold the kid?"

"They're just very protective."

"I'll show them protective."

"Jem."

"I'll be right back."

"Jem, don't get involved, please."

Jem jogged around to the backyard. The adults were clustered together, talking in low voices, obviously enjoying the thrill of dissecting their close call with faggotry. Corom noticed Jem first, and he elbowed Amos and said something sharp but quiet that made the others stop. They all turned toward him, all trying not to look guilty, all trying not to look like kids who'd been caught misbehaving.

"Jem," Robert said. "Is Teancum—"

"If you think he'd hurt your kids," Jem said, and he was shocked at the wave of emotion that came over him, threatening to close his throat, making his voice tight. "If you think he'd let anything happen to them, anything, then you don't know him at all, and you ought to be ashamed of yourselves. If you haven't seen how he interacts with them, how he treats them, how much he loves them, and how much they love him, then you're blind. I don't know what kind of mumbo jumbo you've been working on him, but he deserves better than that. He's the best person I've ever met."

"We love Teancum—" Robert began.

"Be quiet," Jem said, and Robert's mouth snapped shut. "Are you a fucking moron, Robert? He's not a girl. You can cut it out, comparing him to his sisters every time you open your goddamn mouth. You can just cut it out. Did the rest of you know he lives in a run-down apartment, wears cheap clothes, has glasses that won't stay on his face, because he's paying most of the bills for your parents? I didn't think so. Great. So now you can take turns. Hugh can write out next month's check; that's the price for being a bigoted, closed-minded piece of trash." Jem's chest was heaving. The glassy ocean where he'd been swimming felt far away now, and the world had come dangerously close again. "All right, I think we've covered the big talking points. If I've got any luck at all, I'll never have to see you miserable excuses for human beings again. Also, brunch smelled really good, and I think I saw a quiche." Jem could hear himself losing focus, so he flipped them double birds and jogged back to the front of the house.

Tean was standing by the gate, staring, with Scipio in his harness.

"I realize you probably never want to see me again," Jem said, "but those disposable ass plugs needed to hear that at least once."

Tean swallowed. Off in the distance, the engine of a tractor-trailer roared.

"Ok," Jem said. "I'll get out of here."

"I think," Tean said, and then he paused and licked his lips. "I think maybe I could go for some McDonald's."

Jem felt the grin exploding across his face. He tried to make his voice sound respectably butch as he said, "Well, we didn't get brunch."

"Yeah," Tean said. He sounded like he was talking from somewhere far off. "Yeah."

A neighbor family had emerged across the street, and they were singing an annoyingly lilting song that sounded like a show tune; it had something vaguely to do with mothers.

"So maybe we should go to McDonald's," Jem said.

"Yeah," Tean said.

A woman who had to be in her eighties was standing on the porch, dabbing at her eyes as she listened to her children and grandchildren and great-grandchildren singing. Jem was pretty sure he heard a few raunchy lines in the lyrics, but nobody seemed to hesitate.

"Teancum Leon," Jem finally said. "Would you please drive me to McDonald's so I can buy you breakfast?"

Tean smiled, covered his mouth, and nodded.

31

They ate McDonald's. They drove home. Scipio, exhausted, dropped onto the dog bed and immediately fell asleep.

"Be right back," Tean said, tossing his keys on the counter and heading for the bathroom.

Jem opened the sliding glass door. Spring air rushed in, smelling like the flowering trees below, like new grass, a hint of cooking onions from one of the other apartments. The sun was still high in the sky. It seemed impossible that this was the same day. Everything felt like it had shifted, like they'd fast-forwarded a hundred years. Jem glanced at the clock; it wasn't even noon.

When the door opened and Tean came out, his eyes were red.

"Oh no," Jem said.

"No, I'm ok. I just—it kind of caught up with me in there."

"I'm sorry. I know that'll be super awkward when you have to work it out."

"Don't be. Honestly, I don't know if I want to work it out. I don't even know if there's something to work out. They'll probably do what they always do. They'll wait. They'll hold out. Because I've always been the one to apologize. When I came out, I ended up having to apologize. For coming out. I mean, not in those words. But I had to apologize for how I sprang it on them. I had to apologize for not giving them enough time to process it. I had to apologize for not understanding how difficult it was for them."

"Fuck," Jem said, drawing out the word.

"More or less." Tean wiped his eyes; he was crying again, just a little, as he dropped into a dinette chair. "I think I'm done apologizing."

"Hell yes."

"What the fuck is wrong with them? I mean, really. You saw them. You met them. Just tell me what the fuck is wrong with them so I'll quit feeling like something is really fucking wrong with me."

"Nothing's wrong with you." Jem moved to stand behind Tean, putting his hands on Tean's shoulders, and began to rub small circles with his thumbs, fighting the knots he felt there. "They're just who they are. People are who they are, how they're raised, what's been put in their brains, all the way they learn to cope with being alive. And everybody wants someone to dump on. Sorry they tapped you for that, but it's over now."

"It's over."

Scipio let out a snore, and Jem continued to work on Tean's shoulders.

"Sit back," Jem said. "Try to relax. You're like iron."

"Sorry," Tean said.

"No more apologies, right?"

Tean laughed unhappily, but he settled back against Jem's touch. From outside came the sound of a window sliding open, and then a woman talking.

"He's just one of those guys who has to hold the door for you, you know? And he said I have the nicest eyelashes he's ever seen. And he loves dogs, he told me all about the dogs he grew up with, but he can't have dogs now because of his apartment, and I said, well, I can have dogs at my apartment, because, you know, I wanted him to start thinking about the possibility at least." Her runaway narrative was interrupted by an enormous laugh, and she said, "Mama, I didn't see his penis, so I don't know."

"Please never move," Jem whispered.

This time, Tean's laugh sounded more natural. Quiet, yes, but closer to normal. When he spoke, his voice was quiet too, as though he were testing ice underfoot. "Do you know why families are such a big deal for Mormons? Theologically, I mean."

"Families are forever," Jem said. "I picked that up the few times I got dragged to church."

"That's right. Families are forever. Individuals, for Mormons, are incomplete. You're not a full human being until you're packaged with someone else and pumping out babies. Eternally. That's their idea of heaven: this unending existence of creating spirit children."

"Christ, sounds awful if you have a uterus."

"I guess it might. Women have always been second-class citizens. They can't hold any positions of real importance. They can't be priests or bishops, prophets or apostles. Motherhood is the sop they get instead, so there's all this rhetoric about how every woman is a mother, and motherhood is this sacred trust that men wouldn't be worthy of, and how women are so much purer by nature."

"Have any Mormon women ever had an orgasm?"

A laugh exploded out of Tean. "Gosh, I hope so. It's all about family. We're all one human family going back to Adam. Eternal families. Creating families. And, of course, fags can't have families."

"I know you want to talk this out," Jem said, "but maybe you should give yourself some time to get some distance from what happened today."

"No. No, I'm not even talking about it the right way. I'm not even saying what I want to say. I guess . . . I guess I'm trying to tell you what it's supposed to be, and then I want to tell you what it's like."

"Ok."

"There's this fantasy of transparency that's tied up with being a family. Your parents are supposed to have special, divinely given insight into who you are. And then that percolates throughout the whole institution. Your spiritual leaders are supposed to have the same divine insight into who you are. And you have to go through these interviews where you're asked all sorts of personal questions, and supposedly the bishop will know if you're lying. And you get up every month and bear testimony of the spiritual knowledge you've received, and that's supposed to be a form of transparency too, your soul exposed to the community. And the most important part is that God knows you too. Elements of the same fantasy exist in most religions, I guess: there is something greater than you, and it knows you, the real you. Before I formed you in the womb. The Lord looketh on the heart. If anyone loves God, he is known by God. That kind of thing, you know?"

Jem didn't know, but he rubbed Tean's shoulders.

"And the end of all that transparency, the paradisiacal existence under Christ's millennial reign, is supposed to be Zion: when all the righteous will be of one heart and one mind. That's the ultimate fantasy. Not only are we known, but we're one. Seen and loved and bound together. That's why the most extreme punishment in so many religions is excommunication: being cut off from family, from community, from God." Tean shook his head. He was looking off at something Jem couldn't see, something Jem couldn't even glimpse. "Of course, if you're gay, you probably never felt like you belonged. If you're gay, then your whole life, you're lying, and this doubt keeps building: why haven't they caught me yet? How can they not know? And then you realize they don't know you. They don't know anything about you. You realize that you'll never share one heart and one mind with anybody. There's nothing in the universe that knows you, nothing that sees inside. Maybe there's nothing in there to be seen, just neurons going off like fireworks. We're never known, never seen. The glass stays dark. You realize even your family doesn't know you; maybe especially not your family, and they're supposed to be the litmus test, the spiritual nucleus of the universe. You figure out it's all bullshit—the sanctity of families, the divine calling of motherhood. Mothers cannibalize their children. Fathers chain their daughters up in basements and rape them for decades. Family is just biology; it's nothing magical or special or sacred unless you make it that way."

"Is that really what you believe?" Jem asked, his hands tightening on Tean's shoulders.

"I don't know. Sartre would say that family is one of the past determinants that rarely tells us anything about the choices we're most interested in. The really big decisions, in other words. The ones that matter. He would say we have to look elsewhere for answers. And he would say otherwise we're abdicating our responsibility to make choices. Existence precedes essence. We have to determine who we are through our choices."

"But did Sartre's parents thoroughly mindfuck him?" Jem asked.

"He was a philosopher, so probably." Tean reached back, resting his hand on Jem's, and Jem stopped massaging. "For existentialists, the world is absurd. We want meaning, but the world is chaotic and random, and it defies our demands for rational, reasonable explanations. And part of the absurdity is that we are irreparably alienated. We're strangers to each other, strangers to the world. But we're also strangers to ourselves."

"Crypsis," Jem said; his smile felt crooked.

"Yeah. Yeah, I hadn't thought about it that way. Maybe that's the human condition, that inability to know or be known. The ultimate evolutionary defense mechanism against meaninglessness. Maybe we keep ourselves safe by being hidden even from ourselves. Sartre would like that, I think. He said the authentic life was so terrifyingly free that most people chose an inauthentic life rather than face it."

Jem combed his fingers through Tean's hair.

"I don't even know why I let them treat me that way." Tean's voice broke at the end. "If you put me in a room with anybody else in the world, I wouldn't put up with that."

"I know."

"It's humiliating, and it's worse that you saw."

"Stop it, Tean. You need to stop thinking like that right now."

"But the really bad part, the awful part, is I don't know why I let it happen. I don't know why I let it go on like that for all these years. I'll talk to strangers about how well my family and I get along. I tell my friends. Ask Hannah—well, if she weren't in jail you could ask her. Jeez. How in the fuck am I supposed to understand anything when I don't even understand myself?"

Jem squeezed the back of his neck lightly, and then he said, "You're doing an awful lot of swearing, and I appreciate that you're rapidly filling up our Disneyworld fund, but right now, you're overthinking things."

Tean shook his head.

"Yes, you are. You need to get out of your own head." Jem took out his phone and tapped it. Music started. A good beat, chill melody. Jem let his hand slide down Tean's arm, and he took him by the hand and pulled him to his feet.

Tean shook his head again.

"I believe you told me I'm very white," Jem said, guiding Tean's hands to his hips. "So you'll probably have to help out."

Tean was starting to cry, but he sniffed and tried to smile. Jem brought their foreheads together. After a moment, Tean adjusted their rhythm, and Jem could feel it, feel how they met each other, how they met the music. He could feel the spring air, cool on the back of his neck. He could feel Tean, the wiry lines of his body, his warmth, the tiny tremors as his crying slowed. He could feel something he'd never felt, never in his whole life, before meeting this man.

"I like this song," Tean said.

"DJ Khaled," Jem said. "'I'm The One.'"

A beat passed, and Tean whispered, "I think you are."

Then the song ended, and "Monster Mash" came on.

Tean fell back against the table, laughing. "What in the world is this?"

"It's 'Monster Mash.' What do you mean, what is it?" Jem grabbed his phone, but Tean had a huge smile on his face, so Jem let the music keep playing. "You've never heard 'Monster Mash' before?"

"Of course I have. Just not on Mother's Day."

"Well, I made this playlist in October. It's the perfect song for dancing with friends."

"What if I don't want to be friends?"

Jem laid his phone down.

"What if I don't want to be normal friends," Tean asked, "or regular friends or best friends? Not anymore."

"Then you should probably come over here and kiss me."

Tean nodded.

"Glasses," Jem said.

Tean caught them before they fell and laid them on the table. Then he stepped forward. His hand found Jem's arm, his fingers tentative, tracing Jem. "I don't want to mess things up."

"We've already messed things up plenty of times."

"I don't want to lose you."

"You're stalling," Jem said, "because you think I'm going to kiss you first if you hold out long enough."

A tiny smile darted across Tean's face. He tilted his head and kissed Jem. Then he broke away.

"Look at that," Jem breathed. "Nuclear winter didn't happen. Nobody murdered a herd of sea cows. The dog didn't explode."

Tean's hand came to rest over Jem's heart. Jem was breathing faster, his vision blurring. Tean kissed him again, and this time, Jem couldn't stop himself: he wrapped his arms around Tean. He pulled the doc against him, ignoring Tean's squeak of surprise. This was how it was supposed to be—the way they fit together, the smell of the high plains grasses in Tean's hair, those full lips soft under his own, the taste of his mouth. The sensation sent cracks spiderwebbing through the ice that Jem had buried himself under, and everything he'd tried not to feel came rushing in.

When Tean broke the next kiss, his hands fumbled with Jem's waistband.

"Hold on," Jem said.

"I don't need to hold on. We've done this before. We're good at this." Tean hesitated and smiled—afraid and still hoping, the combination that seemed to sum up the doc. "Right?"

"Definitely. But give me a minute. Just one minute." Jem pecked him with another kiss and stepped back, loosening Tean's hands from his clothes. Then he sprinted to the bathroom. When he'd shut the door behind him, he leaned on the counter, taking huge breaths. He didn't understand why it was all happening now. He couldn't have said y because of x, b because of a, I'm crying because he kissed me, and because he loves me, and because I don't know if anyone has ever loved me in my whole life. He couldn't have even said that it was all tied up with Brigitte Berger Fitzpatrick, with two towheaded kids, with an inflatable swimming pool and a house where they felt safe and protected and loved. He just knew it was all hitting him at once, a tidal wave of emotion crashing over him, the undertow dragging him out to sea. He opened the mirrored cabinet and shook out two Xanax and placed them under his tongue.

"Jem? Are you ok?"

"Just peeing."

A moment passed. "Really?"

"Yes. Yep. Be right out." Jem ran the water for a minute, although he wasn't sure he was fooling anyone. Then he turned it off and opened the door.

At the same time, a knock came at the front door. Scipio shot up from his bed, his head whipping around, barking a warning. Tean stood up from the couch and took a few steps toward the door.

"Don't," Jem said.

Tean stopped and looked back. "What?"

"Don't open that door."

"Why? Who is it?"

"Just don't open it. Please. We'll ignore it. We'll go into the bedroom and shut the door, and we'll ignore it."

"Jem, what's going on?"

"Please don't answer the door. Please. This can all still be good. This is perfect, right now. We can be happy." Jem had trouble with the next word; he couldn't get enough air, and the glassy weight of the benzos was crashing down on him. "Please."

"It's ok," Tean said, smiling softly. "It's probably just Mrs. Wish."

When he opened the door, though, it was Ammon. He was in joggers and a BYU t-shirt, and he was smiling as he waved a measuring cup. His gaze moved around the apartment. Scipio had gone berserk, his legs locked, barking ferociously. Jem was frozen in the bathroom doorway. Ammon's eyes slid over him, taking him in like he was nothing—a piece of furniture, another of Tean's pets like Scipio.

"Hi," Ammon said to Tean, flashing a smile. "How about that sugar?"

Tean laughed. "What?" He shifted his weight. "Ammon, it's not that I don't want to see you, but what are you doing here?"

Jem watched it all play out in his head. He tried to figure out how to stop what was coming next, but he was too tired.

"Ok, it's a lame joke," Ammon said. "I just wanted to say hi."

"Hi," Tean said.

Outside, sprinklers came to life, hissing, and someone swore and said, "No, not that one, the other one." Then the sound of sprinklers died.

"It's just not a very good time," Tean finally said. "Can we talk later?"

The worst part was that Ammon looked genuinely hurt. "You're just going to pretend—what? That this isn't happening? That I didn't do this for us? I'm not saying you have to jump up and down and celebrate, but a little acknowledgment would be nice."

"You came over here, ok? I don't know why. No, I think I know why. And I told you I'm not going to do that with you anymore while you're married."

"I came over here, Tean, because you haven't said one word about me moving into the building. You won't even admit that it happened. Maybe that doesn't seem important to you, but it's important to me. I want to at least hear you validate me on that."

Outside, the woman was continuing her instructions: "Yep, that's the switch. Now turn it off again."

Turn it off, Jem thought. Turn it all off. Where's the master switch to turn this shitshow off?

"What do you mean you moved into the building?"

Ammon drew a breath and then froze. His gaze cut toward Jem. And then, slowly, Tean turned. The look on his face was that of a man who'd already stepped off a cliff and was just now realizing it.

"Make him go away," Jem said, "and I can explain."

"Explain what?" Tean asked.

"I can explain. I can explain. Just—just tell him to leave, and I can explain."

"Explain what?" Then a spasm contracted Tean's face, and he said, "Scipio, shut up!"

The dog whined and curled up on his bed.

"I live here," Ammon said. "I moved into this building to be close to you, so we could try to do things right. I left you a note. I left you a key. I wanted you to have time to process it before we talked about it, which is why I didn't call."

"I don't understand," Tean said quietly.

"It's simple. He was here that day; I saw him in the parking lot. He came upstairs. He found the note. He destroyed it. What'd you do with the key?"

"I don't understand," Tean said, blinking rapidly and then dashing one hand across his eyes. "I don't understand."

"It's simple," Ammon said again. "He did this."

But that wasn't what Tean meant, of course. And, of course, Ammon hadn't understood what Tean was saying. Had never understood. But Jem did. Jem knew that what Tean was really saying was, *I don't understand how you could do this to me again.*

And Jem couldn't bear the look on Tean's face. He grabbed his sneakers, his wallet, his keys, and his phone. He jammed a finger against the screen until the music stopped. Then he made himself look at Tean and say, "You deserve better than him."

"Get out," Tean said.

"You don't believe me, not yet. But you're starting to realize it. Part of you has always known you deserve better than this."

"Get out of my apartment right now."

"And you deserve better than somebody like me too."

For a moment, it looked like Tean was about to cry. Then he nodded and said, "Yeah. I do."

It hurt so much that anger was the only defense. Jem dropped his sneakers. He tossed his wallet and keys and phone on the table. Pulling the rental application from his back pocket, where he'd carried it since the day Tean had left it for him, he said, "Good. Good. Glad you figured that out. Because it was fucking unbearable having to deal with all your Boy Scout bullshit. Do you have any idea how demeaning it is to be your fucking charity case?"

Ammon surged forward, but Tean caught his shirt. "You need to go," Tean said to Jem. "Right now."

"Do you even know how stupid you are sometimes? Cosigning something for me? Jesus, do you know how easy you are as a mark? I could have gotten you to cosign a car. I could have gotten you to cosign a house. Fuck, Tean. Open your fucking eyes." Jem ripped the rental application into pieces, letting them flake down to the floor. He was vaguely aware of something else that had fallen, another piece of white paper that had slipped out of his pocket, but he was too focused on this moment to give it any attention. "I did you a favor, throwing his note away, because you're too goddamn stupid to look out for yourself. I did you a favor, making it so you didn't have to choose. And here's the last favor I'm ever going to do you: I'm cutting you some slack from your own fucking stupidity." He dusted the last scraps of the application from his hands. "You're welcome."

"Anything else you want to say?" Tean asked.

"I think that's it."

"Goodbye, Jem."

"Yeah. Fuck both of you. I hope you're fucking miserable together."

Grabbing the essentials again, Jem bulled toward the door. At the last moment, Ammon lunged, but Tean just forced him out of the way, giving Jem a clear path to the door. Then he was outside, the hall carpet rough under his bare feet. The door slammed shut behind him. Jem hopped into his sneakers, stumbled down to the bike, and drove.

32

Tean spent the rest of Sunday in a blur. It took a long time to get Ammon to leave, in spite of the litany of therapist talk—*What I'm hearing is that you want some time alone. Is that right?* Yes, Tean wanted to answer, yes that's right, and if you're hearing it so fucking clearly, then why are you still in my fucking living room? Then, once Ammon was gone, he went into a frenzy of activity: starting a load of laundry, mostly Jem's clothes; a long walk with Scipio, whose feelings were still hurt from the way Tean had shouted; then finishing laundry, folding clean clothes, setting Jem's aside. He was packing Jem's clothes in the duffel when he touched plastic and pulled out a baggie full of pills. When he searched on the computer, he learned that they were clomiphene citrate, and he wondered what Jem was doing with fertility meds. Another scam. Another lie. Another way to cheat people who needed hope.

It was near the end of this frenzy that he found a credit card notification, and his first thought was that this was another scam, another way Jem had found to steal from people who weren't as clever as him. Tean spotted the name, Brigitte Berger Fitzpatrick, right as he was going to throw away the paper. He thought of how suddenly Jem's behavior had changed, the terrifying pain under the dope in his eyes. Then he curled up on the couch and cried until Scipio climbed up next to him and licked his face.

He must have slept because he woke in the dark. He walked and fed Scipio, and then he drove out to Wasatch Hollow, to Hannah's parents' house, and pounded on Howard and Virgie's front door. He was shouting something, although he didn't know what. The lights were on inside, and footsteps moved, but the door didn't open. Then Virgie's face floated in the glass, a phantasm. Air and ether. She had a phone to her ear, and when she hung up, Tean's phone buzzed. Ammon's name showed on the screen. He dismissed the call.

Next, he went to Heber. After parking the truck on a dark stretch of road, he retrieved a length of nylon rope from the back of the cab. A loop with a two-half hitch, nothing fancy. Normally he would have used a catch pole, but he thought about a hundred ways things might go wrong, and a catch pole might point back at him. He walked a quarter mile to Zalie's farm, and then he picked a spot on the east side of the barn where the shadows were thickest and waited. He wasn't sure if it would be tonight, but if not tonight, he'd come back again, and again, and again.

The footsteps broke the silence two hours later. Tean had learned from Jem, and he waited until the person was busy trying to force open the door on the barn. Inside, the pigs stirred, making noises of distress and warning. It was hard to gauge distance in the darkness. Tean got as close as he could, and then kicked out with one foot. He connected with the back of the man's knee, and he staggered and dropped onto his other knee. Tean tossed his improvised lasso over the man's head and yanked on the nylon rope. The knot drew tight. The man rocked back, making choking noises. This was still the moment of surprise, and Tean still had the advantage. Tean kicked wildly, aiming low. Several times he caught the man in the back. When he fell, Tean climbed on top of him, pinning him to the ground.

"Hold still," Tean said, no longer caring about quiet. He jerked on the rope. "Stop it, or I'll let you asphyxiate."

With what must have taken a great deal of effort, the man stilled, and Tean loosened the rope. The man took a shuddering breath. His voice was rough when he said, "What the fuck—"

"Be quiet." Tean dug out a penlight and turned it on. John Sievers squinted into the light. Grabbing a handful of his short hair, Tean forced his face away. "You've been coming around the farm for weeks now, haven't you? You're the one Zalie keeps hearing prowling around out here."

"Fuck you, you fucking psycho, I'm going to—"

Sievers bucked before he had finished, trying to catch Tean off guard and throw him off. Tean just yanked on the rope, and after a few moments, Sievers collapsed again, making those horrible choking noises.

This time when Tean loosened the rope, he said, "Do that again, and I'll leave you here. They'll chalk it up to autoerotic asphyxiation. I'll make sure of it."

Sievers was breathing raggedly.

"Do you understand me?"

"Yes."

"You've been coming around here at night. Is that right?"

It took longer this time, but Sievers said, "Yes."

"For the afterbirth."

"Yes. Fuck, get this fucking rope off me, I can't breathe."

"And you've been using the afterbirth to bait your traps. That's how you're catching so many coyotes."

The breeze off the mountains whistled through the night. Tean tugged lightly on the rope.

"Yes, fine. I watch the sows, keep track of how many are carrying. I wait until I know they've farrowed. The dykes just bury the afterbirth; they don't even want it. I can use it. It's not like it's a crime."

"Actually, you've committed several crimes. I want to know if murder is one of them."

"Get off me."

"Did you kill Joy Erickson?"

"You're fucking insane. Do you realize that? When I'm done with you, there won't be enough left for the cops to put in a matchbox. I'm going to—"

Again, he bucked. This time, Tean wasn't prepared. Sievers threw him clear, and Tean rolled across the scrub and dirt. The flashlight flew out of his hand, glass cracked, night swept back in. He could hear Sievers wheezing, getting to his feet. Tean scrambled upright and got his back to the barn. Everything was swallowed up by the darkness. His heartbeat was so loud that he lost track of Sievers's breathing. Adrenaline made Tean shake. He took a step, as silent as he could. Then another. The uneven boards of the barn dug into his back. The pigs were squealing.

When he reached the end of the structure, he turned and ran. He couldn't tell if Sievers followed. He got to the truck, threw himself inside, and jammed the key into the ignition. Tires squealed; the stink of burning rubber filled the cab as he peeled out. He drove blind until he was out of the valley, and then he pulled onto the shoulder and slumped there, shaking, his clothes sweat-soaked and gritty with dirt.

Eventually he stopped shaking enough that he could drive. He got home. He slept a handful of hours and woke before dawn, Scipio draped halfway over him, the Lab snoring contentedly. Tean worked his way free, cleaned up in the bathroom, and made tea. He carried it out to the balcony. Peppermint steam wafted up to him, and the mug was warm between his hands, the ceramic smooth and glossy with the reflected light from the street. The mountains were a vast presence in his mind, but he found himself replaying that afternoon in the Heber Valley, the look of wonder on Jem's face when he saw the coyote, really saw it, the way everything had suddenly opened onto something else, something greater.

When the tea was cold, he went inside and poured it down the drain. He took a walk with Scipio. When they got back, he fed the Lab and poured himself a bowl of Cookie Crisp. He stirred it around, tried a few bites, and wondered how anybody could eat the stuff. And then he thought that he should stop buying milk, stop buying cereal, because Ammon wasn't going to eat this stuff. Ammon probably ate something hearty and responsible for breakfast like steel-cut oats and fresh fruit, maybe a protein shake to round things out. That was good. Tean needed to learn how to eat like that. He knew Ammon liked him thin, but there was such a thing as too thin, and Tean was straddling the line. Yes, he thought as he poured the uneaten cereal down the disposal. Yes, steel-cut oats and fresh fruit and protein shakes. No Cookie Crisp. No Lucky Charms. No McDonald's.

When he got to work, he had to face the fact that he'd been letting things slide. He looked at Miguel's reports on the coyote population along the Wasatch Back, including Heber, and made a plan to have a conversation with Miguel. The canine distemper outbreak was serious, as was the threat to the kit fox population, and Tean thought he could use it as an excuse to get onto Sievers's land, nominally to look for affected animals. It would also be a chance to look for the black bear that Sievers purportedly kept. Maybe Jem and Tean could search one part of the property while Miguel —

No, Tean thought, tapping out the email slowly. Of course not. Not like that, anyway.

He looked at a report from the Bureau of Land Management on wild horse populations in the state. The federal agency oversaw huge swaths of Utah, and a ranger had reported several tourists being injured when they got too close to a mustang. Now a BLM bureaucrat wanted to know what the Utah Division of Wildlife Resources was going to do about it. Tean decided to pretend to ignore the bureaucratic side of the problem and, instead, think about some realistic solutions. Better educational programs, maybe. Was it possible to teach a federal bureaucrat how to pull his head out of his butt? That sounded like it needed some serious funding.

The next email took up the rest of his morning: a poultry farm along the Idaho border had reported an outbreak of avian influenza, which spread like wildfire and could quickly get into wildlife populations. Tean had to coordinate with inspectors, officials from the Utah Department of Agriculture and Food as well as the United States Department of Agriculture, the farm's owners, and, of course, his own conservation officers.

By the time he'd gotten things in motion, his head was hurting pretty bad and he felt spacey. He wasn't sure when he'd eaten last—possibly McDonald's with Jem, the day before, but that felt like another lifetime—and he realized he probably needed food. He passed Hannah's office, which was still dark. He had the brief thought that he might dig through her files and find something that would give him new insight into the case, but of course, the police had already searched everything, and he couldn't imagine what he might find.

He drove to Rancherito's, ordered a breakfast burrito in the drive-thru, and ate it in the parking lot. He had his window down, and the air smelled clean, the seared meat fragrance drifting over from the restaurant, a hint of the asphalt warming in the sun. He kept turning the puzzle around in his mind. Brigitte Berger Fitzpatrick. Tean's initial thought had been that she was Jem's mother, but now he could imagine other possibilities: a sister that Jem hadn't known about—or hadn't told Tean about—or an aunt, a cousin, a grandmother.

I did you a favor, Jem had said. *You're too goddamn stupid to look out for yourself.*

There was a perverse kind of logic there. Jem had a narrow but fierce protective streak. It had originally only included Benny, his foster brother. When Benny had died, that protectiveness had transferred to Tean. Tean had noticed it in a million ways: Jem checking to see if he was eating, Jem calling if Tean had to travel for work, Jem pacing around the apartment and muttering about security. Tean had found it mostly gratifying and only occasionally annoying. He could see how Jem might have thought he was protecting Tean by destroying the note, although Tean didn't like to follow that train of thought, didn't like to consider why Jem might think Ammon was dangerous or why Tean could, at the edge of consciousness, understand that assessment.

What held Tean's attention, though, was that Jem must have known at some level that he'd be caught. And that hadn't mattered. What had mattered was keeping someone safe. Tean didn't like what Jem had done, and he didn't approve of it or condone it. But he was starting to understand it. And while Jem undoubtedly acted out of a mix of motives, not all of them pure, the bottom line was that he had done something stupid, knowing he would pay for it down the line, to push danger away for a few more minutes. It was the way, Tean intuited, you might live if you had always faced danger day to day. A few more minutes were what mattered, not the big picture, definitely not the distant future.

And then Tean understood something else. The baggie of stolen clomiphene. Sievers watching the sows. He keyed the ignition, crammed the last of the burrito in his mouth, and headed south and east. The Salt Lake County Jail was located about ten minutes from Tean's office in the Division of Wildlife Resources. Both the jail and the sheriff's department, which shared a lot, could have passed for commercial office buildings. The sheriff's building was pale stone and glass that was blue with the reflected sky. The jail lacked windows, but it otherwise followed the same design. Tean found a parking space and jogged up to the building.

He hadn't been sure if Hannah's unit—pod, as they were called at the county jail—would have visiting hours that day, but he was in luck. He showed his ID, stowed his belongings in a locker, passed through a metal inspector, and then endured a pat-down because his glasses had triggered the alarm.

After that, he had to wait almost half an hour, his butt going numb on the hard bench. Voices echoed against the cement, making the space seem vast, and the air smelled like disinfectant and metal.

When a corrections officer opened a door and said, "Teancum Leon," he shot up from the bench, winced, and limped toward the opening.

They led him into a narrow room like the ones he'd seen on the bad movies Jem made him watch: a row of seats with stainless-steel partitions, and a glass barrier separating the inmates from the visitors. Instead of phones, the glass was perforated in places to allow voices to carry. Signs taped to each partition reminded visitors and inmates alike that YOU ARE NOT THE ONLY ONE IN THIS ROOM – PLEASE KEEP THE VOLUME DOWN! – PRIVACY IS NOT GUARANTEED. The CO directed Tean to one of the partitions, and Tean sat on a padded stool. The bad movies had gotten some of it right, but not the human element. Not the way every exhalation sounded trapped and echoing between the partitions and the glass. Not the smudges on the stainless steel. Not the tiny rip in the stool's upholstery, right where the vinyl met the chrome banding, where who knew how many people had picked at it restlessly during visits. Even the tape on the sign had been worried and peeled away in places.

Then Hannah came into view on the other side of the glass. She still looked like Hannah, with her mop of chestnut-colored hair, her intelligent eyes, all the familiar freckles and sunspots. She wore a loose blue shirt and blue trousers, both of them faintly resembling scrubs, although both were printed with SALT LAKE COUNTY JAIL. She smiled, a nervous twisting of her lips, as she dropped onto the seat.

"I wasn't sure I should talk to you."

"I should have come sooner."

She shook her head. "If you had, I definitely wouldn't have talked to you. My lawyer said she didn't want me talking to anyone except Caleb."

"What changed?"

"Well, she ought to spend a few days in here herself. Most of the women are in here for drugs, a few for fraud, only a couple for anything close to violence. I think they robbed a gas station with a pair of water pistols. I'm the badass of the bunch. The crazy hatchet lady."

"You've always been a badass." Tean leaned closer. "Are you ok?"

She shook her head and a tear escaped, but she said, "Yeah. I am. I don't even feel unsafe, if you can believe that. I just don't want to be here. I can't figure out how it came to this. I can't figure out how I got here. My brain—something's wrong with my brain, Tean. I can't even think straight anymore."

"I couldn't ever think straight."

A real smile flickered in and out.

"You're under a lot of stress," Tean said, "and your brain is coping, trying to protect you. Once we've got you out of here, you'll be back to normal. Jem would say something about how you'll be kissing June suckers, I think."

Another of those lightning-flash smiles. Then Hannah said, "And I can tell by your face that you screwed everything up with him again, didn't you? Friends my butt. How long did you think you were both going to be able to keep pretending?"

"A long time, I hoped. Long enough for me to figure things out."

"And what happened?"

He told her, and she nodded and offered an occasional, "Sorry," or, "Oh, Tean," that was half frustration and half commiseration. When he'd finished, he said, "I understand some of why he did it. I have guesses about the rest of it."

"I don't think you should be looking for reasons to excuse that kind of behavior. It's a really unhealthy sign of jealousy."

"From the outside, I guess it looks like that. But I don't think that's what it is. Ok, ok, don't get revved up. I know he's jealous. But I honestly don't think that's why he did what he did. And it'll take too long to explain all of it. Once you're out of here, you can hunt him down. You terrify him, just so you know."

"Well," Hannah said, crossing her arms and looking vaguely pleased with herself, "good."

"Hannah, who are you protecting?"

She shook her head. "I'm not going to talk about the case with you, Tean. I wanted to see you because—because you're you, and I love you, and I miss you. But I won't talk about it."

"Ok. How about I talk? The Hannah I know wouldn't hurt anyone. And you can make a face, and you can pretend I don't know you well enough, and you can hide behind a few reckless things you did when you were young. You're letting Zalie string out the rope they're going to hang you with; she's telling a story about you calling to plead with Joy, and the Kneaders video seems to back that up. It looks like she was blackmailing you, and you decided to get rid of her. But that's not what was happening. And I think I know why you're doing this, who you're trying to protect, but I want you to be the one to say it. I don't want to take it away from you."

Hannah shook her head again. She was crying now.

"This isn't protecting Caleb from anything," Tean said. "You don't know how badly this is hurting him."

She drew in a shaky breath and said, "I messed up. I really, really messed up. And now I'm in too deep, and I'm going to lose him, or I'm going to go to prison, and then I'll lose him anyway."

"I love you. And Caleb loves you. And you've got to trust that both of you are going to make it through this. But you can't do that if you're lying to him. Even if you think it's to protect him."

She put her fingers to her temples and added, "I can't do this."

"When did you get the abortion?"

Hannah went very still.

"I'm not asking why you did it," Tean said, "and I'm not asking you to justify it or defend yourself. It's your body. It's your choice. You know I support you. But I need to know when."

"Monday," she said in a faint whisper. "The sixteenth. After I met Joy at the Kneaders."

Tean let out a breath he hadn't realized he was holding.

"How did you know?" Hannah asked.

"It was a guess," Tean said. "A lot of little things that added up."

"I'd called her when—when I realized I couldn't do it. Have the baby. She'd had an abortion a long time ago. She was the only person I knew who might understand. And I—I did love her at one point, and I knew I could trust her. But I couldn't make up my mind. I called her several times. And we fought because she was telling me I could do whatever was right for me, and I hated her for saying that. I hated her for letting it be an option for me. I finally decided to go through with it. We met at the Kneaders because I needed someone to go with me and I had this idea that if I drove out to Heber, Caleb wouldn't be able to figure out what I was doing. Like I was laying a false trail. Jeez, it all sounds so stupid when I talk about it. Caleb didn't even know I was pregnant; I hadn't told him, and I wasn't showing. Not much."

"And what happened at the Kneaders."

"She handed me that money in the parking lot and told me she wanted me to use it. I was frozen. I was furious, actually. I don't know why; I guess because she was so supportive, which doesn't really make any sense, but I was already so conflicted about it. That's why I threw it back at her. We talked some more outside of the restaurant. She put her purse and the money in the car and said she wanted to ride with me to the clinic and then she'd drive me home in my own car. I asked her how she was going to get back home, and she said she had other things to do in Salt Lake, and a friend would give her a ride."

"What friend?"

"Someone named Becca. I—" Hannah hesitated. "I got the impression they were more than friends, maybe."

"And?"

"And she drove me to the clinic, and after, she drove me home. It was early evening, but Caleb wasn't there. I got in bed and went to sleep. When Caleb woke me up, I told him I was sick and just needed to rest. I'd left my phone at the house all day, so no one could prove I'd been anywhere else."

"Hannah, that's the same day Joy was killed. Do you know where she was going? What was she going to do in the valley after she took you home?"

Tucking her hair behind her ears, Hannah nodded slowly. "But I can't say anything, Tean. If I say where she was going, then I have to explain the rest of it: why she left her car there, why she drove me home, what she told me. I was under medication, so they might not even believe me."

"But you'd at least have an alibi. The clinic will have records."

"You don't understand. My parents. Caleb. Church is everything to them. Do you have any idea what it's like to have a secret that will change how they look at you forever, that will make them think you're—you're a monster?"

Tean just waited.

"I'm sorry," Hannah said. "I'm sorry, I didn't even think about that. But you understand, right?"

"Yes." There was no clock to mark the passing seconds, but Tean's heart thumped out the moments. "I'm sorry, Hannah. I'm not going to tell you it was easy or that it turned out all right. For me, though, it's better than the alternative. I couldn't live with the alternative. You've got to decide if you can."

Crying again, Hannah nodded.

They talked in fits and starts until the end of the visit, when the CO instructed Tean to step away from the glass and make his way to the door.

He met Hannah's gaze and tried once more. "Where was Joy going that night, Hannah?"

Hannah wiped her face and said, "Her father's."

33

Jem lay on the couch in Tinajas's living room. It was an old couch. It had a loose weave on the upholstery. A couple of times that morning he'd staggered into the bathroom to pee and seen the waffle print on his cheek. One of Tinajas's kids—he was pretty sure it was Guillo— was jumping up and down on his back, screaming, "Uncle Jem, Uncle Jem, Uncle Jem!"

In the other room, Tinajas was talking angrily into the phone. She peered through the opening to the kitchen long enough to snap, "Guillo, get off him. He's sick."

"Uncle Jem," Guillo said as he bounced to a stop. "Are you sick?"

Jem made a tiny groan as an answer.

"He's sick," Guillo screamed with excitement, running off to inform the rest of the house. "Uncle Jem is sick!"

In the other room, Tinajas was trying to be quiet. Quiet wasn't exactly one of her skills, though. "I don't care what you're doing. Get over here and get this dumb white boy off my couch. Right now!"

Jem felt a little sorry for whoever was on the other end of the line. He wondered if there was a specialized service that extracted dumb white boys from couches. Maybe they were like TaskRabbit. Maybe they were called White Boy No More. It sounded like a pretty good idea, actually, and if Jem weren't currently in the process of dying, he would have put some more effort into figuring out how it might work.

After the fight with Tean, Jem had made it to Chaquille's. Chaquille had taken one look at him and closed the door, and no matter how long or how hard Jem had knocked, Chaquille wouldn't let him inside. Then Jem had gone to Petrano's, a dive bar where he'd gotten drunk and tried to read about crypsis and weird animals until he was willing to do something reckless, and then he'd scored oxy and taken it all at once. He'd woken up in a weed-choked lot a little after sunrise. At some point during the night he'd cut his face, probably on the mangled can of Bud Light next to him, and a feral dog had been sniffing his sneaker with suspicious intent. Jem shouted and kicked until the damn thing ran away. Then he'd tried to die. When that didn't work, he'd stumbled to the bike, puked, driven a few blocks, puked, and made his way to Tinajas's place in more or less that manner.

Tinajas clomped into the room. She was wearing wedges, and she seemed to be putting a lot of extra emphasis into each step. She sat on the couch near Jem's knees, and the cushions dipped. Then something thunked onto the coffee table. Jem groaned.

"Don't be such a baby."

"I'm dying."

"Good. Die. Then you won't ever show up at my house on a Monday morning looking so fucking pathetic that I have to use a sick day to stay home and take care of you." She slapped his hip. "On your back."

Jem rolled onto his back.

"What the actual fuck," Tinajas paused here as though unsure of how to complete the question, "is wrong with you?"

"I'm really, definitely dying."

"I'm not talking about that."

"Something is messed up. In my brain, I mean."

"I already knew about that. I already knew about all of that. You've been fucked up since you were eleven years old and you thought nobody knew that you took the VHS case for *Saved by the Bell* into the bathroom to jerk off."

"Zack has his shirt off. Mostly. You can see a nipple."

She took his chin and swore under her breath. Then she opened an antiseptic wipe and began scrubbing at the cut on Jem's face. She ignored his howls as she said, "I'm talking about this recent rise in your fuck-uppish-ness."

Guillo and Dionica came into the room, swinging a pair of wooden canes like swords and screaming.

"Probably shouldn't talk like that in front of the kids," Jem tried.

"What the fuck are you doing with Grandma's canes?" Tinajas shouted. "Put those back where you found them and get your asses back downstairs."

The kids just laughed, their combat carrying them away from the stairs and toward the bedrooms at the back of the house.

"They're not scared of you," Jem said.

"They will be, but first I've got to deal with your miserable, garbage-covered, dog-piss-smelling, freckled white ass."

"Ow, ow, ow, Tin, that's my face!"

She finally stopped with the wipe; when she released his chin, Jem swore he could feel bruises starting to form. She applied ointment and taped a bandage in place. Then her shoulders sagged. "Jeremiah Berger, I cannot do this with you. I'm not going to watch you OD or crash your bike because you refuse to take care of yourself."

"I don't do that kind of stuff," Jem said. "Last night was last night."

"I'm talking about why you did that stuff last night. I'm talking about this guy, and how deep he's gotten in your head, and what it's doing to you. There is a lot of hot ass out there. Even for a weird, pathetic piece of shit like you. Find somebody who likes you back. Find somebody who's going to treat you right. Kike—"

"Please don't do this."

She made a disgusted noise as she wadded up the medical waste. "Go take a shower. I'll leave some of Tony's clothes outside."

"Yes, ma'am."

"Don't get your face wet."

"Yes, ma'am."

"Be a smartass one more time and I'll go get one of Grandma's canes and whip your ass raw."

Jem was surprised to find he could still grin. He sat up, kissed Tinajas's cheek, and grinned a little more when she elbowed him away and made the same disgusted noise again. He showered. He washed his hair in the sink to keep his face dry. He looked at himself as the fog cleared from the mirror, the old scars, the new wounds. He needed his hair cut again. Tinajas had provided him with an XXL Corona t-shirt that smelled like the Dobbs where he worked and board shorts big enough for two Jeremiah Berger's. He tied the waistband as tight as he could and hoped the shorts didn't fall and turn him into an impromptu your-growing-body object lesson.

"Do you think you could trim my hair?" Jem called as he moved back into the living room. "It's getting shaggy. I hate when it gets shaggy."

"I could try," Tean said. "You might not like it when I'm done, though."

The doc was sitting on the edge of the couch, hands on his knees, every line in his body tight. He had a little furrow between his eyebrows. He looked sad and hopeful, which meant he looked normal. He was wearing Keens, cargo pants, and a DWR shirt. All khaki again.

"Oh," Jem said. "Hi."

"Hi."

"I guess Tinajas isn't up here."

"She said something, but it was mostly swear words, so I don't really know what she was telling me."

"That sounds about right." Jem moved to stand where he could see Tean better. He leaned on an armchair, keeping the furniture between them. "I guess she called you."

"Yes."

"I shouldn't have done what I did," Jem said.

At the same moment, Tean said, "I shouldn't have done what I did."

Jem smiled. Tean laughed nervously and then covered his mouth.

"Me first," Jem said. "I'm sorry for what I said to you, for all those horrible things. I've been trying to figure out a way to explain it. First I thought about that dog Toby, the one at the tow yard. Then I tried to read about animals; I wanted to find a way to make it make sense. The best I could come up with was the Malaysian ant."

"Oh," Tean said, his eyes suddenly wet. "Jem."

"You know about them?"

"Autothysis. Suicidal altruism. They explode in self-defense, covering predators with toxic chemicals."

Jem nodded. "I knew you would. Everything . . . everything was closing in on me. Ammon. You. Other things. And I exploded. I wanted somebody else to hurt for a while, even if it was self-destructive. Maybe because it was self-destructive. That doesn't make it ok; that's not what I'm trying to say. Hell, I don't even know what I'm trying to say."

"Jem—"

"And the thing with Ammon and the key and the note, I don't know why I did it. I'm sorry I did it. I know trust is a big thing for you—I mean, I guess it's a big thing for everyone—and I just keep breaking your trust. So, I just wanted to say I'm sorry and I know we probably can't be friends anymore.

"I know why you did it," Tean said. "You thought you were protecting me."

Jem gave a one-shouldered shrug. "I think I did it for a lot of reasons. I also did it because if I'm being perfectly honest, I hate Ammon. I hate him. I don't ever want you to be around him again. But I know that's not my choice."

"No," Tean said. "It's not." Then he drew a deep breath and said, "I shouldn't have—I shouldn't have said what I did. I shouldn't have thrown you out. You're my best friend, and I should have listened to you. I should have at least given you the benefit of the doubt."

"I'm your best friend?" Jem said, feeling a real smile start.

"Only for the extent of this conversation. Then I'm downgrading you to normal, regular friend again."

"I'm ok with that." Jem blew out a breath. "And in the interest of full disclosure, I was also tired of seeing how Ammon has all the things you want in a guy, and I'm this fuck up who needs you to cosign for an apartment."

"Ammon has all the things I want in a guy?"

"He's got a job, he's got health insurance, he's got a checking account, he's got a 41k."

"401k," Tean said with a smile. "And actually, he doesn't. He has a pension."

"And then he got the apartment, and it was too much. I mean, fuck, I can't even get a Kohl's credit card. I know that's important to you, and I'm trying to figure it out, but it's just such a fucking mess."

"That stuff doesn't matter to me."

"Ok."

"It doesn't. Why do you think that? Did I tell you that it did? Is that how I act?"

"Aside from your extravagant lifestyle, you mean? The shopping. The designer clothes. The expensive wine. The mini mansion."

"Jem."

"Aside from working on reading, that's what you're always trying to fix in my life. An apartment. Insurance. A job. God, that job at Snow's? I hated that job. Hated it. I mean, I wasn't bad at it. But I hated it. That's not me, but I did it because I knew you wanted me to be that kind of person, and I'm honestly afraid that I can't."

"Jem, I don't want you to be anything but what you are. I just—" Tean cocked his head, as though trying to evaluate something. "I honestly didn't realize I was pressuring you. I'm sorry. What I said the other day, what I said about living in a world that doesn't have any meaning, about choosing who you want to be and then being authentic—that's what I want for you. Well, for me too."

"I guess liars aren't very authentic."

"I think you're the most authentic person I've ever met," Tean said quietly. "I don't want you to be like everyone else; I want you to be you, the real you. I want you to be happy. After you told me some of the stuff you went through growing up, I did some reading."

"Oh no."

"Kids who go through foster care, they have so many extra challenges. Substance dependency, criminal convictions, learning disabilities, unemployment, limited education—the rates for foster care kids are astronomically high in all those areas. I thought if I helped you, you could, you know, have a happy, fulfilling life."

"Tean, I am happy. Well, I'm miserable right now, but most of the time I'm happy."

"I know. I'm sorry. I don't know—I just get scared, and I want your life to be better, and I know that's messed up and wrong."

"No," Jem said. "I mean, I have sometimes thought about college. Fuck, finishing high school, I guess. Or my GED. But maybe I need to be able to get through Dick and Jane first. And I like that you want to make my life better. That's one of the many things I like about you. I'm just going to tell you when I need you to back off a little, starting now."

Tean nodded. Then suddenly he looked like he was about to cry, and his voice broke as he said, "Jem, why didn't you tell me about your mom?"

"Oh," Jem said. "Shit."

Squaring his shoulders, Tean took a deep breath. Jem recognized that look. Tean intended to wait.

Jem said, "What was I supposed to say? 'Hey, remember the heartless bitch who ran out on me? The same one who left me in those shithole care homes, the same one who probably never even knew I spent years in Decker? Well, funny story, turns out she also stole my identity and ruined my credit. Oh, and she's rich now. And she remarried. And she's got two kids, and the new batch must have turned out better because you should have seen the way she was looking at them. She definitely loves the little sons of bitches.' Is that how I should have introduced the subject?"

"Something like that, I guess."

"Fuck, Tean, I don't know. I don't want to think about it, much less talk about it. It's not like it changes anything. Maybe if I watch enough TV, that part of my brain will die and I won't have to remember it anymore."

Tean hooked a finger in his collar. "I'm going to tell you I did something, and I think you're going to be mad."

"That's ok. I know a great place to get more oxy."

"I—I might have called her."

"You called her?"

"When I couldn't find you. I got worried, and you dropped that piece of paper, so I found her phone number."

"Oh my God."

"But I didn't tell her who I really was. I pretended I was with a service that helped people track down their biological parents. She said—she said she'd like to meet you. If you're interested."

"Oh my God," Jem whispered between his fingers.

"And I didn't give her any information about you."

"But she can call you. She has your phone number. She can figure out who you are. She can track me down."

"No." Tean actually looked like he was trying to shrink inside his polo. "I bought a disposable prepaid cell phone."

Jem dropped his hands. "You bought a burner?"

"I thought it might be safer."

"Like a drug dealer?"

"More like an off-the-grid but nobly minded rugged individualist."

For a moment, Jem thought about this. "You are one devious motherfucker."

"Jem!" Then, sitting up straighter, "I am?"

"Definitely. I'm honestly flattered I've had this kind of influence on you."

"Then you're going to love this next part." Tean stood up and held his arms out, Frankenstein's monster-style, and took a few steps towards Jem.

"What is this? What are you doing?" Jem backed up a few steps, which he distantly realized meant sacrificing his improvised barricade of the armchair. "We already did the 'Monster Mash,' and legally we can't do it again until October."

"It's not the 'Monster Mash.'" Tean kept coming. "You told me sometimes you need to know people care about you. Especially when you're hurting. And it's not about words."

"Well, that was more of a 'Jem-teaching-Tean' thing, not really something we need to—" Jem moved back again. "Look, I know this isn't your style. I appreciate the thought."

"It's happening whether you like it or not."

"I'm going to like it. I think. But it's slightly terrifying because your eyes are now closed and you look like you're in physical pain."

With a final lurch, Tean reached him, his arms wrapping around Jem. He was what he always was: a wiry bundle of heat and muscle, wild hair pushed back, the smell of the steppes, sagebrush and pine. He was crying, and Jem laughed quietly as he smoothed down Tean's hair and returned the hug. Then the laugh ended, and Jem had to blink hard to clear his eyes. He let his chin rest against Tean's shoulder. He thought, again, of how rarely anyone had ever touched him like this.

"You smell like a car tire," Tean whispered.

Jem laughed again, wiped his eyes, and said, "I get that a lot."

Then, over Tean's shoulder, he saw Dionica, her little face screwed up in horror. "Mom," she screeched, her voice pitched to a level that normally only dogs could hear. "They're kissing!" Then she turned and ran.

Clomping footsteps made their way through the house. Tean tried to twist free of the hug, but he only got halfway, and he had to settle for standing with Jem's arm across his shoulders. Jem watched the panic build in Tean's face; when the footsteps were almost to them, Jem whispered, "All khaki."

Tean's face went blank. He glanced down and said, "Dang it. How?"

"What the fuck do you two think you're doing?" Tinajas demanded as she came into the living room.

Trying to weasel out from under Jem's arm again, Tean said, "We weren't kissing."

"There are children in this house. Do you realize that? Children. They shouldn't have to watch you make bad choice after bad choice. For some reason, they like you."

"Because I'm adorable," Jem said.

"We were not kissing," Tean said more loudly.

"They like you because they're already smarter than you and they feel sorry for you," Tinajas said. "And they definitely don't need to get a front-row seat to this toxic relationship. Tony and I are already doing just fucking fine on that end, thanks very much."

"I just want to point out," Tean said, "that you called me. And, more importantly, no kissing of any kind—"

"Those kids are lucky to have a cool uncle like me," Jem said. "Tean was just telling me how I've been this amazing influence, and I've helped him find joy in life and live outside the tiny margins he let himself exist in."

"No, I said I bought a disposable cell phone—"

"That's what you want to teach my children?" Tinajas said. "To use burner phones like your drug-dealer boyfriend who has to come pick your ass up from my couch? That's the life lesson you want to impart to my children?"

"Not boyfriend," Tean said. "Or a drug dealer, although really that's not the part I'm worried—"

"I already told you he's not my boyfriend—" Jem said.

"Then why are you kissing him?"

" —he's my best friend."

"Again, not kissing," Tean said. "And really more of an ordinary, normal, regular friend. Like the kind you know at work, and you can have those short, meaningless conversations. And then forty years later he dies of a heart attack and you find out he had a second family in Canada."

Tinajas stared at him. Then, turning to Jem, she said, "What the fuck is this?"

"I have no idea," Jem said. "Isn't he fantastic?"

34

As usual, Jem couldn't get out of Tinajas's house without a sandwich. She made them tuna salad, but with something smoky and spicy in the fish, and she served it on the bread she usually used for tortas. She made mac and cheese, the good kind, for the kids, and Jem bartered half his potato chips with Guillo for some of the mac.

At Tean's insistence, they left Jem's bike at Tinajas's house and drove south.

"Where are we going?"

"Joy's dad's place."

"Want to fill me in on that?"

So Tean did. And as Tean talked, Jem felt himself trying to pay attention, thinking about Hannah and Joy, the secrets kept, all the ways people tried to protect each other and only made things worse. He thought about himself, of course, and how some part of his brain had gotten locked in overdrive when it came to watching out for Tean. And he thought about Hannah and Caleb. He thought about Tean's brother-in-law, the douche who had followed them, determined to make sure his kids were safe from the fags. And then, because it was a bruise he couldn't stop touching, he thought about his mom, the question that he pummeled back under the surface of consciousness as soon as it broached: did she think she was keeping me safe?

"But why was Joy going to see her father?" Jem asked. "Why leave her car in Heber?"

"I think she left the car because she didn't want to be in a vehicle that she owned. Plus, we already know that she loved the drama of imagining herself in an action movie, dodging corporate and government hit men, that kind of thing."

"Ok, fine, I'll buy that up to a point. But you didn't answer me about her dad."

"I don't know. Hannah didn't know either, or she would have told me."

"But you have an idea."

"It's not even really an idea."

"Let's hear it anyway."

"I just keep thinking that the last place anyone knows that Joy went was her father's. And he lied to us about the last time he saw her—he told us he hadn't seen her in a long time."

"You think he killed her."

"I don't know why he would have lied."

Jem considered this for a minute. The valley spread out in front of them; the scrub brush of the desert had been transformed into glass and steel, low and sprawling in every direction, bristling with the same persistence that kept sage and bitterbrush and ephedra growing in alkali soil.

"I don't disagree with you," Jem said, "but we saw him at the funeral. He was acting like a horny old goat, but I just can't imagine him doing that to his daughter."

"Really?" Tean said, head cocked as he turned to examine Jem.

"What's that supposed to mean?"

"Nothing. I just—I just think you're kind of wonderful."

"Of course."

"Right now."

"And in general."

"No, I'm pretty sure just right now. And I don't disagree with you about how he was acting at the funeral, celebration of life, whatever you want to call it."

"Ok, you softened me up. Now go for the kill."

"Jem, family violence is tremendously common. Horrifyingly common. Approximately a third of all men and women will experience violence from an intimate partner. At least one in seven children has experienced abuse in the last year, and in those cases, the perpetrator is a parent over three-quarters of the time. Family violence accounts for eleven percent of all total violence. And that number doubles, twenty-two percent, for murders. More than one in five murders is in a family." Tean blew out a breath. "Sometimes, parents kill their children out of twisted motives. They think they're doing it for a good reason. A mother in Missouri recently killed her children because she planned on committing suicide. She knew that they'd have difficult lives growing up without a mother, and she wanted to spare them that. Animals do it too. Cats will eat their kittens if they're under a great deal of stress, but it's also been observed in lots and lots of species of mammals, insects, fish, amphibians, reptiles, and birds. Frick, human parents eat their children alive in a figurative sense all the time, in a million different ways."

They drove almost a mile, the tires humming, the vents blowing the scent of pineapple air freshener. Jem thought about the sound of the bathroom door jiggling as a foster dad tried to force his way inside. He put his hand on Tean's nape, rubbing his thumb in a small circle.

"I don't want you to have to carry that stuff around inside your head anymore," Jem said.

"I'm not the one who grew up—I just mean, I grew up fine. It doesn't change the facts."

"Tean, I don't want you carrying it around. I met your family. I understand, a little. But you're going to make yourself sick with stuff like that."

A Mack truck whipped past them, the Ford rocking slightly in the air from its passage.

"I already am sick," Tean said. "I think I'm already way too sick." Then he shook his head. "Look, all I'm saying is that it's not outside the bounds of possibility that Leroy killed Joy. I actually don't even think it's impossible that he killed her and genuinely felt remorse later. At some level, unless he's a total psychopath, he must have felt some connection to her. She's his daughter."

"What's his motive?"

Tean ran his hands around the wheel.

Tapping on the doc's nape with his thumb, Jem said, "Why'd he kill her?"

"I don't know. And don't do that; it's annoying."

"Unless he's a pure and total psycho, he had to have a reason—hell, even psychos have reasons. Maybe he gets off on hurting. Maybe he's always been abusive. Maybe he was worried she was going to reveal something about him. The blackmail angle already cropped up in this case, and maybe we weren't too far off."

Tean shook his head. "I feel like it must have been connected to Sievers. That bear he's got on his property —"

"Allegedly."

"The bear he's allegedly got on his property, based on videos and a lot of testimony —"

"From a bunch of redneck hippies who were probably all on shrooms."

" —that bear is the only animal we've even heard of that might have been able to rip off Joy's arm."

"Do bears normally attack humans?"

"No, not really. But a bear that has been tortured, the way that bear has been treated in the videos, is definitely capable of it. Also, bear attacks on humans typically are an escalation from bear attacks on dogs. If Sievers was forcing the bear to fight coyotes, for example, the bear could already be conditioned to attack."

Jem made a noise.

"It has to be connected to Sievers," Tean insisted. "Joy went to see her dad. Somehow, he gets her out to Sievers's property. Maybe he's just offering her a ride back to her car. Together, he and Sievers force her into the pen with the bear. She's killed. Maybe that's it. Maybe the dad doesn't stick around for the dismemberment. Maybe he didn't even know what would happen after he got her to Sievers's property."

"That's a lot of maybes," Jem said, tracing circles on the light brown skin again with his thumb.

"I might have done something." And he told Jem about his nighttime struggle with Sievers.

"Did you go out of your fucking mind temporarily?" Jem said.

"Temporarily, yes."

"What the fuck were you thinking?"

"I don't know. I wasn't thinking, I guess. But you should have heard him. He was scared."

"But he didn't confess."

"He killed her. I know he did. It's the only thing that pulls the pieces together."

"It's real life, Tean. Things don't always pull together."

When they got to the aging house in Sandy, it looked exactly as Jem remembered it: the patchy lawn, the peeling trim, the stickers layered over the door jambs. They got out of the truck, and while the engine ticked, Jem tried to listen.

"I don't think—"

"Shush."

Tean waited almost a full minute before saying, "I don't think you'll be able to hear him through the walls."

"If I were Superman I could."

"Never mind."

"I was trying to hear Roger."

"Who's Roger?" Tean asked as he approached the door.

"The vicious, bloodthirsty, murderous hound who tried to rip me to pieces last time."

As they got to the door, Tean knocked. "The dog stayed in the back the whole time. We never even saw the dog."

"Yeah, but it was thinking about murdering me. Also, I don't hear him."

Tean sighed and knocked again. The spring day was mild. It was early afternoon—it seemed impossible that the whole day wasn't over; it felt like a lifetime had passed—and the sun was warm on Jem's back, and the air smelled like the tulip tree in the next yard. A minivan rolled past on the street, the windows down, and a woman was yelling, "Richard, if you don't pull your pants up and sit down right now, I'm going to park this car and come back there. Don't wag your derriere at your sister!"

"I probably should have asked what our plan was," Jem said.

"Our plan is for you to be silently supportive while I ask him questions." Tean seemed to think about this and added, "Occasionally you can lean forward and look menacing, but only if you want."

"That plan sucks. Let's tie him to a chair and interrogate him. You can tell him about how he's eating beaver ass every time he eats raspberry-flavored ice cream."

"That's not—Castoreum isn't—" Tean took a huge breath, knocked again, and muttered, "More like tie him up and make him watch those Avengers movies."

From inside the house, still nothing.

Tean glanced over. "I guess—"

"How dare you."

"—nobody is home—"

"Those movies are fantastic. You liked them. You jumped, Tean, you literally jumped in your seat when Ultron started talking."

"Because you put your hand down my shorts!"

"I thought you had an itch. I was trying to be a good friend."

"Stay here," Tean said, stepping off the porch.

"Maybe I should—"

"Not if Roger the dog is hanging out in the backyard."

"You know what? I should probably keep watch out here. If there's any trouble, I'll make the call of the Great Australian desert bird, *vegemitus enormous*."

"No such bird," Tean called without looking back.

"But if the coast is clear, I'll do three whooping cries like the tiger-faced bull walloper of Sierra Leon."

He could hear Tean's sigh all the way from the porch. When the doc had passed out of sight, Jem pulled out his picks and went to work on the locks. He listened for any sounds of alarm, but the neighborhood remained quiet. After a few minutes, the door popped open—the locks were old, and they didn't give any trouble.

Leaving the door open behind him, Jem moved into the smell of cheesy processed snacks, body odor, and wet dog. The lights were off, but enough sunlight made its way through the windows that Jem could tell that the living room was empty except for the wall of photographs. The eyes of dogs, cats, hamsters, gerbils, ponies, parakeets, and more stared down at Jem. He passed into the kitchen, which was long and galley style, with melamine countertops the color of old ivory. Shelf-stable food covered the counters: jars of peanut butter, loaves of bread, bags of potato chips, jars of pickles and olives and pimentos. In the sink, two plates and a dog's bowl waited to be washed. A breakfast table had been crammed up against the back wall, where a sliding door opened onto the yard. Jem rapped on the glass.

Tean's head whipped up, and his glasses flew off his face. Then he patted the grass around where he was squatting, grimacing, and — to judge by the shape of his mouth—swearing.

After knocking loose the dowel that lay in the track, Jem opened the door and said, "Sorry. To your left. No, your other left. Oh, I mean, to your right."

Tean definitely said something that time.

"Was that a naughty word?" Jem said.

Shoving the glasses onto his face, Tean got to his feet. He was holding something. "What are you doing?"

"Investigating. I'm a private detective now."

"No, you're not. Private detectives are licensed and don't break the law. You're—"

Jem waited.

"Well, I don't know what you are. A lot of trouble."

"The f-word is a dollar in our Disneyworld fund."

Tean glared as he approached.

"In case you forgot," Jem offered.

"What do you think about this?" Tean asked, holding up white fluff.

Jem touched it. It was synthetic, matted in places, dirty from where it had lain in the yard. "Dog toy guts. Scipio was covered in this stuff the other day after he ripped open your sex doll."

"What?"

"That sex doll. The guy with the big muscles and skimpy shorts, you know, you can kind of see his dick."

"That was a dog toy. And you can't see his—never mind."

"I know, I know. Good cover. Like those dildo melon ballers."

"It came in a themed package."

"What was the theme? 'I'm eating melon balls while riding this schlong?'"

"It was a beach theme package. Of dog toys. He's a lifeguard. He came with a toy whistle."

"I don't know," Jem said, rubbing his chin. "I've never seen anybody use a dildo on a beach. Not in public anyway."

Tean was making a high-pitched noise in his throat as he pushed Jem out of the way and went into the house. Jem tried not to laugh as he pulled the door shut and kicked the dowel back into place.

They moved through the house together: a hall bathroom, a bedroom that had been converted to an office—judging by the ancient computer and the amount of dust, not much work was getting done—and then the next bedroom. Jem gagged when Tean opened the door.

"Geh. What is that?"

"Dog," Tean said, waving a hand to clear the air as he stepped into the room. The only item was a dog kennel, which Tean inspected for a moment. Then he moved to the closet, slid open the doors, and glanced around. After a few more minutes, he looked back at Jem. "You're just going to stand there?"

Jem nodded.

"Is it the smell?"

Jem nodded. Pinprick sweat had broken out on his forehead, and he had to fight the urge to wipe it.

"Just close the door. You can look in the next room if you want."

"No, I'll wait." Then, because he couldn't resist, "This smell, I've kind of—is he neglecting the dog? Keeping it trapped in here? LouElla never let her dog out of the basement. That's why the poor thing was insane."

Tean shook his head. "I hate people like that. I don't understand it, the cruelty of it. And I know—I know she was a lot worse to you, I know animals aren't people. But I just hate thinking about it, about an animal that can't help itself. I hate it so much."

"The good thing is that it prepared me to deal with a menacing brute like Scipio. Do you realize he actually tried to put his paw in my mouth when we were asleep? No. Do not get that look on your face. It was not cute."

"Of course not," Tean murmured. "To answer your question, I don't think so. I mean, the kennel is clean and well maintained, no evidence of distress—clawing, chewing, trying to force the door. There's no sign of urine or feces. I think he's just had the dog sleep in here for a long time, and he probably keeps the door closed. That's why the smell is so strong."

Tean finished the sentence by closing the door, and Jem could breathe easier when it was just the cheesy-potato-chip funk again. They moved into the master bedroom, and they searched it, balancing speed against efficiency. The bathroom was a grim, older single man's bathroom: shaving cream and a bag of disposable razors; a toothbrush with flattened bristles; a tube of Equate toothpaste; a bag of single-use flossers.

"I should buy him some lotion," Jem said.

"I should buy him some bleach," Tean said.

The basement was the last place they checked. It was small—a portion of the house must have been built on a slab—and it contained several shelves of canned food, an enormous plastic barrel full of water, and storage totes. They opened the totes to get a quick look, but it looked like the usual family memorabilia: photographs, schoolwork, a vacuum-packed wedding dress, soccer trophies awkwardly nested.

"I think those trophy girls are scissoring each other," Jem said.

Tean snapped the tote's lid back into place. Then he let out a sharp, frustrated breath. "I don't understand. There's nothing here."

"Well, we don't know that he killed her. We don't know that they struggled." Jem shrugged. "Even if we go with your theory, there's not any reason to expect evidence here. You said she showed up, he drove her out to Sievers's place, and Sievers killed her. I mean, it would have been nice to find a signed confession or an IOU to Sievers or blackmail pictures of Leroy dancing the can-can, but the reality is that she could have walked into the house, hung out five minutes, and left with her dad. That's not going to leave any evidence."

"Yes," Tean said. "But where are the dog toys?"

"What?"

After digging around in his pocket for a moment, Tean produced the synthetic stuffing. "Where are the dog toys?"

Jem hesitated. "Maybe that was the last one."

"You've seen my house. You've seen the toy basket. And I'm relatively level-headed when it comes to my dog—"

Jem made a slight catching noise.

" —so where are the rest of the toys?"

"I don't know. Ok. It's weird. I'll give you that."

"And something else. Something else is weird."

"What?"

"I don't know. There's just something weird."

"Ok. I got kind of, um, focused on other stuff when we went in the dog's room. Let's go look through the house again. Quick."

They moved upstairs, and this time, they split up. Tean headed to the back of the house. Jem worked his way through the living room, tossing the cushions off the couch, replacing them, rifling the DVD cabinet in the entertainment center. He gave the wall of photographs a cursory look.

"Tean!"

Rapid footsteps. "Yes? What? Are you ok?"

"I need a drink of water."

Tean pushed his glasses back into place and sounded like he was struggling to control his breathing. "Jem, I thought you were—"

"Humans."

"What?"

"He doesn't have any pictures of people. Not anywhere. Not in the whole house."

For a moment, Tean's face was blank. Then he nodded. "But there are people in those pictures."

"No, there are people in the background. The pictures are of animals."

"That's what I couldn't figure out," Tean said, the words tumbling out with his excitement. "That's what didn't make any sense. He talked about his rescue operations. He talked about taking care of animals. But all he's got is a kennel and a food and water bowl. He doesn't have any dog toys. He doesn't have a fenced yard. He doesn't have any sign that other animals have been here, not even temporarily. If you've been to an animal hoarder's house, they're full of cages, bowls, perches, cat mansions. Where is all that stuff?"

"Maybe he's not an animal hoarder," Jem said.

Tean gestured at the photographs.

"Those could be old," Jem said.

"Nobody has that many animals at one point in their life and then stops. Not without someone forcing them. Dang it, I should have thought of this earlier. I'm going to call back to the office and see if anybody can dig up Leroy Erickson in our records."

Digging out his phone, he dropped onto the couch and talked quietly into the phone. Jem continued to study the pictures. As he had noticed on their last visit, the photographs spanned decades, some of them instant-develop prints like Polaroids, some of them from 35mm cameras, some of them obviously digital printouts that someone had trimmed by hand. In the earliest pictures, Leroy Erickson was probably in his late teens or early twenties, with wild hair and overalls. Others were much more recent, with Leroy's head shaved and the black-ink Fozzie tattoo on his neck. The same party-loving side that Jem had noticed at the funeral/celebration, when Leroy had been dancing and drinking, emerged in the photographs. In one, Leroy and a tabby cat were dressed in matching Bubba Wallace NASCAR racing uniforms. In another, Leroy was Stockton and a black hound was Malone, the picture obviously taken in the 90s, man and dog both wearing Jazz jerseys.

"Ok," Tean was saying. "Thank you, that's very helpful. Yes, I'll let you know if I'm coming back—"

"Tean."

"Just a second, Norbert." To Jem, he said, "Yes?"

"You need to look at this."

"Be right there."

"No, Tean. Right now."

The couch springs creaked, and Tean said something into the phone, but Jem's focus was entirely on the photograph in front of him. He'd noticed it on their first visit, but now he was seeing it as something else. In the photograph, Leroy was dressed as Captain Hook. Featured in the foreground was an alligator with a miniature clock on his back—obviously meant to be the crocodile from *Peter Pan*, although according to Tean, you could tell an alligator from a crocodile just by looking at it. It was a birthday party, with several other faces visible in the background, and was easy to see that the celebration had been recent: the photograph was unfaded, and in spite of the costume, it was easy to see that Leroy looked close to his current age.

"The crocodile," Jem said.

"I told you, it's an alligator."

"Fine. Whatever. The alligator. Tean, the teeth. Could that thing rip off someone's arm?"

Tean was silent a moment. Then he said, "Definitely. Alligators don't chew their food. They can't chew, actually. With bigger prey, they rip it apart and swallow the pieces whole."

"This is it," Jem said. He felt alive with the realization, crackling with the energy of it. "This is it."

"I heard you," Tean said into the phone. "Norbert, I'm right in the middle of something, but I might need you in a minute. Please stay on the line." To Jem, he said, "I don't understand, though. The alligator could have done that kind of damage to Joy's body, including amputating the arm. And the shape of the mouth is right; its teeth are capable of leaving the marks I saw on the bone, although we'd need to take a dental impression to see if the imperfections match. But what's his motive?" An angry voice buzzed on the other end of the phone, and Tean snapped, "I told you I'd just be a minute. Please hold on."

"I don't know," Jem said. "I don't know, but we're right on the edge of it."

More angry buzzing from the phone.

"Excuse me?" Tean said. "Do you want to try that again without a homophobic slur?"

For a moment, Jem forgot about the alligator and the dead woman and the rest of it. He reached for the phone. "Let me talk to him. Give me five minutes with him, and that walking case of crotch rot won't ever talk to you like that again."

Tean waved him away.

"Holy shit," Jem said. He clutched Tean's arm. "Holy shit!"

"Hold on, Norbert. Jem, I've got to —"

"He wasn't trying to kill Joy. He was trying to save the crocodile. He was protecting it."

Tean froze. Slowly, he pulled the phone from his ear. The voice on the other end continued to buzz.

"You see it?" Jem said.

"He doesn't have pictures of humans," Tean said. "He has pictures of animals. He doesn't have a relationship with his daughter. He has animals. And he doesn't have any animals here, which means —"

"He keeps them somewhere else," Jem shouted, unable to help himself with his excitement. "That's what Joy meant when she said she was going to her dad's. She wasn't coming here. She was going to wherever he keeps the animals. She was — oh shit. She was going to let them out. Set them free. Something like that. That's why father and daughter didn't get along. He loved animals. So did she. But he kept them, and she wanted to release them."

"She must have — she must have made a mistake," Tean said. "Gotten too close to the alligator. Gotten attacked. An injury like the one she suffered, with the arm amputated — she would have lost consciousness in fifteen seconds. She would have been dead shortly thereafter."

"And nobody else was there. She got clear of the tank or wherever the alligator was being held, so it didn't do any further damage to the body, but then she died. The next time Leroy shows up, he finds her dead, and he knows the gator did it. He's lost his daughter, and I'm sure that's a blow, but he can't stand the thought of the state taking the alligator and killing it."

"Worse than that," Tean said. "He would have faced criminal charges, and he would have lost all his animals. He couldn't let that happen."

"So he covered it up. He chopped up her body to hide how she died, and then he tried to frame Zalie and Sievers. When that didn't work, and he knew the police had their eye on someone else, he planted the hatchet at Hannah's."

"Holy shit," Tean said, a huge smile growing.

"Quarter in the swear jar," Jem said.

The voice was still buzzing on the phone. Tean lifted it to his ear, listened, and then broke in. "Yes, Norbert. As a matter of fact, I am with my boyfriend. Now, if you don't want to lose your pension and job in a sexual harassment lawsuit, shut the fuck up. I need you to look something up in the computers for me."

"Your boyfriend," Jem whispered.

Tean pointed a finger at him and mouthed, *Be quiet*.

"This is the best day of my life," Jem said.

35

"He's still not answering," Tean said.

Jem said, "Not a good quality in a future boyfriend."

Tean grimaced and put a finger to his lips. They were still standing in front of the wall of photographs in Leroy Erickson's home. Tean waited for his third call to Ammon to go to voicemail, and then he left a message explaining what they believed they had figured out.

When Tean disconnected, Jem said, "I just think, as your future boyfriend, he ought to—"

"Jem, now is not the time."

"God, but I have so many good ones."

With his phone, Tean took pictures of the photographs, moving along the wall in regular increments, making sure he got overlapping shots so they could reconstruct the arrangement if necessary. Eventually, this would be a crime scene, or at least part of a police investigation, but there was no telling what might happen in the meanwhile. If Leroy Erickson came home and decided to dispose of his mementos—

"So how are we going to find him?" Jem said.

"We're not. We're done. Let's get out of here, and we'll lock the door behind us, and that's the end of it. Ammon and Kat can take over from here."

"Hold on, hold on, hold on," Jem said, scrambling to bar Tean's path. "What about Hannah?"

"What do you mean? She's going to be fine. Once they can prove what happened—"

"But we don't know that they'll be able to prove it," Jem said. "They didn't get this far, did they?"

"Because Hannah lied to them."

"She might keep lying to them."

"But we'll tell Ammon, and he and Kat will find—"

"How?"

"They can access police records."

Jem rolled his eyes. "Do you really think that Leroy's secret animal kingdom is in a building he owns or rents under his own name? He's got light and water in his name? Maybe a trash pickup for all the severed limbs?"

"He might be renting. There's no central database for rental agreements, and they often include utilities."

"And his landlord isn't going to care about the kiddie pool with the alligator inside?"

Tean frowned.

"Look," Jem said. "We find Leroy. That's all. As soon as we know where the animals are, we call Ammon. It's an anonymous tip. The police come out, hey, illegal animals, and you get called in. You, because you're a genius vet, realize the alligator might have killed Joy, and you get X-rays of its teeth—"

"Dental impressions."

"—and Hannah gets to come home, and I get to open my own business as a first-class detective. My slogan is going to be, 'I'm better than Ammon Young at three things: solving crimes, making conversation, and sucking—'"

"Ok," Tean said.

"Wait, really? I am better? Because—"

"Ok," Tean said more forcefully. "I see your point. I think it might be—it might be better if we brought the whole thing to Ammon, all the loose ends tied up first."

"Because he'll probably screw it up."

"Because I want this to move as quickly as possible."

"Because he's incompetent."

"Because he's got a huge case load, and because you and I work well together."

"That's so sweet. I was thinking the same thing about the blow jobs."

Tean turned and headed back to the home office. Jem didn't laugh, but he was radiating amusement as he trailed after him. In their search of the home, Tean hadn't paid much attention to the office — a thick layer of dust covered everything, and the carpet still had vacuum tracks in it. If Leroy ever used this room, he didn't do so frequently. Tean opened drawers in the desk, rifled through old Scotch tape, a yellowing plastic container of paperclips, a jumble of pens and pencils and rubber bands, utility bills (all for the house in Sandy), and the usual detritus of a home office. Jem poked around in a filing cabinet for a few minutes and then left.

"Don't you dare go get Ring Dings," Tean shouted after him.

"You're my Ring Ding," Jem called back.

When Jem returned, he was carrying a map from the Ford. He knelt on the floor and spread it out, the paper crinkling as he smoothed it. Then he spent a moment considering it before turning it. Tean had just finished another desk drawer — this one full of stale granola bars and a bottle of water that had been Sharpied EMERGENCY DO NOT DRINK — and decided whatever Jem was doing had to be more interesting.

"Ok," Jem said. "Where would you keep your private zoo of animals?"

"It's not a zoo."

"It's animals in cages. It's a zoo."

"No, zoos have taken on an important role in conservation and preservation. This is more like a menagerie."

"Ok, where would you keep your menagerie?"

"I'd release them in stages back into the wild."

Jem groaned and slumped down on the map. "Never mind. I'll do this myself."

"Norbert said Leroy had a misdemeanor charge for possessing a protected species — a desert tortoise. Someone reported him keeping it in a storage unit in Glendale."

"Ok," Jem said, sitting up again. "That's good to know. Anything else?"

"Not in DWR records. Ammon might —"

"No, that's fine. Glendale makes sense. It's more industrial than residential, and it's not exactly a desirable area. So let's start with the assumption that Leroy is going to use a similar area again. And let's also assume that he doesn't want to leave the valley."

"We don't know that."

"That's why it's an assumption." Jem considered the map and then snapped his fingers. "Give me a pen."

"Excuse me?"

Jem grinned up at him, the crooked front teeth fully exposed. "Please?"

Tean passed him a pen, and Jem began marking off parts of the valley.

"Nothing too suburban," Jem said, scratching out swaths of territory. "Especially these days, with property values so high and people desperate to find a home that isn't all the way out in Bumfuck, Utah. The last thing Leroy needs is for a neighbor to see him hosing down his pet hyena in the backyard. Besides, we already said it's not going to be a property in his own name."

"He could rent a house."

"Would the layout of a typical home be a good setup for keeping an alligator and whatever other animals he's 'rescued'?"

"No, probably not."

"So, let's assume no house."

"But we don't know—"

"That's why it's an assumption. Ok, no house. And he's not going to use a storage unit again because he got busted last time. Besides, with storage units, you've got people coming and going at all hours, it's not always easy to get water, and even on the exterior units, the doors are thin—anybody walking past would be able to hear the animals. Not just people renting units. Even in a shitty place, they have people walk the grounds, and they've got security cameras everywhere because they don't want anybody cooking meth."

"You know a lot about storage units."

"I lived in one for six months. Winter. Christ, it was so cold." Jem was still crossing out portions of the valley. "You'd better wipe that expression off your face before I look up."

Tean wasn't sure how well he managed, so he said, "No storage units."

"Nope. So, he might have leased a warehouse, but then you've got the problem of paperwork, landlords, and probably utilities. Besides, there's also the problem of money. Even if he's cutting corners and being a cheap-ass son of a bitch, it's got to cost a lot of money to feed all those animals."

"That's one of the major problems with animal hoarders, actually. Very few of them can actually afford to provide nutrition and veterinary attention. Some of them can see the problem, but they still keep collecting. Psychologically, they can't let go of the animals, even if a part of them recognizes that they aren't providing adequate care and quality of life. That's one of the ways you can tell it's a mental illness."

"So he's strapped for cash. That's why the house is empty and he's eating those gross Takis."

"You like Takis."

"Not the chili-lime ones. God, pay attention. Ok, so he's got no money, he needs to be off the grid, and he's operating in Utah, where everybody's nose is halfway up everybody else's anal canal. So he's squatting." Jem sat back on his heels and pointed with the pen. "Here, here, or here."

"Wait, what?"

"Do you know Glendale?"

"Not really."

"West Valley?"

"Just when I've been to visit you and go to Benny's place."

"This part," Jem sketched out a section with the pen, "belongs to Los Bastardos, and they'd be all over Leroy if he was in and out of there, fucking Canada geese or whatever he's doing."

"Dear Lord, I hope that's not what he's doing."

"And this part has a lot of activity. It's close enough to the airport that companies want to use the buildings, but there's a high turnover. Especially with the airport expanding, there's no way a property manager or owner would have a building sit vacant long enough for Leroy to set up shop."

"Jem, you're really good at this."

"I know. Try not to bone up. So here are some possibilities. This area has a few industrial parks with warehouses that might be empty. And I know that there's one over here that's completely abandoned because—put on your politely interested expression—I spent a couple of years here. They have this sweet little office on a platform overlooking the warehouse, and the power was still on. Space heater and mini fridge. It was awesome."

"What happened?"

"Some douche decided he wanted it, and I was nineteen and didn't want my guts spilled all over the floor."

Tean could hear the unsteadiness in his voice. "Oh. Ok."

"And this last one," Jem said, "backs up to a canal, and it's been closed for years."

"It feels like we're guessing," Tean said.

"Kind of," Jem said. "But we're making educated guesses. If they're all wrong, what's the worst that can happen?"

"I hate that question."

36

The first location turned out to be a bust; the grounds were well maintained, with grass that was obviously watered and freshly mulched flowerbeds. Near the road, a shiny new sign proclaimed the administrative offices of Follicle Funk, Ltd. In a jaunty script at the bottom, the company slogan read *Not enough bush by your tush? Put our funk on your junk!*

"I don't want to know," Tean said as he flipped around.

Jem, twisting to look back at the sign, said, "I do."

They drove to the next place that Jem had suggested — where he had lived for two years, Tean thought; two years in a warehouse, and he'd been happy to have a space heater and a mini fridge — and this time, things looked a little more likely. The building was relatively small for a warehouse, painted cinderblock, and the gate was chained shut. They parked on the shoulder, and Jem gave Tean a leg up. On the other side, weeds grew up through cracks in the asphalt — spindly millet grass, big yellow clumps of St. John's wort. A moment later, Jem landed next to Tean, the chain-link gate chiming behind him, and they headed toward the building.

It was late afternoon. The air smelled like prairie dust and sun-warmed cement, with a hint of Jem — whatever he'd used at Tinajas's house to shower. The day was warm without being hot, and the sky was robin's egg blue, a few clouds scruffy on the ridge of the Oquirrh Mountains. The only sound was their footsteps, sometimes muffled where they had to trample weeds, sometimes ringing out against the pavement. Halfway around the building, Jem broke left and moved into the mixture of weeds and buffalo grass beyond the curb. He made a face and came back. Then an eddy stirred, and Tean smelled something like an open sewer.

"What's that?"

As they resumed walking, Jem planted his hand on Tean's face, forcing him to look away, and then said, "That's the bathroom."

His hand was soft against Tean's face. His thumb was at the corner of Tean's lips.

"Someone's still staying here," Jem said. "In case you're wondering. And not Leroy. That was definitely, uh, human."

Tean tried to think of the right thing to say. He settled for, "You need to trim your nails."

After a heartbeat, Jem gave a little shove, sending Tean stumbling a step.

"I'll lend you the clippers I use on Scipio."

"Oh my God."

"And there's a grinder too. To round them. We should definitely use the grinder."

"Perfect. I'm taking my grooming tips from the guy who gets the dog-and-daddy haircut combo at the puppy salon."

"Hey, I like my hair."

"Good, because you've got enough of it."

"Not everybody needs to have their hair buzzed down to their scalp."

"No. Ladies are perfectly welcome to have their hair as long as they want."

"Jem!"

Grinning, Jem threw an arm around Tean's shoulders, and after a few minutes of trying to squirm away, Tean let him have the small victory.

When they got back to the truck, Jem said, "Third time's the charm."

"Let's hope so."

The third possibility that Jem had indicated was farther south, almost where Glendale gave way to West Valley, and Tean was surprised to see that instead of an industrial park, they were looking at acres of overgrown weeds and grass, with a few cinderblock buildings breaking up the vegetation. A chain-link fence ran around the property as far as Tean could see, and a gate and warning sign told people to buzz off.

"I don't see a car," Tean said. "And the gate is locked."

"He might not be here right now, but it's a big property — if he's using this place, he might have another way to access it. A couple of these buildings have rollup doors big enough for a box truck. He could park inside."

"I don't know," Tean said.

"What do you mean? Of course you don't know. That's why we're checking it out."

"I just mean maybe we should call Ammon."

"Tean, we've already checked two of the three. Come on. We'll check this one. If we see any sign that the animals are here, we'll come back to the truck and call Ammon."

Tean wrapped his hands around the steering wheel.

"This one backs up to the canal," Jem said. "This was always our best bet. Let's at least take a look."

Groaning, Tean killed the engine and opened his door. After getting another leg up from Jem, Tean landed easily on the other side of the fence. Jem hopped down next to him a moment later. When Jem took a step forward, Tean grabbed the XXL Corona t-shirt and pointed.

"Some of these are nettles."

"Ok."

"Stinging nettles. Try not to let them touch your skin."

"Which ones are nettles?"

Tean shrugged. "Most of them. There's some junegrass in there, that's the stuff that's really green, and I see a few thistles. But lots of nettles, so be careful."

"This is why people invented things like lawnmowers," Jem said as they picked a path through the waist-high weeds, both holding their bare arms in the air. "This is why people invented magical, wonderful things like weed wackers and Roundup and, Jesus Christ! Jesus Christ, my hand!"

"Jem, what the heck?"

"It stung me!"

"It didn't sting you. I watched you grab that nettle."

"Well, I wanted to see what it felt like. Fucking dicksucking monkeycock plants. Why the fuck didn't you warn me? Oh my Christ, my hand."

"I did warn you. I literally just told you not to touch them. Let me see."

"I meant, why didn't you warn me that it hurt so much?"

"Let me see your hand."

"No, I'm fine." Jem made a whining noise. "I'll just wait for the poison to make my hand shrivel up and fall off."

It went like that for a while until Tean gave up and finally started moving toward the closest building again. Jem came after him, still moaning about his hand. A breeze had picked up, stirring the nettles and the junegrass, combing lines through the thick growth and then stirring it all into disorder again. When they got to the first building, Jem quieted down, and they moved around it slowly. The glass was old and speckled with dirt, but Tean could see some sort of machinery inside the small structure. He tried the door and found it locked.

As they moved to the next one, Jem said, "I really think you could have told me how much it was going to hurt."

"Don't be a baby. We'll wash it and put ice on it, and you'll be fine."

"This is why somebody needs to come through here with a flamethrower and Agent Orange."

"I can't believe I wanted to go camping with you," Tean said.

"I love camping," Jem said, perking up.

"Also, Agent Orange caused an unbelievable amount of environmental damage to Vietnam. Thousands of square miles of forest were destroyed. And Vietnamese people and U.S. soldiers experienced long-lasting effects, including birth defects."

"But I bet it got rid of all the nettles, so, kind of a fair trade."

At the next building, which was much larger, they stopped again at a series of windows on the south wall. Tean stretched up onto his toes, scrubbed with the heel of his hand to clear a patch of glass, and looked inside. He dropped back down.

"Leroy is in there," Tean whispered.

"I was right. Fucking hallelujah, I was right. Go on, you can tell me I'm a genius."

"You're a genius. He's in there. And he's got animals. Now let's go."

"The alligator?"

"I don't know; it's a bad view because something is stacked in front of the window. I just saw a dog with him."

Cradling his hand, Jem made a face. "Always with the fucking dogs. I bet dogs love nettles."

"Come on," Tean whispered, yanking on Jem's tee. "Let's go."

"We saw him with one dog. Let's see if we can spot anything else."

"No way. We're leaving."

"Do you really want to call Ammon and tell him you saw one man and a dog, and hey, he should probably investigate just in case a killer alligator has teamed up with the world's most poisonous nettles?"

"I literally have no idea what you're saying."

"Five more minutes," Jem said. He was grinning, crooked front teeth showing, his eyes bright and boyish. "I'll check the windows at that end. You stay here."

"I'm not staying here."

"Then check the windows around the other corner. We'll meet back in five."

"Jem, no—"

But Jem was already moving.

Tean noticed another sound, a low rumbling. It got into his head, mechanical and regular, as he crept along the side of the building. Part of him recognized it as an engine. Another part, though, was thinking about bee swarms, how swatting them released a pheromone that only made things worse. It was the smell of their fellow bees dying that made them crazy. Instead of retreating, they became berserkers.

When he reached the next set of dirt-specked windows, he had almost made his way to the front of the building. Looking through the glass, he realized he could see clear through to the other side, where a rolling door had been raised. The smudged glass gave only a wavy image of Leroy Erickson, his shaved head pink and dull like a thumb sticking out of his overalls. The dog was gone.

Then Tean heard the snarl: low and vicious. He glanced around. Nothing but nettles and buffalo grass and Queen Anne's lace that had burned up in the sun.

"Get him!" Leroy shouted

And Jem screamed.

37

The scream unlocked Tean's muscles, and he ran. He reversed course, sprinting along the perimeter of the building in the direction Jem had gone. He forgot about the nettles; he was only distantly aware of the heat in his arms, the backs of his hands, like he'd rolled in ground-up glass. The scream went on and on, partially pain, mostly terror.

When Tean skidded around the next corner, he saw them. Jem was on his back, one arm raised to protect himself. That arm was already a bloody mess. The dog lunged, caught Jem's arm again, and bit down. He shook Jem's arm the way Scipio sometimes shook his avocado, a squishy dog toy that a friend had given him.

"Get him, Roger," Leroy was yelling from the rollup door. "Kill that motherfucker!"

Like a snapshot, Tean's eye captured in an instant what was happening: the dog, Jem, the tiny comets of blood on Jem's cheeks and forehead, his eyes squeezed shut, Leroy flushed with excitement, and beyond Leroy, a box truck half-loaded with crates and pens that held turtles, foxes, jackrabbits, an angry tom that kept hissing. He was moving them. Another day—another few hours—and the animals would have been gone.

Then Tean kept moving, running toward Roger and Jem. The dog had dropped Jem's arm and was lunging and snapping again, wild with excitement.

"Cover your head and belly," Tean shouted as he ran. "Jem, cover your head and belly. Potato-bug style! Fingers in, fingers in, make a fist!" Then he was pulling his polo over his head, the sun hot on his skin, the sensation of moving air, the stinging brush of the nettle.

"Tean," Jem was screaming, "Tean! Tean!"

If he had heard Tean, or if he had understood the instructions, he was too lost in panic to respond. Roger leaped forward, nipping at Jem's face, testing to see how Jem would respond. Jem's arm was still in the way, and Roger savaged the arm instead. Bloody foam gathered at the corners of the dog's mouth. Not rabid, but full of a predator's love for the fight, and from what Tean knew of dogs — he thought of the synthetic padding he had found in Leroy's yard — thrilled to be doing what his owner had trained him to do: attack.

Opening his shirt at the hem, Tean darted forward in the next lull. Roger heard him too late. When the dog swung around to glance at the noise, Tean shoved the polo over his head. Roger made a noise that was half snarl, half surprise. He snapped at the air, but the polo blinded him. Roger was still turning in a circle, trying to figure out what was going on, but Tean didn't give him the opportunity. He seized the dog by the back legs and lifted him into the air. Roger let out another of those startled barks, his weight now only supported by his front legs, a position he'd probably never been in before. Tean looped one arm under the dog's hips, freeing his other hand and worked his belt free.

"Hey!" Leroy shouted. "Hey! Let Roger go!"

"Tean?" Jem said through panicked breaths, on the verge of hyperventilating. He was still on the ground. Bites had ripped his arm open in a dozen places, but Jem had it locked in place, still trying to defend himself. "Tean?"

"I'm here," Tean said. "You're going to be ok."

"You're hurting him," Leroy shouted. "You're hurting his legs!"

By then, Tean had the belt free. He forced Roger onto the ground, on his side, using one knee and his body weight to pin him. Then he tied the belt tight around Roger's back legs. The dog kicked once and whined, thrashing inside the polo.

"Don't touch my dog," Leroy roared.

"Tean, it was a dog," Jem said, still taking those rapid, shallow breaths, his voice breaking on the last word.

"I know," Tean said, he took a step toward Jem.

Until then, Leroy had stayed in the shadow of the rollup door. Now he sprang at Tean. Tean had forgotten how big he was: taller and bigger than Jem, who was already much bigger than Tean. He crossed the distance between them in two steps, his shaved head shining in the sun. When the punch came, Tean tried to dodge. He was close enough that he could see the chicken skin caught in Leroy's thick beard. On the side of Leroy's neck, the tattoo of Bo was snarling at Tean.

Tean didn't quite get clear of the punch, but it landed at a bad angle, catching him too far forward on the side of his head and clipping along the bone of his forehead. It still hurt like hell. Tean stumbled back. The tall grass and nettles hissed against his legs. Leroy came after him.

"Don't. Hurt. My. Dog."

"I didn't hurt him," Tean said. "He's fine. But he attacked my friend, and—"

The next punch was faster, and Tean didn't get out of the way in time. It caught him full in the face. For an instant, Tean thought his nose had exploded. The world snapped off for a minute, and when it came back, Tean was lying in the nettles, his face throbbing and already feeling twice its normal size. He stared up at the sky. The sun was very bright. The robin's egg blue looked darker. A bird of prey circled, too far away for Tean to make out what it was. When he sat up, blood dripped from his face onto his chest.

He got to his feet and hobbled toward Leroy and Roger. Leroy was kneeling next to the dog, trying to undo the belt.

"I'm not going to let you do that," Tean said. The words were thick in his throat, and some of the sounds weren't right. He wanted to touch his nose, but he had a picture in his mind of an overripe tomato that had fallen onto a tile floor. "Get away from the dog."

"Fuck off," Leroy said without looking back. "Next time, I'm putting you down for good."

"Tean," Jem was saying. He'd finally dropped his arm, and under the constellation of blood spatter, his face was pale and strangely numb. "Tean, I think a dog bit me."

"You're ok," Tean said. "You're going to be just fine. You handled that dog like nothing. Now all you've got to do is rest." His throat tightened. "We're going to get you some McDonald's on the way home."

"That sounds nice," Jem said. "I think a dog bit me."

"Don't worry about that," Tean said. The pain in his head was in crescendo. It wasn't just a feeling now; it had a dimension of light too. It was like watching a star being born in slow motion right inside his head. "Just think about what you're going to get at McDonald's."

"I like a Big Mac."

"I know you do." Tean could see what was taking Leroy so long: Tean had knotted the belt, and when Roger had thrashed around, he'd pulled the leather even tighter. Leroy couldn't get the knot undone.

"I think a dog bit me."

"I bet you want a chocolate shake too."

"Yeah." Then, hesitantly, "Was it Scipio?"

"No, it wasn't Scipio."

"Oh." Jem said. "Good. Tean, I feel really funny. I think I'm going to pass out."

"Take some deep breaths. You don't need to talk right now. Just take deep breaths." And then he had reached Leroy and Roger. "Get away from the dog. You're finished. If you—"

For an old man, Leroy struck like a viper. He rotated at the waist and swung. Tean turned his head in time—he was picturing the tomato again—but Leroy's big fist smashed into his ear, and the force of the blow made Tean stagger. He stayed up, but he felt like somebody had a finger on the light switch inside his head, ready to flip it if things got any wilder.

"Get away from that dog," Tean said. The voice was somebody else's. Somebody who probably needed his nose realigned. "I won't tell you again."

"Come near me," Leroy said, "and I'll beat you to death. I won't tell you again either."

Tean wobbled, tried to stand straight, and settled for not falling over. He knew how things would go: Leroy would keep trying to release Roger. Tean would try to stop him. Leroy, who was stronger and obviously a much better fighter would win. Impossible odds. Tean didn't like fights, but if he had to fight, he preferred everything stacked in his favor. Then his gaze shifted to Jem, who was pale and bloody, who had never had a single fight with the odds on his side.

With one shaking hand, Tean got his pocketknife out. He opened the blade and said, "Get away from the dog."

Something in his voice must have attracted Leroy's attention because the big man glanced over his shoulder. "That'll do," he said. Rising to his full height, he added, "Let me have that."

"Go sit against the wall," Tean said.

"I'm only going to ask you the one time," Leroy said.

"Do you know what they do to dogs who attack people? They put them down. It's a humane process; they use a barbituric acid derivative. Sodium pentobarbital is the most common."

"Shut your mouth," Leroy said.

"It has a rapid onset leading to loss of consciousness. Most animals barely have time to feel even the prick of the needle."

"Shut your mouth."

"It shuts down the central nervous system. Eventually, they can't breathe, and they go into cardiac arrest." Tean ran his tongue over his teeth and tried to smile. "I'm going to ask them to let me stick the needle in Roger."

Leroy roared and charged. Tean dropped into a crouch to meet him. He got in one good slice across Leroy's belly before the other man clobbered him with a huge, two-handed blow that landed on the top of Tean's head. It was like somebody had run lightning down Tean's spine. His legs gave out, and he fell. When he hit the ground, Leroy kicked him in the gut, and the air exploded from Tean's lungs. He flopped onto his back, struggling to breathe.

The old man settled down onto Tean's chest, his weight pinning him to the ground. Then he grabbed Tean by the hair and punched him. There was no finesse. No art. Just all the force Leroy could muster delivered to a fist-sized area of Tean's face. His head rebounded from the ground. Whoever was in charge of the lights flipped them on and off like crazy.

When Tean could see somewhat clearly again, he realized that Leroy had been waiting for him.

"Say that again about Roger," Leroy said. Spittle flecked Tean's face. "Say it!"

Tean drove the knife into Leroy's thigh.

Leroy howled, but instead of releasing Tean, he punched him again. This time, the lights went off for longer. When Tean came back, Leroy was waiting. He was holding the bloody knife. The tattoo of Bo the Goldendoodle was stretched over the straining cords in his neck. He was screaming something, Tean realized, although the volume inside his head was all the way down. It took a moment for Tean to understand the two words being repeated: "Say it! Say it! Say it!"

Tean popped him in the mouth. It was a nothing blow; he was pinned on the ground, without the ability to generate any serious force behind the punch. But it snapped Leroy's head back for a moment. Then Leroy looked down again, and the knife stabbed toward Tean.

It never reached him.

Leroy jerked backward and then glanced around, the expression on his face comically surprised. He put one hand to the side of his head and then waved the other, still holding the knife, as though warding off a horsefly. He jerked again, and this time, Tean saw it: the flash of metal before a hex nut cracked against the side of Leroy's head. It opened a bloody gash in his scalp, judging by the way Leroy flinched and then screamed, Jem had put a serious amount of force behind the blow. Leroy swung himself off Tean, turning toward Jem, who had come up behind him. That was as far as he got. A tube sock full of something heavy cracked against the side of his head, and Leroy went down.

Jem dropped onto his knees and released the tube sock. Cradling his injured arm, he crabbed toward Tean. His face was shiny, almost translucent, like waxed paper. In his eyes, Tean could see that he was on the brink of falling off into a horrible place.

"Did you at least put a can of Tab inside that sock?"

After a moment, Jem shook his head, and a tiny sob that was also kind of a laugh slipped free. Tean managed to sit up, and he put his arm around Jem, pulled his head down to his shoulder.

"Aquarium gravel," Jem finally managed to whisper. "He had a whole bag of it."

"Mine was better," Tean said.

He didn't start breathing again until he heard another of those broken laughs.

38

For Jem, things got better by stages. First and most important was that Tean was safe. Then the police taking away Leroy and Roger. When the ambulance finally arrived, the paramedic was a tiny girl with a mound of curly hair, and she gave him a shot and made him lie down. Then, at the hospital, they gave him something even better while they worked on his arm. It crashed over him, dead dark waters like the Salt Lake, until he came up screaming because the dog was back, the dog was going at his arm again. Then they gave him something else, and when he woke, he was in Tean's bed.

It took him a while to understand where he was. The light coming through the window meant early morning, the mountains just a blue haze, as though they might smoke away in the dawn. The smell of Gain on the sheets. And the faint dustiness of range grass, the hint of crushed resin. Through the open window came the sounds of a city getting started: tires, brakes, a distant horn.

Snapping jaws.

Teeth.

Worst was the sound, the snarl building in its throat.

On the nightstand was a vial of Valium, and Jem shook out two and held them under his tongue. He considered the closed door. Tean would be on the other side with Scipio, and for a moment, Jem had to rest his head in his hands. It wasn't until then that he noticed the flash of pain, and his forearm swathed in bandages. But he couldn't stay in here forever, and the Valium was coming down on him like a snowdrift, so he made his way to the door and opened it.

No Scipio. No Tean.

Jem went into the bathroom. He peed. He used a washcloth and soap to give himself a cat bath at the sink—he didn't feel up to wrapping his arm in a bag and showering. He fixed his hair. Then he opened the mirrored cabinet and saw that the Xanax were gone.

When he came out of the bathroom, he smelled the food first: definitely a McGriddle, maybe a biscuit too. The paper sack rustled in the kitchen. The footsteps of someone trying to be quiet. The clink of glass. Jem stood in the doorway, unable to take the next step.

"Could you—could you just hold on to Scipio for a minute?"

Racing footsteps, no attempt at quiet. Tean rushed out of the kitchen and then stopped. Then he rushed a few more steps. Then he stopped again. He looked awful. His nose was huge and swollen, with a bandage across the bridge and another, smaller tear along one nostril. He had a black eye, and one ear was still puffy. His hair was crazier than ever, and his glasses had been updated with electrical tape over the bridge and one earpiece. For once, he'd ditched his DWR gear and was wearing a blue SAMANTHA'S 5K CHARITY – RACE FOR A CURE t-shirt and blue jeans. His eyes, though, were red.

"He's not here. I'm sorry, I should have told you; I thought I'd be back before you woke up."

"Oh."

"You don't have to worry about that." Tean put his hands on his hips. Shoved them into his pockets. Back to his hips. "You don't have to see him ever again. Do you want to sit on the couch for a while? Do you want to eat? I got—um, I got everything, actually. I wasn't sure what you'd want."

"I think I'll just lie down again."

"You don't want a sausage biscuit?"

"I'm still really tired."

"You don't want a bacon, egg, and cheese McGriddle?"

Jem tried to smile and moved toward the bedroom.

"What about a hash brown? I got a dozen of them."

"That was really sweet. Thank you."

In the bedroom, he lowered the blinds and climbed under the covers.

Footsteps moved up and down the hall. Paper rustled. The oven door shut with a hollow boom. Then the footsteps were back, stopping at the end of the hall.

When Jem rolled onto his side, Tean was standing in the doorway, his face broken with helplessness.

"You didn't put Scipio down, did you?"

"Jeez, no. He's at my parents."

"Good. That's good. He's a really good dog."

"Do you want to talk? I can bring the TV in here and we can watch TV."

"I don't know what I want. I think I'm just tired."

"Jem, if you're—if you're still scared, still upset, it's ok."

"I can feel whatever I want to feel?" Jem asked with another of those aborted smiles.

Nodding, Tean wiped his face. "But you don't have to, either. Not right now. I just want you to do whatever is best for you right now."

"When did you figure out about the Xanax?"

"I—I didn't want you mixing them."

"When did you realize I was taking them?"

"When we first met, back in October, I wondered. I thought some were missing. Then, when you passed out the other day, I thought about it again. I didn't check until we got home from the hospital yesterday."

"I took two Valium."

"I don't think you should take more than what the doctor prescribed."

"I know." Jem flopped onto his back, his arm over his eyes. As the morning light gained strength, it shone through his eyelids red, and the bandage smelled like sweat and something else, something Jem associated with hospitals.

Near the door, Tean was managing to make a lot of sound for someone who was supposedly standing still.

"Why don't you tell me what you're feeling?" Jem said.

"I'm really, really scared. For you."

"I'm ok. I think the doctors told me none of the bites are that serious. Some scarring, probably. It's going to be a bitch to pay those bills, but they're going to have to catch me first. Maybe I'll forward them to Mommy."

"I'm not scared about your arm. I'm scared about all the trauma you carry around, and the fact that a dog attacked you again, and I let it happen. And I'm scared—frick, this is so fricking selfish—I'm scared you won't want to hang out with me anymore because of Scipio. Or because I couldn't keep you from getting hurt. Or because

I asked you to get into this mess. I know I say stupid things all the time, but you matter more to me than anyone else in the whole world, and I don't know what I'll do when you realize you don't want to see me anymore."

The thing about light, Jem realized staring up at the ceiling, was that it wasn't all big changes—light to dark, black to white. It was little shifts too. Nuances. The gray of the walls looked blue. Very soft blue. It made him think of a pair of Reeboks he'd owned before going to Decker. He thought Tean would compare it to the sky over the Salt Lake a few minutes after dawn.

"So, before you make any rash decisions," Tean continued, sounding like a man who knew he was poking a bear, "I wanted to tell you that Scipio's going to split his time between my parents and my siblings. I told them they either did this for me, or I'd never talk to them again. And I'll go visit him and go on long walks, but he loves those kids. He really does. And he's going to be so much happier with a yard to run in, with people around him all day."

The same room. The same paint. The same sun. And then, somehow, it could be different.

"Before I do anything rash?" Jem said.

"I just wanted you to know that—"

"Scipio is not going to live with your parents and your siblings. For one thing, they'd raise him Mormon, and I'm not going to have a Mormon goddog."

"What?"

"Goddog. It's like a godson. And for another thing, you love him, and he's your best buddy. So he's not going anywhere."

"Jem, after—"

"It's not like I hadn't been attacked before. I'll be nervous for a while. Scared shitless is the medical term, I believe. I'll probably need you to introduce us again. And maybe run interference for a while. But it's not like that attack broke my brain. I know Scipio's a different dog. I know he likes me."

"He loves you."

"So that's settled," Jem said. "And don't ever do something stupid with my goddog again. Understand?"

"Not even close." In a quieter voice, Tean asked, "Do you want to tell me what you're feeling now?"

"Nothing," Jem said. "I'm feeling nothing. That's why I took two Valium."

"Oh."

Outside, below the apartment, kids were laughing, and a woman said, "I will beat your asses with a belt if you don't give me my pop back," and the kids just laughed harder, and then the woman started laughing too.

"I helped LouElla get kids back in her house."

"What?"

"I helped her do it. I went to the home inspection or whatever they call it. I lied through my teeth. I made it possible for her to have kids in that house. I was crazy, I think. I can't believe I did it. But I wanted to know who had fucked up my life so badly. And I wanted those things, a job and an apartment and all that stuff, because you wanted me to have them. I thought maybe if I had those things—I don't know. I guess I thought things would be different."

"I don't want you to have those things because I want you to be different," Tean said. "I want you to be happy and safe. I just—I just don't know any other way to do it."

"She's going to hurt those kids. She's going to fuck them up. And I put them there. And you know what the really messed up part is?" Jem rolled onto his side. Tean was crying, his hands dashing furiously at his tears. "The really screwy part is that I did it for nothing. I think LouElla got a good laugh about that. I thought I was going to find the son of a bitch who stole my identity. I thought I was going to fix things. And then, Christ, it's my own mom. How's that for a kick in the ass?"

"I don't know. I can't even imagine. I'm sorry, Jem, I'm so sorry that's what happened."

"You know. You do. I saw how your family treats you. You just got to experience it all from a different angle." Jem was watching Tean, studying the out-of-control eyebrows, the taped glasses that had slid to the end of his nose, the slender lines of his body. The light was still coming in at an angle, and deep shadows lay across Tean's face, hid his hands—strong, capable hands, even though he always seemed so unsure. This wasn't the right place for the doc; he ought to be outside, with sagebrush and a wide open sky, with the light pooling in the hollow of his throat, with the desert sun bright on his hair, bright in his eyes. "You know what I wanted when I was growing up?"

"Those kangaroo shoes combined with the shoes that you could pump up with air."

"Oh my God, I did. I forgot I told you that. But I wanted something else too. I wanted a house with a yard, instead of an apartment. For a lot of reasons. Cosmic joke: one of those reasons was that I wanted a dog. But the big reason was that for some reason, and I had to have been four or five, I got fixated on having an inflatable swimming pool, the kind you can have in your backyard. I just thought they looked like so much fun. I don't know if I ever told my mom I wanted one. But that's what she's got now: the house she wanted, the yard she wanted, the kids she wanted."

"Jem."

"She even got the motherfucking pool."

"Jem, it's not that she didn't want you."

"It doesn't matter," Jem said, wiping his face on the pillow. "None of it matters. I think I better go to sleep again."

He lay back against the pillow, which was now damp, and closed his eyes. Tean was still there; Jem could feel him, waiting.

"I guess with the dog," Jem said. "With Antony, I mean, back at LouElla's house, I guess when you're a kid, you think your mom is going to protect you. Then for a long time, I thought I was over that. I thought I could take care of myself. Jesus, I even thought I could take care of you. But when it came down to it, when that dog was lunging at me, snapping, poof. I might as well have been five years old again." He opened his eyes. The room was darker; the sun had moved again. "Big surprise, she wasn't there when I needed her yesterday either."

"No," Tean whispered.

"But you were."

Nodding, Tean wiped his face some more. "Maybe you don't need to take care of yourself for a while. Maybe you can let someone else do that. That's part of loving someone: taking care of them."

Jem closed his eyes again. The Valium snow was falling on him, deeper and deeper. "I can remember what it felt like to be next to her. She let me sleep with her sometimes." He smiled in spite of himself. "She'd scratch my back."

He must have already been at the edge of sleep because he didn't hear the footsteps. The shifting mattress pulled him back for a moment, and he grumbled as Tean pressed against him, both of them moving around until Tean was sitting with his back to the wall and Jem was stretched out, snugged up against Tean's side. The last thing he remembered was fingers running over his back lightly and slowly.

39

Each day was a little bit better, but Tean left Scipio with his parents for now. They assured him that the Lab was having a great time trying to catch a mole in the yard. That was a relief; in spite of Jem's insistence, Tean wasn't ready to bring him back into contact with a dog. Not yet. The Xanax had gone down the toilet, which Tean knew wasn't the responsible way to dispose of a prescription but had seemed the best option in a bad situation, and after the first two days—and after several uncomfortable conversations—Jem had eased up on the Valium.

They were eating In-N-Out burgers at the dinette table when the knock came. Tean wiped his mouth and hands—animal style was messy, no matter how much you tried to keep clean—and waved Jem back into his seat. He got up and answered the door.

Hannah was standing there. She was wearing a DWR polo and jeans, and she'd had her hair cut. No makeup, which was a good thing because Hannah wouldn't have been Hannah with makeup. Tucking the chestnut-colored hair behind her ears, she said, "Hi."

"Hi," Tean said. "Oh my gosh, you're out. That's fantastic. Come in."

She shook her head. Then Tean noticed Caleb standing farther down the hall. "I just wanted to give Jem his money and say thank you."

"You didn't need to do that," Jem said. He had moved up behind Tean without Tean noticing, and he shook his head when Hannah held out the check. "Really, I promise. I'm just glad we could help."

"Please take it," Hannah said. "I'll never be able to pay you both back for helping me, but at least let me try. Besides, you're good at what you do, and my dad always said that you should pay a man what he's worth. This doesn't come close to what you're worth; consider it a down payment." Then her mouth quivered. "I've heard myself repeating a lot of my parents' little sayings over the last few days. That's probably a coping mechanism since they won't ever talk to me again."

"Hannah, I'm so sorry," Tean said.

"No, it's ok. Caleb and I—we're going to try to make it work. It'll be hard. I knew it would hurt him; I didn't know how bad. But we're going to try." When Tean opened his mouth, she raised a hand to stop him and said, "And it's better that he learned this way. It's better all around, in fact. I was so tired of trying to hide parts of myself."

"I hope you both find a way to be happy," Tean said. He was surprised to feel Jem's hand on his nape, a faint squeeze of reassurance. "We tried to visit at the jail, but—"

"After they arrested Leroy, thanks to both of you, my lawyer made me swear not to see anyone. It was crazy for forty-eight hours. Zalie admitted she'd exaggerated a lot of the details of my conversations with Joy. She even admitted that she'd been following me, trying to catch Joy and me together; that's who I saw on the path that night near my house. She's the one who sent Ammon to my house the night you were waiting outside. Then my lawyer managed to track down Becca, the woman Joy met on the Playmates app. The night Joy died, Becca picked her up at my house and drove her to where her dad was keeping his animals. Joy was planning on releasing them while Leroy was out of town. Becca gave a statement, her side of things. I guess she left after dropping off Joy; she lost her nerve and didn't wait around.

"The big break, though, is that Leroy finally confessed. Unofficially, the version I heard from my lawyer, who heard it from a friend inside the police, is that Leroy came back from a trip and found Joy dead—the alligator had ripped off her arm, and she'd bled out. I guess you figured that out on your own. He tried to make it look like a murder to save his animals. When nobody took the bait and arrested Sievers or Zalie, he dressed up as a Dominion Energy employee and stashed the hatchet in my garage. I guess nobody looked twice at someone walking around the house to read the gas meter."

"Bingo bango bongo," Jem said, squeezing Tean's neck again. "You're lucky your boss is a veterinary stud."

"Stud has a different kind of meaning," Tean said, squirming to get free of the touch. "For vets, anyway."

"I know," Jem said.

To Tean's surprise, Hannah laughed. Then, her smile fading, she said, "He's not my boss anymore. I resigned today. Caleb and I are going away for a while. When I come back—well, I guess I'll see. There's got to be a job for a biologist somewhere in this state."

"There'll be one at DWR," Tean said, "if I can do anything about it."

"Thank you." She looked around. "I heard you got Sievers."

"What? Oh. Yes. We got a warrant because of the canine distemper outbreak. He was keeping that bear just like people thought, although he killed it before we got there. He had a lot of illegal game trophies. He'll get something, but it won't be close to what he deserves."

"I'm not sure anyone does," Hannah said slowly. "I guess that's all. Thank you, both of you, for giving me my life back." Then she hugged Tean and kissed Jem on the cheek and walked away.

As Tean shut the door, Jem said, "I got a kiss."

"I saw."

"You only got a hug, but I got a kiss."

"She was just being polite. That was like the *besitos* in Latin America. It's basically a handshake. A hug is much more meaningful."

"No, it was a kiss. And I think she gave me a little bit of cheek tongue."

"What is wrong with you?" Tean said. "Cheek tongue? Does that mean she licked your cheek?"

"Wouldn't you love to know?"

When they'd finished eating, Tean cleaned up the mess. He'd bought groceries, but aside from the milk and breakfast cereal, Jem preferred eating out. To build up his strength, he said, although his eyes had looked very alarmed when Tean had suggested trying to make burgers at home out of diced mushrooms and some leftover scrambled eggs. After washing up, Tean joined Jem on the couch. Jem was watching an old cartoon: *Visionaries*. Apparently, they were knights who turned into animals. Or something like that.

"Jem," Tean said. "Can I ask you for something?"

"Not cheek tongue. Not on the first date, mister."

Tean took the remote and turned off the TV. "I'd like you to go somewhere with me." He took a breath. "And Ammon."

"A threesome?"

"No, not a threesome."

"Because that's not really my thing. I like a guy's full attention."

"Please?"

"Why Ammon?"

"If I tell you, I'm afraid you'll say no."

Jem chewed his lip. "That's not a great sign."

"I know. But please?"

"Yes, ok."

"Really?"

"Stop smiling. Think about your carbon footprint or how many ducks were boiled alive to get the feathers for your pillow or something like that."

Tean managed to stop smiling; all he had to do was look at the bandages on Jem's arm.

Ammon came downstairs that afternoon, and they loaded up in his car, which smelled like farts and fast food and industrial cleaner. Jem described these smells at great length and insisted on rolling the window down. Ammon didn't say anything, but the muscles in his jaw got tighter and tighter.

"Thank you for doing this," Tean said in one of the lulls in Jem's monologue. He touched Ammon's arm. "I know it's a gray area."

"I want to be part of your life," Ammon said. "Whatever part you'll let me be. If that means keeping you out of trouble, well, I'm just happy you'll talk to me." He reached over and brushed a thumb, feather light, up the black-and-blue bridge of Tean's nose. "All I want is to keep you safe, make sure you're happy. I don't ever want to see you hurt like this again. It's killing me."

Jem was making gagging noises in the back seat.

Tean reached back to poke him. "Jem, be nice to Ammon, please. He heard there was a warrant out for you after what happened at Snow's, and he got it taken care of."

Jem didn't say thank you, but he did stop making noises.

They drove west out of the city, following I-80 out of the valley and then turning south along the back of the Oquirrh Mountains. The Tooele Valley was green with blue grama and junegrass and buffalo grass, tender stalks fluttering in the breeze. They passed a pasture with a herd at rest, and one cow was leaning against a fence post near the highway, trying to clear a path. Her black-and-white coat made Tean think of a Rorschach test. A shingle beach, he would have said. Islands in the sea. A galaxy.

"Where are we going?" Jem said.

"To see LouElla," Tean said.

"Oh no. Oh fuck no."

"You don't even have to get out of the car," Tean said. "I promise. I just wanted you to see this. I thought—I thought maybe you needed to see this."

"What the fuck does that mean?"

"Just wait. Just try to relax and wait. I promise, you won't have to do anything."

"As usual," Ammon said. "You can sit in the car while Tean gets the shit beaten out of him."

"Hey! I got mauled by a dog!"

"You got nipped a few times. Jesus Christ. You probably didn't even need stitches."

"Enough," Tean said.

"Oh yeah?" Jem said. "Where were you when that inflatable ass toy was beating Tean's face into the ground? Where were you?"

"Enough," Tean said. "Enough, Ammon! Let it go!"

From the look on Ammon's face, that was a bitter pill to swallow, but Tean didn't back down. He'd backed down his whole life with Ammon. If they were going to find a way forward—if—then he had to learn to hold his ground.

A few miles later, Ammon said, probably in what he thought was a neutral tone, "I saw your Prowler profile."

"No," Tean said. "We are not going to talk about that."

"I was just surprised. I thought you were dating the shrinking violet back there."

"We're just friends," Tean said.

"Best friends, motherfucker," Jem said, leaning into the front of the car. "How do you like that?"

Ammon was grinding his teeth again. After another moment, he managed to say, "I really liked that you put the World Wildlife Fund as the charity you would donate money to. I thought that was perfect for you. It shows how compassionate you are and what you really care about."

"Thank you," Tean said. He didn't look in the rearview mirror; he didn't need to. He could feel Jem grinning.

Ammon wanted to talk about Prowler the rest of the drive, circling around the questions Tean could tell he wanted to ask: have you gone out with anybody, how many, how often, why. Tean kept his gaze locked forward, the landscape blurring into browns and greens around him, and focused on keeping up his end of the conversation. He didn't look back at Jem. Not once.

Guided by the app on his phone, Ammon stopped the car outside of a 70s-era split-level home, with the exposed timbers and stucco of a vaguely Tudor design. Although the paint looked relatively new, the garage door was dinged in places, and the basketball hoop to one side of the garage lacked a net. The curtains were drawn in every window. In the back seat, Jem was breathing faster.

"This part is up to you," Tean said. "You and I can get out of here and talk for a minute. Or Ammon volunteered to get out if you felt safer staying here."

"I didn't volunteer," Ammon said. "You told me I wasn't allowed to come if I didn't agree."

"Jem?" Tean said.

"I can get out of the car. Are we going to talk to her? I just need to get ready if we are."

"No."

"Ok." He sat there, drying his palms against his jeans. "Ok," he said again, and he pushed open the door and got out.

"Stay here, please," Tean said to Ammon.

Ammon grimaced and nodded.

When Tean got out of the car, the first thing he noticed was the mountain breeze, the smell of evergreens and exposed rock and gasoline. A small engine hummed off in the distance—a four-wheeler or ATV—punctuated by whoops of excitement. Kids having fun. Tean shut the door and moved to the front of the car, where Jem stood with his arms folded, staring at the house. The day was warm, and the first hint of sweat glistened at his nape along the short blond hairs.

"We're here. What do I need to see or do or talk about? If this is supposed to be some sort of armchair psych shit, I'm not going to be a very good patient."

"She's never going to have kids in that house again."

"Unfortunately, the DWR doesn't get to make that decision. And I helped her pass the inspection. Hell, I probably could have given that lady a guided tour of Satan's dildo collection, and she still would have passed LouElla; LouElla's not bad at these kinds of games herself."

"Jem, I'm telling you, she's never going to have kids here again." Tean took a deep breath. "She was arrested this morning for possession with intent to distribute. It's a felony charge. The max is fifteen years, but she won't get anywhere close to that. Still, it'll keep her from having foster kids again. Ever."

"LouElla doesn't do drugs. She's devoutly Mormon, at least as far as that stuff goes."

"Jem, she was arrested. They found the drugs. It's an open-and-shut case."

Scratching the back of one arm, Jem cocked his head. Maybe he was listening to the kids on the four-wheeler. One of them was telling Philip to "Just do it, do it, do it!"

"Why is Ammon sitting in the car?"

"This doesn't have anything to do with him."

"Bullshit. He came because he doesn't want to let you out of his sight. You couldn't make him stay home, so you left him sitting in the car because you did something illegal, and you're trying to keep him from being an accessory after the fact."

Tean shrugged.

"Tell me what you did. Right now."

"Jem—"

"Tell me, or I swear to God I will walk back to Salt Lake."

"That's really more punishing yourself."

"Tean, God damn it."

"Ok, ok. I called Tinajas. It turned out that someone might have made a mistake and pressed the wrong button in a program somewhere, and all of a sudden LouElla didn't have the right plates registered to her car. Some industrious patrol cop must have noticed and pulled her over, and during the stop, he found a kilo of Mexican brown."

"I've never heard someone say Mexican brown not ironically. You don't even know what Mexican brown is."

"Oh. Never mind, then."

"Where did you get it?"

"I don't know what you're talking about."

"You're on thin fucking ice right now. If you went out and bought from a dealer and put yourself in danger for this stupid stunt, I'm going to have a lot to say. And so will Ammon." Then, seeming unable to help himself, he said, "Glasses."

Pushing the taped frames back up his nose, Tean said, "I remembered you mentioned a friend named Chaquille."

"Oh my God. And how did you get into her car?"

"I'm done talking about this. I'm pleading the Fifth."

"Teanemone Mahi-Mahi Leon, explain yourself."

"There are YouTube videos! It's not rocket science!"

A tiny smile slipped out as Jem's gaze slid back to the house. Down the street, a woman leaned out from her front door and shouted, "Philip, Peter, get back here and clean your rooms this instant!" If the boys heard her over the four-wheeler's rumble, they gave no sign of it, and after a moment the woman slammed the door.

"Thank you," Jem said.

"For what?" Tean said, opening his eyes as widely as possible.

Jem caught his glasses before they could fall. As he resettled them, his smile got even bigger, and he said, "I've created a monster."

40

A few days later, they were sitting in the DWR's white Ford F-150, Tean behind the wheel as they drove up toward Emigration Canyon and the park where they had arranged this meeting. They wove through neighborhoods of older homes, where oak trees lined the sidewalks, already leafed out, their shadows dancing across the pavement. Jem smelled like something new, grapefruit and white musk, and he was wearing a button-up printed with dinosaurs: stegosaurus, brontosaurus, tyrannosaurus, velociraptor. He had changed pants four times before settling on his favorite jeans. Now he was checking his hair in the mirror.

"Can I have the emergency comb?"

"What is an emergency comb?"

"It's a comb used in emergencies. What does it sound like?" Jem opened the glove box and began tossing its contents on the floor: the vehicle owner's manual, a pack of Orbit gum, two pencils, disinfectant wipes, tissues that were so old they had turned gray. "Where do you keep it?" When Tean didn't answer, he twisted in his seat. "Tean, where is it?"

"I'm sorry, this is too fascinating. It's like making first contact, only it happens over and over again. I wonder what Captain Picard — wait. Do you actually have an emergency comb?"

"Just one?" Jem said with a disgusted noise. "Never mind. This is a mistake. Let's turn around."

"Jem."

"My hair is ridiculous."

As far as Tean could tell, Jem's hair was perfect. He'd had the hard side part recently cut again, and on the sides and back it was that low, bristly texture that Tean wanted to rub. He resisted the urge and said, "Your hair looks great."

Another of those disgusted noises. "I'll trust a mirror over you. You look like you let Scipio groom you."

"Hey! That's not fair!"

"You're right. Scipio would have done a better job. You know what? Right there. That's the perfect spot to flip a u-ey. Tean, you missed it. Is something wrong with your head? Are you beating yourself up because you didn't have an emergency comb?"

"Yes. Yes, that's what I'm doing."

"Please stop the truck."

Tean slowed and pulled up to the curb. He looked over at Jem. Beneath the beard, the color was high in his cheeks, and his eyes moved restlessly.

"I shouldn't have agreed to this," Jem said. "I'm not ready."

"Ok," Tean said. "I'm not going to force you, but can I make a suggestion?"

"Yeah," Jem said, and then he laughed explosively. "Yes, please tell me what to do because I'm about to have a nervous breakdown."

"I can't even imagine how scary this is, but I think you're going to regret it if we turn around. My suggestion is that we at least get to the park. Then we can reassess how you're feeling. I also think you should do some deep breaths. And I know you're out of Valium—"

"Actually, I stole a bunch from Caleb, and I've been rationing them."

Tean took a deep breath.

"Don't be mad," Jem said. "I didn't take any today because—because I don't know, but I just think I need to be clean for this."

After another moment, Tean managed to say, "That's probably a good idea. And I know this is easy for me to say, but I still think it's the right thing to tell you: you need to—"

"Feel what I need to feel," Jem muttered.

"That's all. You don't have to do anything with it. You don't have to fight it or control it or make it go away. Just feel it and realize it's just one part of you, and there are all these other parts too, and together they make up this amazing, wonderful person who happens to be my casual acquaintance."

Jem tried to smile, but he mostly just swallowed. He put his hands to his face. His head dropped back. Then, sitting up straight again, he nodded.

"Would it be ok if I held your hand?" Tean said. He hadn't even realized he was going to ask until the question had emerged. He wasn't even sure where the question came from.

Jem nodded.

Tean took his hand carefully, lacing their fingers together loosely, surprised by how clammy Jem's skin was. He squeezed once.

After a moment, Jem squeezed back. Then he turned and faced out the window; when he spoke, his voice was rough. "Let's get this over with."

The closer they got, the tighter his grip. Tean bore it without saying anything.

When they stopped, Jem's whole body locked up. Tean barely spared the park a glance—scrub and sage and thistles giving way to a perfect lawn, perfect flowerbeds, perfect families enjoying a perfect day. A sign said THIS IS THE PLACE. Then his gaze moved back to Jem.

Jem was facing forward again, as though refusing to look at the park, and chewing his lip. He was clutching Tean's hand hard enough to hurt. Then something changed, and his eyes were full, and he had to blink rapidly to clear them before the tears spilled.

"Jem," Tean began, "we don't have to—"

"What if she doesn't love me? I don't even know why it matters. She abandoned me, and I never thought she loved me, never once thought it, and now it's the only thing in my head. Christ, I'll be lucky if I get up there and can remember my own name."

Tean waited to see if it was a genuine question. "That's her decision. You can't make somebody love you. And it's your decision to love her. If you want to forgive her, if you want to try to have a relationship, you own that, and nobody can take that away from you. All you can decide is what you're going to do."

"Yeah," Jem said. He flipped down the mirror, wiped his eyes, and checked his hair one last time. "I guess I should do this."

"Jem?"

"I'm feeling my feelings, Tean. If I feel them any more, I'm literally going to explode."

"No, I just wanted to tell you—" Tean drew a breath. "Did you know that crypsis isn't always beneficial? Like any evolutionary development, it has costs too. Sometimes it's the cost of investing too many resources, too much energy, at the expense of other possibilities. Many forms of crypsis lock a species into an environmental niche, and then they're stuck. And . . . and one of the most common forms of crypsis is simply remaining motionless. All sorts of animals do it; it improves their camouflage, of course, but it's also a form of hiding on its own."

"Oh boy," Jem whispered. "You're about to go megadark, aren't you?"

"I've been hiding for a long time. Hiding in plain sight. Trying to be invisible. And I did it by . . . by not moving, not changing, not taking any risks or trying anything new. I ended up getting stuck. And then I met you, and—and I just want you to know that I love you. So much. I know it might not be the way either of us thought it was going to be, but I'm not going to make it sound like less than what it is by saying we're just friends. We've both been trying to get to the same place, but maybe this, what we have right now, this is the place, this is where we're supposed to be together. I love you. You're the most important person in my life. I love your great big old purple grandma t-shirt. I love the Power Rangers DVDs you think are hidden in your duffel. I love that one time I caught you kissing your comb. I love how hard you try to make yourself better every day, when anybody else would have given up. And I love that you're kind and caring, and that you took all the hate and brutality in your life and found a way to be gentle. I know you've said, in the past, that you wanted us to be more than this. But for me, this is everything. I want you to know that."

Jem suddenly smiled, the real one, with the crooked front teeth. "Can I tell you something now?"

"Of course."

"You know what you were talking about? About how the universe is absurd because it's orderless, no matter how much we work to impose order on it, and how that absurdity alienates us from each other and even alienates us from ourselves, how we come into existence without really being anything, and we have to decide what we're going to be, and then all we can do is be authentic, and that's how we live a good life in a broken cosmos?"

"Hmm. That must have been something you and Tinajas talked about. Ow!" Tean tried to pull his hand free, and he rubbed the line of teeth marks on his wrist. "You can't bite people, you mongrel."

"Well, apparently I can, because I just did. Do you remember now?"

"Vaguely. I never would have said something like 'broken cosmos,' though."

"I went to church a few times, you know. And I remember this phrase because it's got a cool ring to it: 'Stranger in a strange land.' That's it, right?"

"That's it."

"Maybe you're right. Maybe the universe is meaningless, and maybe life is absurd, and maybe all we can do is try to decide who we want to be, and then be authentic about it. Maybe we really are strangers in a strange land. Maybe we're even strangers to ourselves. But you, Teancum Leon, are not a stranger to me." Releasing Tean's hand, he slid out of the truck and shut the door. Through the open window he said, "Stick with me. We'll be strangers in a strange world together."

"I think I'd like that," Tean said, his voice thick.

Jem glanced over his shoulder. Then back. His eyes were the eyes of a child for one brief moment. "You won't go anywhere?"

The breeze carried the smell of Jem's new cologne, the smell of the warming asphalt, the smell of the park's freshly watered grass, the smell of the scrub oak and lodgepole pines on the mountains. Where the park ended, ephedra and bitterbrush and Russian thistle grew in pale, cracked earth. The sun, high overhead, made the valley huge and bright, as though the sky went on forever. When pioneers had come, they had wanted everything to be different: they had wanted the green grasses and old trees of the lands they had left. They had wanted to make this place something else. For the desert to blossom like the rose. But they had gotten one thing right. They had seen, in the desert, the burning bush. They had seen the valley and known it was home.

Tean shook his head. "I'll be right here."

THE SAME END

Keep reading for a sneak preview of *The Same End,* book three of
The Lamb and the Lion.

1

"I don't want to kill anything," Tean said into the phone as he unlocked the door and stepped into his apartment. "You know that. I haven't been hunting in twenty years, probably more."

His brother Amos sighed. "You don't have to kill anything. I'm not inviting you to go hunting."

Scipio, Tean's black Lab, bounded off the sofa, stretched, and then crashed into him. A wet nose found his hand, and Scipio did some happy whining to fully communicate how thrilled he was that Tean had returned. "You, Corom, Timothy, Seth, and Dad go hunting every Pioneer Day weekend."

"We go camping. And every year we invite you, and every year you refuse to go."

"Because you're not just going camping. You're going hunting."

"We go hiking. We cook potatoes in the Dutch oven. We try to find constellations. We eat s'mores and listen to Dad's dumb jokes. Like we did when we were kids."

"And you do some hunting."

On the other end of the call, Amos made an irritated noise that he suppressed quickly. "I'm just trying to get you to see the big picture. Yes, we go hunting."

"And fishing."

Another of those noises. "And fishing," Amos said; it sounded like he was gritting his teeth. "But you're missing the point. The point is that this year, we're not going camping."

"Hunting."

"Teancum, please!"

"Fine. What are you doing instead?"

"We're going to Vegas."

"Sin City? Bold choice. What does your wife think about that?"

"It was Bailey's idea, actually. She won some sort of KSL giveaway. Five tickets to Celine Dion. She's taking Mom and the sisters-in-law; Sara and Miriam opted out to give the other girls a chance to bond. They're even taking the kids for four days; we come back late on Pioneer Day."

"I hope you have a great time."

"And you know Bailey, so she called the hotel and talked them into reserving a block of rooms for all of us. It's an unbelievable rate."

Tean tried to repress a shudder. He'd once seen Bailey break down a Hobby Lobby clerk, leaving the poor man in tears, over a ten-cent price adjustment on a baby-Jesus-themed wreath. "Even better. I hope you all have a great time."

"A block of rooms for all of us, Tean. That includes you. Come on, please. This is a chance for us to bond, just the guys, while the girls do their thing."

Tean cradled the phone against his shoulder as he helped Scipio into his harness. "I've got too much work. A moose injured a hiker, we're still trying to figure out how bad the damage from the Beaver Mesa fire really is, and we've got to inspect close to fifteen thousand boats for invasive mussels on the hulls. I've got enough work for the rest of the year."

"Great. You're never going to catch up on it, so you might as well take a few days off and hang with your brothers."

"What about Jem?"

"I don't think even Baily can get another free ticket to Celine." Doubtfully, Amos added, "Not this late."

Scipio led the way out of the apartment, and Tean pulled the door shut behind him. They went downstairs. "Do you want to try that again?"

"I was just joking."

"Jem isn't my wife. He's not even my boyfriend. He's my friend."

"Nobody else is bringing friends."

"Why can't I bring him?"

"You just said he's not even your boyfriend. He was unbelievably rude last time he came around, and he made everyone feel horrible—Mom cried, by the way. And I don't know why you feel like you need a bodyguard so you can attend family events. If you've got a problem with us, you can tell us yourself. We don't need your friend sticking his nose into our family business."

"He's not sticking his nose—"

"Does he even allow you to go places by yourself? Are you permitted to see your family on your own?"

"Goodbye, Amos."

They stopped at the first available stretch of grass so Scipio could relieve himself, and then they headed south. Salt Lake City was an oven in July, the dry heat baking the air. The whole city felt gritty with dust—they might not have precipitation again until the first snowfall—and where the sun danced on glass and stucco, it was so bright that Tean had to squint.

Everyone was looking for ways to beat the heat. He passed a kebab shop, its doors propped open, two fans humming to circulate air—and, as a bonus, the smell of seared meat, probably in the hopes of attracting customers. Scipio was definitely interested. A glitzy, upgraded hipster version of the old-fashioned ice-cream truck was parked at the next corner, and the line of people ran for half a block. Tean had no idea what mochi balls were, but if they were this popular, Jem had probably already tried them and fallen in love with them. Catty-corner, a pair of Latina girls were running an ancient shaved-ice machine, their only client a middle-aged woman who was digging through her purse while the kids threw murderous looks at the mochi truck.

Tean and Scipio were halfway to Liberty Park when his phone buzzed. It was Amos again. Tean dismissed the call. At the next crosswalk, it vibrated again. Cor, the next brother in line. Then, when they got under the shade of an elm, Timothy. At this rate, they'd burn through the immediate family before dinner, and then Tean would be ignoring calls from his ailing, elderly great-aunts until he put his head under the wheel of a mochi truck.

When Seth called, Tean answered and said, "What?"

"Oh. I didn't think you were going to answer, so I honestly wasn't ready."

"Goodbye, Seth."

"No, wait. Can I start with Amos is a jerk, and we're all sorry?"

"How often do you talk to each other? Is there a group chat I don't know about?"

"Yes, obviously. Except you do know about it. It's on that app you refuse to download. I've sent you ten invites."

"I'm not going to Vegas."

"Please?"

"I'm not going."

"Ok. That's fine. I mean, we'll miss you, but that's fine." Someone had set up sprinklers in one of the open fields of the park, and kids were darting through the spray, laughing, shrieking, slipping, coming up muddy and grinning. "Would you at least think about it, though?"

"You know that you guys do this with everything? You invite me, invite me, invite me, and you don't want me there, but then I'm the bad guy if I don't go."

A diesel dump truck rumbled past, the engine so loud that it obliterated other sounds.

"Do you really feel that way?"

"Never mind. I'm tired. I've got a lot going on." When they got to the fenced section of the park, Tean knelt to unhook the leash from the harness. He opened the gate and let Scipio race inside. "Thanks for the invitation, but I'm not going to be able to make it."

"You know what?" Seth said.

Tean shook his head and didn't answer.

"Your friend was right about a lot of stuff. But you're not giving us a chance to make it better."

"Right. Got it. It's my fault again."

"Don't do that. You know this was Dad's idea, right? This is all about you. Just like every conversation we have in this family is about you. He's told everyone who would listen that he wants you there."

"Dad's freaking out because I stopped writing Mom blank checks," Tean said.

"Jeez, Tean, I get it! Dad's an asshole! Quit letting him screw up your relationship with people who love you."

At the other end of the fenced area, Scipio was playing tag with a Pomeranian. The Lab would get as close as he dared, and when the Pomeranian would whirl around, Scipio would shoot off in the other direction.

Tean started to laugh. Then Seth started to laugh too.

"I honestly don't know if I've ever heard you use a bad word before," Tean said.

"Well, it's not the first time."

Tean sat on a bench; the back was hot from the sun, and he rested his elbows on his knees, watching Scipio play. "So, what? Everybody resents me because I'm the black sheep and you have to talk about me and think about me and pray about me?"

"You are an extremely frustrating person sometimes. Did you know that? If this is what you put Jem through, somebody honestly ought to give that man a medal."

"You should hear him when I make him wash the dishes. You'd think he was the victim of a war crime." Then Tean's face heated. "We're just friends, you know."

"Why?"

"What?"

"He's crazy about you; that's obvious. He stood up for you. Heck, you dragged him to a family party, and he didn't run away screaming. You should probably just jump straight to marrying him."

"It's complicated."

"Is it because of Ammon?" Seth sounded hesitant. "Just so you know, well, everybody knows. More or less."

"It's complicated. That's all."

"That's your way of saying you don't want to talk about it."

"Seth, if I'm being totally upfront, I don't think I can talk about it. Not with you, anyway."

Scipio had taken up position near the fence and was barking at joggers.

"I'm really sorry to hear that," Seth said.

"I'll think about Vegas," Tean said. "I need to go. Please don't make Great-aunt Gilda call me."

The call ended in taut silence.

After collecting Scipio, Tean headed back to the apartment. The line for the mochi truck was longer. The Latina girls had packed up, maybe to try their luck somewhere else. Tean considered stopping at the kebab shop, but then he remembered he had a brick of tofu and a few cloves of garlic at home, and he figured he could make something out of that.

As he neared the apartment building, he heard Mrs. Wish screaming.

"Stop it right this minute! I absolutely will not tolerate this behavior. You are both gentlemen, and you will behave — no, Senator Borah, don't you dare, I will not — " And then more screams.

His neighbor was an older woman in a housedress printed with sailboats, her white hair up in a bun. She was currently trying to wrangle three of the Irreconcilables. The cats' leashes had gotten tangled, and two of them — Senator Poindexter, a Siamese, and Senator William Borah, a Bengal — were hissing at each other, lunging, trying to fight. The third cat, Senator Frank B. Bandegee, a domestic short hair with a white patch on her chest, was pulling in the opposite direction. Mrs. Wish was yanking on the tangled leashes and screaming.

Tean secured Scipio's leash to the trunk of a short-needled pine, and the Lab flopped onto his stomach, obviously curious to see how Tean sorted this out. Tean got his leg between the fighting cats, clapped his hands loudly a few times, and when Senator Poindexter retreated and hissed at him, Tean retrieved the leashes from Mrs. Wish's hands. He untangled Senator Poindexter's, passed it to Mrs. Wish, and said, "Take him back to the apartment, please."

"No, no, we're going to work this out. They just need more time together."

"That's only going to make things worse. Take him back, please."

"I really think they'll be the best of friends if they'd just — "

Senator William Borah hissed and lunged again, and Mrs. Wish let out a shriek. She stumbled back, dragging Senator Poindexter with her, only barely managing to keep her balance.

"I am very disappointed," she announced, straightening the housedress. "I am very disappointed in all of you."

Still untangling Senator William Borah and Senator Frank B. Bandegee, Tean had the suspicion that he was included in that statement. Mrs. Wish trundled back to the apartment. Tean retrieved Scipio. The Lab had watched the proceedings with disinterest, but when Senator Borah got within range, he bent and sniffed at the Bengal.

"Leave him alone," Tean said, using the leashes to force the animals apart.

Scipio sneezed. He was still eyeing Senator Borah.

"I know," Tean said. "This is why we don't have cats."

On his way back to the apartment, he got a text from Ammon: *Want to grab dinner?* Tean dismissed the message without replying.

By the time he made it upstairs, Mrs. Wish had gotten Senator Poindexter inside, and she stood in the hallway with her hands on her hips.

"This is absolutely unacceptable behavior, Senator William Borah," she said. "I will not stand for it." To Tean, she said, "I'm sorry you had to see that, Dr. Leon. I thought we'd reached a détente, but it seems they're determined to act like little boys instead of gentlemen."

"Mrs. Wish, they're not acting like boys or men. They're acting like cats. Unneutered cats. And if I had to guess, I'd say Senator Frank B. Bandegee is in estrus. This is why you should have all of the Irreconcilables fixed; you're not going to be able to socialize them out of this. It's instinct."

"Well, I should hope not."

"I'm sorry, but it is. You can't fight nature."

"Senator Frank B. Bandegee is an excellent young lady, but the boys have other choices, and I'm sure they can find a way to—"

"It's not about choices, Mrs. Wish. And it's not about logic or reason. You've got two males who are fighting over a mate. That's not going to end well; you need to take care of this, even though I know you don't like your options."

Mrs. Wish frowned, the lines around her mouth deepening. Then she shook her head. "We'll just continue to go on walks. They'll work things out between them."

Sighing, Tean passed over the leashes. Then he led Scipio to their apartment. As he was heading inside, he got another text, this one from Jem. It was a GIF of a woman eating an enormous bowl of pasta, which was Jem's way of asking if Tean wanted to get dinner. Tean dismissed that message too.

Tean shook his head, already thinking about Mrs. Wish again as he helped Scipio out of his harness. He wasn't sure why so many people fooled themselves into thinking that if they ignored a problem, it would eventually go away.

2

"Hold on," Jem said into the phone. "This might be them."

"I don't care," Tinajas said. Keys clicked on her end of the call. "I'm hanging up now."

"Just hold on." Eyeing the white Mercedes GLE through the window, Jem decided these were the people he'd been waiting for. "It's them, but they're not getting out of the car for some reason."

"I don't care. Really. I do not care at all. I have a rich, fulfilling life that has nothing to do with you."

"Really? It sounds boring. Wait, wait, I think they're arguing."

"Again: do not care. You called me at work to bother me —"

"I called you at work to harass you."

" — and complain about how bored you are —"

"Well, I like to keep you updated."

More clicking from Tinajas's end of the call. " — in spite of me repeatedly telling you not to bother me at work. Great. Consider me officially updated. Goodbye, Jem. Sell a house, make lots of money, and pay me back the five hundred dollars I loaned you."

"Loaned me? I thought that was a birthday present."

"It wasn't. It was a loan. Which is what I told you when I gave you the money and made you sign an IOU to pay me back."

"I thought that was my birthday card."

"Really? You thought you were signing your own birthday card?"

Sensing that he might have spun things out a little too far, Jem said, "This guy looks really douchey. He keeps checking his sunglasses lanyard."

"Goodbye, Jem."

"And the wife is way too young for him. Oh, maybe she's a mistress?"

"Sell a house. Pay me my money."

"She looks like she's got fake boobs."

"Do not call me at work ever again," Tinajas said and disconnected.

From inside the house that was currently for sale, Jem took one last look at his prospective clients. They were definitely arguing. He made a quick tour of the ground floor — everything was in order, but it felt creepy to stand at the window, watching them — and settled himself in the kitchen. He checked his phone. He sent Tean a GIF of a woman eating pasta. He considered doing this showing with an accent. Maybe Swedish. Or — or he could pretend to keep getting lost. That was a new one. He could walk straight into a closet and pretend to be completely baffled that it wasn't the butler's pantry or whatever these fucking jackals wanted. He was willing to do anything, at this point, that made the game even the tiniest bit less boring.

It had been different at the beginning. When he hadn't known what he was doing, when he'd been figuring everything out. First, making a fake license. Then making fake business cards. Then making a fake website. Then making contact with other agents, pitching himself as a client broker, which he was incredibly proud of himself for having invented. Utah was in the midst of the biggest housing boom in its history. New houses were going up all over the state, but construction couldn't keep up with demand. More importantly, the new houses were often an hour or two away from Salt Lake, which meant houses that were closer in were going for unimaginable sums. And Jem had figured out how to get a nice little cut of that business.

When the knock came at the door, he sent Tean a GIF he had made of Scipio wagging his tail, and then he went and answered.

"Hello," he said, showtime grin, already shaking hands. "Jake Brimhall. Jake Brimhall. Nice to meet you both, you must be Sam and Diane."

The man was fifty, too tan, and the sunglasses lanyard was just the tip of the iceberg. Not golf, Jem decided after a moment. Boating. The woman was probably skating close to thirty, too tan, and the boobs were definitely fake. Dancer, Jem decided after a moment. Former cheerleader.

"No," the man said. "Dwayne and Leslie Rae."

Leslie Rae gave Jem a limp flutter of her fingertips and a dead-eyed smile.

"God, of course. Sorry. I've got Sam and Diane a little later. Then Jerry and Elaine. And Ross and Rachel. It just doesn't stop, you know? Come in, come in. God, look at you, you guys belong here. Have you seen the neighbors? You're going to fit right in."

"I don't know about that," Dwayne said, hands on his hips. "This place has sure seen better days."

Leslie Rae looked like she was trying to pop her gum, only she didn't have any gum at the moment.

Jem walked them through the house.

"A/C needs to be replaced," Dwayne said, fanning the warm air.

"Don't worry, it's only five years old," Jem said with an easygoing smile. "I just turned it on when I got here, that's all."

Upstairs, Dwayne pointed at a cracked window.

"Two words," Jem said, holding up two fingers to drive the point home. "Home warranty. You make sure the seller writes it into the contract, and then you get that taken care of first thing."

In the basement, Dwayne kicked the furnace, apparently under the impression that this was the homebuyer equivalent of kicking the tires on a car. The hollow boom echoed back from bare cement.

"Doesn't sound good," Dwayne said, frowning.

Jem nodded. "You know what? I've got an agent in mind. If you want me to put you in touch, you just say the word. He'll make sure you get a few grand off the price to cover that furnace."

Back in the kitchen, Dwayne flipped the lights on and off. "Bulb's burned out."

"I've got one in the car," Jem said. "I'll swap it out after you go."

Dwayne opened his mouth.

"Dwayne, Leslie Rae, now's the time to make a decision. I've got Homer and Marge coming in twenty minutes, and I need to know if you want me to make things happen for you."

That was the magic phrase, *make things happen*. It could mean anything. It meant whatever people like Dwayne and Leslie Rae wanted it to mean. They'd already paid two hundred dollars for pre-screened access to elite homes, a back network of agents managed by a client broker. At least, that's what Jem had said they were paying for. He didn't even know what it meant himself, but people like Dwayne and Leslie Rae ate it up.

Dwayne and Leslie Rae glanced at each other. Leslie Rae made that gum popping movement with her mouth again. Dwayne started to nod.

Then Leslie Rae said, "What do you even do?"

Jem smiled and raised his eyebrows. "I'm a client broker." It was the tone that sold it, sounding slightly embarrassed that he had to explain.

"But what do you do? That's what I was asking Dwayne the whole way over. What does he do? And Dwayne couldn't tell me."

"I told you," Dwayne said, coloring under his tan. "He's a client broker. He pre-screens. He's got a back network of agents."

Jem nodded, shrugged, spread his hands.

"Isn't that what a normal real estate agent does?" Leslie Rae said. Her mouth popped invisible gum again.

He'd made a mistake, Jem realized. He'd miscalculated. He'd been so focused on Dwayne kicking the goddamn furnace that he might have overplayed his hand.

He laughed. "In a normal world," Jem said. "Five years ago, ten, maybe. But that's just not the way things happen anymore. You want a house?" He snapped his fingers. "It's gone before you even find it. If you're using a normal agent, I mean. You've got to get one step ahead of the game. You've got to pre-buy. You've got to beat the market curve, anticipate, outfox. Dwayne knows what I mean."

"I told her about pre-buying," Dwayne said, shooting a look at Leslie Rae. "I couldn't think of the word, but that's what I was telling you about."

For a moment, Leslie Rae looked like she might argue. Then she shrugged.

Jem could have left it there. Another two hundred in cash. But his blood was pounding, and he felt awake and alive for the first time in months, having to think on his feet, having to riff. Riffing was what he did best. And now he was riffing again, the words spilling out of him.

"I don't want to overstep," he said. "But I've got to warn you, this place is going to go fast. I think it might go today, if I'm being totally honest."

Dwayne shifted his weight. "We'd have to have that furnace looked at."

"Absolutely. And you should, you absolutely should." Jem hesitated. He let the moment hang, and then he lowered his voice. "Look, I shouldn't do this, but the owner is a friend of the family. Practically family; I call them my aunt and uncle. He and my dad were on the high council together for thirty years, and he was the stake patriarch when I got my patriarchal blessing. He and his wife were on their third mission to Georgia—that's the country, not the state—when the cancer came back." Jem shook his head. "We haven't given up on a miracle, but that's about what it's going to take."

"Jeez," Dwayne said.

"I'm sorry to hear that," Leslie Rae said in the vocal equivalent of ordering at a drive-thru.

"Normally, as a client broker, I'm supposed to hand you off to an agent at this point, but—Uncle Dan and Aunt Roseanne, they need money bad. They'd be willing to consider selling without an agent just to save a commission." Jem shook his head. "I can't even believe I'm telling you this, but they'd be willing to take half what the house is worth, just to get the cash in their hands."

"I thought homes were selling too fast these days," Leslie Rae said. "I thought that's why we needed a client broker."

"Homes are going fast. Agents, banks, and wire transfers, they're still taking their sweet time."

"What's the catch?" Dwayne said, narrowing his eyes. It furrowed his too-tan face like an old baseball mitt.

"If they don't make a mortgage payment today, the bank repossesses the house. It's got to be cash, and if I'm totally honest—it's got to be cash because it's a gray area, if you get what I mean."

"There it is," Dwayne trumpeted. "There's the other shoe. Did you hear it drop?"

Jem shrugged. "It is what it is. I thought maybe—well, it could have worked out for everybody: you get a house that instantly doubles in value, Uncle Dan gets his chemo. But you're right. I'm not really comfortable with it either. I'm sorry I brought it up."

Dwayne was breathing a little faster. He was tapping the kitchen counter. "Now let's just think about this for a minute."

"It seems pretty awful," Leslie Rae said. "That's what I think about it. Giving them half what they deserve just because they need it now."

"If they didn't need it so badly," Jem said, and then he stopped, as though unable to go on.

"Well, you heard him, didn't you?" Dwayne gestured at Jem. "You heard how bad they need it. We're doing them a favor. How low do you think they'll go?"

"Dwayne Mapes, can you even hear yourself?"

"I'm not made of cash, and this is a business transaction. I want to do these people a solid turn, but it's business first. How low will they go?"

"This house came in at four twenty-five," Jem said. "They've got to have two hundred thousand by the end of the month. Goll', I'm getting sick just talking about this. I don't know, I don't think —"

"Young man, listen up. You're feeling sick because you're thinking about all the money they'd be leaving on the table. That's a young man's way of looking at things. That's a healthy man's way of looking at it. Where's your Uncle Dave —"

"Dan," Leslie Rae said.

"Where's your Uncle Dan going to be if he holds out for the full value?"

"Dwayne Mapes, you are sleeping on the couch tonight."

"Let the men talk, please. Well, sir?"

"I know," Jem said. "I know. And I get it. But it still makes me sick. I shouldn't have said anything."

"You're thinking about it all wrong. You're doing them a favor. You're saving your uncle's life. That's how you ought to be seeing this."

Jem shook his head.

"What are we talking with that outstanding mortgage payment? Sixteen hundred? Two thousand?"

"Jeez, no," Jem said with a laugh. "Five-oh-five. They bought this place twenty-five years ago. It wasn't worth anything back then."

Dwayne practically licked his chops. "Well, that's nothing. We can handle that."

"But it's got to be cash. This is a real fine line, and if it makes you uncomfortable at all, knowing you're walking it, I'd rather not put you through that."

"You ought to be thanking us, young man. And your uncle ought to be thanking you. This is a square deal all around, and I'd say the Lord put us in each other's path. Now, I'm going to get that cash. What I need from you is for you to talk to Uncle Don—"

"Dan," Leslie Rae said, "Dan, it's like you don't even listen."

"Talk to that Uncle Dan and get things in order for me."

"Done," Jem said. "Should I cancel my other showings? Frick, I feel like I'm making a huge mistake."

"Son, you tell those people this place is as good as sold."

He walked them to the door. Leslie Rae stopped to measure the opening into the living room and said, "It's like they built this place for ants."

When they stepped outside, Jem moved to the window. He held his phone to his ear and waved. The closest ATM was five blocks away, and if he had to go by the gleam in Dwayne's eye, Jem thought the greedy old lech would sell a kidney to get that five hundred in cash. Once they were out of sight, Jem scrolled through GIFs until he found one of Scrooge McDuck swimming in gold coins. He sent it to Tinajas.

She sent back a middle-finger emoji.

3

Tean stacked the boxes from The Pie. Then he set them side by side. Then he stacked them again. Scipio leaned hard into him, his muzzle poking up over the counter, drawn by the smell of tomato sauce, hot cheese, and a variety of cured meats. Tean kneed the Lab gently away from the pizzas and offered him, instead, a rawhide-substitute treat. Scipio took it gingerly and then dropped it on the floor, fixing Tean with a look of pure disgust.

Tean didn't have time to soothe the dog. He straightened the plates and forks and knives. Did anybody need forks and knives with pizza? He put out spoons too, just in case. He checked the Bristlecone, which was on ice, the glass beaded with condensation. He thought Jem liked brown ale. He thought Ammon liked brown ale. He had put a single bottle of cider for himself in the ice, but then he'd thought maybe that was too much, and he'd put the whole pack of cider in a bottom cabinet behind a roll of trash bags.

Scipio had his muzzle on the counter again.

"Right," Tean said. "Xanax."

But he'd only taken two steps toward the bedroom—he now kept the bottle hidden, although he wasn't convinced he could successfully hide anything if Jem really wanted to find it—when someone knocked at the door.

Scipio lunged toward the noise, barking.

Tean followed, and when he opened the door, he smiled and said, "Come in."

Ammon Young, childhood friend, former lover, and one of the immense complications in Tean's life, stepped into the apartment. Scipio backed up a few steps, his whole body stiff, growling. Ammon gave an embarrassed grin, rubbed a hand through blond hair that was starting to thin, and said, "Hi. And hi, Scipio."

"Ignore him, he's — oh. Hi."

Ammon's hug lasted a moment too long for it to be a simple, friendly hug. When he released Tean, his smile looked more like the one Tean remembered from high school. "I didn't even try to kiss you."

"I noticed."

"How's that for progress?"

"Well, you did have to point it out."

Ammon's grin got bigger, but instead of answering, he squatted and said to Scipio, "Come on, I'm your buddy. Can I give him a treat?"

"You can try. He looked at me like I was insulting his family honor when I gave him one earlier. Here, see if he wants one of these."

Taking a small, liver-flavored treat from the pouch that Tean held out, Ammon said, "Skip, Skip, let's have a treat. I'm your friend." He held out the treat, and Scipio forgot to growl as he leaned forward to sniff the offering. He accepted it grudgingly and then turned and dropped it on the linoleum.

"Hey!"

"I know, that's what he did to me too."

Scipio slunk over to the couch and curled up on a cushion.

"I thought he wasn't allowed on the furniture."

Tean was saved from having to explain by the door opening. Jem stopped in the doorway. He'd gotten his hair cut again, and the hard side part was perfect as always. He had broad shoulders and a muscular build that the jacket and trousers couldn't hide. Ammon was bigger; if Tean were being fair, Ammon was probably better looking all around, with more classically handsome features, and over the last few months he'd regained the gym-toned body that had filled Tean's fantasies as a teenager and his bed as a younger man. But Jem was Jem.

Scipio charged across the room. The Lab didn't notice how Jem flinched, and he crashed into Jem's legs at full speed. By then, Jem had recovered, and he was crouching to rub Scipio's ears. Scipio was whining with excitement, licking Jem's face, crashing into him so many times that he finally managed to knock Jem on his butt. Tean was trying to get the dog to back up, and he didn't notice until too late that Ammon had put an arm around him.

"Fuh, fuh, he put his nose in my mouth. Tean, why are there treats on the floor?" Jem snatched up the liver one and held it out; Scipio took it and swallowed it. When Jem collected the rawhide substitute, Scipio took it out of his hand before Jem even had a chance to offer it. The Lab carried it over to the couch and curled up again, gnawing on his treat.

"I'm sorry," Tean said, and Ammon held on a little too tightly before Tean managed to get free. "I swear we've been working on staying." He gave Jem his hand and helped him up. "Are you ok?"

"I know what a dog's nose tastes like. No, I'm not ok."

"I'll put him in the bedroom next time."

"It's too late. I can never un-know what a dog's nose tastes like." Then Jem's gaze slid past Tean to Ammon. "And I think I misunderstood your message, so I'll come back another day."

"You didn't misunderstand. We're going to have dinner. Together. You're both my friends, and you need to be able to spend five minutes in a room together."

"Five minutes," Ammon said. "Starting now."

"You said we were having pizza," Jem said. "You didn't say we were also having a torrential douche."

"I want to point out that he started it."

"You started it by being you and having your dumb face—"

"Ok," Tean said.

"Calling me names," Ammon said. "Really mature."

"I can be mature," Jem said. "You haven't even seen me try to be mature."

"Ok, that's enough," Tean said.

"If it's too much to have a civilized dinner with friends—"

"You're not my friend. Tean is my friend. My best friend."

"Just a normal friend," Tean said. "And I really think—"

"Best friend? I've known Tean for more than twenty years. You haven't even known him for twenty months."

"Ok!" Tean slapped the counter. "That's enough."

Scipio looked up from his treat long enough to woof once.

Jem was staring back defiantly. Ammon was studying his sneakers.

"I'm tired of the pissing matches. I don't want to date you." He pointed at Ammon. "I don't want to date you." He pointed at Jem. "I've had just about enough of all the men in my life. Eat your damn pizza, and if you can't be decent human beings, go home."

"Nickel in the swear jar," Jem whispered. Then, to Ammon, "It's our Disneyworld fund."

"Sorry," Ammon muttered.

"Don't tell me," Tean shouted. With a little more control, he added, "Also, I'm sorry I'm still shouting."

"I'm sorry, Jem. And Tean, I'm sorry too."

"Well, now I have to say I'm sorry or I look like an asshole," Jem said. "So I guess I'm sorry."

Tean covered his face.

"But if you had to pick one of us," Jem said. "Like, a desert-island type of situation. Just in theory."

"Oh my gosh."

"It would really speed things along if you could just tell us."

"Neither of you. I would pick the moldy skeleton in the shipwreck."

"He's already in a relationship with the mermaid statue thingy on the front of the boat."

"It would probably be a ship," Ammon said. "Not a boat." When Tean and Jem both looked at him, he raised his hands and said, "I'm trying to be helpful."

"Then I'd swim out into the ocean. That would be better than this conversation. I would throw away my Julia-Child brand shark repellant, and I would swim straight into a garbage current, and I'd paddle until I ran out of strength. And then I'd drown. And my bloated corpse would float there until a shark came along and ripped me apart."

Ammon made a face and, probably trying to cover it, reached for a beer.

"What about your guts and stuff, though?" Jem said. "You didn't talk about your guts."

"They'd get sucked up in a ship's engine, obviously." Tean considered it for a moment. "Some kind of gull might get my eyeballs."

"Ok," Ammon said, and the Bristlecone hissed as he opened it. "Let's talk about something else."

"But your bones would probably jam a ship's propeller, right?" Jem said. "And then a Carnival cruise ship would be stuck adrift for months on the garbage current. And they'd eventually have to start eating each other. And then they'd get smeared in the news as the Cannibal cruise lines."

"New topic, please," Ammon said and took a swig of beer.

"There'd definitely be some executive suicides," Tean said, his eyes narrowed in thought. "And a trickle-down effect. Maybe huge swaths of coastal regions shut down because the cruise industry has collapsed. Are you happy? You just shattered Port-au-Prince's economy because the two of you had to measure your, um. You know."

"All right. There. You got it out of your system." Ammon opened a box, and steam and the aroma of garlic and sausage wafted up. "Can we eat now?"

"Cocks," Jem said.

Ammon choked on pizza.

"He was talking about our cocks," Jem said.

"I wasn't talking — you two were the ones — " Tean jerked a slice of pizza free, slapped it onto a plate, and shoved it at Jem. "Eat. And be quiet."

For a few blessed moments, the only sounds were chewing, beer caps pinging against the counter, and Scipio's drool dripping. Jem kept sneaking the Lab pieces of sausage when he thought Tean wasn't looking, and Ammon kept taking long drinks of Bristlecone.

"I thought you were Mormon," Jem said.

"Don't — " Tean began.

"No, it's fine." Ammon held out the brown-glass bottle, eyeing it, and then he shrugged. "I spent a long time convincing myself I could have everything I wanted. Turns out, I can't. So I'm picking the things I want the most and trying to be honest about it, which is what normal, healthy people do. Or so I understand."

"God, I wouldn't have any idea," Jem said. "It sounds awful, though."

The laugh must have caught Ammon by surprise because suds burst out of his nose, and then he staggered to the sink, coughing and wiping his face while Tean patted him on the back. Then he got him a wet cloth, and Ammon wiped his face, still chuckling. Jem was letting Scipio lick invisible traces of sauce from between his fingers, and he was wearing a small smile.

"I haven't seen you laugh that hard since you convinced Clyde Kerry that he got his girlfriend pregnant by letting her wear his 501s."

"Oh my God," Ammon said, squeezing his eyes shut. "I was such a dick in high school."

"In high school?" Jem murmured.

"What was that?" Tean said.

"That was a private conversation with Scipio. I was telling him about . . . something."

Tean fixed him with a glare. Jem smiled and stroked Scipio's ears.

"You're not going to tell me you were a saint in high school, are you?" Ammon said.

"Jem probably doesn't want to talk about—"

Waving Tean to silence, Jem said, "I was in juvie. We had classes. Kind of. A lot of workbooks, which, well, I could make fuck-all sense out of. You were supposed to get a GED or high-school equivalency diploma if you finished everything."

"You don't have a high-school degree?"

"Ammon!"

"It's a question, Tean. If you want us to be friends, fine. But if I can't even ask him a question, we might as well go back to measuring our cocks."

Tean groaned.

"No, no degree." Jem played with Scipio's scruff. "And in case Tean hasn't told you, I can't read either."

"He can read. You can read."

"He didn't tell me that. He doesn't tell me anything about you, just so you know."

"He didn't tell you how much better I am at sex?"

"That's not what—I never—"

Ammon's hand settled on his shoulder, and he squeezed once. "He's just messing with me." Then, to Jem, "God, you really know how to wind him up, don't you?"

"It's too easy."

"I just want to point out," Tean said, "that Jem Berger is the one who got drunk and called me last weekend to make a series of indecent proposals, and so if anyone is easy, it's him."

"I wasn't drunk. I was high. And I put a lot of thought into those ideas."

Ammon gave a tiny half-shake of his head, and he was smiling as he turned to Tean. "Do you want to watch Daniel's baseball game with me tomorrow?"

"Wow. Is—are you sure?"

"Is Lucy going to be there? Is that what you were going to ask?"

"I think it's a fair question."

"It's completely fair. Yes, she will be. But you're my friend, and I can ask my friends to do stuff with me."

"He's my best friend," Jem put in.

"Casual, you-had-high-school-shop-together-and-didn't-see-each-other-again-until-your-twentieth-high-school-anniversary level of friends," Tean said, unable to look away from Ammon's eyes. "I can't, Ammon. It means a lot to me that you'd ask, and I'd love to go another time, but I can't."

"Another time," Ammon said. "Sure."

"He's got a date."

The only change was a slight furrow between Ammon's eyebrows.

"Well," Tean said, his face heating. "Yes, actually. Maybe Jem could go with you."

"No!" they both shouted at the same time.

"I'm sure he's got better things to do," Ammon said.

"I do." Jem nodded vigorously. "I've got to pick lint out of my crotch hair."

Ammon didn't seem to hear him; his gaze was fixed on Tean, and the struggle on his face was painful to watch. Finally, with what seemed like remarkable control, he said, "Am I allowed to ask questions?"

"Half a question," Jem said. "And you have to say it backwards."

"Will you stop it? You can ask questions. I might not answer them."

"Did you meet him on Prowler?"

"Yes."

"What's his name?"

"I'm not going to answer that."

"Name his?" Jem suggested in what he obviously thought was a helpful tone.

"Where are you going?" Ammon asked.

"Going you?"

"Enough," Tean snapped. "I'm not answering that one either."

"I'm not being nosy for kicks and giggles," Ammon said. "Online dating isn't necessarily safe."

"He's right," Jem said. "You should borrow his diaphragm. And his asshole-bleaching kit. Ammon, be a pal and lend him your asshole-bleaching kit, please?"

Tean leaned against the counter. He glanced at the lower cabinet where he'd hidden the cider. He rarely wanted to be drunk, but the thought was a parachute right then. "Fireflies—"

"No," Jem groaned, dropping his head onto the table. "You made him start with the firefly thing again."

"Please don't tell me this is more animal trivia," Ammon said. "I'm being serious right now."

"I'm being serious too. Fireflies of the species *Photuris* prey on fireflies of the species *Photinus*. The females mimic the light signals of *Photinus* fireflies. When they show up to mate, instead of sex, they get murdered. And eaten."

"Great. Right now, I don't want to talk about fireflies. I want to talk about you being safe."

"Put a condom on a banana," Jem said. "Show him how to do it."

"And it's not just interspecies violence." Tean grabbed a Bristlecone. "Open this, please?" Sexual cannibalism is rife in the animal world. Chinese mantises. Black widow spiders. Some animals kill their sexual partner before consummating the act. Some consume them during sex."

"It's like having a sandwich in bed," Jem said. "Like on *Seinfeld*."

When Ammon handed back the open Bristlecone, he said, "Fine. We'll do this the little-kid way. What are you going to do when a praying mantis tries to eat you after sex?"

"I'll probably pretend to have a heart attack."

At the table, Jem choked on something and managed to wheeze, "Please record this."

"That's not going to stop a crazy person from killing you."

"It worked when I went to Try-angles. This guy kept trying to buy me a drink, and he wouldn't take no for an answer, so I pretended to fall asleep."

Jem's eyes were huge and bright. He was biting his lip. Ammon covered his face with two big hands.

"It's a proven tactic," Tean said, trying to square his shoulders. "Female dragonflies fake sudden death to avoid male advances."

"Never stop," Jem breathed.

"Stop what?"

"Any of this."

"You don't have to stop," Ammon said, "but if we could press pause for a minute. I'm going to ask you again: what's his name, and where are you going?"

"I don't—"

"I'm your friend, right? And you're not going to go out with a stranger without providing some basic information in case something happens to you. You could have a stroke. You could get hit by a car. You could get mugged. And nobody would know where you'd been."

Tean closed his eyes. Then, after letting out a slow breath, he said, "Ammon, please don't make me regret trusting you."

"If we're going to figure out how to be friends again, we have to start somewhere."

"His name's Ragnar."

"Oh my God," Jem said.

"For fuck's sake," Ammon said. Then, almost immediately, "Sorry."

"See? This is why I didn't tell you."

"No, no. I'm sorry. It won't happen again. And where are you guys going?"

"Stanza."

Ammon's eyebrows went up. "A little pricey for a first date, don't you think?"

"Yeah, well," Tean pulled on his collar, "I finally have disposable money for the first time in my life, and I want to spend some of it on myself."

"Buy some sex toys," Jem said. "Some really scary ones."

"Will you be quiet for five seconds?"

"What is a scary sex toy?" Tean said. "No, please, don't answer that."

"Too late—"

"Thank you for trusting me," Ammon said. He downed the rest of his beer and met Tean's eyes. "Will you tell me if you go home with him? I'm not asking for details. I just want to know if I should come down and take care of Scipio."

Scipio raised his head at the sound of his name, his expression wary as he studied Ammon.

"That seems like too much."

"If we're friends—"

"No, Ammon. I don't feel comfortable talking to you about that yet."

Something Tean couldn't describe flitted across Ammon's face. Then he nodded. "Thanks for being honest about your feelings. I appreciate that you respect me enough to do that."

Jem pretended to throw up into his beer bottle.

"Enough," Tean said.

Jem continued the gagging noises.

Tean pegged him with a crumpled-up ball of foil, and Jem slumped sideways on the table, dead.

"Now," Jem said, "can I please ask one question?"

"No."

"Ammon got to ask questions."

"Ammon isn't going out of his way to make my life more difficult."

"I think I should get a turn. I want to ask a question."

"Fine, jeez, before I lose my mind."

"I want you to be completely, devastatingly honest: does Ragnar have a better beard than me?"

Acknowledgments

My deepest thanks go out to the following people (in alphabetical order):

Kate Collopy, for implanting in my brain a vision of Bradley Cooper's, Jared Leto's, and Jonathan Van Ness's DNA chimera, for helping me think about how I write banter, for keeping track of Scipio's paws, and for doing all this on top of an extraordinary amount of high-stress work of her own!

Austin Gwin, for catching a multitude of grammatical and spelling errors that slipped past others, for giving me feedback on the characters, and for providing so much encouragement and support that helped me feel like what I was doing in this book, even if imperfectly, was very much worth doing.

Dr. Anne Justice-Allen, for her expert knowledge—anything I got correct related to Tean's veterinary expertise is due to her guidance, and anything I got wrong is my own fault; for her feedback on the mystery itself and the mechanism of death; for her insight into the office manueverings inside an agency like the DWR; for suggesting kit foxes and avian influenza; and for her kindness and patience with the innumerable questions I sent her way.

Steve Leonard, for remembering Scipio was in the truck, for telling me about Abercrombie & Fitch calendars, for reminding me that Jem isn't a good speller, for tracking all my condensed timelines and suggesting that people sometimes don't move as quickly as I think, for helping me pace Ammon's revelations, and for providing excellent feedback on how to restructure Jem's introduction to Tean's parents.

Cheryl Oakley, for being (as usual) the first to read a version of this story and get back to me with assurances that it held together (for the most part) and with suggestions for how to fix it (where it didn't), for keeping track of where everybody was (when I forgot and put them back inside the apartment), for helping me introduce Linda more effectively, and for a million more little things.

Tray Stephenson, for catching the usual miscellaneous errors that slipped past everyone else, for helping me keep track of characters changing names, and for checking in to make sure I was doing ok.

Dianne Thies, for her sensitive, thoughtful reactions to the text, at the level of the word (bullpucky and menswear, for example), character (Ammon smashing his phone, Jem standing up for Tean), and plot (turns out I had the brachial artery right except in that one, critical instance!), and for providing kind encouragement when it was needed.

Jo Wegstein, for her careful reading and for catching so many errors, but above all for her helpful feedback regarding Ammon. Although Ammon's internal struggle takes place off the page, it forms an important part of this book, and I'm deeply indebted to Jo for helping me think through the factors behind Ammon's behavior, including his identity as a police officer.

About the Author

Learn more about Gregory Ashe and forthcoming works at **www.gregoryashe.com**.

For advanced access, exclusive content, limited-time promotions, and insider information, please sign up for my mailing list at **http://bit.ly/ashemailinglist**.

Made in United States
Orlando, FL
27 November 2022

25105133R00228